生活實用**英語**

腦中延伸
的人事物

檸檬樹

出版前言

無邊無際的英文單字，如何有效歸納記憶？

【圖解生活實用英語】全系列三冊，
系統化整合龐雜大量的英文單字，分類為：

「眼睛所見」（具體事物）
「大腦所想」（抽象概念）
「種類構造」（生活經驗）

透過全版面的圖像元素，對應的單字具體呈現眼前；
達成「圖像化、視覺性、眼到、心到」的無負擔學習。

第 1 冊【舉目所及的人事物】：眼睛所見人事物的具體單字對應
第 2 冊【腦中延伸的人事物】：大腦所想人事物的具體單字對應
第 3 冊【人事物的種類構造】：生活所知人事物的具體單字對應

「各種主題」的「相關人事物」與「大腦所想」實境呼應，
將英語學習導入日常生活，體驗大腦創造的英文風景，

適合「循序自學」、「從情境反查單字」、「群組式串連記憶」。

觀賞「馬戲團表演」，你會看到……

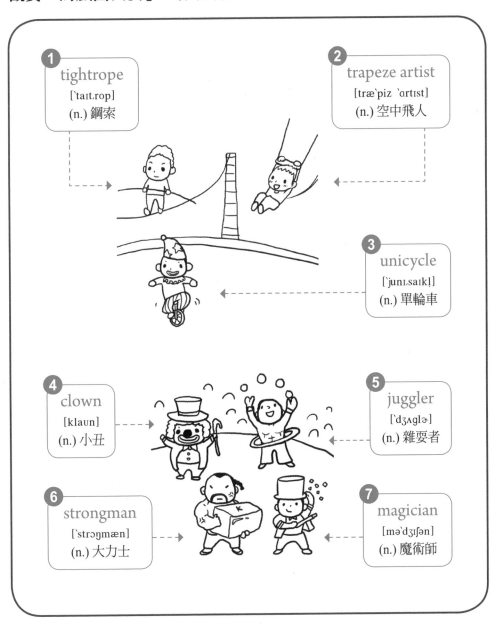

1 tightrope
[ˋtaɪtˏrop]
(n.) 鋼索

2 trapeze artist
[træˋpiz ˋɑrtɪst]
(n.) 空中飛人

3 unicycle
[ˋjunɪˏsaɪkl̩]
(n.) 單輪車

4 clown
[klaʊn]
(n.) 小丑

5 juggler
[ˋdʒʌglɚ]
(n.) 雜耍者

6 strongman
[ˋstrɔŋˏmæn]
(n.) 大力士

7 magician
[məˋdʒɪʃən]
(n.) 魔術師

第 2 冊：大腦延伸的人事物
從這個主題，容易連想到的英文單字。

從「學生百態」，可能連想到……

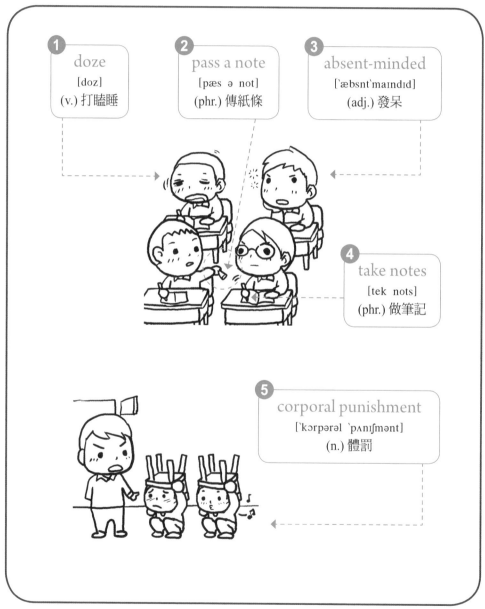

1 doze
[doz]
(v.) 打瞌睡

2 pass a note
[pæs ə not]
(phr.) 傳紙條

3 absent-minded
[`æbsnt`maɪndɪd]
(adj.) 發呆

4 take notes
[tek nots]
(phr.) 做筆記

5 corporal punishment
[`kɔrpərəl `pʌnɪʃmənt]
(n.) 體罰

第 3 冊：人事物的種類構造

〔種類〕彙整「同種類、同類型事物」英文說法。

「奧運項目」的種類有……

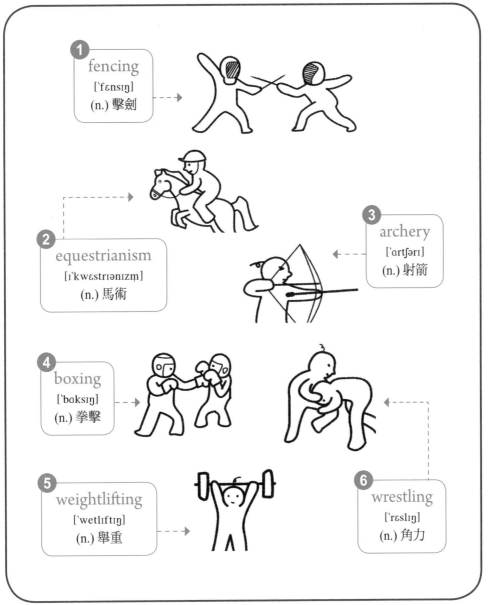

1 fencing
[ˋfɛnsɪŋ]
(n.) 擊劍

2 equestrianism
[ɪˋkwɛstrɪənɪzm̩]
(n.) 馬術

3 archery
[ˋɑrtʃərɪ]
(n.) 射箭

4 boxing
[ˋbɑksɪŋ]
(n.) 拳擊

5 weightlifting
[ˋwetlɪftɪŋ]
(n.) 舉重

6 wrestling
[ˋrɛslɪŋ]
(n.) 角力

〔構造〕細究「事物組成結構」英文說法。

「腳踏車」的構造有⋯⋯

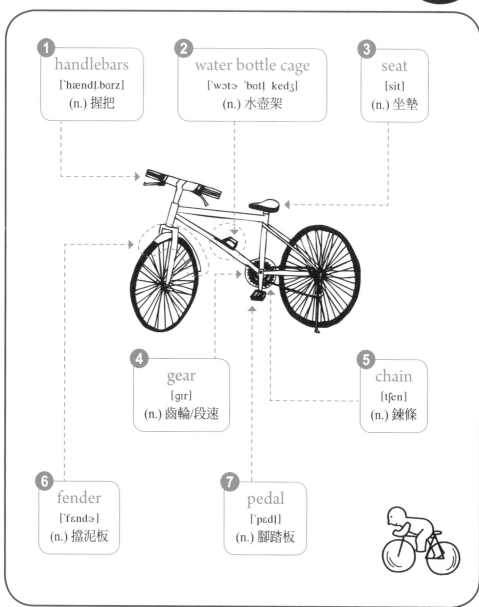

1 handlebars
[ˈhændḷˌbɑrz]
(n.) 握把

2 water bottle cage
[ˈwɔtɚ ˈbɑtḷ kedʒ]
(n.) 水壺架

3 seat
[sit]
(n.) 坐墊

4 gear
[gɪr]
(n.) 齒輪/段速

5 chain
[tʃen]
(n.) 鍊條

6 fender
[ˈfɛndɚ]
(n.) 擋泥板

7 pedal
[ˈpɛdḷ]
(n.) 腳踏板

本書特色

【腦中延伸的人事物】：
「各種主題」的「小群組單字」，與大腦所想實境呼應！

◎ 以【畢業】（單元 012、013）相關插圖，對應學習單字：
畢業證書（diploma）、畢業典禮（graduation ceremony）、學士服（academic robes）、畢業論文（dissertation）、畢業旅行（graduation trip）。

◎ 以【看電影】（單元 091、092）相關插圖，對應學習單字：
上映日期（release date）、電影分級（movie rating）、票房（box office）、爛片（bad movie）、熱門鉅片（blockbuster）、片長（length）。

◎ 以【敵對】（單元 036、037）相關插圖，對應學習單字：
惡意（malice）、憎恨（hate）、敵人（enemy）、敵意（hostility）、談判（negotiate）、對質（confront）。

各單元有「4 區域學習板塊」，點線面延伸完備的「生活單字＋生活例句」！
「透過圖像」對應單字，「透過例句」掌握單字用法，就能將英文運用自如。
安排「4 區域學習板塊」達成上述功能：

1. 【單字圖解區】：
   各單元約安排 5～7 個「具相關性的小群組單字」，以「全版面情境插圖」解說單字。

2. 【單字例句區】：
   各單字列舉例句，可掌握單字用法、培養閱讀力，並強化單字印象。

3. 【延伸學習區】：
   詳列例句「新單字、時態變化、重要片語」。

4. 【中文釋義區】：
   安排在頁面最下方，扮演「輔助學習角色」，如不明瞭英文句義，再參考中譯。

採「全版面情境圖像」解說單字：
插圖清晰易懂，腦中延伸的人事物，留下具體英文印象！

【單字圖解區】

全版面情境插圖，對應的「人、事、物」單字具體呈現眼前。

【學習單字框】

包含「單字、KK音標、詞性、中譯」；並用虛線指引至插圖，不妨礙閱讀舒適度。

(4) run a red light ← （單字）
[rʌn ə rɛd laɪt] ← （KK音標）
(phr.) 闖紅燈 ← （詞性、中譯）

【小圖示另安排放大圖】

讓圖像構造清楚呈現。

（單元167：選票放大圖）

(7) display one's ballot
[dɪˋsple wʌns ˋbælət]
(phr.) 亮票

【情境式畫面學習】

透過插圖強化視覺記憶，能減輕學習負擔，加深單字印象。

可以「從情境主題查詢單字」，任意發想的單字疑問，都能找到答案！

全書「217個生活情境」，「蘊藏217種英文風景」。生活中想到的場景，都能透過查詢主題，「呈現該場景蘊藏的英文風景」。

<u>最熟悉的生活百態，成為最實用的英語資源。</u>

適合親子共讀，利用插圖誘發學習興趣，將英語導入日常生活。

本書「以圖像對應英語」適合親子共讀。可透過圖像開啟學習興趣，藉由「圖像英語」解釋抽象性詞彙、激發腦中人事物的聯想，並增長英語知識。

單字加註背景知識，同步累積生活知識，提升英語力，豐富知識庫！

受限於生活經驗，許多生活中所知的人事物，可能「只知名稱、不知背景知識與內涵」。本書透過圖解指引英文單字，對於常聽聞、卻未必了解本質的單字，加註背景知識，有助於閱讀時加深單字印象。同步累積生活知識，對於聽說讀寫，更有助力。

◎ 單元 054【用電】的【short circuit】（短路）：

short circuit
[ʃɔrt `sɝkɪt]
(phr.) 短路

兩極直接碰觸產生放電現象，引起火花及熱，造成電器損壞或失火。

◎ 單元 126【山難】的【altitude sickness】（高山症）：

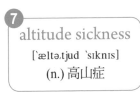

altitude sickness
[`æltə.tjud `sɪknɪs]
(n.) 高山症

人體在高海拔狀態因為氧氣濃度降低，而出現耳鳴、頭痛、嘔吐、呼吸困難等症狀。

書末增列【全書單字附錄】：
詞性分類×字母排序，清楚知道「從這本書學到了哪些單字」！

依循「詞性分類＋字母排序」原則，將全書單字製作成「單字附錄總整理」。有別於本文的「情境式圖解」，「單字附錄」採取「規則性整理」，有助於學習者具體掌握「學了哪些單字、記住了哪些單字」。

<u>讓所經歷的學習過程並非蜻蜓點水，而是務實與確實的學習紀錄。</u>

目錄 Contents

※ 本書各單元 MP3 音軌 = 各單元序號

天災人禍

身心狀態

136	懷孕 (1)	pregnancy (1)
137	懷孕 (2)	pregnancy (2)
138	減肥 (1)	weight loss (1)
139	減肥 (2)	weight loss (2)
140	健康 (1)	healthy (1)
141	健康 (2)	healthy (2)
142	不健康 (1)	unhealthy (1)
143	不健康 (2)	unhealthy (2)
144	眼睛 (1)	eye (1)
145	眼睛 (2)	eye (2)
146	血液 (1)	blood (1)
147	血液 (2)	blood (2)
148	看診 (1)	see the doctor (1)
149	看診 (2)	see the doctor (2)
150	心情不好 (1)	bad mood (1)
151	心情不好 (2)	bad mood (2)
152	感冒 (1)	catching a cold (1)
153	感冒 (2)	catching a cold (2)

球類＆運動

154	籃球賽 (1)	basketball game (1)
155	籃球賽 (2)	basketball game (2)
156	足球賽 (1)	football game (1)
157	足球賽 (2)	football game (2)
158	棒球場 (1)	baseball field (1)
159	棒球場 (2)	baseball field (2)
160	棒球選手	baseball player
161	運動 (1)	sports (1)
162	運動 (2)	sports (2)
163	游泳 (1)	swimming (1)
164	游泳 (2)	swimming (2)

社會政經

165	競選 (1)	election (1)
166	競選 (2)	election (2)
167	投票 (1)	vote (1)
168	投票 (2)	vote (2)
169	離婚 (1)	divorce (1)
170	離婚 (2)	divorce (2)
171	親子關係 (1)	parent-child relationship (1)
172	親子關係 (2)	parent-child relationship (2)
173	國家＆政治 (1)	nation & politics (1)
174	國家＆政治 (2)	nation & politics (2)
175	犯罪行為 (1)	crime (1)
176	犯罪行為 (2)	crime (2)
177	社會福利 (1)	social welfare (1)
178	社會福利 (2)	social welfare (2)

金融

179	借貸 (1)	loan (1)
180	借貸 (2)	loan (2)

001~019
學術

020~050
日常場合

051~072
生活

073~090
交通＆飲食

091~120
娛樂＆購物

121~135
天災人禍

136~153
身心狀態

154~164
球類＆運動

165~178
社會政經

179~187
金融

188~193
職場

194~199
電腦操作

200~205
創作

206~217
特殊場合

學生百態

MP3 001

1 doze
[doz]
(v.) 打瞌睡

2 pass a note
[pæs ə not]
(phr.) 傳紙條

3 absent-minded
[`æbsnt`maɪndɪd]
(adj.) 發呆/心不在焉

4 take notes
[tek nots]
(phr.) 做筆記

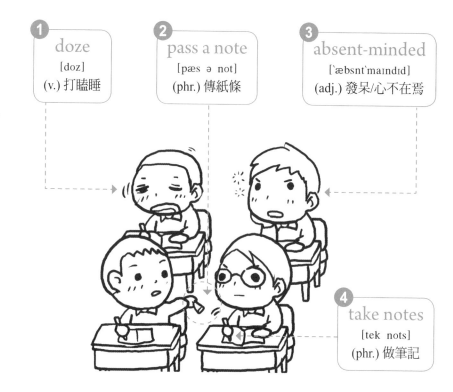

5 corporal punishment
[`kɔrpərəl `pʌnɪʃmənt]
(n.) 體罰

6 focus
[`fokəs]
(v.) 專心

7 not focus
[nɑt `fokəs]
(v.) 不專心

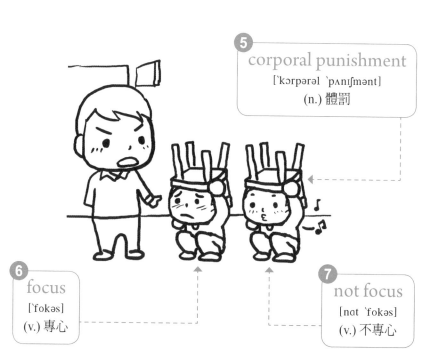

❶ 打瞌睡

Angela was so sleepy that she began to doze during the lecture.
她開始打瞌睡

❷ 傳紙條

The two boys were in trouble when the teacher saw them passing a note
那兩個男孩身陷麻煩

in class.

❸ 發呆 / 心不在焉

Sammy's very absent-minded. He's always forgetting things.

❹ 做筆記

The students all took notes during the lecture.

❺ 體罰

Do you agree with corporal punishment? I don't think it's right for
同意體罰

teachers to hit children.

❻ 專心

Gina never focuses in class, so she always gets bad grades.
拿到不好的成績

❼ 不專心

If you do not focus in class, you will fail your exams.
你的考試不及格

學更多

❶ sleepy〈想睡的〉‧ began〈begin（開始）的過去式〉‧ lecture〈課堂、授課〉
❷ in trouble〈在困境、險境中〉‧ passing〈pass（傳遞）的 ing 型態〉‧ note〈便條〉
❸ absent〈心不在焉的〉‧ minded〈有…傾向的〉‧ forgetting〈forget（忘記）的 ing 型態〉
❹ student〈學生〉‧ note〈筆記〉‧ during〈在…期間〉
❺ agree〈同意〉‧ corporal〈身體的〉‧ punishment〈處罰〉‧ right〈對的〉‧ hit〈打〉
❻ never〈從未〉‧ get〈得到〉‧ bad〈不好的〉‧ grade〈成績〉
❼ if〈如果〉‧ fail〈不及格〉‧ exam〈考試〉

中譯

❶ Angela 太想睡覺，以至於她在課堂中開始打瞌睡。
❷ 當老師看到他們在課堂上傳紙條，那兩個男孩就身陷麻煩了。
❸ Sammy 非常心不在焉，他老是忘東忘西。
❹ 課堂上，學生全都在做筆記。
❺ 你同意體罰嗎？我不認為老師打小孩是對的。
❻ Gina 從未專心上課，所以她的成績一直很差。
❼ 如果你上課不專心，考試就會不及格。

002

上課時

MP3 002

1 roll call
[rol kɔl]
(n.) 點名

2 late
[let]
(adj.) (adv.) 遲到/晚

3 leave early
[liv `ɝlɪ]
(phr.) 早退/提早離開

4 skip class
[skɪp klæs]
(phr.) 蹺課

5 present
[`prɛznt]
(adj.) 出席/在場

6 absent
[`æbsn̩t]
(adj.) 缺席

❶ 點名

The teacher takes roll call so she knows which students are away.
　　　　　　　　 点名　　　　　　　　　　　　　　　哪些學生不在

❷ 遲到 / 晚

Ivan woke up late so he didn't get to school on time.
　　　 很晚起床　　　　　　　　　　　　準時到達學校

❸ 早退 / 提早離開

Cathy was tired, so she left the party early.

❹ 蹺課

Ian skipped class and went to the mall with his friends.

❺ 出席 / 在場

When the students heard their name, they said, "present."

❻ 缺席

Sandy was ill, so she was absent from class.
　　　　　　　 她從課堂上缺席

學更多

❶ teacher〈老師〉．take〈做〉．roll〈名單〉．call〈呼叫〉．away〈不在〉
❷ woke up〈wake up（起床）的過去式〉．get〈到達〉．on time〈準時〉
❸ tired〈疲倦的〉．left〈leave（離開）的過去式〉．party〈派對〉．early〈提早〉
❹ skipped〈skip（不參加）的過去式〉．went〈go（去）的過去式〉．mall〈購物中心〉
❺ heard〈hear（聽到）的過去式〉．name〈名字〉．said〈say（說）的過去式〉
❻ ill〈生病的〉．class〈課堂〉

中譯

❶ 老師會點名，這樣她就知道有哪些學生缺席。
❷ Ivan 起得很晚，以至於他上課遲到了。
❸ Cathy 覺得很累，所以她提早離開派對。
❹ Ian 翹課跟朋友去購物中心。
❺ 當學生聽到自己的名字，會回應「在」（我在場）。
❻ Sandy 生病了，所以她缺席沒去上課。

003

學校生活

1 go to school
[go tu skul]
(phr.) 上學

2 after school
[ˋæftɚ skul]
(phr.) 放學

MP3 003

3 lunch break
[lʌntʃ brek]
(n.) 午休時間

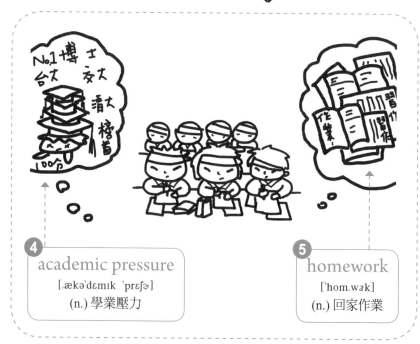

4 academic pressure
[ˌækəˋdɛmɪk ˋprɛʃɚ]
(n.) 學業壓力

5 homework
[ˋhom͵wɝk]
(n.) 回家作業

❶ 上學
What time do you go to school in the morning?

❷ 放學
Jerry walks home with his friends after school.
　　　　走路回家

❸ 午休時間
Andy went to eat with his friend in the lunch break.
　　　　和他的朋友一起去吃飯

❹ 學業壓力
In the weeks before the exams, students have a lot of academic pressure.
　　　　　　　　　　　學生有很大的學業壓力

❺ 回家作業
Ken was doing homework until midnight last night.

學更多

❶ time〈時間〉‧ school〈學校〉‧ morning〈早晨〉

❷ walk〈走路〉‧ friend〈朋友〉

❸ went〈go（去）的過去式〉‧ eat〈吃飯〉‧ lunch〈午餐〉‧ break〈休息〉

❹ week〈一個星期〉‧ before〈在…之前〉‧ exam〈考試〉‧ a lot of...〈許多〉‧
　academic〈學校的〉‧ pressure〈壓力〉

❺ doing〈do（做）的 ing 型態〉‧ until〈到…為止〉‧ midnight〈午夜〉‧ last〈上一次的〉

中譯

❶ 你早上都幾點去上學？
❷ 放學時，Jerry 跟朋友一起走路回家。
❸ 午休時間時，Andy 和朋友一起去用餐。
❹ 在考試前的幾個星期，學生會有很大的學業壓力。
❺ Ken 昨晚寫回家作業寫到半夜。

學校行事

MP3 004

1 winter vacation
[`wɪntɚ ve`keʃən]
(n.) 寒假

2 school start
[skul stɑrt]
(phr.) 開學

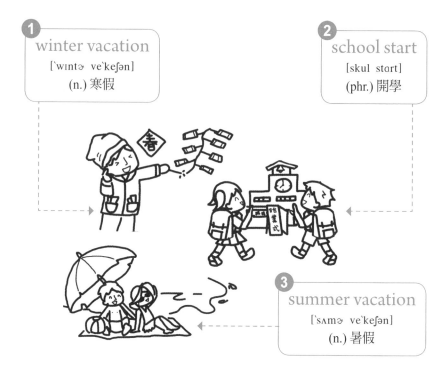

3 summer vacation
[`sʌmɚ ve`keʃən]
(n.) 暑假

4 enroll
[ɪn`rol]
(v.) 註冊

5 tuition
[tju`ɪʃən]
(n.) 學費

6 school birthday
[skul `bɝθ.de]
(n.) 校慶

7 relay race
[rɪ`le res]
(n.) 大隊接力/接力賽跑

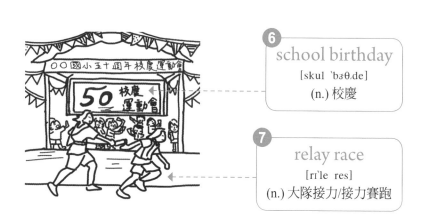

❶ 寒假

People celebrate Chinese New Year in the winter vacation.
　　　　　　　　　　　　農曆新年

❷ 開學

The students are unhappy because school starts today.

❸ 暑假

Emily went to the beach a lot in the summer vacation.
　　　　　時常去海邊

❹ 註冊

Which classes do you want to enroll in this year?

❺ 學費

Lisa's tuition for private school is extremely expensive.
　　　　私立學校的學費

❻ 校慶

On the school birthday this year, the school will be 26 years old.
　　　　　　　　　　　　　　校齡將滿 26 年

❼ 大隊接力 / 接力賽跑

He and his friends decided to enter a 50-kilometer relay race.
　　　　　　　　　　參加全長 50 公里的接力賽跑

學更多

❶ people〈人們〉・celebrate〈慶祝〉・winter〈冬天〉・vacation〈假期〉
❷ student〈學生〉・unhappy〈不開心的〉・start〈開始〉・today〈今天〉
❸ went〈go（去）的過去式〉・beach〈海灘〉・summer〈夏天〉
❹ which〈哪一些〉・class〈課程〉・want〈想要〉
❺ private〈私立的〉・extremely〈極端地〉・expensive〈昂貴的〉
❻ school〈學校〉・birthday〈生日、開始的日子〉・years old〈…歲〉
❼ enter〈參加〉・kilometer〈公里〉・relay〈接力賽跑〉・race〈賽跑、競賽〉

中譯

❶ 寒假時，大家會慶祝農曆新年。
❷ 學生們很不開心，因為今天要開學了。
❸ 暑假時，Emily 經常去海邊。
❹ 今年你想要註冊哪些課程？
❺ Lisa 就讀私立學校的學費極其昂貴。
❻ 在今年校慶時，這間學校就要成立屆滿 26 年了。
❼ 他跟朋友決定參加全長 50 公里的接力賽跑。

005

讀書

1 understand
[ˌʌndəˋstænd]
(v.) 理解

2 recite
[rɪˋsaɪt]
(v.) 背誦

3 underline
[ˌʌndəˋlaɪn]
(v.) 畫重點/畫底線

4 study plan
[ˋstʌdɪ plæn]
(n.) 讀書計劃

bookworm（喜歡看書的人）
沒有貶意，nerd（書呆子）
則帶有貶意。

5 nerd
[nɝd]
(n.) 書呆子

6 study hard
[ˋstʌdɪ hɑrd]
(phr.) 用功讀書

❶ 理解

Chris doesn't understand the lesson, so he'll have trouble doing his
homework.　　　　　　　　　　　　　　　　　　寫功課會碰到問題

❷ 背誦

Millie recited a poem in the school show.

❸ 畫重點 / 畫底線

Rob underlined the important words in his textbook.
　　　　　　將重要的字畫上底線

❹ 讀書計劃

Sandy made a study plan so she would know how much time to spend on
each subject.　　　　　　　　　　　　　　　花多少時間在各科上

❺ 書呆子

Fiona's a real nerd. She loves to study.

❻ 用功讀書

He wishes he'd studied harder in school so that he wouldn't have so many
problems with math now.　　　　　　　　　　在數學上碰到許多困難

學更多

❶ lesson〈課程〉‧ have trouble...〈在⋯有困難〉‧ doing〈do（寫）的 ing 型態〉
❷ recited〈recite（背誦）的過去式〉‧ poem〈詩〉‧ show〈表演〉
❸ underlined〈underline（畫重點）的過去式〉‧ important〈重要的〉‧ textbook〈課本〉
❹ made〈make（做）的過去式〉‧ spend〈花費〉‧ each〈各個〉‧ subject〈科目〉
❺ real〈十足的〉‧ love〈喜愛〉‧ study〈讀書〉
❻ studied〈study（學習）的過去分詞〉‧ harder〈更努力地，hard（努力地）的比較級〉‧
math〈數學〉

中譯

❶ Chris 不理解上課內容，所以他寫功課時會碰到問題。
❷ Millie 在學校的表演上背誦了一首詩。
❸ Rob 將課本裡重要的字畫底線。
❹ Sandy 訂了一個讀書計劃，這樣她就知道要在各個科目上花多少時間。
❺ Fiona 真是個十足的書呆子。她很愛讀書。
❻ 他希望自己以前在學校時更用功讀書一點，這樣現在他就不會對數學這麼頭痛。

006
考試(1)

1 examination sheet
[ɪɡˌzæməˈneʃən ʃit]
(n.) 考卷

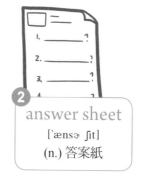

2 answer sheet
[ˈænsɚ ʃit]
(n.) 答案紙

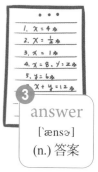

3 answer
[ˈænsɚ]
(n.) 答案

MP3 006

4 pass
[pæs]
(v.) 合格

5 fail
[fel]
(v.) 不合格

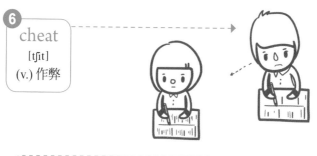

6 cheat
[tʃit]
(v.) 作弊

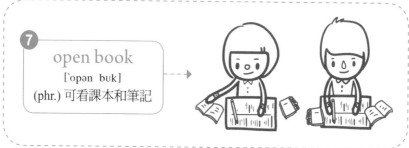

7 open book
[ˈopən bʊk]
(phr.) 可看課本和筆記

❶ 考卷

The teacher handed out the examination sheet at the start of the exam.

老師發考卷

❷ 答案紙

The teacher used the answer sheet to check the student's work.

❸ 答案

Stacey felt happy at the end of the exam because she knew the answer

在考試結束時感覺開心

to every question.

❹ 合格

You need to get over 70% to pass the test.

達到 70% 以上的答對率

❺ 不合格

The student failed the test because she did not study.

❻ 作弊

Sam cheated on the test. He looked at someone else's paper.

其他人的考卷

❼ 可看課本和筆記

This is an open book test; you will be able to take your books with you.

學更多

❶ handed out〈hand out（分給）的過去式〉・examination〈考試〉・sheet〈紙張〉
❷ used〈use（利用）的過去式〉・check〈檢測〉・work〈學業〉
❸ felt〈feel（覺得）的過去式〉・exam〈考試〉・knew〈know（知道）的過去式〉
❹ get〈得到〉・over〈超過〉・test〈考試〉
❺ student〈學生〉・failed〈fail（不及格）的過去式〉・study〈讀書〉
❻ cheated〈cheat（作弊）的過去式〉・someone else〈其他人〉・paper〈考卷〉
❼ open〈打開〉・able〈可以〉・take〈帶去〉

中譯

❶ 考試開始時，老師發考卷給大家。
❷ 老師利用答案卷檢測學生的學習成果。
❸ 考完試後 Stacey 覺得很開心，因為她知道每一題的答案。
❹ 你需要達到 70% 以上的答對率，才能考試合格。
❺ 那名學生考試不及格，因為她沒有唸書。
❻ Sam 考試作弊，他偷看了別人的考卷。
❼ 這是可看課本和筆記的考試，你可以帶著你的書應考。

考試 (2)

MP3 007

1 multiple choice question
[ˈmʌltəpl̩ tʃɔɪs ˈkwɛstʃən]
(n.) 選擇題

2 cloze question
[kloz ˈkwɛstʃən]
(n.) 填充題

3 true or false question
[tru ɔr fɔls ˈkwɛstʃən]
(n.) 是非題

4 short answer question
[ʃɔrt ˈænsɚ ˈkwɛstʃən]
(n.) 簡答題

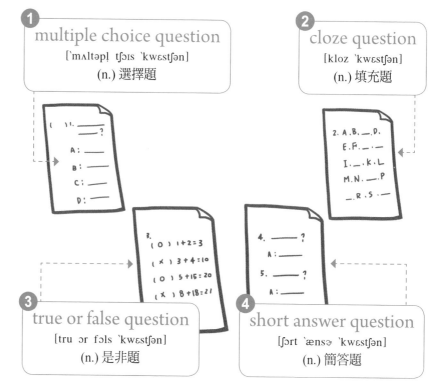

5 midterm exam
[ˈmɪd.tɚm ɪgˈzæm]
(n.) 期中考

6 final exam
[ˈfaɪnl̩ ɪgˈzæm]
(n.) 期末考

7 pop quiz
[pɑp kwɪz]
(n.) 隨堂小考

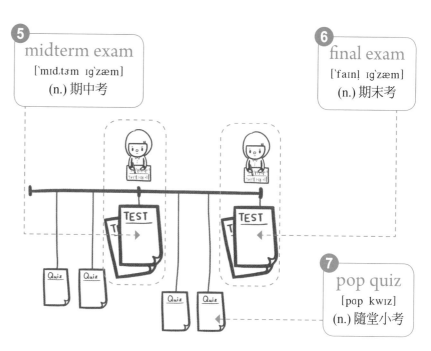

❶ 選擇題
❷ 填充題

He felt nervous and looked at the multiple choice questions and the cloze questions on the examination sheet.
考試卷

❸ 是非題

The history teacher warned his students to prepare for a pop quiz
提醒他的學生

composed of 10 true or false questions.

❹ 簡答題

The midterm exam was mostly short answer questions.

❺ 期中考

You'll take the midterm exam in the middle of the semester.
考期中考

❻ 期末考

The final exam will come at the end of the year.

❼ 隨堂小考

The teacher surprised her class with a pop quiz.

學更多

❶❷ felt〈feel（感覺）的過去式〉·nervous〈緊張不安的〉·multiple〈多樣的〉·choice〈選擇〉·cloze〈填充測驗的、克漏字〉·examination〈考試〉·sheet〈紙張〉

❸ composed〈compose（組成）的過去分詞〉·true〈正確的〉·false〈不正確的〉

❹ mostly〈大多數地〉·short〈短的〉·answer〈答案〉

❺ midterm〈期中的〉·exam〈考試〉·middle〈中間〉·semester〈一學期〉

❻ final〈最後的〉·come〈來臨〉·end〈末尾〉

❼ surprised〈surprise（驚訝）的過去式〉·class〈班級〉·pop〈突然地出現〉·quiz〈測驗〉

中譯

❶❷ 他感到很緊張，看著考卷上的選擇題和填充題。

❸ 那位歷史老師提醒他的學生，要準備進行一個有 10 道是非題的隨堂小考。

❹ 那次期中考大部分都是簡答題。

❺ 當學期進行一半的時候，你要考期中考。

❻ 期末考將於年底的時候來臨。

❼ 老師的隨堂小考，讓班上同學嚇了一跳。

008

成績優異(1)

MP3 008

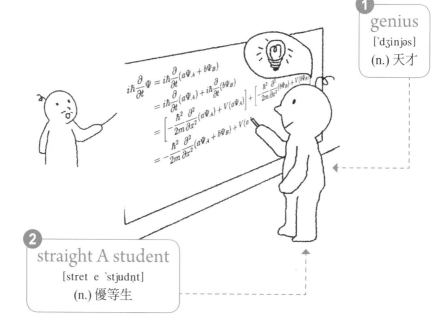

1 genius
['dʒinjəs]
(n.) 天才

2 straight A student
[stret e 'stjudṇt]
(n.) 優等生

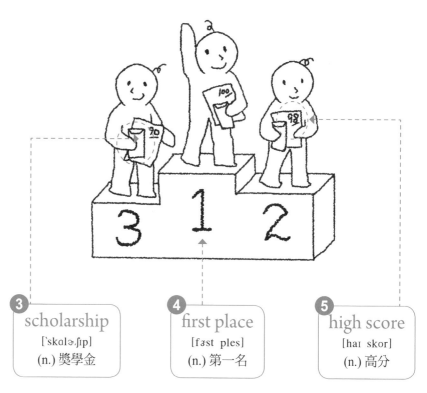

3 scholarship
['skɑləˌʃɪp]
(n.) 獎學金

4 first place
[fɝst ples]
(n.) 第一名

5 high score
[haɪ skor]
(n.) 高分

❶ 天才

Gary's a genius. He finished college when he was 15.
唸完大學

❷ 優等生

Pauline is a straight A student. She always gets good scores.
得到好成績

❸ 獎學金

Ronnie was given a college scholarship; she doesn't pay tuition fees.
付學費

❹ 第一名

Alice is the smartest girl in the class, so she usually gets first place in tests.
考試考第一名

❺ 高分

Frank was happy when he got a high score on the test.

學更多

❶ finished〈finish（完成）的過去式〉‧college〈大學〉
❷ straight〈連續的〉‧straight A〈學業成績都是 A 的〉‧always〈總是〉‧get〈得到〉‧
score〈成績〉
❸ given〈give（給予）的過去分詞〉‧pay〈支付〉‧tuition〈學費〉‧fee〈費用〉
❹ smartest〈最聰明的，smart（聰明的）的最高級〉‧usually〈通常〉‧first〈第一的〉‧
place〈名次〉
❺ happy〈高興的〉‧got〈get（得到）的過去式〉‧high〈高的〉‧score〈分數〉

中譯

❶ Gary 是個天才，他在 15 歲時就讀完了大學。
❷ Pauline 是一位優等生，她的成績一直都很好。
❸ Ronnie 獲得了大學的獎學金，她不需要付學費。
❹ Alice 是班上最聰明的女孩，所以她考試通常都是第一名。
❺ 當 Frank 在考試中拿到高分時，他感到很開心。

009 成績優異(2)

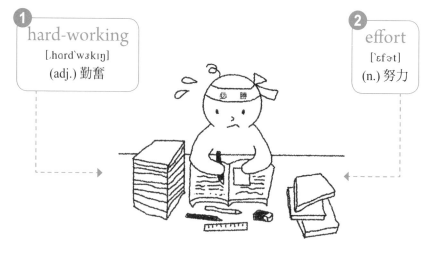

1 hard-working
[ˌhɑrdˈwɝkɪŋ]
(adj.) 勤奮

2 effort
[ˈɛfɚt]
(n.) 努力

MP3 009

3 brainy
[ˈbrenɪ]
(adj.) 聰明的

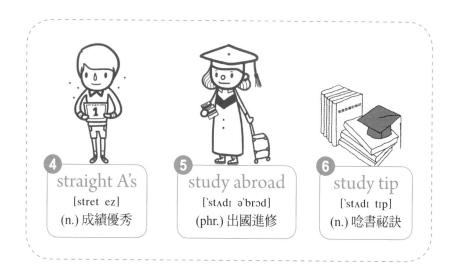

4 straight A's
[stret ez]
(n.) 成績優秀

5 study abroad
[ˈstʌdɪ əˈbrɔd]
(phr.) 出國進修

6 study tip
[ˈstʌdɪ tɪp]
(n.) 唸書祕訣

❶ 勤奮

Hard-working students usually do better in school.

❷ 努力

Danny felt his efforts were rewarded when he got an A on the assignment.

他的努力得到了回報

❸ 聰明的

Teresa is very brainy. She knows lots about everything.

知道很多事

❹ 成績優秀

Joe's a good student. He gets straight A's.

成績全部拿 A

❺ 出國進修

Carol signed up for a study abroad program. She wants to study in the UK.

在英國唸書

❻ 唸書祕訣

With these study tips, you should be able to prepare for the test much better.

更充分地準備考試

學更多

❶ usually〈通常〉‧ better〈比較好地〉

❷ felt〈feel（感覺）的過去式〉‧ rewarded〈reward（報償）的過去分詞〉‧
   got〈get（得到）的過去式〉‧ assignment〈作業〉

❸ know〈知道〉‧ everything〈一切事物〉

❹ good〈好的〉‧ get〈得到〉‧ straight〈連續的〉‧ A〈學業成績 A 等〉

❺ signed up〈sign up（登記、報名）的過去式〉‧ abroad〈到國外〉‧ program〈課程〉

❻ tip〈祕訣〉‧ able〈可以〉‧ prepare〈準備〉‧ test〈考試〉

中譯

❶ 勤奮的學生在學校的表現通常都比較好。

❷ 當 Danny 的作業得到最高分的 A 時，他覺得所有的努力都獲得了回報。

❸ Teresa 非常聰明，她通曉許多事。

❹ Joe 是個好學生。他成績優秀（全部都拿 A）。

❺ Carol 報名了出國進修的課程，她想要到英國留學。

❻ 運用這些唸書祕訣，你應該就能為考試作更充分的準備。

大學生活(1)

010

1 optional course
[`ɑpʃənl̩ kors]
(n.) 選修課

2 required course
[rɪ`kwaɪrd kors]
(n.) 必修課

3 credit
[`krɛdɪt]
(n.) 學分

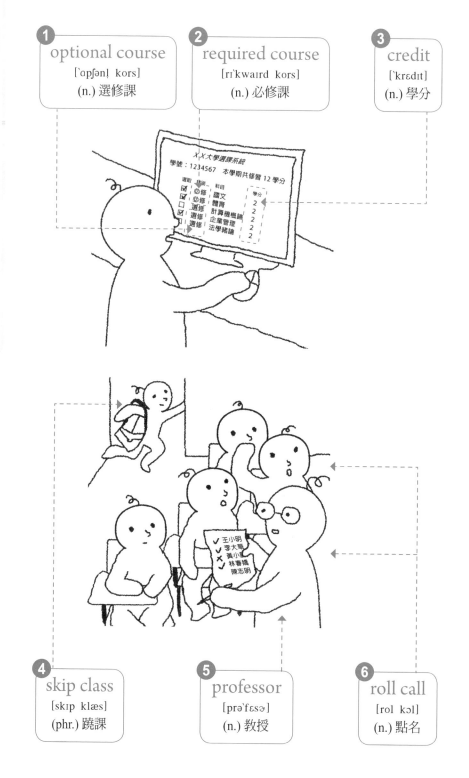

4 skip class
[skɪp klæs]
(phr.) 蹺課

5 professor
[prə`fɛsɚ]
(n.) 教授

6 roll call
[rol kɔl]
(n.) 點名

034

❶ 選修課

This is an optional course. You don't have to take it.

不一定要修這門課

❷ 必修課

This is a required course. You have to do it.

❸ 學分

Doing this course will get you a lot of credits.

❹ 蹺課

You shouldn't skip class or you'll fall behind in your course.

跟不上你的課程

❺ 教授

The college professor enjoyed giving lectures to his students.

對他的學生進行授課

❻ 點名

The teacher takes roll call at the start of the class to find out who's there.

會在開始上課時點名

學更多

❶ optional〈非必須的〉・course〈課程〉・have to〈必須〉・take〈修課〉

❷ required〈必修的〉・do〈學習〉

❸ doing〈do（學習）的 ing 型態〉・get〈得到〉・a lot of〈許多〉

❹ skip〈不參加〉・fall behind〈落後、跟不上〉

❺ college〈大學〉・enjoyed〈enjoy（喜愛）的過去式〉・giving〈give（給予）的 ing 型態〉・lecture〈講課〉

❻ take〈做〉・roll〈名單〉・call〈呼叫〉・start〈開始〉・find out〈找出〉

中譯

❶ 這是選修課，你不一定要修這門課。

❷ 這是必修課，你一定要修這門課。

❸ 選修這門課，你會得到很多學分。

❹ 你不該翹課，不然你會跟不上這門課的進度。

❺ 這名大學教授樂於授課教導學生。

❻ 開始上課時，老師會點名確認有誰出席。

大學生活(2)

MP3 011

1 club
[klʌb]
(n.) 社團

2 group dating activity
[grup `detɪŋ æk`tɪvətɪ]
(n.) 聯誼活動

3 part-time
[`part`taɪm]
(adj.) 打工/兼差

4 internship
[`ɪntɜn.ʃɪp]
(n.) 實習

5 leave of absence
[liv ɑv `æbsn̩s]
(n.) 休學/休假

6 drop out
[drɑp aʊt]
(phr.) 退學

❶ 社團

Ian joined a chess club when he was at college.

❷ 聯誼活動

Nine boys and nine girls got together for the group dating activity.

❸ 打工 / 兼差

Janine had a part-time job when she was at college. She worked at a drinks store at night time.

❹ 實習

Dean did an internship at a newspaper when he left college. He wasn't paid for the work he did there.

他沒有被支付薪水

❺ 休學 / 休假

The worker took a leave of absence when his wife had a baby.

請了休假

❻ 退學

Annie dropped out of university in her second year.

在她二年級的時候

學更多

❶ joined〈join（加入）的過去式〉‧ chess〈西洋棋〉‧ college〈大學〉

❷ got together〈get together（聚集）的過去式〉‧ group〈團體〉‧ dating〈約會的〉‧ activity〈活動〉

❸ had〈have（有）的過去式〉‧ part〈部分的〉‧ job〈工作〉‧ drink〈飲料〉

❹ newspaper〈報社〉‧ left〈leave（離開）的過去式〉‧ paid〈pay（支付）的過去分詞〉

❺ worker〈員工〉‧ leave〈假期〉‧ absence〈缺席〉‧ wife〈太太〉‧ baby〈嬰兒〉

❻ dropped〈drop（丟棄）的過去式〉‧ out〈出來〉‧ university〈大學〉‧ second〈第二的〉

中譯

❶ Ian 在大學時參加了西洋棋社團。

❷ 9 名少年和 9 名少女聚在一起進行聯誼活動。

❸ Janine 讀大學時有份兼差的工作，當時她晚上都在飲料店工作。

❹ Dean 大學畢業後到報社實習，當時他在那兒工作是沒有薪水的。

❺ 那名員工在他太太生產時請了休假。

❻ Annie 在大學二年級時退學。

012

畢業 (1)

1 diploma
[dɪˋplomə]
(n.) 畢業證書

2 graduation ceremony
[ˌɡrædʒʊˋeʃən ˋsɛrə.monɪ]
(n.) 畢業典禮

3 academic robes
[ˌækəˋdɛmɪk robz]
(n.) 學士服

MP3 012

4 dissertation
[ˌdɪsəˋteʃən]
(n.) 畢業論文

5 graduation trip
[ˌɡrædʒʊˋeʃən trɪp]
(n.) 畢業旅行

6 graduation examination
[ˌɡrædʒʊˋeʃən ɪɡ.zæməˋneʃən]
(n.) 畢業考

❶ 畢業證書
At the graduation ceremony, the students were handed their diplomas.
被給予他們的畢業證書

❷ 畢業典禮
The graduating students were all happy at their graduation ceremony.

❸ 學士服
Academic robes are worn by those receiving university degrees at the
graduation ceremony.
那些接受學士學位的人

❹ 畢業論文
The student had to write his dissertation before he could graduate.

❺ 畢業旅行
My classmates and I are going on a graduation trip to Thailand.
要去畢業旅行

❻ 畢業考
Kirsty was happy to pass the graduation examination. She was looking
forward to graduating.
通過畢業考

學更多

❶ graduation〈畢業〉・ceremony〈典禮〉・handed〈hand（給）的過去分詞〉

❷ graduating〈畢業的〉・all〈全部〉・happy〈高興的〉

❸ academic〈大學的〉・robe〈長袍〉・worn〈wear（穿著）的過去分詞〉・
receiving〈receive（接受）的 ing 型態〉・university〈大學〉・degree〈學位〉

❹ had to〈have to（必須）的過去式〉・write〈寫〉・graduate〈畢業〉

❺ classmate〈同學〉・trip〈旅行〉・Thailand〈泰國〉

❻ examination〈考試〉・looking forward to〈look forward to（盼望…）的 ing 型態〉

中譯

❶ 畢業典禮時，學生們領取了他們的畢業證書。

❷ 畢業典禮時，畢業生全都很開心。

❸ 畢業典禮時，獲得學士學位的人都身穿學士服。

❹ 學生必須撰寫畢業論文才能畢業。

❺ 我和班上同學要去泰國畢業旅行。

❻ Kirsty 很開心能通過畢業考，她很期待畢業。

畢業(2)

MP3 013

1 yearbook photo
[`jɪr͵bʊk `foto]
(n.) 畢業照

2 yearbook
[`jɪr͵bʊk]
(n.) 畢業紀念冊

3 look for a job
[lʊk fɔr ə dʒab]
(phr.) 找工作

4 career counseling
[kə`rɪr `kaʊnslɪŋ]
(n.) 就業諮詢

5 life plan
[laɪf plæn]
(n.) 生涯規劃

6 freshman
[`frɛʃmən]
(n.) 社會新鮮人/
大學一年級新生

❶ 畢業照

Kate had fun looking at the yearbook photos of her old classmates.

看畢業照看得很開心

❷ 畢業紀念冊

The students asked their friends to sign their yearbooks.

要他們的朋友簽名

❸ 找工作

After graduating, the young women are all looking for a job.

❹ 就業諮詢

Eric had career counseling because he doesn't know what he wants to do.

他要做什麼

❺ 生涯規劃

The teacher talked to us about career choices based on our life plans.

根據我們的生涯規劃

❻ 社會新鮮人 / 大學一年級新生

He's in his first year; he's a freshman.

在讀一年級

學更多

❶ had fun＋動詞-ing〈have fun＋動詞-ing（做…很開心）的過去式〉・old〈舊交的〉

❷ asked〈ask（要求）的過去式〉・friend〈朋友〉・sign〈簽名〉

❸ graduating〈graduate（畢業）的 ing 型態〉・young〈年輕的〉・
women〈woman（女性）的複數〉・looking for〈look for（尋找）的 ing 型態〉・
job〈工作〉

❹ counseling〈諮詢服務〉・know〈知道〉・want〈想要〉

❺ career〈職業〉・choice〈選擇〉・based on〈base on（以…作為基礎）的過去分詞〉

❻ first〈第一的〉・year〈學年〉

中譯

❶ Kate 看老同學們的畢業照看得很開心。

❷ 學生們要求朋友在畢業紀念冊上簽名。

❸ 畢業之後，所有的年輕女生都在找工作。

❹ Eric 接受了就業諮詢，因為他不知道自己要做什麼。

❺ 老師告訴我們，要根據個人的生涯規劃來選擇職業。

❻ 他現在是一年級；他是位大學新鮮人。

014

留學

1 exchange student
[ɪksˋtʃendʒ ˋstjudn̩t]
(n.) 交換學生

2 advisor
[ədˋvaɪzɚ]
(n.) 指導教授

MP3 014

3 language barrier
[ˋlæŋgwɪdʒ ˋbærɪr]
(n.) 語言隔閡

5 homesick
[ˋhom͵sɪk]
(adj.) 想家

4 culture shock
[ˋkʌltʃə ʃɑk]
(n.) 文化衝擊

6 not acclimatize
[nɑt əˋklaɪmə͵taɪz]
(v.) 水土不服/不適應

7 racial discrimination
[ˋreʃəl dɪ͵skrɪməˋneʃən]
(n.) 種族歧視

❶ 交換學生

The exchange student loves being in another country.
待在其他國家

❷ 指導教授

The advisor told me that I should try to get some work experience.
得到一些工作經驗

❸ 語言隔閡

As he can't speak Chinese well, he finds there's a language barrier between himself and many of the people he meets.
他自己和許多他所遇見的人之間

❹ 文化衝擊

When you go to a very different country, you can sometimes feel culture shock.

❺ 想家

The girl was homesick when she first moved away to go to college.
搬出去讀大學

❻ 水土不服 / 不適應

She comes from a cold country, and she has not acclimatized to the hot weather yet.
仍對炎熱的氣候水土不服

❼ 種族歧視

The Chinese man was told he couldn't join the club because he was
被告知他不能加入俱樂部
Chinese. That kind of racial discrimination is awful.

學更多

❶ exchange〈交換〉・student〈學生〉・another〈另外的〉・country〈國家〉
❷ told〈tell（告訴）的過去式〉・try〈試圖〉・work〈工作〉・experience〈經驗〉
❸ as〈因為〉・find〈發現〉・language〈語言〉・barrier〈障礙〉・meet〈遇見〉
❹ different〈不同的〉・sometimes〈有時〉・culture〈文化〉・shock〈衝擊〉
❺ first〈第一次〉・moved away〈move away（搬走）的過去式〉・college〈大學〉
❻ acclimatized〈acclimatized（服水土、適應）的過去分詞〉・weather〈天氣〉・yet〈依然〉
❼ club〈俱樂部〉・racial〈種族的〉・discrimination〈歧視〉・awful〈糟糕的〉

中譯

❶ 這名交換學生喜歡在不同的國家生活。
❷ 指導教授告訴我，我應該試著增加工作經驗。
❸ 因為無法說出流利的中文，他發現自己和許多他所接觸的人之間，存有語言隔閡。
❹ 當你前往一個完全迥異的國家，有時候會感受到文化衝擊。
❺ 這名女孩在她第一次離家讀大學時很想家。
❻ 她來自寒冷的國家，目前仍對炎熱的氣候水土不服。
❼ 這名中國男子被告知因為他是中國人，所以無法成為俱樂部會員。這種種族歧視是很糟糕的。

015

作文 (1)

MP3 015

① structure
[`strʌktʃɚ]
(n.) 結構

【起承轉合】指「作文的章法」、「文章的佈局」。

② middle
[`mɪdl]
(n.) 承（承接）/中間的段落

【承】：文章的承接。承接「起」並加以論述。

③ beginning
[bɪ`ɡɪnɪŋ]
(n.) 起（開頭）

【起】：文章的開頭。在起頭處提出自己的主張和看法。

④ argument
[`ɑrɡjəmənt]
(n.) 論點

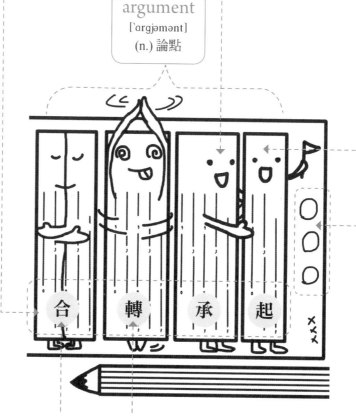

【合】：文章的總結。綜合前面所述，並提出結語。

【轉】：文章的轉接、轉折。從不同面向論述，創造文章的高潮。

⑤ conclusion
[kən`kluʒən]
(n.) 合（總結）

⑥ climax
[`klaɪmæks]
(n.) 轉（轉折）

⑦ topic
[`tɑpɪk]
(n.) 主題/標題

❶ 結構

To write a complete dissertation requires a solid structure.
<u>一篇完整的論文</u>

❷ 承（承接）/ 中間的段落

My English professor said the middle of my report had too many grammatical errors, so I needed to rewrite it.
有太多文法錯誤

❸ 起（開頭）

I've written a good beginning in which I introduce the topic. I'm not sure what to write next, though.
<u>接下來要寫什麼</u>

❹ 論點

Denise presented her argument very well in her essay.
闡述她的論點

❺ 合（總結）

The conclusion of the essay summed up the writer's opinions.

❻ 轉（轉折）

The climax of the story came when the detectives found the killer.
故事出現了轉折

❼ 主題 / 標題

What topic is your essay going to be about?

學更多

❶ complete〈完整的〉・dissertation〈論文〉・solid〈紮實的〉
❷ professor〈教授〉・report〈報告〉・grammatical〈文法的〉・error〈錯誤〉・rewrite〈修改〉
❸ written〈write（寫）的過去分詞〉・introduce〈介紹〉・sure〈確信的〉・though〈然而〉
❹ presented〈present（描述）的過去式〉・well〈很好地〉・essay〈論說文〉
❺ summed up〈sum up（總結）的過去式〉・writer〈作者〉・opinion〈意見〉
❻ story〈故事〉・detective〈偵探〉・found〈find（找到）的過去式〉・killer〈兇手〉
❼ about〈關於〉

中譯

❶ 要寫作一篇完整的論文，須具備紮實的結構。
❷ 我的英文教授說，我報告裡中間的段落有太多文法上的錯誤，所以我必須修改它。
❸ 我已經寫了一個很好的開頭來介紹主題，但我不確定接下來該寫些什麼。
❹ Denise 在論說文中，極佳地闡述了她的論點。
❺ 這篇論說文的總結，歸納出了作者的看法。
❻ 當偵探找出殺人兇手的時候，故事出現了轉折。
❼ 你的論說文主題會是什麼？

016

作文(2)

1 paragraph
[ˋpærə͵græf]
(n.) 段落

2 title
[ˋtaɪtl]
(n.) 主題/標題

3 sentence
[ˋsɛntəns]
(n.) 句

4 word
[wɝd]
(n.) 字

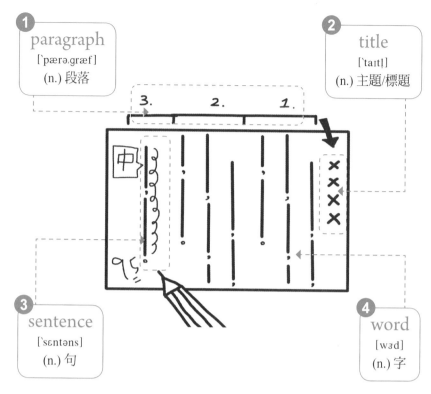

5 plagiarism
[ˋpledʒə͵rɪzəm]
(n.) 抄襲

6 reference
[ˋrɛfərəns]
(n.) 參考資料

❶ 段落

Paragraphs group together sentences about the same subject.
把句子聚集在一起

❷ 主題／標題

The title of an essay should say what has been written about.
寫了什麼

❸ 句

Sentences are usually ended by periods.

❹ 字

"The" is one of the most common English words.

❺ 抄襲

Plagiarism is wrong; don't copy other people's work.

❻ 參考資料

When you write essays, make sure you use trustworthy references.
可靠的參考資料

學更多

❶ group〈聚集〉‧same〈同樣的〉‧subject〈主題〉
❷ essay〈論說文〉‧say〈說明〉‧written〈write（寫）的過去分詞〉
❸ usually〈通常〉‧ended〈end（結束）的過去分詞〉‧period〈句號〉
❹ most〈最〉‧common〈常見的〉
❺ wrong〈錯誤的〉‧copy〈抄襲〉‧work〈作品〉
❻ make sure〈確保〉‧use〈使用〉‧trustworthy〈可靠的〉

中譯

❶ 段落將相同主題的句子聚集在一起。
❷ 論說文的標題必須說明文章的內容。
❸ 句子通常以句號作為結尾。
❹ 「The」是最常用的英文字之一。
❺ 抄襲是不對的；請勿抄襲他人的作品。
❻ 當你撰寫論說文時，要確定你使用的是可靠的參考資料。

017
書 (1)

MP3 017

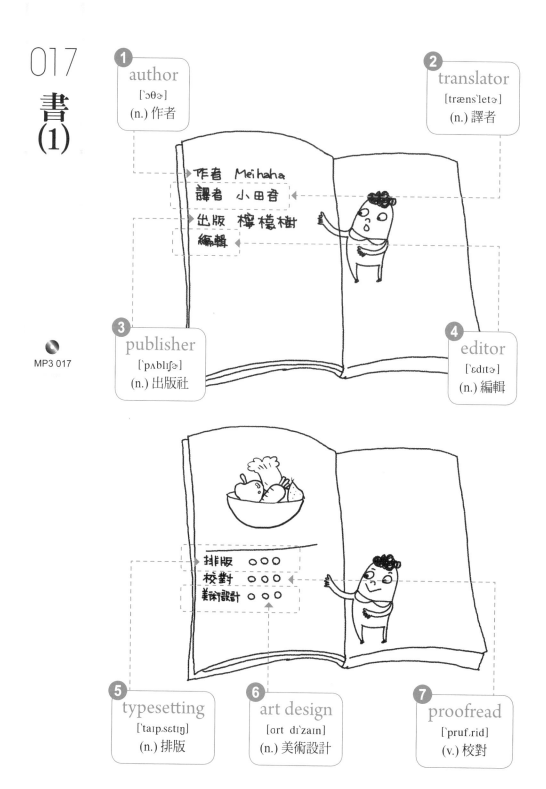

1 author
[ˈɔθɚ]
(n.) 作者

2 translator
[trænsˈletɚ]
(n.) 譯者

3 publisher
[ˈpʌblɪʃɚ]
(n.) 出版社

4 editor
[ˈɛdɪtɚ]
(n.) 編輯

5 typesetting
[ˈtaɪpˌsɛtɪŋ]
(n.) 排版

6 art design
[ɑrt dɪˈzaɪn]
(n.) 美術設計

7 proofread
[ˈprufˌrid]
(v.) 校對

作者 Meihaha
譯者 小田音
出版 檸檬樹
編輯

排版 ○○○
校對 ○○○
美術設計 ○○○

❶ 作者

Stephenie Meyer is the author of the Twilight books.
<u>暮光之城的書籍</u>

❷ 譯者

The translator changed the words from English into Chinese.
<u>從英文變成中文</u>

❸ 出版社

The publisher agreed to print Danny's novel.

❹ 編輯

The editor asked the writer to make some changes to his book.
<u>對他的書做一些改變</u>

❺ 排版

The typesetting is messed up, so the paragraphs don't fit on the page.
<u>不符合頁面</u>

❻ 美術設計

The art design was done by a great young artist.
<u>一位優秀的年輕藝術家</u>

❼ 校對

Dawn proofread the book to look for mistakes.

學更多

❶ twilight〈薄暮〉・book〈書籍〉

❷ changed〈change（更改）的過去式〉・word〈字〉

❸ agreed〈agree（同意）的過去式〉・print〈出版〉・novel〈小說〉

❹ asked〈ask（要求）的過去式〉・writer〈作家〉・change〈改變〉

❺ messed up〈mess up（弄糟）的過去分詞〉・paragraph〈段落〉・fit〈相稱〉・page〈頁面〉

❻ design〈設計〉・done〈do（製作）的過去分詞〉・young〈年輕的〉・artist〈藝術家〉

❼ proofread〈proofread（校對）的過去式〉・look for〈尋找〉・mistake〈錯誤〉

中譯

❶ Stephenie Meyer 是暮光之城系列小說的作者。

❷ 這位譯者將文字內容從英文翻譯成中文。

❸ 出版社同意出版 Danny 的小說。

❹ 編輯要求這位作家對他的書的內容稍做更動。

❺ 排版弄得亂七八糟，導致段落沒有放在該放的地方。

❻ 這個美術設計是出自一位優秀的年輕藝術家之手。

❼ Dawn 校對書籍來找出錯誤。

018

書
(2)

1 printing
[ˋprɪntɪŋ]
(n.) 印刷

2 bookbinding
[bʊkˋbaɪndɪŋ]
(n.) 裝訂

MP3 018

印刷 – ○○○印刷公司
裝訂 – 平裝本

3 version
[ˋvɝʒən]
(n.) 刷次/版本

4 second-hand book
[ˋsɛkəndˋhænd bʊk]
(n.) 二手書

5 out of print
[aʊt ɑv prɪnt]
(phr.) 絕版

❶ 印刷

Thanks to the elimination of paper and printing costs, e-books sell for

省去紙張和印刷的成本

about half the price of regular books.

大約是一半的價錢

❷ 裝訂

The bookbinding process turns separate pages into an actual book.

把各書頁做成

❸ 刷次 / 版本

The new version of the book leaves out some chapters. I don't like it.

省去一些章節

❹ 二手書

This is a second-hand book. That's why it looks a bit old.

這就是為什麼…

❺ 絕版

The book's out of print. They don't make it any more.

學更多

❶ thanks to〈幸虧〉‧ elimination〈除去〉‧ paper〈紙〉‧ cost〈費用〉‧ e-book〈電子書〉‧
sell〈賣〉‧ about〈大約〉‧ half〈一半的〉‧ price〈價格〉‧ regular〈一般的〉

❷ process〈過程〉‧ turn...into〈使…變成…〉‧ separate〈個別的〉‧ page〈頁〉‧
actual〈實際的〉

❸ leave out〈省去〉‧ some〈某些、一些〉‧ chapter〈章節〉‧ like〈喜歡〉

❹ second-hand〈二手的〉‧ a bit〈有點〉‧ old〈舊的〉

❺ print〈出版〉‧ make〈製作〉‧ not...any more〈不再…〉

中譯

❶ 歸功於省去紙張及印刷的成本費用，電子書的售價約是一般書籍（紙本書）的一半。

❷ 在裝訂的流程中，會把個別的書頁加工成一本真正的書。

❸ 這本書的新版本將某些章節刪減了。我不喜歡這個版本。

❹ 這是一本二手書。這就是它為什麼看起來有點舊的原因。

❺ 這本書絕版了，他們今後將不再印刷。

019

書 (3)

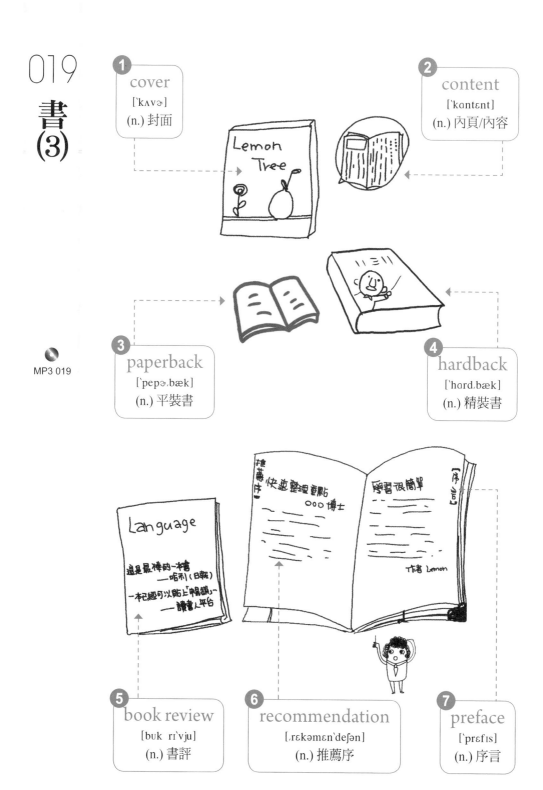

1. cover
['kʌvɚ]
(n.) 封面

2. content
['kɑntɛnt]
(n.) 內頁/內容

3. paperback
['pepɚ,bæk]
(n.) 平裝書

4. hardback
['hɑrd,bæk]
(n.) 精裝書

5. book review
[bʊk rɪ'vju]
(n.) 書評

6. recommendation
[,rɛkəmɛn'deʃən]
(n.) 推薦序

7. preface
['prɛfɪs]
(n.) 序言

MP3 019

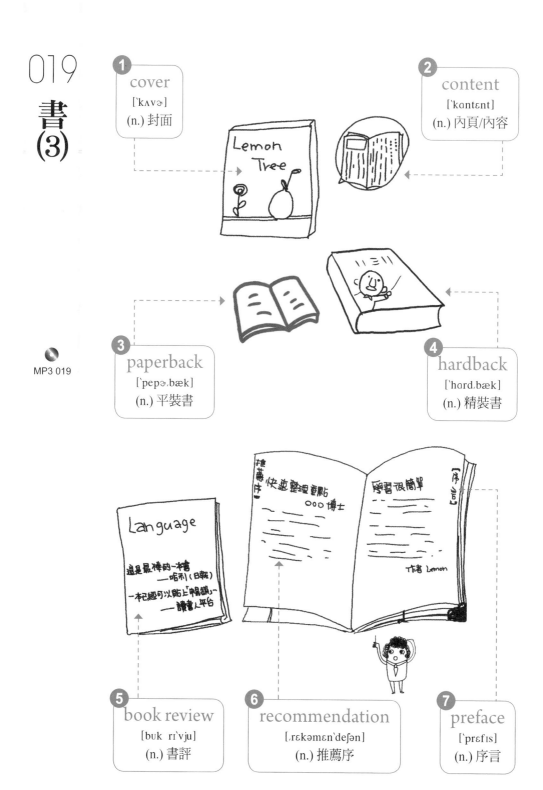

Lemon Tree

Language

這是最棒的一本書
——咕利 (日森)
一本絕可以貼上鴨頭」
——讀書人平台

推
薦
序

快速整理重點
OOO博士

學習很簡單

作者 Lemon

序

❶ 封面
❷ 內頁 / 內容
Don't judge a book by its cover. Open it, and look at some of the content.
<u>看一下內容</u>

❸ 平裝書
Paperbacks have a soft cover.

❹ 精裝書
Hardbacks are usually more expensive than paperbacks.
<u>比平裝書更貴</u>

❺ 書評
I read a book review about this novel. Apparently it's very good.

❻ 推薦序
This book was a recommendation from my brother. He said it's good.
<u>來自我哥哥的推薦</u>

❼ 序言
I never read the preface at the start of a book.
<u>書本一開始的地方</u>

學更多

❶ ❷ judge〈判斷〉‧ open〈打開〉‧ look at...〈看…〉‧ some〈一些〉
❸ have〈有〉‧ soft〈軟的〉
❹ usually〈通常〉‧ expensive〈昂貴的〉
❺ read〈read（閱讀）的過去式〉‧ review〈評論〉‧ novel〈小說〉‧ apparently〈顯然地〉
❻ brother〈兄弟〉‧ said〈say（說）的過去式〉
❼ never〈從未〉‧ read〈讀〉‧ start〈開頭〉

中譯

❶ ❷ 不要憑封面來評判一本書的好壞。要打開它，並看一下內容。
❸ 平裝書的封面是軟的。
❹ 精裝書的價格通常比平裝書貴。
❺ 我看了有關這本小說的書評，很明顯地，它的評價非常好。
❻ 這本書是我哥哥推薦的，他說這本書很讚。
❼ 我從來不看書本前面的序言。

020

初次見面(1)

MP3 020

1 shake hands
[ʃek hændz]
(phr.) 握手

2 self-introduction
[sɛlf.ɪntrə`dʌkʃən]
(n.) 自我介紹

3 name card
[nem kɑrd]
business card
[`bɪznɪs kɑrd]
(n.) 名片

兩個單字都是「名片」。

4 greeting
[`gritɪŋ]
(n.) 寒暄

5 break the ice
[brek ði aɪs]
(phr.) 打破沉默

❶ 握手

After you've been introduced, shake hands.
你們已經互相介紹了

❷ 自我介紹

At the start of the meeting, I had to give a self-introduction.

❸ 名片

Here's my name card. It has my contact details on it.
聯絡方式

❹ 寒暄

There are many kinds of greetings, but "Hi!" is one of the most
有很多種打招呼的方式

common.

❺ 打破沉默

Nobody was talking, so, to break the ice, Lindsey told a joke.

學更多

❶ after〈在…之後〉‧introduced〈introduce（介紹）的過去分詞〉‧shake〈握手〉‧
hand〈手〉

❷ start〈最初〉‧meeting〈會議〉‧had to〈have to（必須）的過去式〉‧give〈做〉‧
self〈自我〉‧introduction〈介紹〉

❸ name〈名字〉‧card〈卡片〉‧business〈商務〉‧contact〈聯絡〉‧detail〈細節〉

❹ kind〈種類〉‧most〈最〉‧common〈常見〉

❺ nobody〈沒有人〉‧talking〈talk（講話）的 ing 型態〉‧break〈打破〉‧ice〈冰〉‧
told〈tell（講）的過去式〉‧joke〈笑話〉

中譯

❶ 在你們互相介紹完之後，就握個手。

❷ 在會議開始時，我必須做自我介紹。

❸ 這是我的名片，上面有我的聯絡方式。

❹ 寒暄的方式有很多，但「嗨！」是其中最普遍的。

❺ 沒有人開口說話，所以，為了打破沉默，Lindsey 講了一個笑話。

021

初次見面(2)

MP3 021

1 déjà vu
[ˌdeʒɑˈvu]
(n.) 似曾相識

2 stranger
[ˈstrendʒɚ]
(n.) 陌生人

3 awkward silence
[ˈɔkwəd ˈsaɪləns]
(n.) 冷場

4 get along well
[gɛt əˈlɔŋ wɛl]
(phr.) 合得來

5 don't get along
[dont gɛt əˈlɔŋ]
(phr.) 合不來/不對盤

❶ 似曾相識

Steve had a feeling of déjà vu when he saw the black cat outside. He was
<u>有種似曾相識的感覺</u>
sure he'd seen it before.

❷ 陌生人

It's not safe for children to talk to strangers.
<u>對小孩來說是不安全的</u>

❸ 冷場

There was an awkward silence after Tom told us the rude joke.
<u>告訴了我們這個粗俗笑話</u>

❹ 合得來

Amy gets along well with her mother. They chat quite often.

❺ 合不來 / 不對盤

I don't get along with my brothers. We don't see each other very often.

學更多

❶ had〈have（有）的過去式〉・feeling〈感覺〉・saw〈see（看）的過去式〉・
outside〈在外面〉・sure〈確信的〉・seen〈see（看）的過去分詞〉

❷ safe〈安全的〉・children〈child（小孩）的複數〉・talk〈講話〉

❸ awkward〈尷尬的〉・silence〈沉默〉・told〈tell（講）的過去式〉・rude〈粗俗的〉・
joke〈笑話〉

❹ get along〈和睦地相處〉・chat〈聊天〉・quite〈相當〉・often〈時常〉

❺ brother〈兄弟〉・see〈看見〉・each other〈互相〉

中譯

❶ Steve 看到外面那隻黑貓時，有種似曾相識的感覺。他確定自己曾經看過牠。

❷ 讓小孩子跟陌生人交談是不安全的。

❸ 在 Tom 對大家講了個粗俗的笑話之後，現場一片冷場。

❹ Amy 和媽媽很合得來，她們時常聊天。

❺ 我和我的兄弟合不來，我們不常見面。

022

初次見面(3)

MP3 022

1 first impression
[fɝst ɪmˈprɛʃən]
(n.) 第一印象

2 good feeling
[gʊd ˈfilɪŋ]
(n.) 好感

3 bad feeling
[bæd ˈfilɪŋ]
(n.) 反感/不好的感覺

4 wary
[ˈwɛrɪ]
(adj.) 戒心

5 nervous
[ˈnɝvəs]
(adj.) 緊張

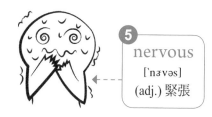

❶ 第一印象

My first impression of her was good. I'd like to get to know her.
<u>想了解她</u>

❷ 好感

I had a good feeling about her. I think she's nice.

❸ 反感 / 不好的感覺

I've got a bad feeling about this. I think it will go badly.
有不好的感覺　　　　　　　　　　進展不順利

❹ 戒心

Ginny was hurt by her last boyfriend, so she's wary of starting a new relationship.
展開新戀情

❺ 緊張

Many people get nervous when they meet someone for the first time.
和人初次見面

學更多

❶ first〈第一的〉‧ impression〈印象〉‧ know〈認識〉
❷ had〈have（有）的過去式〉‧ feeling〈感覺〉‧ nice〈好的〉
❸ got〈get（得到）的過去式〉‧ bad〈不好的〉‧ go〈進行〉‧ badly〈不好地〉
❹ hurt〈受傷的〉‧ last〈上一個的〉‧ starting〈start（開始）的 ing 型態〉‧ new〈新的〉‧ relationship〈關係〉
❺ meet〈見面〉‧ someone〈某人〉‧ first time〈第一次〉

中譯

❶ 我對她的第一印象很好，我想要更了解她。
❷ 我對她很有好感，我覺得她人很好。
❸ 我對這件事有不好的感覺，我覺得事情不會進展順利。
❹ Ginny 的前男友傷透了她的心，使得她對展開新戀情充滿戒心。
❺ 許多人在與人初次見面時，都會感到緊張。

023

生日
(1)

MP3 023

1 birthday song
[ˋbɝθ.de sɔŋ]
(n.) 生日快樂歌

2 birthday party
[ˋbɝθ.de ˋpɑrtɪ]
(n.) 生日派對

Happy Birthday to You…

3 surprised
[səˋpraɪzd]
(adj.) 感到驚喜

4 candle
[ˋkændḷ]
(n.) 蠟燭

5 make a wish
[mek ə wɪʃ]
(phr.) 許願

6 birthday cake
[ˋbɝθ.de kek]
(n.) 生日蛋糕

❶ 生日快樂歌

All around the world, people use the same birthday song.

❷ 生日派對

It's Ben's birthday tomorrow. We should have a birthday party for him.

❸ 感到驚喜

I was so surprised when my friends gave me a cake on my birthday.

❹ 蠟燭

Ted blew out the candles on his cake.

吹熄蠟燭

❺ 許願

After you blow out the candles, you should make a wish.

❻ 生日蛋糕

The little boy wanted to cut his own birthday cake at his party.

學更多

❶ around〈到處〉．same〈同樣的〉．birthday〈生日〉．song〈歌曲〉

❷ tomorrow〈明天〉．have〈進行〉．party〈派對〉

❸ friend〈朋友〉．gave（give（送給）的過去式〉

❹ blew out〈blow out（吹熄）的過去式〉．cake〈蛋糕〉

❺ after〈在…之後〉．make〈做〉．wish〈願望〉

❻ little〈小的〉．wanted〈want（想要）的過去式〉．cut〈切〉．own〈自己的〉

中譯

❶ 全世界的人都唱同一首生日快樂歌。

❷ 明天就是 Ben 的生日，我們應該為他辦個生日派對。

❸ 生日時朋友送我一個蛋糕，我感到非常驚喜。

❹ Ted 吹熄了蛋糕上的蠟燭。

❺ 吹熄蠟燭後，你要許願。

❻ 這個小男孩想在派對上切他的生日蛋糕。

024

生日 (2)

MP3 024

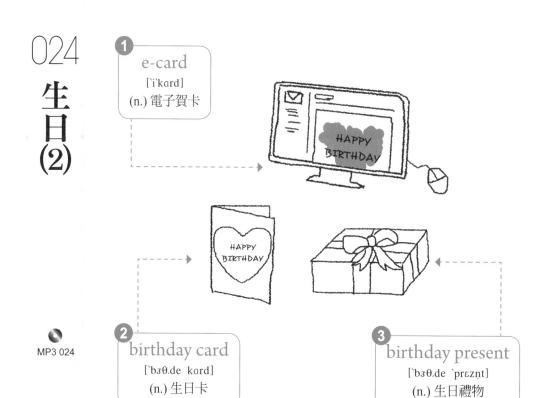

1 e-card
[ˋiˋkɑrd]
(n.) 電子賀卡

2 birthday card
[ˋbɝθˎde kɑrd]
(n.) 生日卡

3 birthday present
[ˋbɝθˎde ˋprɛzn̩t]
(n.) 生日禮物

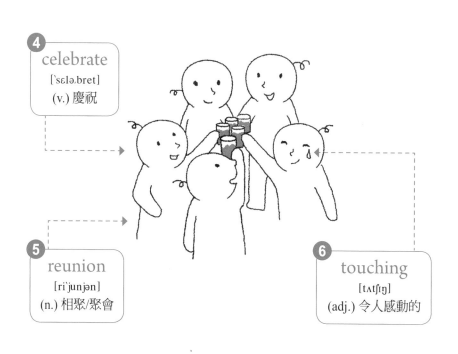

4 celebrate
[ˋsɛləˎbret]
(v.) 慶祝

5 reunion
[riˋjunjən]
(n.) 相聚/聚會

6 touching
[tʌtʃɪŋ]
(adj.) 令人感動的

❶ 電子賀卡
To save paper, you can send people e-cards through the Internet.
透過網路

❷ 生日卡
Do you want to write a message in Ben's birthday card?

❸ 生日禮物
The little girl was happy when she opened her birthday presents.

❹ 慶祝
We're having a party to celebrate Wendy's birthday.

❺ 相聚／聚會
The old classmates are going to have a reunion next weekend.
將舉辦一個聚會

❻ 令人感動的
The kind message Eva wrote in the card was very touching.
Eva 寫下的貼心話

學更多

❶ save〈節省〉・paper〈紙〉・through〈憑藉〉・Internet〈網際網路〉
❷ write〈寫〉・message〈訊息〉・birthday〈生日〉・card〈卡片〉
❸ little〈小的〉・opened〈open（打開）的過去式〉・present〈禮物〉
❹ having〈have（進行）的 ing 型態〉・party〈派對〉
❺ old〈舊交的〉・classmate〈同班同學〉・weekend〈週末〉
❻ kind〈親切的〉・wrote〈write（寫）的過去式〉

中譯

❶ 為了節約用紙，你可以透過網路寄送電子賀卡。
❷ 你想在 Ben 的生日卡上寫些什麼嗎？
❸ 拆開生日禮物時，小女孩很開心。
❹ 我們將舉辦一個派對來慶祝 Wendy 的生日。
❺ 老同學們將在下週末舉辦一場聚會。
❻ Eva 寫在卡片上的貼心話，非常令人感動。

025

打
電
話
(1)

MP3 025

1 dial
[`daɪəl]
(v.) 撥打（電話）

2 call log
[kɔl lɔg]
(n.) 通話記錄

3 wrong number
[rɔŋ `nʌmbə]
(n.) 打錯電話

Mr. A
?

Mr. B

4 leave a message
[liv ə `mɛsɪdʒ]
(phr.) 留話

message:

5 no answer
[no `ænsə]
(phr.) 無人接聽

Doo…
Doo…

6 telephone scam
[`tɛlə.fon `skæm]
(n.) 詐騙電話

$

7 con man / con artist
[kɑn mæn] / [kɑn `ɑrtɪst]
(n.) 詐騙分子

兩個單字都是
「詐騙分子」。

❶ 撥打（電話）

Dean picked up the phone and dialed his friend's number.
　　　　　拿起電話

❷ 通話記錄

Check your call log to see whether you have any missed calls.
　　　　　　　　　　　　　　　　　　　你是否有未接來電

❸ 打錯電話

You dialed the wrong number. I don't know you.
　　　　　　　打錯電話

❹ 留話

This is Nicky's voicemail. Please leave a message.

❺ 無人接聽

I tried calling him, but there was no answer.
　　　　　　　　　　　　　沒有人接聽電話

❻ 詐騙電話

That call was part of a telephone scam. Don't trust what they say.
　　　　　　　　　是一通詐騙電話　　　　　　　　　他們所說的

❼ 詐騙分子

I can't believe that con man was not prosecuted!
　　　　　　　　　　　　沒有被起訴

學更多

❶ picked up〈pick up（拿起）的過去式〉‧ dialed〈dial（撥號）的過去式〉‧ number〈號碼〉
❷ check〈檢查〉‧ call〈通話〉‧ log〈記錄〉‧ whether〈是否〉‧ missed〈錯過的〉
❸ wrong〈錯誤的〉‧ know〈認識〉
❹ voicemail〈語音信箱〉‧ please〈請〉‧ leave〈留下〉‧ message〈訊息〉
❺ tried〈try（嘗試）的過去式〉‧ calling〈call（打電話給…）的 ing 型態〉‧ answer〈接聽〉
❻ part of〈一部分〉‧ telephone〈電話〉‧ scam〈詐騙〉‧ trust〈信任〉
❼ con〈詐欺的〉‧ artist〈騙子〉‧ prosecuted〈prosecute（起訴）的過去分詞〉

中譯

❶ Dean 拿起電話，撥打他朋友的電話號碼。
❷ 查看你的通話記錄，看看有沒有未接來電。
❸ 你打錯電話了，我不認識你。
❹ 這是 Nicky 的語音信箱，請留話。
❺ 我試著打電話給他，但都無人接聽。
❻ 那是一通詐騙電話，不要相信他們所說的。
❼ 我真不敢相信，那名詐騙分子居然沒有被起訴！

026

打電話(2)

MP3 026

1 answer
[ˋænsɚ]
(v.) 接聽

2 operator
[ˋɑpəˏretɚ]
(n.) 總機

3 extension
[ɪkˋstɛnʃən]
(n.) 分機

4 transfer
[trænsˋfɝ]
(v.) 轉接

5 busy
[ˋbɪzɪ]
(adj.) 忙線

6 incoming call
[ˋɪnˏkʌmɪŋ kɔl]
(n.) 來電

7 call back
[kɔl bæk]
(phr.) 回電

066

❶ 接聽

My phone's ringing. I should answer it.

❷ 總機

Please dial the extension or wait for an operator.
<u>請撥打分機</u>

❸ 分機

After you call the company, dial my extension number. It's 619.

❹ 轉接

I'm just going to transfer you to my supervisor. Please hold.
請稍候

❺ 忙線

Oh, Sarah's phone's busy. I'll have to call her back later.
Sarah 的電話正在忙線中

❻ 來電

I have an incoming call; I should answer it.

❼ 回電

Tommy called about your date tonight. He wants you to call him back ASAP.

學更多

❶ phone〈電話〉・ringing〈ring（響）的 ing 型態〉
❷ please〈請〉・dial〈撥號〉・wait〈等待〉
❸ after〈在…之後〉・call〈打電話〉・company〈公司〉・number〈號碼〉
❹ supervisor〈主管〉・hold〈等待〉
❺ have to〈必須〉・back〈返回〉・later〈晚些時候〉
❻ have〈有〉・incoming〈進來的〉・call〈電話〉
❼ date〈約會〉・tonight〈今晚〉・ASAP〈as soon as possible（越快越好）的縮寫〉

中譯

❶ 我的電話響了，我得要接聽。
❷ 請撥打分機，或等待總機為您服務。
❸ 當你打電話到公司後，撥我的分機號碼 619。
❹ 我幫您轉接給我的主管，請稍候。
❺ 噢，Sarah 的電話正在忙線。我得之後再打電話給她。
❻ 我有一通來電，我得先接聽一下。
❼ Tommy 今晚打電話來問你有關約會的事情。他希望你盡快回電。

027

戀
愛
(1)

MP3 027

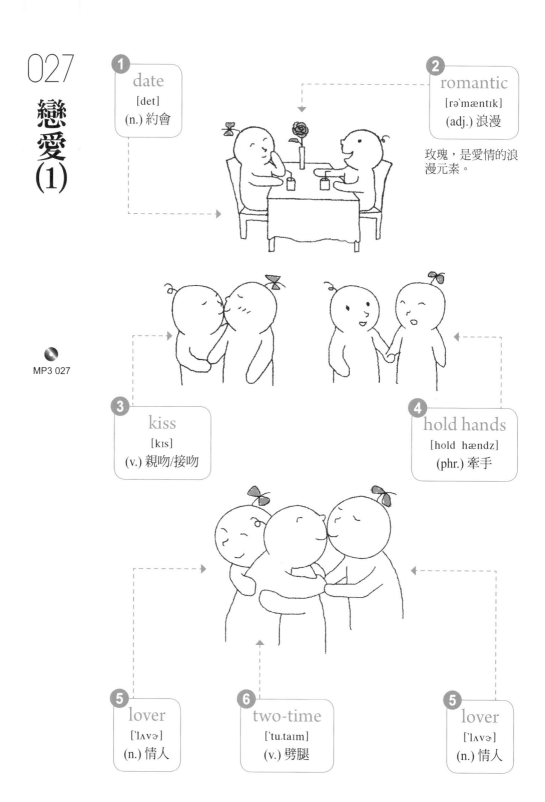

1 date
[det]
(n.) 約會

2 romantic
[rəˋmæntɪk]
(adj.) 浪漫

玫瑰，是愛情的浪漫元素。

3 kiss
[kɪs]
(v.) 親吻/接吻

4 hold hands
[hold hændz]
(phr.) 牽手

5 lover
[ˋlʌvɚ]
(n.) 情人

6 two-time
[ˋtu.taɪm]
(v.) 劈腿

5 lover
[ˋlʌvɚ]
(n.) 情人

❶ 約會

Joan and John are going on a date tonight. They really like each other.
今天晚上要約會

❷ 浪漫

Alex is very romantic; he's always buying his girlfriend flowers and gifts.
買花和禮物給他的女朋友

❸ 親吻 / 接吻

At the end of their date, Rick and Beth kissed.
在他們的約會結束時

❹ 牽手

Some guys don't like holding hands with their girlfriends.
和他們的女朋友牽手

❺ 情人

Emma wants to be with her lover all the time.
和她的情人在一起

❻ 劈腿

Erica is two-timing her boyfriend; she's seeing someone else.
她還有跟別人約會

學更多

❶ tonight〈今晚〉‧ really〈很〉‧ each other〈互相〉
❷ always〈總是〉‧ buying〈buy（購買）的 ing 型態〉‧ flower〈花〉‧ gift〈禮物〉
❸ end〈末尾〉‧ their〈他們的〉
❹ some〈一些〉‧ guy〈男人〉‧ holding〈hold（握著）的 ing 型態〉‧ hand〈手〉
❺ want〈想要〉‧ all the time〈一直〉
❻ two-timing〈two-time（劈腿）的 ing 型態〉‧ boyfriend〈男朋友〉‧
   seeing〈see（和…約會、交往）的 ing 型態〉‧ else〈其他〉

中譯

❶ Joan 和 John 今晚要約會，他們彼此很相愛。
❷ Alex 十分浪漫，總是買花和禮物送女朋友。
❸ 在約會結束時，Rick 和 Beth 接吻了。
❹ 有些男人不喜歡和女朋友牽手。
❺ Emma 無時無刻都想和她的情人在一起。
❻ Erica 對男朋友劈腿，她還有跟別人約會。

028

戀愛(2)

MP3 028

1 love at first sight
[lʌv æt fɜst saɪt]
(phr.) 一見鍾情

2 fall in love
[fɔl ɪn lʌv]
(phr.) 墜入愛河

3 live together
[lɪv təˈgɛðɚ]
(phr.) 同居

4 promise
[ˈprɑmɪs]
(v.) 承諾

一生相守，是愛情的最終承諾。

5 anniversary
[ˌænəˈvɜsərɪ]
(n.) 紀念日

❶ 一見鍾情
When Joe met Nikki, it was love at first sight.

❷ 墜入愛河
Ian fell in love with Annie when he began spending more time with her.
　　　　　　　　　　　　　　　　　　　　他開始花更多時間

❸ 同居
They're not married, but they do live together.

❹ 承諾
Simon promised his girlfriend that he would love her forever.
　　　　　　　　　　　　　　　　　　他會永遠愛她

❺ 紀念日
Mr. and Mrs. Nielson celebrated their fifth wedding anniversary with dinner.
Nielson 先生和 Nielson 太太　　　　　　　　　五周年結婚紀念日

學更多

❶ met〈meet（遇見）的過去式〉‧ love〈愛情〉‧ first〈第一的〉‧ sight〈看見〉
❷ fell〈fall（墜落）的過去式〉‧ began〈begin（開始）的過去式〉‧
spending〈spend（花費）的 ing 型態〉
❸ married〈已婚的〉‧ live〈居住〉‧ together〈一起〉
❹ promised〈promise（承諾）的過去式〉‧ girlfriend〈女朋友〉‧ love〈愛〉‧ forever〈永遠〉
❺ celebrated〈celebrate（慶祝）的過去式〉‧ fifth〈第五的〉‧ wedding〈婚禮〉‧
dinner〈晚餐〉

中譯

❶ 當 Joe 遇見 Nikki ，就對她一見鍾情。
❷ 當 Ian 開始用更多的時間陪伴 Annie 的時候，就是他墜入愛河的時候。
❸ 他們還沒結婚，但是他們同居。
❹ Simon 承諾他的女朋友，他會永遠愛她。
❺ Nielson 夫妻共進晚餐，慶祝他們五周年的結婚紀念日。

029

戀愛(3)

MP3 029

1 approach
[əˋprotʃ]
(v.) 追求

2 chocolate
[ˋtʃɑkəlɪt]
(n.) 巧克力

3 rose
[roz]
(n.) 玫瑰

4 love letter
[lʌv ˋlɛtɚ]
(n.) 情書

5 jealous
[ˋdʒɛləs]
(adj.) 嫉妒

❶ 追求

Sometimes a person approaches the one he or she loves wholeheartedly but still fails in the end. 有人全心全意地追求所愛

❷ 巧克力

Joe likes sweet food like ice cream and chocolate.

❸ 玫瑰

On his girlfriend's birthday, Harry gave her roses and chocolates.

❹ 情書

Chris wrote a love letter to his girlfriend.
　　　　　　　　　寫情書

❺ 嫉妒

Tina is jealous of Fiona because she likes her boyfriend, Neil.

學更多

❶ sometimes〈有時候〉‧ person〈人〉‧ wholeheartedly〈全心全意地〉‧ still〈仍然〉‧ fail〈失敗〉‧ in the end〈最後〉

❷ sweet food〈甜食〉‧ ice cream〈冰淇淋〉

❸ girlfriend〈女朋友〉‧ birthday〈生日〉‧ gave〈give（送）的過去式〉

❹ wrote〈write（寫）的過去式〉‧ love〈愛情〉‧ letter〈信件〉

❺ because〈因為〉‧ like〈喜歡〉‧ boyfriend〈男朋友〉

中譯

❶ 有時候，人全心全意去追求所愛，到最後卻仍是一場空。

❷ Joe 喜歡冰淇淋和巧克力這類的甜食。

❸ Harry 在女朋友生日時，送她玫瑰花和巧克力。

❹ Chris 寫情書給他的女朋友。

❺ Tina 很嫉妒 Fiona，因為她喜歡 Fiona 的男朋友 Neil。

030

搬
家
(1)

1 truck
[trʌk]
(n.) 卡車

2 moving company
[`muvɪŋ `kʌmpənɪ]
removal company
[rɪ`muvḷ `kʌmpənɪ]
(n.) 搬家公司

兩個單字都是「搬家公司」。

3 removal man
[rɪ`muvḷ mæn]
(n.) 搬家工人

MP3 030

4 luggage
[`lʌgɪdʒ]
(n.) 行李

5 pack / package
[pæk] / [`pækɪdʒ]
(v.) 打包/裝箱

兩個單字都是「打包/裝箱」。

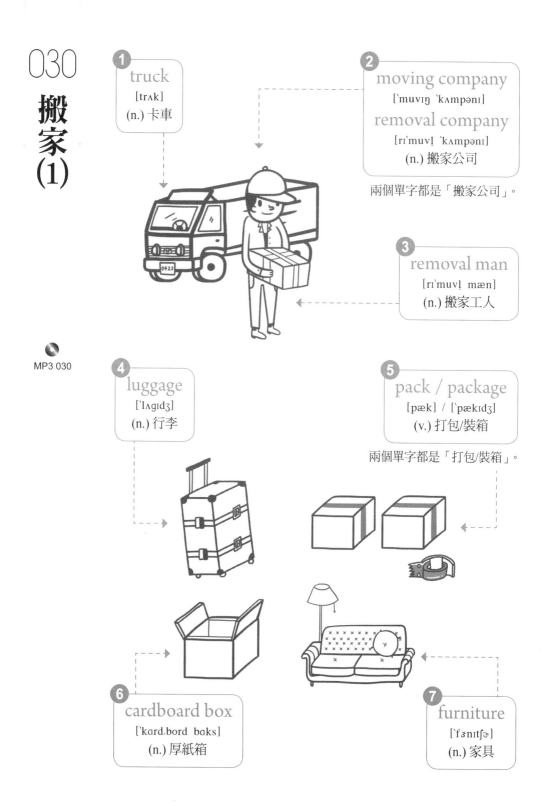

6 cardboard box
[`kɑrd.bord bɑks]
(n.) 厚紙箱

7 furniture
[`fɝnɪtʃɚ]
(n.) 家具

① 卡車
Paul's things were loaded into a truck and taken to his new house.
　　　　　　　　　被搬上卡車

② 搬家公司
The moving company will take your things to your new house.

③ 搬家工人
The removal man carried the chairs into the house.

④ 行李
Rose doesn't have many clothes. She's only got one piece of luggage.
　　　　　　　　　　　　　　　　　　　帶著一件行李

⑤ 打包 / 裝箱
He's packed all of his things into cardboard boxes.
他已經打包所有的東西（= He has packed all of his things）

⑥ 厚紙箱
Dan doesn't use shopping bags. When he goes to the supermarket, he
puts his things into cardboard boxes.
　　　　　　把他的東西放進厚紙箱裡

⑦ 家具
We only have one piece of furniture: an old sofa.
　　　　　　　　一件家具

學更多

① loaded〈load（裝載）的過去分詞〉・taken〈take（帶去）的過去分詞〉・house〈房子〉
② moving〈搬家的〉・company〈公司〉・thing〈物品〉・new〈新的〉
③ removal〈搬遷〉・carried〈carry（搬運）的過去式〉・chair〈椅子〉
④ many〈許多的〉・clothes〈衣服〉・only〈只〉・piece〈一件〉
⑤ packed〈pack（打包、裝箱）的過去分詞〉・all〈所有的〉・cardboard〈硬紙板〉
⑥ use〈使用〉・shopping bag〈購物袋〉・supermarket〈超級市場〉・put into〈把…放進〉
⑦ old〈舊的〉・sofa〈沙發〉

中譯

① Paul 的東西被搬上卡車，載往他的新家。
② 搬家公司會把你的東西載往新家。
③ 搬家工人把椅子搬進了屋裡。
④ Rose 的衣服不多，她只有一件行李。
⑤ 他把所有的東西都打包裝入厚紙箱。
⑥ Dan 不使用購物袋，當他去超市時，他把東西都放進厚紙箱裡。
⑦ 我們只有一件家具：一張舊沙發。

031

搬家(2)

①

transfer
[trænsˋfɝ]
(v.) 轉學

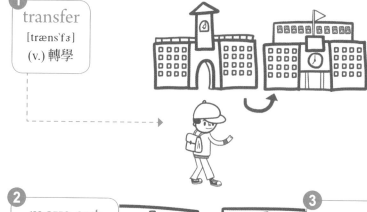

②

move out
[muv aut]
(phr.) 遷出/搬離

③

move in
[muv ɪn]
(phr.) 遷入/搬入

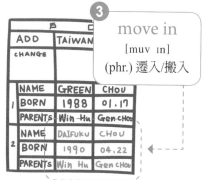

④

new home
[nju hom]
(n.) 新家

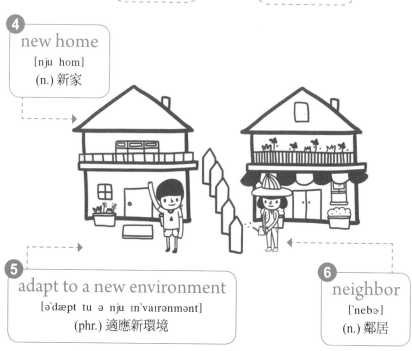

⑤

adapt to a new environment
[əˋdæpt tu ə nju ɪnˋvaɪrənmənt]
(phr.) 適應新環境

⑥

neighbor
[ˋnebɚ]
(n.) 鄰居

❶ 轉學

The student had to transfer schools when his parents moved.
學生必須轉學

❷ 遷出 / 搬離

When she got married, Mandy moved out of her parents' house.
她的娘家

❸ 遷入 / 搬入

Grace will move in to her new house next week.

❹ 新家

Sam and Sue bought a new home. They wanted somewhere that no one had lived in before.
之前沒有人住過的地方

❺ 適應新環境

Lily hasn't adapted to her new environment, so she's feeling homesick.
她很想家

❻ 鄰居

After moving in to her house, Lisa went next door to meet her neighbor.
去隔壁戶

學更多

❶ had to〈have to（必須）的過去式〉‧ parents〈父母〉‧ moved〈move（搬家）的過去式〉
❷ got married〈get married（結婚）的過去式〉‧ out〈在外面〉
❸ in〈進〉‧ new〈新的〉‧ house〈房子〉‧ next〈接下去的〉‧ week〈一星期〉
❹ bought〈buy（買）的過去式〉‧ somewhere〈在某處〉‧ lived〈live（住）的過去分詞〉
❺ adapted〈adapt（適應）的過去分詞〉‧ environment〈環境〉‧
feeling〈feel（感覺）的 ing 型態〉‧ homesick〈想家的〉
❻ moving〈move（搬家）的 ing 型態〉‧ next〈緊鄰的〉‧ meet〈認識〉

中譯

❶ 當父母親搬家了，學生就必須跟著轉學。
❷ Mandy 結婚後，就搬離她的娘家。
❸ Grace 下星期將搬入她的新家。
❹ Sam 和 Sue 買了新房子。他們想要一個之前沒有人住過的地方。
❺ Lily 還沒有適應新環境，因此她很想家。
❻ 搬進新家後，Lisa 就去隔壁認識她的鄰居。

032

說話(1)

MP3 032

1 speed
[spid]
(n.) （說話）速度

2 intonation
[ˌɪntoˈneʃən]
(n.) 語調

3 dialogue
[ˈdaɪəˌlɔg]
(n.) 對話

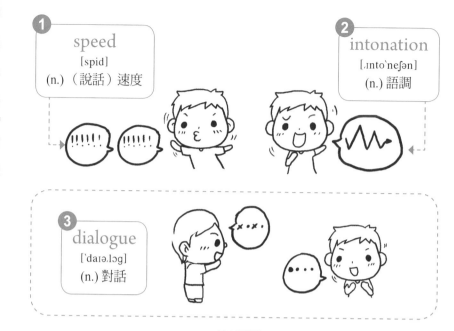

你記得那個人嗎？他就是…

4 speak slowly
[spik ˈsloli]
(phr.) 說話緩慢

我…好…像…

5 speak in haste
[spik ɪn hest]
(phr.) 說話急促/倉促發言

揮棒落空！

6 lisp
[lɪsp]
(n.) 口齒不清

飛棒落空！

7 clearly
[klɪrlɪ]
(adv.) 口齒清晰

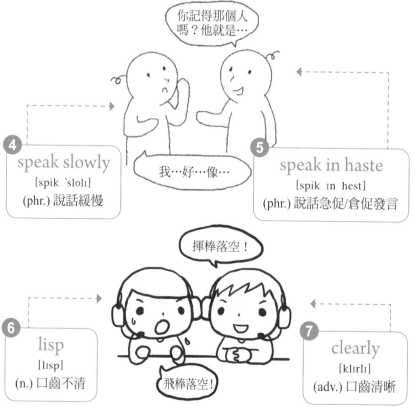

❶（說話）速度
He talks at a high speed. It's hard to understand him.

❷ 語調
Many people ask questions with a rising intonation.

❸ 對話
The dialogue between the two characters in the movie is very interesting.
兩個角色之間的對話

❹ 說話緩慢
Trevor spoke slowly and chose his words carefully.
注意他的用字遣詞

❺ 說話急促 / 倉促發言
Don't speak in haste. You might regret what you say.
你說的話

❻ 口齒不清
People with a lisp have trouble saying the letter "s."
說話口齒不清的人

❼ 口齒清晰
My English teacher is easy to understand because she speaks very clearly.

學更多

❶ talk〈講話〉・high〈高速的〉・hard〈困難的〉・understand〈懂〉
❷ many〈許多的〉・people〈人們〉・ask〈問〉・question〈問題〉・rising〈上升的〉
❸ between〈在…之間〉・character〈角色〉・movie〈電影〉・interesting〈有趣的〉
❹ spoke〈speak（說話）的過去式〉・chose〈choose（選擇）的過去式〉・carefully〈小心地〉
❺ in haste〈匆忙地〉・might〈可能〉・regret〈後悔〉・say〈說〉
❻ trouble〈困難〉・saying〈say（說）的 ing 型態〉・letter〈字母〉
❼ teacher〈老師〉・easy〈容易的〉

中譯

❶ 他講話的速度很快，很難聽懂他所說的。
❷ 很多人會用上升的語調來發問。
❸ 這部電影中，這兩個角色的對話非常有趣。
❹ Trevor 說話緩慢，而且謹慎地選擇用字遣詞。
❺ 別倉促發言，你可能會對說出口的話感到後悔。
❻ 說話口齒不清的人，在英文字母「s」的發音上有困難。
❼ 我的英文老師說的話很好懂，因為她說話口齒清晰。

033

說話(2)

MP3 033

1 murmur
[ˈmɝmɚ]
(v.) 喃喃低語

2 nonsense
[ˈnɑnsɛns]
(n.) 胡言亂語

3 whisper
[ˈhwɪspɚ]
(v.) 說悄悄話/竊竊私語

4 bite one's tongue
[baɪt wʌns tʌŋ]
(phr.) 盡力忍住不說

5 stutter
[ˈstʌtɚ]
(n.) 口吃

6 interrupt
[ˌɪntəˈrʌpt]
(v.) 插嘴

什、什麼事

好想說…

先聽我說…

❶ 喃喃低語

The little boy murmured quietly in his sleep.

❷ 胡言亂語

He's talking nonsense. It's just rubbish.

❸ 說悄悄話 / 竊竊私語

The employees are all whispering about what is happening.
發生了什麼事

❹ 盡力忍住不說

I had to bite my tongue and not say anything.

❺ 口吃

I have a stutter, so I sometimes repeat words or sounds.

❻ 插嘴

She kept interrupting me. I could never finish a sentence.
她一直打斷我說話　　　　　　　　從未說完一句話

學更多

❶ little〈小的〉・murmured〈murmur（喃喃低語）的過去式〉・quietly〈輕聲地〉・
sleep〈睡覺〉

❷ talking〈talk（說）的 ing 型態〉・just〈只是〉・rubbish〈廢話〉

❸ employee〈員工〉・happening〈happen（發生）的 ing 型態〉

❹ had to〈have to（必須）的過去式〉・bite〈咬住〉・tongue〈舌頭〉・anything〈任何事〉

❺ have〈有〉・sometimes〈有時〉・repeat〈重複〉・word〈字詞〉・sound〈聲音〉

❻ kept〈keep（持續不斷）的過去式〉・finish〈完成〉・sentence〈句子〉

中譯

❶ 小男孩在睡夢中，輕聲地喃喃低語。

❷ 他在胡言亂語，說的都是廢話。

❸ 員工們全都在竊竊私語，討論發生了什麼事。

❹ 我必須盡力忍住不說，不說出任何事。

❺ 我有口吃，所以有時候會重述字詞或聲音。

❻ 她一直插嘴打斷我，讓我沒辦法說出完整的一句話。

034

發言(1)

MP3 034

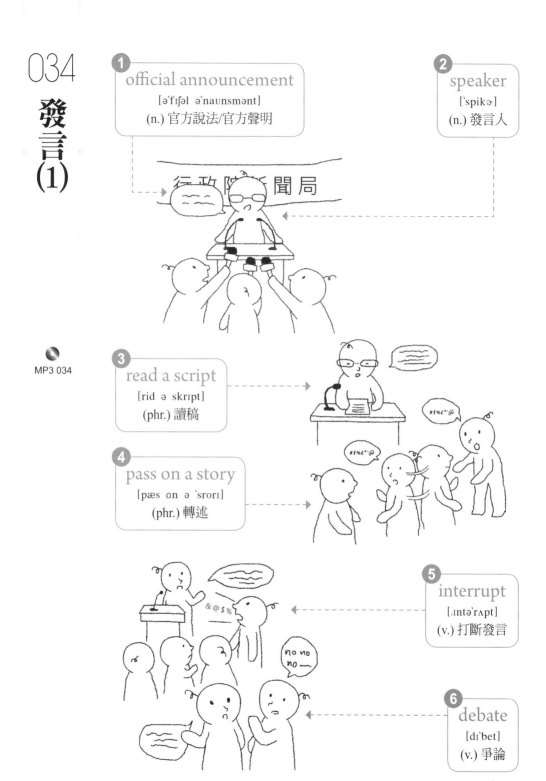

1 official announcement
[ə'fɪʃəl ə'naʊnsmənt]
(n.) 官方說法/官方聲明

2 speaker
['spikə]
(n.) 發言人

3 read a script
[rid ə skrɪpt]
(phr.) 讀稿

4 pass on a story
[pæs ɑn ə 'srorɪ]
(phr.) 轉述

5 interrupt
[ˌɪntə'rʌpt]
(v.) 打斷發言

6 debate
[dɪ'bet]
(v.) 爭論

❶ 官方說法 / 官方聲明

In an official announcement, the police said that they had caught the criminal.

他們已經逮捕犯人

❷ 發言人

The speaker looked nervous during her speech.

在她發言時

❸ 讀稿

The actor read his script before going on stage.

上舞台之前

❹ 轉述

Dave loves passing on stories. He's always telling others what people have told him.

人們告訴他的事情

❺ 打斷發言

Don't interrupt people when they're speaking. Let them finish what they want to say.

讓他們講完他們想說的話

❻ 爭論

The two men debated the issue, but they still couldn't agree.

仍然無法意見一致

學更多

❶ official〈官方的〉・announcement〈宣布〉・police〈警察〉・
said〈say（說、聲稱）的過去式〉・caught〈catch（逮捕）的過去分詞〉・criminal〈罪犯〉

❷ looked〈look（看起來）的過去式〉・nervous〈緊張的〉・speech〈演講、公開發言〉

❸ actor〈演員〉・read〈read（讀）的過去式〉・script〈劇本、底稿〉・stage〈舞台〉

❹ passing〈pass（傳遞）的 ing 型態〉・others〈其餘的人〉・told〈tell（告訴）的過去分詞〉

❺ speaking〈speak（說話）的 ing 型態〉・finish〈完成〉・want〈想要〉

❻ men〈man（男人）的複數〉・issue〈議題〉・still〈還是〉・agree〈意見一致〉

中譯

❶ 在一次官方聲明中，警方聲稱他們已經逮捕犯人。
❷ 這位發言人在發言時看起來很緊張。
❸ 演員上台前，先讀了稿。
❹ Dave 喜歡轉述。他總是把別人告訴他的事又告訴其他人。
❺ 不要在別人說話時打斷發言，要讓他們把話說完。
❻ 這兩個男人爭論這個問題，但始終無法達成共識。

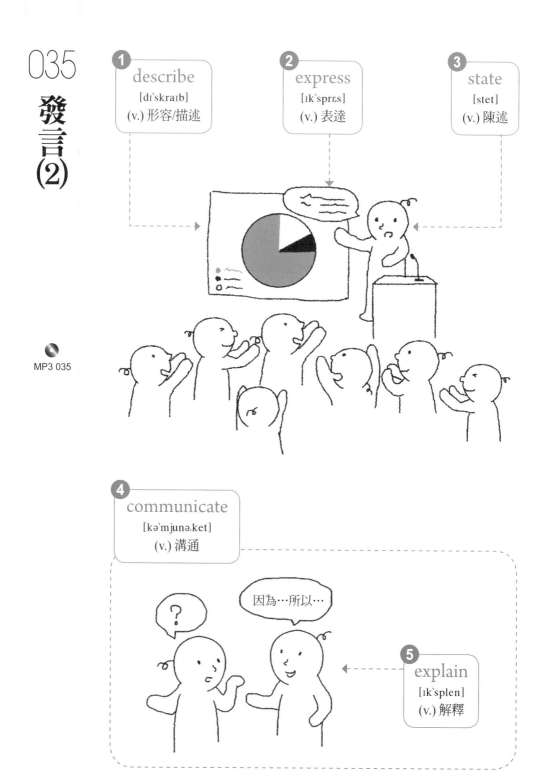

035

發言(2)

MP3 035

1 describe
[dɪˋskraɪb]
(v.) 形容/描述

2 express
[ɪkˋsprɛs]
(v.) 表達

3 state
[stet]
(v.) 陳述

4 communicate
[kəˋmjunə͵ket]
(v.) 溝通

5 explain
[ɪkˋsplen]
(v.) 解釋

因為⋯所以⋯

?

❶ 形容 / 描述
Amy described her new car to her friends.

❷ 表達
He expressed his view that cats are nicer than dogs.
                          貓比狗更好

❸ 陳述
The president stated her opinions on the issue.
                  主席陳述她的意見

❹ 溝通
Since Liz doesn't speak German, she can't communicate easily with people
in Berlin.
                          她無法順利地與人溝通

❺ 解釋
The teacher explained the new word to his students.

學更多

❶ described〈describe（形容、描述）的過去式〉‧car〈車子〉‧friend〈朋友〉
❷ expressed〈express（表達）的過去式〉‧view〈看法〉‧cat〈貓〉‧
   nicer〈更好的，nice（好的）的比較級〉‧dog〈狗〉
❸ president〈主席〉‧stated〈state（陳述）的過去式〉‧opinion〈意見〉‧issue〈議題〉
❹ since〈因為〉‧speak〈講〉‧German〈德語〉‧easily〈容易地〉‧Berlin〈柏林〉
❺ teacher〈老師〉‧explained〈explain（解釋）的過去式〉‧word〈單字〉‧student〈學生〉

中譯

❶ Amy 向朋友們描述她的新車。
❷ 他表達了他的看法 —— 認為貓優於狗。
❸ 主席陳述她對這個議題的見解。
❹ 因為 Liz 不會講德語，所以她在柏林無法順利地與人溝通。
❺ 老師對學生們解釋新單字。

036

敵對 (1)

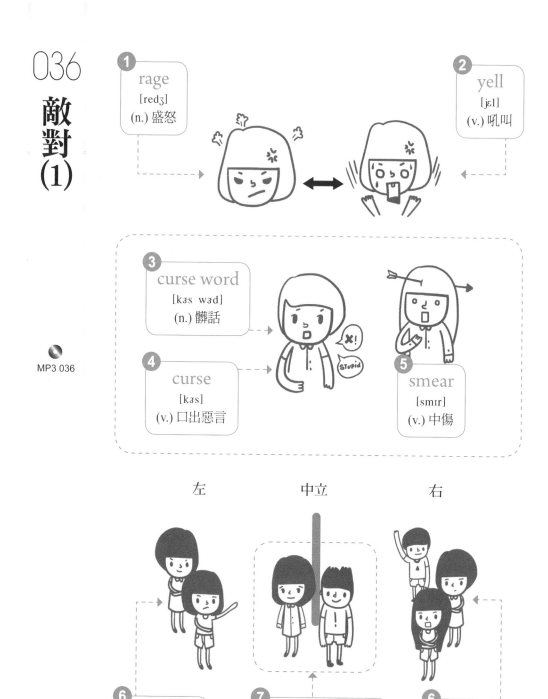

1 rage
[redʒ]
(n.) 盛怒

2 yell
[jɛl]
(v.) 吼叫

3 curse word
[kɝs wɝd]
(n.) 髒話

4 curse
[kɝs]
(v.) 口出惡言

5 smear
[smɪr]
(v.) 中傷

MP3 036

左　　　　　中立　　　　　右

6 take sides
[tek saɪdz]
(phr.) 選邊站

7 sit on the fence
[sɪt ɑn ðə fɛns]
(phr.) 保持中立

6 take sides
[tek saɪdz]
(phr.) 選邊站

❶ 盛怒

Brian was in a rage earlier. I wonder what made him angry.
　　　　　　　勃然大怒　　　　　　　　　　　　　什麼事情讓他生氣

❷ 吼叫

Don't yell at me. I didn't do anything wrong.
　　　　對我吼叫

❸ 髒話

My mom says that curse words are dirty. She never uses them.
　　　　　　　　　　　髒話很不雅

❹ 口出惡言

You shouldn't curse around children.

❺ 中傷

Steve tried to smear his opponent by saying bad things about him.
　　　　　　　　　　　　　　　　　　　　說他的壞話

❻ 選邊站

Rupert didn't want to take sides in the argument. He liked both people too
much to do that.　　　　　　　　　　　　　太喜歡雙方的人，而無法…

❼ 保持中立

She always sits on the fence. She never gives an opinion.
　　　　　　　　　　　　　　　　　　給予意見

學更多

❶ earlier〈早先的時候〉・wonder〈想知道〉・made〈make（使）的過去式〉・angry〈生氣的〉

❷ do〈做〉・anything〈任何事情〉・wrong〈錯誤的〉

❸ mom〈媽媽〉・say〈說〉・dirty〈不雅的〉・never〈從未〉・use〈使用〉

❹ around〈在…周圍〉・children〈child（小孩）的複數〉

❺ tried〈try（嘗試）的過去式〉・opponent〈對手〉・saying〈say（說）的 ing 型態〉

❻ side〈一方〉・argument〈爭執〉・both〈雙方的〉・too...to...〈太…，而無法…〉

❼ always〈總是〉・sit〈坐〉・fence〈籬笆〉・give〈給予〉・opinion〈意見〉

中譯

❶ Brian 稍早時盛怒，我想知道他在氣什麼。

❷ 別對我吼叫，我沒有做錯任何事。

❸ 我媽媽說，髒話很不雅，她從來不說髒話。

❹ 你不該在小孩面前口出惡言。

❺ Steve 試圖說對手的壞話來中傷他。

❻ Rupert 不想在這場爭執中選邊站。兩邊的人他都非常喜歡，所以無法抉擇。

❼ 她總是保持中立，從來不給予意見。

037

敵對(2)

MP3 037

1 malice
[`mælɪs]
(n.) 惡意

2 hate
[het]
(v.) 憎恨

導致

3 enemy
[`ɛnəmɪ]
(n.) 敵人

4 hostility
[hɑs`tɪlətɪ]
(n.) 敵意

5 confront
[kən`frʌnt]
(v.) 對質

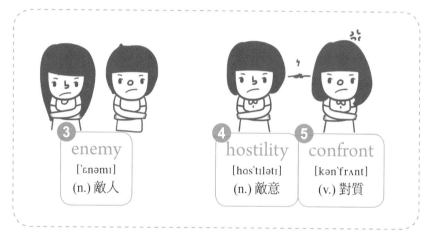

6 negotiate
[nɪ`goʃɪˌet]
(v.) 談判

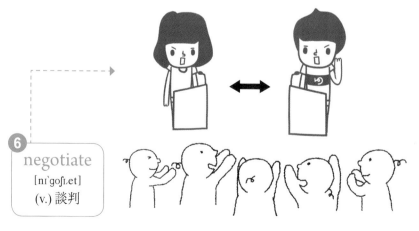

❶ 惡意

I know she offended you, but there wasn't any malice in her words.

她說的話裡

❷ 憎恨

I hate that song. It's terrible.

❸ 敵人

The two boys have been enemies since they were little. They're always

從他們小時候就是敵人

trying to beat each other.

❹ 敵意

Peter has a lot of hostility towards me. He really doesn't like me.

對我充滿敵意

❺ 對質

After the boy said something bad about her, she confronted him and

講了她的壞話

asked him why he did it.

❻ 談判

The worker negotiated with his boss to get a bigger salary.

得到更多的薪水

學更多

❶ know〈知道〉‧ offended〈offend（冒犯）的過去式〉‧ word〈話語〉
❷ song〈歌曲〉‧ terrible〈糟糕的〉
❸ since〈自…以來〉‧ little〈幼小的〉‧ trying〈try（嘗試）的 ing 型態〉‧ beat〈打〉
❹ a lot of〈大量〉‧ towards〈對於〉‧ really〈真地、確實〉‧ like〈喜歡〉
❺ bad〈壞的〉‧ confronted〈confront（對質）的過去式〉‧ asked〈ask（問）的過去式〉
❻ worker〈員工〉‧ negotiated〈negotiate（談判）的過去式〉‧ boss〈老闆〉‧
　 get〈獲得〉‧ bigger〈較大的，big（大的）的比較級〉‧ salary〈薪資〉

中譯

❶ 我知道她冒犯了你，但她的話並沒有惡意。
❷ 我憎恨那首歌，它很糟糕。
❸ 這兩個男孩從小就視對方為敵人，他們總想揍對方。
❹ Peter 對我充滿敵意，他真的很不喜歡我。
❺ 那個男孩講了她的壞話之後，她便與他對質，質問他為何這樣做。
❻ 員工跟他的老闆進行談判，以求取更高的薪資。

038

吵架(1)

1 silent treatment
[ˈsaɪlənt ˈtritmənt]
(n.) 冷戰

2 terminate the relationship
[ˈtɝmə.net ðə rɪˈleʃənˌʃɪp]
(phr.) 絕交

3 wrangle
[ˈræŋgl̩]
(n.) 口角

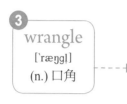

4 complain
[kəmˈplen]
(v.) 抱怨

5 argue
[ˈɑrgju]
(v.) 爭辯

6 point the finger at
[pɔɪnt ðə ˈfɪŋɡɚ æt]
(phr.) 指責

7 curse
[kɝs]
(v.) 咒罵

❶ 冷戰

Serena's giving me the silent treatment. She hasn't spoken to me for days.
正在跟我冷戰

❷ 絕交

We used to be friends, but I generally disagree with his actions so I
過去曾是朋友　　　　　　　　　　　　　不認同他的行為

terminated the relationship.

❸ 口角

After their cars collided, the drivers had a bit of a wrangle.
發生了一些口角

❹ 抱怨

The mother is complaining about how messy her daughter's bedroom is.
她女兒的房間有多亂

❺ 爭辯

The boy's arguing with his girlfriend because she saw him looking at other girls.
看到他在看其他女生

❻ 指責

Joe never takes responsibility; he always points the finger at other people.
負責任

❼ 咒罵

Paul cursed the man who knocked into him on the street.
撞到他的男人

學更多

❶ silent〈沉默的〉・treatment〈對待〉・spoken〈speak（講話）的過去分詞〉
❷ generally〈總體上〉・terminated〈terminate（結束）的過去式〉・relationship〈關係〉
❸ collided〈collide（相撞）的過去式〉・driver〈司機〉・a bit of a〈有些〉
❹ about〈關於〉・messy〈凌亂的〉・daughter〈女兒〉・bedroom〈寢室〉
❺ saw〈see（看見）的過去式〉・looking at...〈look at（看…）的 ing 型態〉
❻ responsibility〈責任〉・point at〈指向〉・finger〈手指〉・other〈其他的〉
❼ knocked into〈knock into（撞上）的過去式〉・street〈街道〉

中譯

❶ Serena 正在跟我冷戰，她已經好幾天不跟我說話。
❷ 我們以前曾經是朋友，但總體而言我並不認同他的行為，因此跟他絕交了。
❸ 車子相撞之後，車主們發生了一些口角。
❹ 媽媽正在抱怨她女兒的房間有多麼雜亂。
❺ 男孩正在跟女朋友爭辯，因為她看到他在注視其他女生。
❻ Joe 從不負責任。他總是指責其他人。
❼ Paul 咒罵在街上撞到他的那個男人。

039

吵架(2)

MP3 039

1 yell
[jɛl]
(v.) 吼叫

2 outraged
[ˋaut.redʒd]
(adj.) 憤怒的

3 out of control
[aut ɑv kənˋtrol]
(phr.) 情緒失控

4 cry
[kraɪ]
(v.) 哭泣

5 apologize
[əˋpalə.dʒaɪz]
(v.) 道歉

6 make up
[mek ʌp]
(phr.) 和好

❶ 吼叫

The teacher yelled at the student who didn't do his homework.
　　　　　　對學生吼叫

❷ 憤怒的

Emily was outraged when her friend started dating her boyfriend.
　　　　　　　　　　　　　　　　開始和她男朋友約會

❸ 情緒失控

I feel like she's out of control. She says whatever she wants and never
thinks about others.　　　　　　　她說任何她想說的話

❹ 哭泣

After being shouted at, the boy sat down and cried.
　　　　　被呵斥

❺ 道歉

I apologize for what I said before. I was very rude.
　　　　　　　　我之前說的話

❻ 和好

After their fight, the two boys shook hands and made up.
　　　　　　　　　　　　　　　　握手言和

學更多

❶ teacher〈老師〉・yelled〈yell（吼叫）的過去式〉・student〈學生〉・homework〈作業〉

❷ friend〈朋友〉・dating〈date（約會）的 ing 型態〉・boyfriend〈男朋友〉

❸ feel like〈感覺好像〉・out of〈脫離〉・control〈控制〉・whatever〈不管什麼〉・
others〈其餘的人〉

❹ shouted〈shout（叫嚷）的過去分詞〉・sat down〈sit down（坐下）的過去式〉

❺ said〈say（說）的過去式〉・before〈之前〉・rude〈無禮的〉

❻ fight〈打架〉・shook hands〈shake hands（握手）的過去式〉

中譯

❶ 老師朝這名沒做作業的學生吼叫。

❷ 當 Emily 的朋友開始跟她男朋友約會時，她很憤怒。

❸ 我覺得她已經情緒失控，她想說什麼就說什麼，完全不考慮其他人。

❹ 被呵斥之後，那名男孩坐下來哭泣。

❺ 我為我之前說的話道歉，我太失禮了。

❻ 打完架之後，這兩個男孩便握手和好了。

040

討論事情(1)

MP3 040

1 debate
[dɪˋbet]
(v.) 爭論

2 argue
[ˋɑrgjʊ]
(v.) 爭執

3 perfectly calm
[ˋpɝfɪktlɪ kɑm]
(phr.) 心平氣和

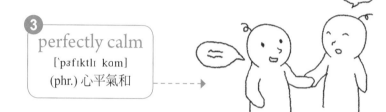

4 agree
[əˋgri]
(v.) 同意

5 disagree
[͵dɪsəˋgri]
(v.) 不同意

6 no comment
[no ˋkɑmɛnt]
(phr.) 不予置評

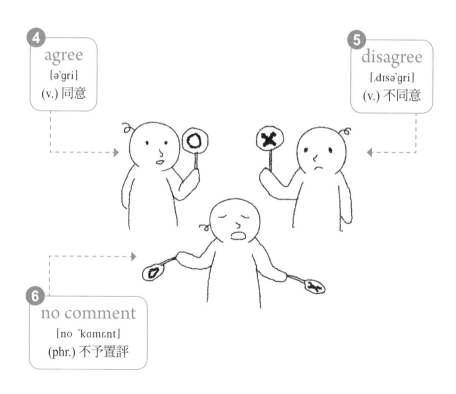

❶ 爭論
The two women debated which designer was better, Louis Vuitton or Gucci.

❷ 爭執
Jeff and his girlfriend are always arguing; they don't seem happy together.
他們在一起似乎不太開心

❸ 心平氣和
I'm not angry. I'm perfectly calm.

❹ 同意
I usually agree with Dan, but I thought he was wrong today.

❺ 不同意
I disagree with what you said; I think you're wrong.
你說的話

❻ 不予置評
When asked for his opinion, the president wouldn't answer. He just said,
問及他的意見時
"No comment."

學更多

❶ women〈woman（女人）的複數〉‧ designer〈設計師〉‧ better〈較好的〉
❷ always〈總是〉‧ arguing〈argue（爭執）的 ing 型態〉‧ seem〈似乎〉‧ together〈一起〉
❸ angry〈生氣的〉‧ perfectly〈完全地〉‧ calm〈平靜的〉
❹ usually〈通常〉‧ thought〈think（認為）的過去式〉‧ wrong〈錯誤的〉
❺ said〈say（說）的過去式〉
❻ asked〈ask（問）的過去式〉‧ opinion〈意見〉‧ president〈總統〉‧ answer〈回答〉‧ just〈只〉‧ comment〈評論〉

中譯

❶ 兩名女子爭論哪邊的設計比較好，是 Louis Vuitton 還是 Gucci。
❷ Jeff 和他的女朋友總是在爭執，他們在一起似乎不太開心。
❸ 我沒有生氣，我很心平氣和。
❹ 我通常會同意 Dan，但我覺得他今天是錯的。
❺ 我不同意你所說的，我覺得你錯了。
❻ 當問及總統的意見時，他不願回答，只說了句「不予置評」。

041

討論事情(2)

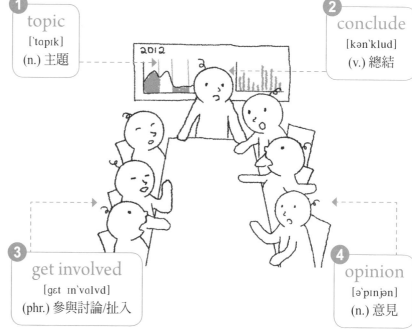

1 topic
['tɑpɪk]
(n.) 主題

2 conclude
[kən'klud]
(v.) 總結

3 get involved
[gɛt ɪn'vɑlvd]
(phr.) 參與討論/扯入

4 opinion
[ə'pɪnjən]
(n.) 意見

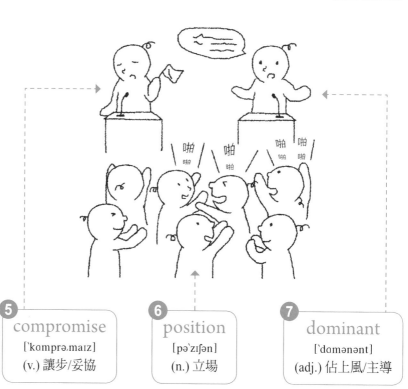

5 compromise
['kɑmprə,maɪz]
(v.) 讓步/妥協

6 position
[pə'zɪʃən]
(n.) 立場

7 dominant
['dɑmənənt]
(adj.) 佔上風/主導

❶ 主題

What's the topic for today's discussion?

❷ 總結

After all that, I just want to conclude by saying that we want to move forward
with this project. 繼續進行這項計劃

❸ 參與討論／扯入

Don't get involved in their argument. Let them sort it out.
讓他們自己解決

❹ 意見

Terry told me what he thought about the story. It was an interesting opinion.
他對這個故事的感想

❺ 讓步／妥協

The worker wanted NT$50,000, the boss wanted to give NT$40,000.
They compromised and agreed on NT$45,000.

❻ 立場

What's your position on these protests? What do you think about them?

❼ 佔上風／主導

Harry's the dominant person in the relationship. He makes the decisions.
做決定

學更多

❶ discussion〈討論〉
❷ after〈在…之後〉・just〈只〉・move〈進展〉・forward〈向前〉・project〈計劃〉
❸ get〈處於某種狀態〉・involved〈牽扯在內的〉・argument〈爭執〉・sort out〈解決〉
❹ told〈tell（告訴）的過去式〉・thought〈think（想）的過去式〉・interesting〈有趣的〉
❺ worker〈員工〉・boss〈老闆〉・agreed〈agree（意見一致）的過去式〉
❻ protest〈抗議〉・think〈想〉
❼ person〈人〉・relationship〈關係〉・make〈做出〉・decision〈決定〉

中譯

❶ 今天討論的主題是什麼？
❷ 經過這些事情之後，我用這句話來總結 —— 我們要繼續進行這項計劃。
❸ 不要扯入他們的爭執，讓他們自己解決。
❹ Terry 告訴我他對這個故事的感想，那是個有趣的意見。
❺ 員工要求 5 萬元台幣，老闆只想支付 4 萬元。他們最後妥協以 4 萬 5 千元達成共識。
❻ 在這些抗議中，你秉持什麼立場？你對他們有何看法？
❼ Harry 是這段關係的主導者，總是由他做決定。

042

送禮 (1)

1 gift shop
[gɪft ʃɑp]
(n.) 禮品店

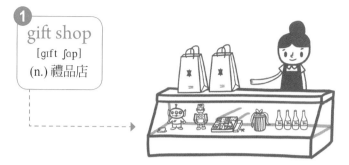

2 kindness
[ˋkaɪndnɪs]
(n.) 善意

3 appropriate
[əˋproprɪ,et]
(adj.) 得體/恰當

MP3 042

4 taboo
[təˋbu]
(n.) 禁忌

（傘）　=　（散）

5 kiss up to someone
[kɪs ʌp tu ˋsʌm,wʌn]
(phr.) 討好別人

❶ 禮品店

Ian went into the gift shop to buy things for his family.

❷ 善意

It was a great kindness for the man to give you his favorite hat.
<u>對那名男子來說這是極大的善意</u>

❸ 得體 / 恰當

It's not appropriate to give teenagers wine.

❹ 禁忌

It's a bit of a taboo to ask someone how much they spent on a gift.
<u>有點算是禁忌</u>　　　　　　　　　　<u>他們花多少錢</u>
Don't do it.

❺ 討好別人

Carly is kissing up to the boss. Maybe she wants more money.
　　　　　　　　　　　　　　　　　　　<u>她想要更多的錢</u>

學更多

❶ went into〈go into（進入）的過去式〉・gift〈禮品〉・shop〈商店〉・family〈家人〉
❷ great〈巨大的〉・give〈送〉・favorite〈特別喜愛的〉・hat〈帽子〉
❸ teenager〈青少年〉・wine〈酒〉
❹ a bit of a〈有些〉・ask〈問〉・spent〈spend（花錢）的過去式〉
❺ kissing up〈kiss up（拍馬屁）的 ing 型態〉・boss〈老闆〉・more〈更多的〉・money〈錢〉

中譯

❶ Ian 去禮品店為家人買些東西。
❷ 對那名男子來說，送給你他心愛的帽子，就是他的極大善意。
❸ 給青少年酒精飲料是不恰當的。
❹ 問人花了多少錢買禮物算是個禁忌。千萬別這麼做。
❺ Carly 一直討好老闆，也許她是想獲得加薪。

043

送禮(2)

MP3 043

1 gift
[gɪft]
(n.) 禮物

2 greeting card
[ˋgritɪŋ kɑrd]
(n.) 賀卡

3 ribbon
[ˋrɪbən]
(n.) 緞帶

4 wrapping paper
[ˋræpɪŋ ˋpepɚ]
(n.) 包裝紙

5 bow
[bo]
(n.) 蝴蝶結

6 exchange gifts
[ɪksˋtʃendʒ gɪfts]
(phr.) 交換禮物

7 unwrap
[ʌnˋræp]
(v.) 拆開（包裝）

❶ 禮物

Sally gave me a gift for my birthday.

❷ 賀卡

The greeting card has "Happy birthday" written on the front of it.

在卡片的正面上

❸ 緞帶

After wrapping the gift, Mollie tied it with red ribbon.

替它繫上紅緞帶

❹ 包裝紙

I don't know what the gift is because it's covered in wrapping paper.

禮物是什麼　　　　　　　　　它被包裝紙包住

❺ 蝴蝶結

Fiona tied her laces into a bow.

❻ 交換禮物

We exchanged gifts before Christmas.

❼ 拆開（包裝）

You can't unwrap your gift until Christmas Day.

學更多

❶ gave〈give（送）的過去式〉‧ birthday〈生日〉

❷ greeting〈祝賀詞〉‧ card〈卡片〉‧ written〈write（寫）的過去分詞〉‧ front〈正面〉

❸ after〈在…之後〉‧ wrapping〈wrap（包）的 ing 型態〉‧ tied〈tie（繫上）的過去式〉

❹ covered〈cover（覆蓋…的表面）的過去分詞〉‧ wrapping〈包裝材料〉‧ paper〈紙〉

❺ lace〈鞋帶〉‧ into〈變成〉

❻ exchanged〈exchange（交換）的過去式〉‧ before〈在…之前〉‧ Christmas〈聖誕節〉

❼ until〈直到…時〉

中譯

❶ Sally 送了我一個禮物，祝賀我的生日。

❷ 賀卡的正面印有「生日快樂」的字樣。

❸ 包裝完禮物後，Mollie 為它繫上紅緞帶。

❹ 我不知道這個禮物是什麼，因為它被包裝紙包起來了。

❺ Fiona 把她的鞋帶綁成一個蝴蝶結。

❻ 我們在聖誕節來臨前交換禮物。

❼ 你要等到聖誕節當天才能拆開禮物。

044

洗衣服

MP3 044

1 care label
[kɛr ˋlebḷ]
(n.) 洗滌標示

2 wash by hand
[waʃ baɪ hænd]
(phr.) 手洗

3 bleach
[blitʃ]
(n.) 漂白/漂白劑

4 dry clean
[draɪ klin]
(phr.) 乾洗

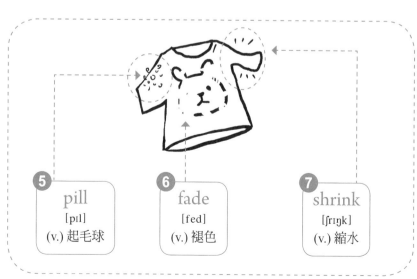

5 pill
[pɪl]
(v.) 起毛球

6 fade
[fed]
(v.) 褪色

7 shrink
[ʃrɪŋk]
(v.) 縮水

❶ 洗滌標示
The care label on the shirt tells you how to wash it.
<u>讓你知道如何清洗它</u>

❷ 手洗
There's a nasty stain on this shirt. I'll have to wash it by hand.
難處理的汙漬

❸ 漂白 / 漂白劑
Valerie used bleach to make her towels white.
<u>使她的毛巾變白</u>

❹ 乾洗
You can't put this top in a washing machine. It needs to be dry cleaned.
洗衣機　　　　　　　　　　　被乾洗

❺ 起毛球
There are little balls of wool on my sweater. It's pilling.
小毛球

❻ 褪色
My black shirt has faded. It's gray now.

❼ 縮水
Wool can shrink easily if you don't wash it properly.

學更多

❶ care〈照料〉‧label〈標籤〉‧shirt〈襯衫〉‧tell〈顯示某訊息〉‧wash〈洗〉
❷ nasty〈難處理的〉‧stain〈汙漬〉‧have to〈必須〉‧hand〈手〉
❸ used〈use（使用）的過去式〉‧make〈使得〉‧towel〈毛巾〉‧white〈白色的〉
❹ put〈放〉‧top〈上衣〉‧dry〈乾燥〉‧cleaned〈clean（清洗）的過去分詞〉
❺ little〈小的〉‧ball〈球狀的物體〉‧wool〈毛織品〉‧sweater〈毛衣〉
❻ black〈黑色的〉‧faded〈fade（褪色）的過去分詞〉‧gray〈灰色的〉
❼ easily〈容易地〉‧if〈如果〉‧properly〈正確地〉

中譯

❶ 襯衫上的洗滌標示會告訴你清洗方式。
❷ 襯衫上有一個頑強的汙漬，我必須手洗它。
❸ Valerie 用漂白劑將她的毛巾漂白。
❹ 你不能把這件上衣放進洗衣機裡，它必須乾洗。
❺ 我的毛衣上有些小毛球。它起毛球了。
❻ 我的黑色襯衫褪色了，它現在變成灰色的。
❼ 若你沒有正確地清洗毛織品，它很容易縮水。

045

朋友 (1)

MP3 045

1 friendship
['frɛndʃɪp]
(n.) 友誼

2 close friend
[kloz frɛnd]
(n.) 好友

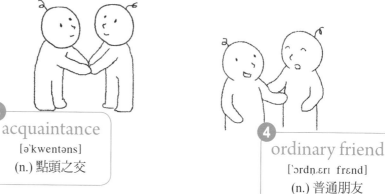

3 acquaintance
[əˋkwentəns]
(n.) 點頭之交

4 ordinary friend
[ˋɔrdn͵ɛrɪ frɛnd]
(n.) 普通朋友

5 fair-weather friend
[ˋfɛr͵wɛðɚ frɛnd]
(n.) 酒肉朋友

6 childhood friend
[ˋtʃaɪld͵hʊd frɛnd]
(n.) 童年好友

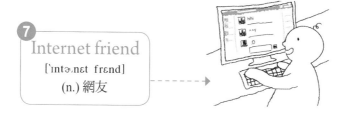

7 Internet friend
[ˋɪntɚ͵nɛt frɛnd]
(n.) 網友

❶ 友誼

I've known Mark for years. We have a good friendship.

❷ 好友

Gina's a close friend. We talk about everything.
聊任何事情

❸ 點頭之交

We're not really friends, just acquaintances.

❹ 普通朋友

We're just ordinary friends, nothing more than that.
除此之外沒有其他的了

❺ 酒肉朋友

She's a fair-weather friend. She's never around when I'm having problems.
她從不在我身旁

❻ 童年好友

Sam is a childhood friend. We met in school.

❼ 網友

Dom's an Internet friend. I met him on Twitter.

學更多

❶ known〈know（認識）的過去分詞〉・good〈好的〉
❷ close〈親密的〉・friend〈朋友〉・talk〈說〉・everything〈每件事〉
❸ really〈真正的〉・just〈只〉
❹ ordinary〈普通的〉・nothing〈沒什麼〉・more〈更多的〉
❺ fair-weather〈不能共患難的〉・never〈從未〉・around〈在附近〉・problem〈問題〉
❻ childhood〈童年時期〉・met〈meet（認識）的過去式〉・school〈學校〉
❼ Internet〈網路〉・Twitter〈推特，一個社群網路的平台〉

中譯

❶ 我認識 Mark 好幾年了，我們有很好的友誼。
❷ Gina 是我的好友，我們無所不談。
❸ 我們算不上是真正的朋友，只是點頭之交。
❹ 我們只是普通朋友，除此之外沒有其他關係。
❺ 她是個酒肉朋友，當我有困難時她從不在身邊。
❻ Sam 是我的童年好友，我們是在學校認識的。
❼ Dom 是我的網友，我是在推特上認識他的。

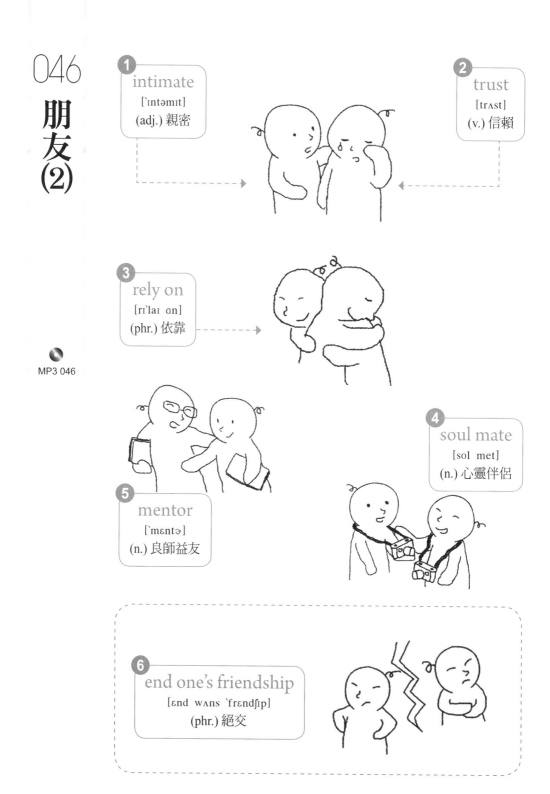

046

朋友(2)

MP3 046

1 intimate
[ˈɪntəmɪt]
(adj.) 親密

2 trust
[trʌst]
(v.) 信賴

3 rely on
[rɪˈlaɪ ɑn]
(phr.) 依靠

4 soul mate
[sol met]
(n.) 心靈伴侶

5 mentor
[ˈmɛntɚ]
(n.) 良師益友

6 end one's friendship
[ɛnd wʌns ˈfrɛndʃɪp]
(phr.) 絕交

❶ 親密

Claire and Emily are intimate. They don't have any secrets.

❷ 信賴

I don't trust Ron. He always lies.

❸ 依靠

I know I can rely on Beth. She's always been there for me when I've
needed her.
　　　　　　　　　　　　　　　　她總是為我在那

❹ 心靈伴侶

Neil's my soul mate. We feel the same way about everything.
　　　　　　　　　　　　　　對…有同樣的想法

❺ 良師益友

Sam's a bit of a mentor to me. He's taught me so much.
　　　有點算是良師益友

❻ 絕交

Tom ended our friendship after I kissed his girlfriend.

學更多

❶ have〈有〉‧ any〈任何〉‧ secret〈祕密〉
❷ always〈總是〉‧ lie〈說謊〉
❸ know〈知道〉‧ been〈be（在）的過去分詞〉‧ needed〈need（需要）的過去分詞〉
❹ soul〈心靈〉‧ mate〈同伴〉‧ feel〈感覺〉‧ same〈相同的〉‧ way〈方式〉
❺ a bit of a〈有些〉‧ taught〈teach（教導）的過去分詞〉
❻ ended〈end（結束）的過去式〉‧ friendship〈友誼〉‧ kissed〈kiss（吻）的過去式〉

中譯

❶ Claire 和 Emily 很親密，他們之間沒有任何祕密。
❷ 我不信賴 Ron，他總是說謊。
❸ 我知道我可以依靠 Beth。當我需要她的時候，她總會在那裡。
❹ Neil 是我的心靈伴侶，我們對每件事都有相同的想法。
❺ Sam 對我來說算是個良師益友，他教導我許多。
❻ 我吻了 Tom 的女朋友之後，他就和我絕交了。

居家裝潢(1)

1 interior designer / interior decorator
[ɪnˋtɪrɪə dɪˋzaɪnə] / [ɪnˋtɪrɪə ˋdɛkəˌretə]
(n.) 室內設計師

2 blueprint
[ˋbluˋprɪnt]
(n.) 藍圖

兩個單字都是「室內設計師」。

3 design
[dɪˋzaɪn]
(v.) 設計

4 decorate
[ˋdɛkəˌret]
(v.) 裝潢/粉刷

5 furnishings
[ˋfɚnɪʃɪŋz]
(n.) 室內陳設/家具

6 lighting
[ˋlaɪtɪŋ]
(n.) 採光

7 partition
[parˋtɪʃən]
(n.) 隔間

❶ 室內設計師

Hillary is an interior designer. She knows how to make a house look good.

<u>讓房子看起來美觀</u>

❷ 藍圖

The builder looked at the blueprint before starting to build the house.

看了藍圖

❸ 設計

Wendy designed a dress for her daughter to wear.

❹ 裝潢 / 粉刷

Andy bought some paint to decorate his room.

❺ 室內陳設 / 家具

Frank needs to buy furnishings, such as chairs and tables, for his home.

❻ 採光

The lighting in this apartment is very bright.

❼ 隔間

Using a partition, we'll separate this room into two spaces.

隔開這間房間成兩個空間

學更多

❶ interior〈內部的〉‧designer〈設計師〉‧decorator〈裝潢的人〉‧look〈看起來〉
❷ builder〈建築工人〉‧starting〈start（開始）的 ing 型態〉‧build〈建造〉
❸ designed〈design（設計）的過去式〉‧dress〈洋裝〉‧daughter〈女兒〉‧wear〈穿〉
❹ bought〈buy（買）的過去式〉‧paint〈油漆〉‧room〈房間〉
❺ need〈需要〉‧such as〈像是〉‧chair〈椅子〉‧table〈桌子〉
❻ apartment〈公寓〉‧bright〈明亮的〉
❼ using〈use（使用）的 ing 型態〉‧separate〈分割〉‧space〈空間〉

中譯

❶ Hillary 是個室內設計師，她知道如何讓房子看起來美觀。
❷ 建築工人開始蓋房子前，先看了藍圖。
❸ Wendy 設計了一件洋裝給女兒穿。
❹ Andy 買了一些油漆來粉刷他的房間。
❺ Frank 需要為家裡添購家具，像是桌椅。
❻ 這間公寓的採光非常明亮。
❼ 使用隔間，我們就能將房間分隔成兩個空間。

048

居家裝潢 (2)

MP3 048

1 renovate
[`rɛnə,vet]
(v.) 整修

2 contractor
[`kɑntræktɚ]
(n.) 承包商

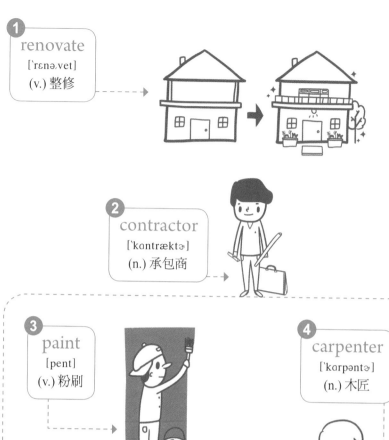

3 paint
[pent]
(v.) 粉刷

4 carpenter
[`kɑrpəntɚ]
(n.) 木匠

5 construction
[kən`strʌkʃən]
(n.) 施工

6 wallpaper
[`wɔl,pepɚ]
(n.) 壁紙

7 construction material
[kən`strʌkʃən mə`tɪrɪəl]
(n.) 建材

❶ 整修

The house is quite old. It needs renovating.

❷ 承包商

I hired a contractor to make some changes to my house.
<u>做一些改變</u>

❸ 粉刷

The little girl asked for her room to be painted pink.

❹ 木匠

The carpenter is busy cutting his wood.

❺ 施工

Construction has taken a long time, and the house still isn't built yet.
<u>房子仍然還沒蓋好</u>

❻ 壁紙

Instead of painting, Lisa used wallpaper on her walls.
<u>代替油漆</u>

❼ 建材

Wood, stone, and steel are all common construction materials.

學更多

❶ quite〈相當〉‧ old〈舊的〉‧ renovating〈renovate（整修）的 ing 型態〉
❷ hired〈hire（雇用）的過去式〉‧ change〈改變〉
❸ asked〈ask（要求）的過去式〉‧ painted〈paint（粉刷）的過去分詞〉‧ pink〈粉紅色的〉
❹ busy〈忙碌的〉‧ cutting〈cut（鋸）的 ing 型態〉‧ wood〈木頭〉
❺ taken〈take（執行）的過去分詞〉‧ built〈build（建築）的過去分詞〉‧ yet〈還沒〉
❻ instead of...〈作為替代〉‧ painting〈油漆〉‧ wall〈牆壁〉
❼ steel〈鋼鐵〉‧ common〈常見的〉‧ construction〈建造〉‧ material〈材料〉

中譯

❶ 這間房子頗為老舊，它需要整修。
❷ 我聘請承包商來改造我的房子。
❸ 小女孩要求將她的房間粉刷成粉紅色。
❹ 這名木匠正忙著鋸他的木頭。
❺ 已經施工很久了，這棟屋子仍然尚未完工。
❻ Lisa 在她的牆壁上貼上壁紙，而非粉刷油漆。
❼ 木材、石頭及鋼筋都是很普遍的建材。

049

清潔環境(1)

MP3 049

1 household hygiene
[ˈhausˌhold ˈhaɪdʒin]
(n.) 居家衛生

2 sweep
[swip]
(v.) 掃地

3 dust
[dʌst]
(n.) 灰塵

4 mop
[mɑp]
(v.) 拖地

5 wax
[wæks]
(v.) 打蠟

6 spider web
[ˈspaɪdɚ wɛb]
(n.) 蜘蛛網

7 spread pesticide
[sprɛd ˈpɛstɪˌsaɪd]
(phr.) 噴殺蟲劑

❶ 居家衛生

Household hygiene is important. If your house is dirty, you're more likely to get sick.
　　　　　　　　　　　　　　　　　　　　　　生病

❷ 掃地

You can sweep the floor with this brush.

❸ 灰塵

These books haven't been read for years. They're covered in a thick layer of dust.
　　　　　已經好幾年沒人看了　　　　　　　　　　　　　一層厚厚的灰塵

❹ 拖地

To mop the floor, you'll need a bucket of water.
　　　　　　　　　　　　　　一桶水

❺ 打蠟

The woman waxed her wooden floors to make them shine.
　　　　　　　　　　　　　　　　　　　讓它們發亮

❻ 蜘蛛網

There's a little bug caught in that spider web.
　　　　　　　　　　　　　　落入蜘蛛網

❼ 噴殺蟲劑

The farmer spread pesticides on his fields to kill bugs.

學更多

❶ household〈家庭的〉‧ hygiene〈衛生〉‧ important〈重要的〉‧ likely〈很可能的〉
❷ floor〈地板〉‧ brush〈掃把〉
❸ covered〈cover（覆蓋）的過去分詞〉‧ thick〈厚的〉‧ layer〈層〉
❹ need〈需要〉‧ bucket〈桶〉
❺ woman〈女人〉‧ wooden〈木製的〉‧ make〈使得〉‧ shine〈發亮〉
❻ bug〈蟲〉‧ caught〈catch（卡住）的過去分詞〉‧ spider〈蜘蛛〉‧ web〈網狀物〉
❼ farmer〈農夫〉‧ spread〈撒〉‧ pesticide〈殺蟲劑〉‧ field〈田地〉‧ kill〈殺死〉

中譯

❶ 居家衛生很重要。如果你的房子髒亂，你很可能會生病。
❷ 你可以用這支掃把掃地。
❸ 這些書好幾年都沒人翻閱了，覆蓋了一層厚厚的灰塵。
❹ 你需要一桶水來拖地。
❺ 那名女子替她的木質地板打蠟，讓它們看起來閃閃發亮。
❻ 有一隻小蟲掉進了蜘蛛網。
❼ 農夫在他的田裡噴殺蟲劑來消滅蟲子。

050

清潔環境(2)

MP3 050

1 filth
[fɪlθ]
(n.) 髒污

2 mildew
[`mɪl.dju]
(n.) 發霉

3 mess
[mɛs]
(n.) 雜亂

4 dirty
[`dɝtɪ]
(adj.) 骯髒

5 sterilize
[`stɛrə.laɪz]
(v.) 消毒

6 virus
[`vaɪrəs]
(n.) 病菌

7 garbage
[`gɑrbɪdʒ]
(n.) 垃圾

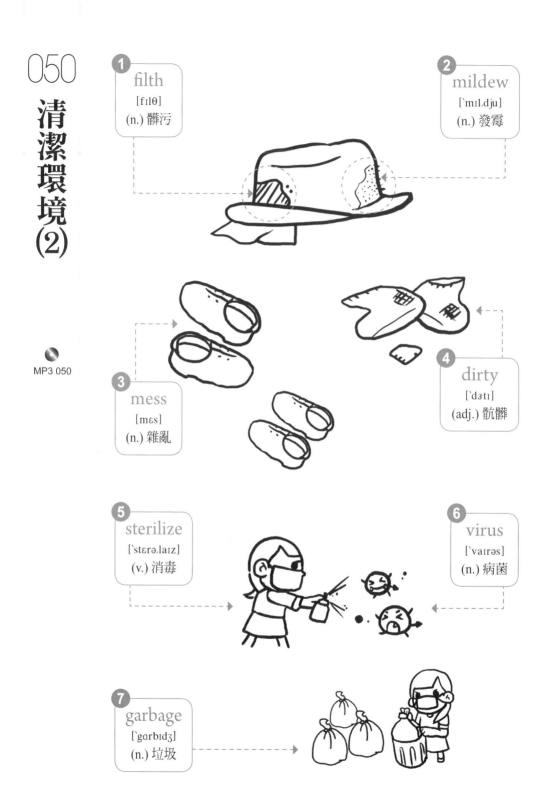

❶ 髒污

After walking in the country, my shoes are covered in filth.
鞋子被髒污所覆蓋

❷ 發霉

This house must be quite damp. There are patches of mildew on the walls.
一塊一塊的發霉

❸ 雜亂

The house is a mess. There are clothes and dirty plates everywhere.

❹ 骯髒

These clothes are dirty. I'm going to wash them later.

❺ 消毒

I'm going to sterilize these jars by putting them in boiling water.
把罐子放進滾燙的水

❻ 病菌

If you don't clean your house, you might become ill with a virus.
因為病菌

❼ 垃圾

We usually take out the garbage every day. Otherwise, it starts to smell.
把垃圾拿出去

學更多

❶ country〈鄉下〉‧ shoes〈shoe（鞋子）的複數〉‧ covered〈cover（覆蓋）的過去分詞〉
❷ quite〈很〉‧ damp〈潮濕的〉‧ patch〈斑塊〉‧ wall〈牆壁〉
❸ clothes〈衣服〉‧ plate〈盤子〉‧ everywhere〈到處〉
❹ wash〈洗〉‧ later〈晚些時候〉
❺ jar〈罐〉‧ putting〈put（放）的 ing 型態〉‧ boiling〈沸騰的〉‧ water〈水〉
❻ clean〈清潔〉‧ become〈變得〉‧ ill〈生病的〉‧ with〈因為〉
❼ usually〈通常〉‧ take out〈帶⋯出去〉‧ otherwise〈否則〉‧ smell〈有臭味〉

中譯

❶ 在鄉間散步後，我的鞋子沾滿了髒污。
❷ 這間房子一定很潮濕，因為牆壁上有一塊一塊的發霉。
❸ 這間房子一團雜亂，到處都是衣物和髒盤子。
❹ 這些衣服很骯髒，我待會要去洗這些衣服。
❺ 我要把這些罐子放入滾水消毒。
❻ 如果你不打掃房子，可能因為病菌而生病。
❼ 我們通常每天倒垃圾，否則它會開始發臭。

051

睡眠(1)

MP3 051

1 light sleep
[laɪt slip]
(n.) 淺睡

未進入真正熟睡狀態,
容易醒來。

2 deep sleep
[dip slip]
(n.) 熟睡

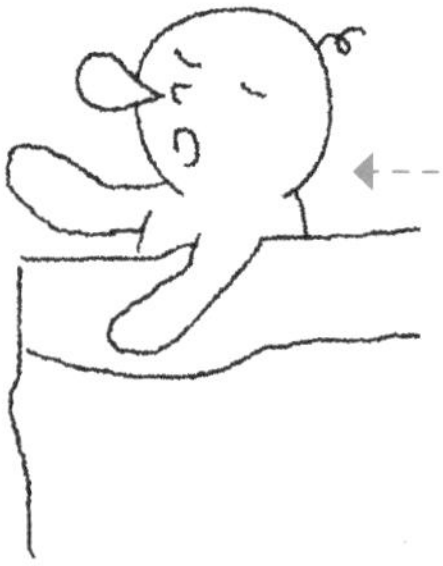

3 dream
[drim]
(n.) 夢/作夢

4 talk in one's sleep
[tɔk ɪn wʌns slip]
(phr.) 說夢話

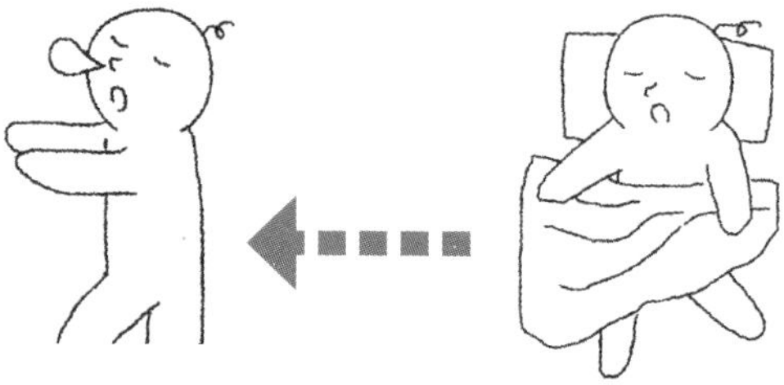

5 sleepwalk
[ˋslipˏwɔk]
(v.) 夢遊

從睡眠狀態中無意識起身,有時會做出複雜的動作。

❶ 淺睡

People can be woken easily when they having a light sleep.
　　　　　　　　人們容易被吵醒

❷ 熟睡

It looks like she's enjoying some deep sleep. We won't easily wake her up.
　　　　　　　　　　　　　　　　　　　　　　　　　　　　　叫醒她

❸ 夢／作夢

I had a strange dream when I was sleeping last night. I was chased by a bear.
　　　　　　　　　　　　　　　　　　　　　　　　　　　我被一隻熊追趕

❹ 說夢話

Susan sometimes talks in her sleep, but she never remembers in the morning.

❺ 夢遊

Sometimes he sleepwalks or has the symptoms of sleep apnea syndrome.
　　　　　　　　　　　　　　　　　　　　　　　　睡眠呼吸中止症

學更多

❶ woken〈wake（弄醒）的過去分詞〉・easily〈容易地〉・having〈have（進行）的 ing 型態〉・light〈輕微的〉・sleep〈睡眠〉

❷ look like〈看起來像是〉・enjoying〈enjoy（享受）的 ing 型態〉・deep〈深的〉・wake up〈使…醒來〉

❸ strange〈奇怪的〉・chased〈chase（追趕）的過去分詞〉・bear〈熊〉

❹ sometimes〈有時〉・talk〈講話〉・never〈從未〉・remember〈記得〉

❺ symptom〈症狀〉・apnea〈窒息〉・syndrome〈併發症狀〉

中譯

❶ 人在淺睡時，很容易被吵醒。
❷ 她似乎正熟睡著，我們無法輕易叫醒她。
❸ 我昨晚睡覺時作了一個奇怪的夢，夢見我被一隻熊追趕。
❹ Susan 有時會說夢話，但早上醒來時，她從不記得自己說過什麼。
❺ 有時候他會夢遊，或出現睡眠呼吸中止症的症狀。

052

睡眠(2)

MP3 052

1 insomnia
[ɪnˋsɑmnɪə]
(n.) 失眠

2 count sheep
[kaunt ʃip]
(phr.) 數羊

3 sleeping pill
[ˋslipɪŋ pɪl]
(n.) 安眠藥

4 oversleep
[ˋovɚˋslip]
(v.) 睡過頭

5 drowsiness
[ˋdrauzɪnɪs]
(n.) 打瞌睡/睡意

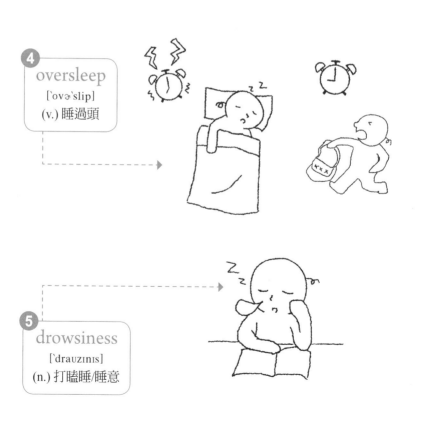

❶ 失眠

I suffer with insomnia, so I have trouble sleeping.
受失眠所擾

❷ 數羊

If you're having trouble sleeping, try counting sheep in your mind.

❸ 安眠藥

Rob takes sleeping pills to help him sleep at night.
吃安眠藥

❹ 睡過頭

My alarm clock didn't ring, so I overslept.

❺ 打瞌睡 / 睡意

I usually feel a bit of drowsiness in the morning, but a cup of coffee wakes me up.
一杯咖啡讓我清醒

學更多

❶ suffer〈受苦〉‧ have trouble〈在…有困難〉‧ sleeping〈sleep（睡覺）的 ing 型態〉

❷ try〈嘗試〉‧ counting〈count（計算）的 ing 型態〉‧ sheep〈綿羊〉‧ mind〈心〉

❸ take〈服用〉‧ sleeping〈睡眠〉‧ pill〈藥丸〉‧ help〈幫助〉‧ sleep〈睡覺〉

❹ alarm clock〈鬧鐘〉‧ ring〈響〉‧ overslept〈oversleep（睡過頭）的過去式〉

❺ usually〈通常〉‧ feel〈覺得〉‧ a bit of〈一點〉‧ a cup of〈一杯〉‧
wake up〈使…醒來〉

中譯

❶ 我飽受失眠所苦，我有睡眠障礙。

❷ 如果你有睡眠障礙，試著在心裡數羊。

❸ Rob 會服用安眠藥來幫助自己夜晚入眠。

❹ 我的鬧鐘沒響，害我睡過頭。

❺ 早上時，我通常會感到些許睡意，但一杯咖啡就可以讓我神智清醒。

053

睡
眠
(3)

MP3 053

1
toss and turn
[tɔs ænd tɜn]
(phr.) 翻身

2
snore
[snor]
(v.) 打呼

3
grind one's teeth
[ɡraɪnd wʌns tiθ]
(phr.) 磨牙

4
sleeping position
[ˈslipɪŋ pəˈzɪʃən]
(n.) 睡姿

5
face down
[fes daʊn]
(phr.) 趴睡

❶ 翻身

He tossed and turned all night, but he just couldn't sleep.

❷ 打呼

Some people snore loudly when they sleep.

❸ 磨牙

George grinds his teeth when he sleeps. It must be bad for his mouth.

<u>對他的嘴巴有不良影響</u>

❹ 睡姿

What's your usual sleeping position? I sleep on my side.

平常的睡姿   側睡

❺ 趴睡

Eric doesn't sleep on his back or side. He sleeps with his face down on the pillow.

平躺或側睡   他的臉埋在枕頭裡趴睡

學更多

❶ tossed〈toss（翻來覆去）的過去式〉・turned〈turn（翻轉）的過去式〉・all night〈整夜〉・sleep〈睡覺〉

❷ some〈一些〉・people〈人們〉・loudly〈大聲地〉

❸ grind〈磨〉・teeth〈tooth（牙齒）的複數〉・must〈一定〉・bad〈不好的〉・mouth〈嘴〉

❹ usual〈平常的〉・sleeping〈睡眠〉・position〈姿勢〉・side〈人體的側邊〉

❺ back〈背部〉・face〈臉〉・down〈向下〉・pillow〈枕頭〉

中譯

❶ 他整晚都在翻身，就是無法入睡。

❷ 有些人在睡覺的時候，會打呼打得很大聲。

❸ George 睡覺時會磨牙，這一定對他的嘴巴有不良影響。

❹ 你平常的睡姿是什麼？我都是側睡。

❺ Eric 不會平躺或側睡，他都把臉埋在枕頭裡趴睡。

MP3 054

1 electric shock
[ɪ`lɛktrɪk ʃɑk]
(n.) 觸電

2 electrical leakage
[ɪ`lɛktrɪkl̩ `lɪkɪdʒ]
(n.) 漏電

3 wire
[waɪr]
(n.) 電線/線路

燈不亮

兩極直接碰觸產生放
電現象，引起火花及
熱，造成電器損壞或
失火。

4 short circuit
[ʃɔrt `sɝkɪt]
(phr.) 短路

5 overload
[`ovɚ͵lod]
(v.) 電量超載

6 charge
[tʃɑrdʒ]
(v.) 充電

7 transformer
[træns`fɔrmɚ]
(n.) 變壓器

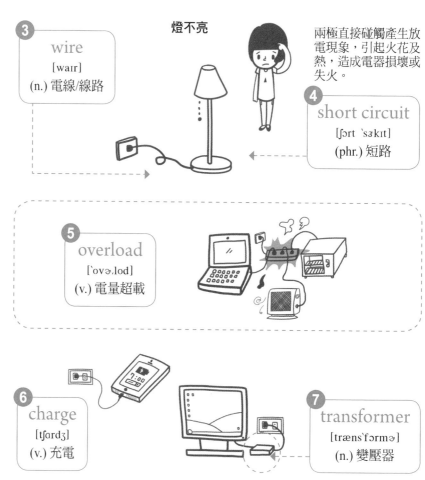

❶ 觸電

Jimmy got an electric shock when he put his finger in the plug socket.
把他的手指伸進插座

❷ 漏電

Leaving cellphone rechargers plugged in will cause electrical leakage.
使手機充電器處於…狀態

❸ 電線 / 線路

Someone cut the telephone wire, so you can't make a call.

❹ 短路

When the wires touched each other, the machine short circuited.

❺ 電量超載

This system was designed for a small amount of electricity. If too much
少量電流

electricity goes through it, it will overload.
通過它

❻ 充電

My battery's dead. I need to charge it up.
為它充電

❼ 變壓器

This machine is meant to be used on a smaller electrical system. You'll
必須被使用於

need a transformer if you want to plug it in here.

學更多

❶ electric〈電的〉．shock〈電擊〉．finger〈手指〉．plug〈插頭〉．socket〈插座〉
❷ recharger〈充電器〉．plugged in〈plug in（接通電源）的過去分詞〉．leakage〈漏出〉
❸ cut〈cut（剪）的過去式〉．telephone〈電話〉．make a call〈打電話〉
❹ touched〈touch（接觸）的過去式〉．each other〈互相〉．circuited〈circuit（環行）的過去式〉
❺ designed〈design（設計）的過去分詞〉．amount〈量〉．electricity〈電力〉
❻ battery〈電池〉．dead〈沒電的〉
❼ machine〈機器〉．be meant to〈必須要…〉．electrical〈電的〉．system〈系統〉

中譯

❶ 當 Jimmy 把手指伸進插座時，他感受到觸電。
❷ 一直讓手機充電器處於充電狀態，會導致漏電。
❸ 有人把電話線路剪斷了，所以你沒辦法打電話。
❹ 當線路互相接觸時，機器發生了短路。
❺ 這個系統是為少量電流而設計的，如果過多電流通過，將會電量超載。
❻ 我的電池沒電了，我需要替它充電。
❼ 這台機器適用於較小的電力系統，如果你要把它插入這裡的電源，你需要變壓器。

055

用
電
(2)

MP3 055

1 nuclear generator
['njuklɪə 'dʒɛnə.retə]
(n.) 核能發電

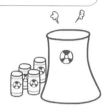

2 wind generator
[wɪnd 'dʒɛnə.retə]
(n.) 風力發電

3 water generator
['wɔtə 'dʒɛnə.retə]
(n.) 水力發電

4 fire generator
[faɪr 'dʒɛnə.retə]
(n.) 火力發電

5 blackout
['blæk.aʊt]
(n.) 停電

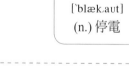

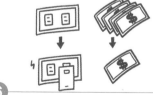

6 electrical savings system
[ɪ'lɛktrɪkl 'sevɪŋz 'sɪstəm]
(n.) 省電裝置

7 power supply
['paʊə sə'plaɪ]
(n.) 電源供應器

❶ 核能發電

The nuclear generator is powered by uranium.
利用鈾來提供動力

❷ 風力發電

The wind generator creates a lot of power when it's windy.
產生巨量的電力

❸ 水力發電

Water generators use the power of water to create electricity.
水力

❹ 火力發電

Fire generators burn things like coal and oil.

❺ 停電

There was a blackout last night. All the lights in the city went out.

❻ 省電裝置

This electrical savings system saves me money on my electrical bill.
節省我許多電費帳單的錢

❼ 電源供應器

Is there a power supply I can use? I need to plug in my computer.
把我的電腦接通電源

學更多

❶ nuclear〈原子核的〉‧ powered〈power（提供動力）的過去分詞〉‧ uranium〈鈾〉
❷ wind〈風〉‧ create〈產生〉‧ a lot of...〈許多〉‧ power〈電力〉‧ windy〈風大的〉
❸ water〈水〉‧ generator〈發電機〉‧ power〈動力〉‧ electricity〈電力〉
❹ fire〈火〉‧ burn〈燃燒〉‧ like〈像〉‧ coal〈煤〉‧ oil〈石油〉
❺ light〈燈〉‧ city〈城市〉‧ went out〈go out（熄滅）的過去式〉
❻ system〈系統〉‧ save〈節省〉‧ money〈錢〉‧ electrical〈電的〉‧ bill〈帳單〉
❼ supply〈供應〉‧ use〈使用〉‧ plug in〈接通電源〉‧ computer〈電腦〉

中譯

❶ 核能發電是利用鈾來發電。
❷ 在強風下，風力發電能產生巨大的電力。
❸ 水力發電利用水的動力來產生電力。
❹ 火力發電燃燒煤和石油之類的東西。
❺ 昨晚停電，城市裡所有的燈火都熄滅了。
❻ 這個省電裝置替我省了不少電費。
❼ 有沒有電源供應器可以使用？我需要接通電腦的電源。

056

美容保養(1)

MP3 056

1
remove makeup
[rɪ`muv `mek.ʌp]
(phr.) 卸妝

2
exfoliating
[ɛks`folɪ.etɪŋ]
(adj.) 去角質

3
massage
[mə`sɑʒ]
(n.) 按摩

4
apply a facial mask
[ə`plaɪ ə `feʃəl mæsk]
(phr.) 敷臉

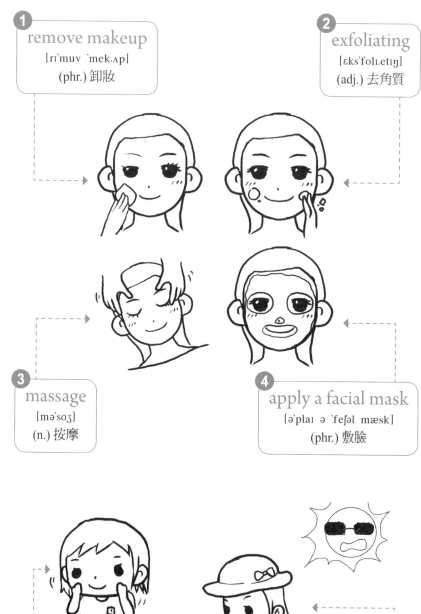

5
skin whitening
[skɪn `hwaɪtnɪŋ]
(phr.) 美白

6
sun block
[sʌn blɑk]
(phr.) 防曬

❶ 卸妝
The girl always removes her makeup before going to bed.

❷ 去角質
The exfoliating face wash will clear away your dead skin.

❸ 按摩
I have so many aches; I could use a massage.

❹ 敷臉
The girl applied a facial mask to moisturize her face.
　　　　　　　　　　　　　　　　　　保濕她的臉

❺ 美白
The skin whitening cream will make your skin paler.
　　　　　　　　　　　　　　　　讓你的皮膚更白皙

❻ 防曬
Put sun block on 30 minutes before going out into the sun.
　　擦防曬

學更多

❶ remove〈去除〉・makeup〈化妝品〉・going to bed〈go to bed（睡覺）的 ing 型態〉
❷ face wash〈洗面乳〉・clear away〈清除〉・dead〈死的〉・skin〈皮膚〉
❸ have〈有〉・ache〈疼痛〉・use〈使用〉
❹ applied〈apply（敷）的過去式〉・facial〈臉的〉・mask〈面膜〉・moisturize〈使濕潤〉・face〈臉〉
❺ whitening〈變白〉・cream〈化妝用乳霜〉・paler〈較白皙的，pale（白皙的）的比較級〉
❻ put on〈在皮膚上塗抹〉・before〈在…之前〉・sun〈陽光〉

中譯

❶ 那女孩總會在睡覺前卸妝。
❷ 這個去角質洗面乳，能清除你的老舊皮膚。
❸ 我身上有多處痠痛；我可以用按摩改善一下。
❹ 女孩敷臉來保濕她的臉部肌膚。
❺ 美白乳液能使你的皮膚更白皙。
❻ 出門曝曬在陽光下的 30 分鐘前，要擦上防曬。

057

美容保養(2)

MP3 057

1 deep clean
[dip klin]
(phr.) 深層清潔

2 oil control
[ɔɪl kənˋtrol]
(phr.) 控油

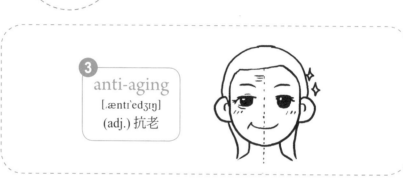

3 anti-aging
[ˌæntɪˋedʒɪŋ]
(adj.) 抗老

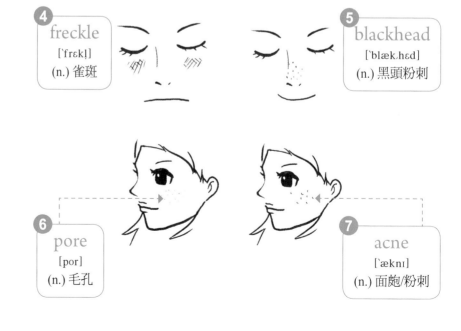

4 freckle
[ˋfrɛkl]
(n.) 雀斑

5 blackhead
[ˋblæk.hɛd]
(n.) 黑頭粉刺

6 pore
[por]
(n.) 毛孔

7 acne
[ˋæknɪ]
(n.) 面皰/粉刺

❶ 深層清潔

This facial gel will deep clean your skin's pores.

❷ 控油

Neil has oily skin, so he finds oil control very difficult.

❸ 抗老

The anti-aging cream will stop you from getting wrinkles.
<u>防止你產生皺紋</u>

❹ 雀斑

Valerie's face is covered in little brown freckles.

❺ 黑頭粉刺

The small black spots on his nose are blackheads.
小的黑色斑點

❻ 毛孔

If you don't want spots, you need to clean out your pores.

❼ 面皰 / 粉刺

Henry's got terrible acne. He's got spots all over his face.
滿臉都是痘痘

學更多

❶ facial〈臉用的〉・gel〈凝膠〉・deep〈深深地〉・clean〈清潔〉
❷ oily〈油的〉・skin〈皮膚〉・oil〈油〉・control〈控制〉・difficult〈困難的〉
❸ anti〈反對〉・aging〈老化〉・cream〈化妝用乳霜〉・stop〈阻止〉・wrinkle〈皺紋〉
❹ face〈臉〉・covered〈cover（覆蓋）的過去分詞〉・little〈小的〉・brown〈咖啡色的〉
❺ small〈小的〉・black〈黑色的〉・spot〈斑點、面皰瘡、痘痕〉・nose〈鼻子〉
❻ if〈如果〉・want〈想要〉・need〈需要〉・clean out〈清除〉
❼ got〈get（得到）的過去分詞〉・terrible〈嚴重的〉・all over〈到處〉

中譯

❶ 這款潔面凝膠會深層清潔你的毛孔。
❷ Neil 是油性肌膚，因此他發現控油對他而言相當困難。
❸ 抗老霜能減緩你的皺紋產生。
❹ Valerie 的臉上佈滿咖啡色的小雀斑。
❺ 在他鼻子上的那些小小黑色斑點是黑頭粉刺。
❻ 如果你不想要長痘痘，就必須徹底清潔毛孔。
❼ Henry 有嚴重的粉刺問題，他滿臉都是痘痘。

058

盥洗(1)

MP3 058

1 rinse one's mouth
[rɪns wʌns mauθ]
(phr.) 漱口

2 brush one's teeth
[brʌʃ wʌns tiθ]
(phr.) 刷牙

3 wash one's face
[wɑʃ wʌns fes]
(phr.) 洗臉

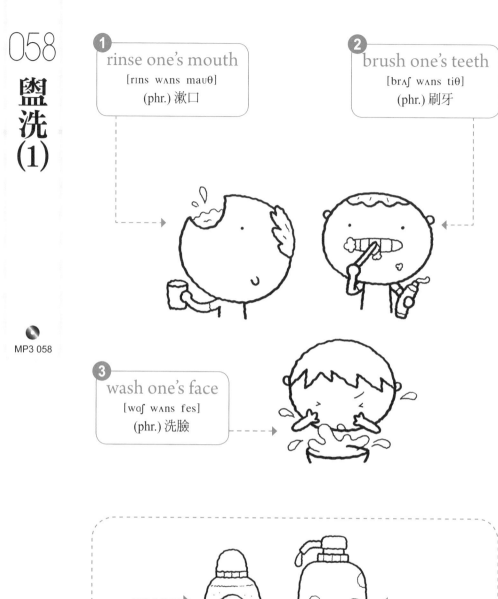

4 bath salt
[bæθ sɔlt]
(n.) 沐浴鹽

5 body wash
[ˋbɑdɪ wɑʃ]
(n.) 沐浴乳

❶ 漱口

Iris always rinses her mouth with a mouthwash.
　　　　　　　　用漱口水漱口

❷ 刷牙

Use toothpaste to brush your teeth.

❸ 洗臉

Oliver washes his face with soap and water.

❹ 沐浴鹽

Cathy put bath salts in the water to make it smell nice.
　　　　把沐浴鹽放入水裡

❺ 沐浴乳

I used body wash to clean myself with.
　　　　　用來清洗我自己

學更多

❶ always〈總是〉・rinse〈漱〉・mouth〈嘴巴〉・mouthwash〈漱口水〉
❷ use〈使用〉・toothpaste〈牙膏〉・brush〈刷〉・teeth〈tooth（牙齒）的複數〉
❸ wash〈洗〉・face〈臉〉・soap〈肥皂〉・water〈水〉
❹ put〈put（放）的過去式〉・bath〈洗澡〉・salt〈鹽〉・smell〈聞起來〉・nice〈好的〉
❺ used〈use（使用）的過去式〉・body〈身體〉・clean〈把…弄乾淨〉・myself〈我自己〉

中譯

❶ Iris 總是使用漱口水漱口。
❷ 要使用牙膏來刷牙。
❸ Oliver 會使用肥皂及清水洗臉。
❹ Cathy 在洗澡水裡灑了沐浴鹽，讓它聞起來有芳香的氣味。
❺ 我使用沐浴乳洗澡。

059

盥洗(2)

MP3 059

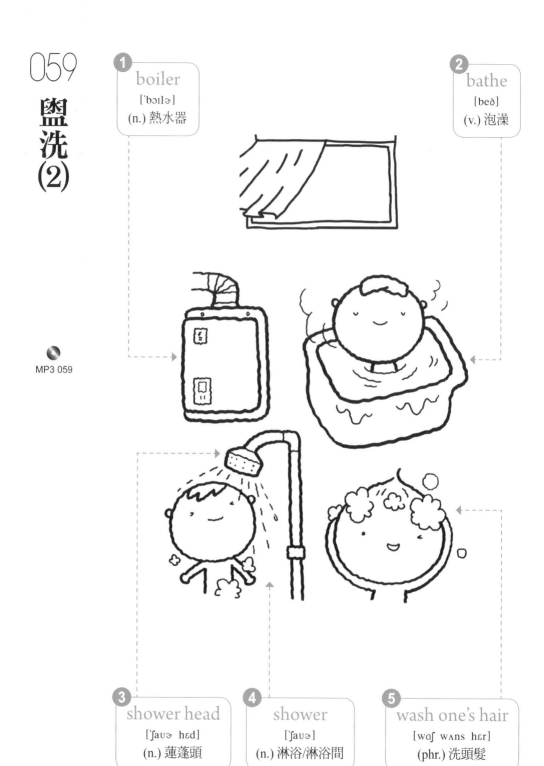

1 boiler
[ˋbɔɪlɚ]
(n.) 熱水器

2 bathe
[beð]
(v.) 泡澡

3 shower head
[ˋʃaʊɚ hɛd]
(n.) 蓮蓬頭

4 shower
[ˋʃaʊɚ]
(n.) 淋浴/淋浴間

5 wash one's hair
[wɑʃ wʌns hɛr]
(phr.) 洗頭髮

❶ 熱水器

You need to make sure the boiler is on if you want a shower.

確認熱水器是開著的

❷ 泡澡

Dean is looking forward to bathing in the hot spring waters.

❸ 蓮蓬頭

Zach always holds the shower head when he takes a shower.

拿著蓮蓬頭　　　　　　　　　　淋浴洗澡

❹ 淋浴 / 淋浴間

There's a shower in the bathroom, but no bathtub.

❺ 洗頭髮

Hillary bought some shampoo to wash her hair with.

用來洗她的頭髮

學更多

❶ make sure〈確定〉・on〈開啟的〉・want〈想要〉

❷ looking forward to〈look forward to（期待）的 ing 型態〉・hot spring〈溫泉〉

❸ always〈總是〉・hold〈拿著〉・head〈物品的頭部〉

❹ bathroom〈浴室〉・bathtub〈浴缸〉

❺ bought〈buy（買）的過去式〉・shampoo〈洗髮精〉・wash〈洗〉・hair〈頭髮〉

中譯

❶ 如果你想沖澡，你需要先確認熱水器的開關是開著的。

❷ Dean 很期待在溫泉裡泡澡。

❸ Zach 淋浴時，總會手拿著蓮蓬頭。

❹ 浴室裡有一個淋浴間，但沒有浴缸。

❺ Hillary 買了一些洗髮精來洗頭髮。

060

個人衛生 (1)

MP3 060

1 dirty
[ˋdɝtɪ]
(adj.) 骯髒

2 hygiene
[ˋhaɪdʒin]
(n.) 衛生

3 sloppy
[ˋslɑpɪ]
(adj.) 邋遢

4 clean
[klin]
(adj.) 乾淨

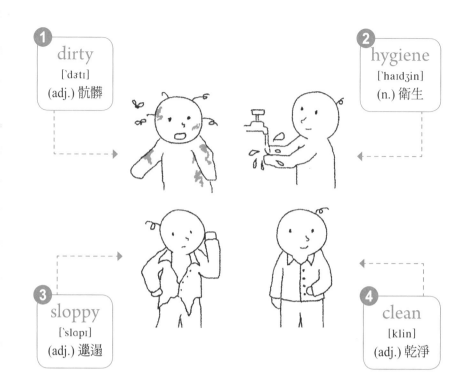

5 clean freak
[klin frik]
(n.) 潔癖

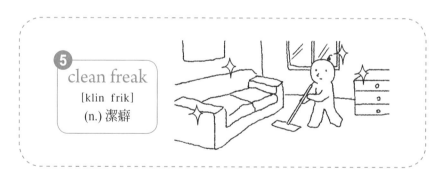

6 toiletries
[ˋtɔɪlɪtrɪs]
(n.) 盥洗用具

7 antiseptic
[͵æntəˋsɛptɪk]
(n.) 抗菌的/抗菌劑

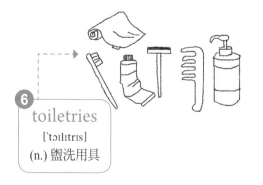

❶ 骯髒

That towel is dirty. Get a new one.

❷ 衛生

Hygiene isn't very important to Joe. He never washes his hands after using the bathroom.

<u>上完廁所之後</u>

❸ 邋遢

Tom's a sloppy eater. He gets food everywhere.

❹ 乾淨

I always put on clean clothes after taking a shower.

穿上乾淨的衣服

❺ 潔癖

My mom's a real clean freak. She's always cleaning the house.

❻ 盥洗用具

Most hotels provide free toiletries like soap and shampoo.

提供免費的盥洗用具

❼ 抗菌的 / 抗菌劑

Alcohol is a good antiseptic. It will kill germs.

學更多

❶ towel〈毛巾〉‧ get〈得到〉‧ new〈新的〉
❷ important〈重要的〉‧ using〈use（使用）的 ing 型態〉‧ bathroom〈廁所〉
❸ eater〈吃東西的人〉‧ get〈使得〉‧ food〈食物〉‧ everywhere〈到處〉
❹ put on〈穿上〉‧ clothes〈衣服〉‧ taking a shower〈take a shower（沖澡）的 ing 型態〉
❺ real〈十足的〉‧ freak〈狂熱者〉‧ cleaning〈clean（打掃）的 ing 型態〉
❻ most〈大部分的〉‧ provide〈提供〉‧ soap〈肥皂〉‧ shampoo〈洗髮精〉
❼ alcohol〈酒精〉‧ kill〈殺死〉‧ germ〈細菌〉

中譯

❶ 那條毛巾很骯髒，去拿一條新的。
❷ 衛生對 Joe 來說不太重要，他如廁後從不洗手。
❸ Tom 是一個吃相很邋遢的人，他會把食物弄得到處都是。
❹ 沖完澡之後，我總是會換穿乾淨的衣物。
❺ 我媽媽有嚴重的潔癖，她總是在打掃家裡。
❻ 大部分的旅館都會提供免費的盥洗用具，像是肥皂及洗髮精。
❼ 酒精是良好的抗菌劑，它會殺死細菌。

061

個人衛生(2)

MP3 061

1 bad breath
[bæd brɛθ]
(n.) 口臭

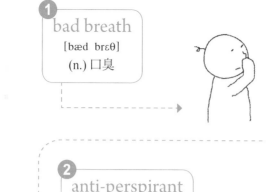

2 anti-perspirant
[ˌæntɪˈpɚspərənt]
(n.) 制汗劑

3 body odor
[ˈbɑdɪ ˈodɚ]
(n.) 體味/狐臭

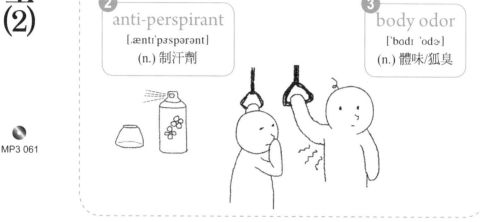

4 contagious disease
[kənˈtedʒəs dɪˈziz]
(n.) 傳染病

5 immunity
[ɪˈmjunətɪ]
(n.) 免疫力

6 parasite
[ˈpærəˌsaɪt]
(n.) 寄生蟲

7 skin disease
[skɪn dɪˈziz]
(n.) 皮膚病

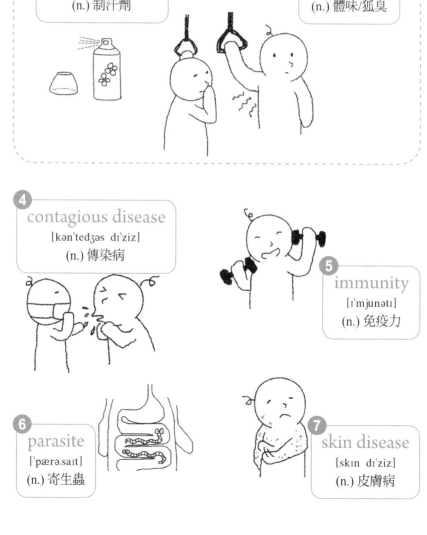

❶ 口臭

If you don't brush your teeth, you'll get bad breath.

❷ 制汗劑

Frank rubbed anti-perspirant under his arms.
<u>在他的腋下</u>

❸ 體味 / 狐臭

Ian went to take a shower after someone told him he had body odor.
<u>沖澡</u>

❹ 傳染病

SARS is a contagious disease, so stay away from other people if you have it.
<u>和其他人保持距離</u>

❺ 免疫力

After receiving the vaccination, Sarah has immunity from the disease.

❻ 寄生蟲

This bug is a parasite that lives inside human bodies.
<u>居住在人體內</u>

❼ 皮膚病

The rash on Dave's hands is a skin disease.

學更多

❶ brush〈刷〉‧teeth〈tooth（牙齒）的複數〉‧bad〈不好的〉‧breath〈氣息〉
❷ rubbed〈rub（擦）的過去式〉‧under〈在…下面〉‧arm〈手臂〉
❸ went〈go（去）的過去式〉‧shower〈淋浴〉‧told〈tell（說）的過去式〉‧odor〈氣味〉
❹ contagious〈接觸傳染的〉‧stay away from...〈和…保持距離〉‧have〈患有〉
❺ receiving〈receive（接受）的 ing 型態〉‧vaccination〈接種疫苗〉‧disease〈疾病〉
❻ bug〈蟲子〉‧live〈居住〉‧inside〈在…的裡面〉‧human〈人類〉
❼ rash〈疹子〉‧hand〈手〉‧skin〈皮膚〉

中譯

❶ 如果你不刷牙，就會有口臭。
❷ Frank 在腋下擦了制汗劑。
❸ 有人告訴 Ian 說他有狐臭之後，他就去沖了澡。
❹ SARS 是一種傳染病，所以如果你染上 SARS，請遠離其他人。
❺ 接受疫苗接種之後，Sarah 對這種疾病有了免疫力。
❻ 這隻蟲是寄居在人體內的寄生蟲。
❼ Dave 手上的疹子，是一種皮膚病。

062

禮儀(1)

1 please
[pliz]
(v.) 請

2 thank you
[θæŋk ju]
(phr.) 謝謝

3 sorry
[`sɑrɪ]
(adj.) 對不起

MP3 062

4 personal space
[`pɝsn̩l spes]
(n.) 人我距離/個人空間

5 privacy
[`praɪvəsɪ]
(n.) 隱私/私人空間

6 intimate
[`ɪntəmɪt]
(adj.) 熱絡

❶ 請

When you ask people to do things for you, say please.

<u>要求別人做事</u>

❷ 謝謝

Make sure you say thank you after someone helps you out.

<u>有人幫助你擺脫困難</u>

❸ 對不起

Don't be too proud to say sorry when you've done something wrong.

<u>太自傲而無法說抱歉</u>

❹ 人我距離 / 個人空間

He was standing too close to me and invading my personal space.

<u>站得太靠近我</u>

❺ 隱私 / 私人空間

Mark enjoys his privacy, so he spends a lot of time at home alone.

<u>花很多時間獨自在家</u>

❻ 熱絡

They have an intimate relationship. They're always together.

<u>他們有很熱絡的關係</u>

學更多

❶ ask〈要求〉‧ people〈人們〉‧ say〈說〉

❷ make sure〈確定〉‧ after〈在⋯之後〉‧ help out〈幫助⋯擺脫困難〉

❸ too...to...〈太⋯而無法⋯〉‧ proud〈有自尊心的、驕傲的〉‧ done〈do（做）的過去分詞〉

❹ standing〈stand（站立）的 ing 型態〉‧ too〈太〉‧ close〈近的〉‧
  invading〈invade（侵犯）的 ing 型態〉‧ personal〈個人的〉‧ space〈空間〉

❺ enjoy〈享受〉‧ spend〈花費〉‧ alone〈獨自地〉

❻ relationship〈關係〉‧ always〈總是〉‧ together〈一起〉

中譯

❶ 當你要求別人為你做事時，要說「請」。

❷ 別人幫你解決困難後，要記得說「謝謝」。

❸ 當你確實做錯時，別因為過多的自尊而無法說對不起。

❹ 他站得太靠近我，侵犯到我的個人空間。

❺ Mark 很享受他的私人空間，所以他長時間獨自待在家裡。

❻ 他們的關係很熱絡，他們總是形影不離。

063

禮儀(2)

1 good manners
[gʊd ˋmænəz]
(phr.) 有禮貌/良好禮儀

2 bad manners
[bæd ˋmænəz]
(phr.) 沒禮貌

MP3 063

3 bow
[baʊ]
(v.) 鞠躬

4 respect
[rɪˋspɛkt]
(n.) 尊敬

5 polite
[pəˋlaɪt]
(adj.) 彬彬有禮

6 rude
[rud]
(adj.) 粗魯

❶ 有禮貌 / 良好禮儀
Lee has good manners, so everyone says he's polite.

❷ 沒禮貌
Jessica has bad manners; she offends lots of people.

❸ 鞠躬
Men should bow when they meet the queen.
　　　　　　　　　　當他們見到女王時

❹ 尊敬
Susie has no respect for anyone. Her attitude is terrible.

❺ 彬彬有禮
Nick's very polite. He always says please and thank you.
　　　　　　　　　　他常說「請」和「謝謝」

❻ 粗魯
That man's so rude. He just pushed past me.
　　　　　　　　擠過去

學更多

❶ manners〈禮貌〉・everyone〈每個人〉
❷ bad〈不好的〉・offend〈冒犯〉・lots of〈很多〉・people〈人們〉
❸ men〈man（人）的複數〉・meet〈遇見〉・queen〈女王〉
❹ anyone〈無論誰〉・attitude〈態度〉・terrible〈糟糕的〉
❺ always〈總是〉・say〈說〉・please〈請〉
❻ just〈剛才〉・pushed〈push（擠出路前進）的過去式〉・past〈經過〉

中譯

❶ Lee 有著良好禮儀，所以大家都說他很有禮貌。
❷ Jessica 很沒禮貌，她得罪很多人。
❸ 人們見到女王時，應該鞠躬。
❹ Susie 對誰都不尊敬，她的態度很糟糕。
❺ Nick 非常彬彬有禮，他總是把「請」和「謝謝」掛在嘴邊。
❻ 這個男人非常粗魯，他剛剛硬是從我身旁擠過去。

064

起床 (1)

MP3 064

1 wake up
[wek ʌp]
(phr.) 醒來

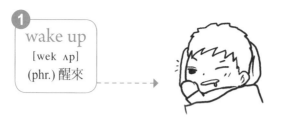

2 get up early
[gɛt ʌp `ɝlɪ]
(phr.) 早起

3 get up late
[gɛt ʌp let]
(phr.) 晚起

4 yawn
[jɔn]
(v.) 呵欠

5 stretch
[strɛtʃ]
(v.) 伸懶腰/伸展

6 sleep in
[slip ɪn]
(phr.) 賴床

7 good morning
[gʊd `mɔrnɪŋ]
(phr.) 早安

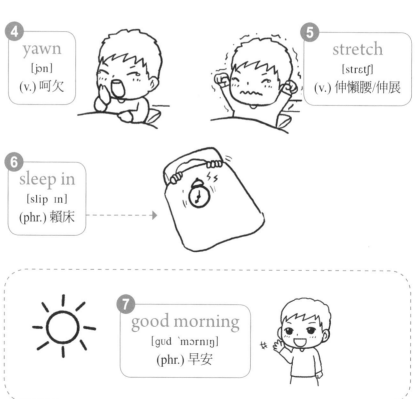

❶ 醒來

Patsy wakes up at 7am every day.

❷ 早起

You'll need to get up early if you want to see the sun come up.

<u>看太陽升起</u>

❸ 晚起

I'm very tired, so I plan to get up late tomorrow.

❹ 呵欠

Gina keeps yawning because she's so tired.

<u>一直打呵欠</u>

❺ 伸懶腰 / 伸展

It's a good idea to stretch your legs before running.

❻ 賴床

I don't need to work today, so I'm going to sleep in.

❼ 早安

Alice usually says good morning to the bus driver on her way to work.

<u>在她上班途中</u>

學更多

❶ every〈每個〉‧ day〈一天〉
❷ get up〈起床〉‧ early〈提早〉‧ see〈看〉‧ sun〈太陽〉‧ come up〈太陽升起〉
❸ tired〈疲倦的〉‧ plan〈打算〉‧ late〈晚〉
❹ keep〈繼續不斷〉‧ yawning〈yawn（呵欠）的 ing 型態〉
❺ idea〈觀念〉‧ leg〈腿〉‧ before〈在…之前〉‧ running〈run（跑步）的 ing 型態〉
❻ need〈需要〉‧ work〈工作〉‧ today〈今天〉
❼ usually〈通常〉‧ morning〈早晨〉‧ bus〈公車〉‧ driver〈司機〉

中譯

❶ Patsy 每天早上 7 點醒來。
❷ 若你想看日出，你就必須早起。
❸ 我感到非常疲倦，所以明天我打算晚起。
❹ Gina 不停打呵欠，因為她非常疲倦。
❺ 跑步前先伸展你的雙腿，是一個良好觀念。
❻ 我今天不用工作，所以我要繼續賴床。
❼ Alice 在她上班途中，總會向公車司機道早安。

065

起床(2)

MP3 065

1 alarm clock
[ə`lɑrm klɑk]
(n.) 鬧鐘

2 oversleep
[`ovə`slip]
(v.) 睡過頭

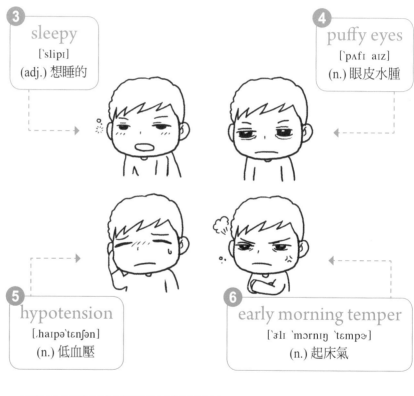

3 sleepy
[`slipɪ]
(adj.) 想睡的

4 puffy eyes
[`pʌfɪ aɪz]
(n.) 眼皮水腫

5 hypotension
[ˌhaɪpə`tɛnʃən]
(n.) 低血壓

6 early morning temper
[`ɝlɪ `mɔrnɪŋ `tɛmpə]
(n.) 起床氣

7 go back to sleep
[go bæk tu slip]
(phr.) 睡回籠覺

1 鬧鐘
Do you need an alarm clock to help you wake up in the morning?
幫助你醒來

2 睡過頭
Joe's alarm clock is broken so he keeps oversleeping.

3 想睡的
I only just woke up, so I still feel sleepy.
剛剛

4 眼皮水腫
Polly hasn't slept well, so she's got puffy eyes.
沒有睡飽

5 低血壓
People with hypotension have very low blood pressure.
非常低的血壓

6 起床氣
Beth has a terrible early morning temper. She gets angry very quickly.
變得生氣

7 睡回籠覺
Nick turned off his alarm clock and went back to sleep.
關掉他的鬧鐘

學更多

1 need〈需要〉・alarm〈鬧鐘〉・clock〈時鐘〉・help〈幫助〉・wake up〈起床〉
2 broken〈損壞的〉・keep〈繼續不斷〉・oversleeping〈oversleep（睡過頭）的 ing 型態〉
3 woke up〈wake up（起床）的過去式〉・still〈還是〉・feel〈覺得〉
4 slept〈sleep（睡）的過去分詞〉・well〈充分地〉・got〈get（變成）的過去分詞〉
5 low〈低的〉・blood pressure〈血壓〉
6 terrible〈嚴重的〉・early〈早的〉・temper〈脾氣〉・angry〈生氣的〉・quickly〈迅速地〉
7 turned off〈turn off（關掉）的過去式〉・went back〈go back（回去）的過去式〉

中譯

1 你需要一個鬧鐘在早晨裡叫你起床嗎？
2 Joe 的鬧鐘壞了，導致他睡過頭。
3 我才剛起床，所以我還是覺得想睡。
4 Polly 沒有睡飽，所以她的眼皮水腫。
5 低血壓的人，血壓會非常低。
6 Beth 有嚴重的起床氣，她會一下子就暴怒。
7 Nick 按掉他的鬧鐘，繼續睡回籠覺。

145

066

寵物 (1)

MP3 066

1 owner
['onɚ]
(n.) 飼主

2 pet hotel
[pɛt hoˋtɛl]
(n.) 寵物旅館

3 pet shop
[pɛt ʃɑp]
(n.) 寵物店

welcome

大麥町犬

柴犬

貴賓狗

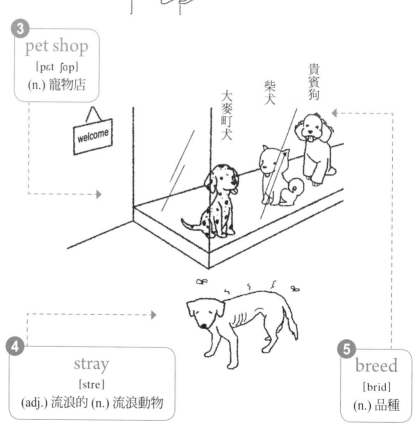

4 stray
[stre]
(adj.) 流浪的 (n.) 流浪動物

5 breed
[brid]
(n.) 品種

❶ 飼主

There's a dog wandering on the streets outside. I think it doesn't have an owner.
在外面的街上遊蕩

❷ 寵物旅館

When some people go on holiday, they put their pets into expensive pet hotels.
去渡假　　　　　　　　把他們的寵物送至昂貴的寵物旅館

❸ 寵物店

Frankie buys pet food for her rabbits at the pet shop.

❹ 流浪的 / 流浪動物

There are a few stray dogs that wander around the streets near here.
在街頭遊蕩

❺ 品種

What breed of dog is that? Is it a bulldog?

學更多

❶ wandering〈wander（遊蕩）的 ing 型態〉‧ street〈街〉‧ outside〈在外面〉
❷ holiday〈假期〉‧ put...into〈把…放進〉‧ expensive〈昂貴的〉‧ hotel〈旅館〉
❸ food〈食物〉‧ rabbit〈兔子〉‧ pet〈寵物〉‧ shop〈商店〉
❹ a few〈一些〉‧ around〈四處〉‧ near〈靠近〉‧ here〈這裡〉
❺ bulldog〈牛頭犬、鬥牛犬〉

中譯

❶ 有一隻狗在外面的街上遊蕩，我想牠應該沒有飼主。
❷ 有些人要去渡假時，會把他們的寵物送去昂貴的寵物旅館。
❸ Frankie 會在寵物店為她的兔子們買飼料。
❹ 這附近有一些流浪狗會在街上遊蕩。
❺ 那是什麼品種的狗？牠是鬥牛犬嗎？

067

寵物(2)

MP3 067

1 feed
[fid]
(n.) 飼料

2 collar
[`kɑlɚ]
(n.) 項圈

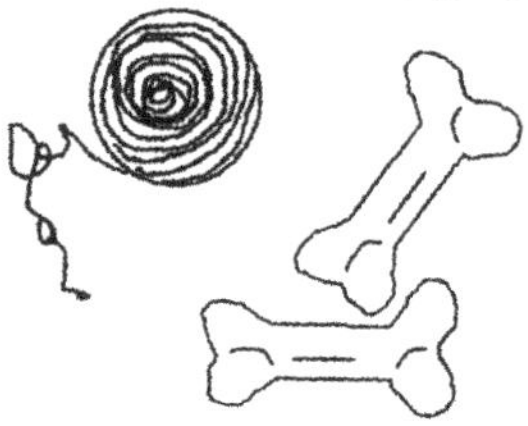

3 pet clothing
[pɛt `kloðɪŋ]
(n.) 寵物衣服

4 pet toy
[pɛt tɔɪ]
(n.) 寵物玩具

毛線球　　狗骨頭

寵物訓練專用跳圈

5 pet trainer
[pɛt `trenɚ]
(n.) 寵物訓練師

❶ 飼料

Steve spends a lot of money on animal feed because his dog eats a lot.
花很多錢在…

❷ 項圈

The cat has a red collar around its neck.
圍繞著牠的脖子

❸ 寵物衣服

Some animals need pet clothing when it gets cold in the winter.
天氣變冷

❹ 寵物玩具

Dwayne bought a new pet toy for his dog to play with.
給他的狗一起玩

❺ 寵物訓練師

Allen is a pet trainer; he teaches animals how to behave.
如何守規矩

學更多

❶ spend〈花費〉・a lot of〈許多〉・animal〈動物〉・a lot〈大量〉

❷ cat〈貓〉・red〈紅色的〉・around〈圍繞〉・neck〈脖子〉

❸ pet〈寵物〉・clothing〈衣服〉・get〈變成〉・cold〈冷的〉・winter〈冬天〉

❹ bought〈buy（買）的過去式〉・toy〈玩具〉・play〈玩耍〉

❺ trainer〈訓練師〉・teach〈教導〉・behave〈守規矩〉

中譯

❶ Steve 在寵物飼料的花費相當大，因為他的狗食量很大。

❷ 這隻貓的脖子上繫著一條紅色項圈。

❸ 當冬季天氣漸冷時，有些動物需要穿上寵物衣服。

❹ Dwayne 買了一個新的寵物玩具給他的狗玩。

❺ Allen 是一位寵物訓練師，他教導動物們如何守規矩。

068

寵物(3)

MP3 068

1 animal hospital
[`ænəml `hɑspɪtl]
(n.) 動物醫院

2 microchip implant
[`maɪkro͵tʃɪp ɪm`plænt]
(n.) 植入晶片

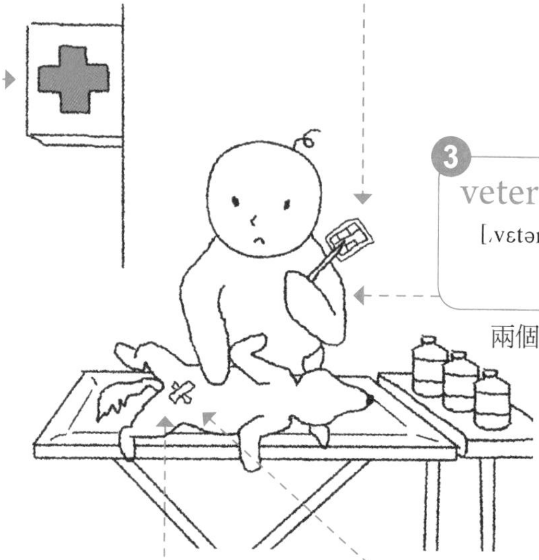

3 veterinarian / vet
[͵vɛtərə`nɛrɪən] / [vɛt]
(n.) 獸醫

兩個單字都是「獸醫」。

4 neuter
[`njutɚ]
(v.) 結紮（公的動物）

5 spay
[spe]
(v.) 結紮（母的動物）

6 adopt
[ə`dɑpt]
(v.) 認養

7 lost
[lɔst]
(adj.) 走失

❶ 動物醫院

Olivia took her parrot to the animal hospital because it seemed ill.
帶她的鸚鵡去動物醫院

❷ 植入晶片

Microchip implants help the authorities find out who an animal belongs to.
動物是屬於誰的

❸ 獸醫

Tom loves animals and he really wants to be a veterinarian when he's older.
實在是屬於要當獸醫

❹ 結紮（公的動物）

We neutered our dog, Maverick, after it had five puppies. We didn't
want to try and find homes for any more. 生了5隻小狗

❺ 結紮（母的動物）

We spayed Miss Fluffy by visiting the local vet last week.
拜訪當地的獸醫

❻ 認養

I went to the dog shelter to look for a dog to adopt and take home.
流浪狗收容所

❼ 走失

Mavis is looking for her dog. It's lost.
正在尋找她的狗

學更多

❶ parrot〈鸚鵡〉‧hospital〈醫院〉‧seemed〈seem（看起來）的過去式〉‧ill〈生病的〉
❷ microchip〈微晶片〉‧implant〈植入〉‧authority〈管理機構〉‧find out〈找出〉
❸ really〈實在〉‧older〈年紀較大的，old（上了年紀的）的比較級〉
❹ neutered〈neuter（結紮（公的動物））的過去式〉‧had〈have（生）的過去式〉
❺ spayed〈spay（結紮（母的動物））的過去式〉‧local〈當地的〉
❻ went〈go（去）的過去式〉‧shelter〈收容所〉‧take〈帶走〉
❼ looking for〈look for（尋找）的 ing 型態〉

中譯

❶ Olivia 帶她的鸚鵡去動物醫院，因為牠看起來好像生病了。
❷ 植入晶片可以幫助相關單位找出寵物的飼主是誰。
❸ Tom 很喜愛動物，他非常想在長大之後當獸醫。
❹ 在我們養的狗 Maverick 生了 5 隻小狗之後，我們替牠做了結紮。我們不想要之後又得試著幫小狗找新家了。
❺ 我們上星期拜訪了當地的獸醫，並把 Fluffy 小姐結紮了。
❻ 我去流浪狗收容所挑選一隻狗狗認養，並帶牠回家。
❼ Mavis 正在尋找她走失的狗。

069

寒冷

MP3 069

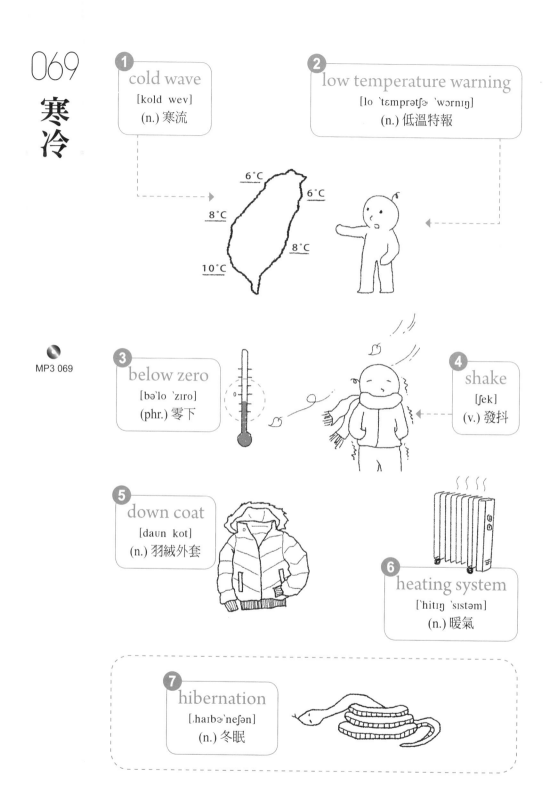

1 cold wave
[kold wev]
(n.) 寒流

2 low temperature warning
[lo `tɛmprətʃə `wɔrnɪŋ]
(n.) 低溫特報

3 below zero
[bə`lo `zɪro]
(phr.) 零下

4 shake
[ʃek]
(v.) 發抖

5 down coat
[daʊn kot]
(n.) 羽絨外套

6 heating system
[`hitɪŋ `sɪstəm]
(n.) 暖氣

7 hibernation
[ˌhaɪbə`neʃən]
(n.) 冬眠

❶ 寒流

It won't be hot all week. There should be a cold wave on Tuesday.

❷ 低溫特報

Put on lots of clothing. There has been a low temperature warning.
多穿一些衣服

❸ 零下

It's going to be very cold. The weatherman said it will fall below zero.
降到零度以下

❹ 發抖

I'm so cold. I'm shaking.

❺ 羽絨外套

This down coat is filled with feathers, so it should keep you warm.
被填滿了羽毛　　　　　　　　　讓你保持溫暖

❻ 暖氣

There's a heating system inside the house, so we should be warm there.

❼ 冬眠

Bears go into hibernation every winter.
進入冬眠

學更多

❶ hot〈熱的〉・all〈整個的〉・week〈週〉・cold〈寒冷的〉・wave〈波〉
❷ put on〈穿上〉・clothing〈衣服〉・low〈低的〉・temperature〈溫度〉・warning〈警告〉
❸ weatherman〈氣象預報員〉・fall〈下降〉・below〈在…以下〉・zero〈氣溫零度〉
❹ shaking〈shake（發抖）的 ing 型態〉
❺ down〈羽絨〉・coat〈外套〉・filled with〈fill with（填滿）的過去分詞〉・feather〈羽毛〉
❻ heating〈暖氣〉・system〈系統〉・inside〈在…的裡面〉・warm〈溫暖的〉
❼ bear〈熊〉・go into〈進入…狀態〉・every〈每個〉・winter〈冬天〉

中譯

❶ 未必整個星期都很熱，週二時應該會有一波寒流。
❷ 多穿一些衣服，已經發布低溫特報了。
❸ 天氣會變得很冷。氣象預報員說，氣溫將降到零度以下。
❹ 我好冷，我一直在發抖。
❺ 這件羽絨外套填滿了羽毛，所以它能讓你保暖。
❻ 那間房子裡有暖氣，所以我們待在那裡應該會很溫暖。
❼ 每年冬季時，熊會進入冬眠。

070

炎熱

MP3 070

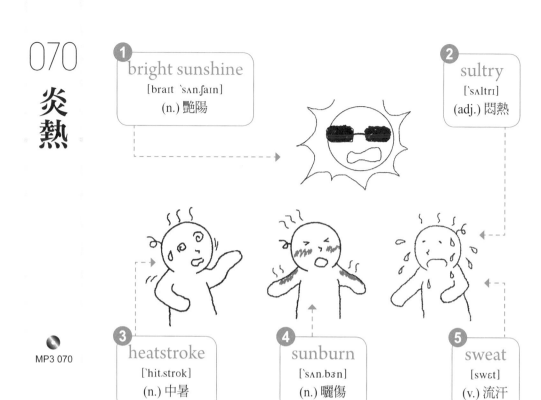

1 bright sunshine
[braɪt `sʌn.ʃaɪn]
(n.) 艷陽

2 sultry
[`sʌltrɪ]
(adj.) 悶熱

3 heatstroke
[`hit.strok]
(n.) 中暑

4 sunburn
[`sʌn.bɝn]
(n.) 曬傷

5 sweat
[swɛt]
(v.) 流汗

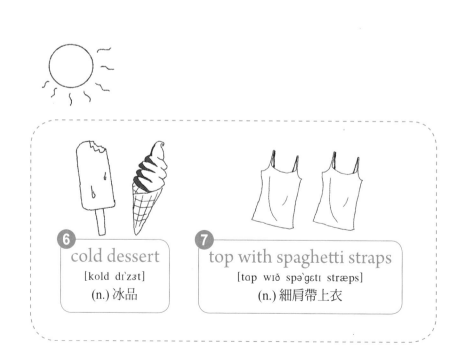

6 cold dessert
[kold dɪ`zɝt]
(n.) 冰品

7 top with spaghetti straps
[tɑp wɪð spə`gɛtɪ stræps]
(n.) 細肩帶上衣

❶ 艷陽

Make sure you put on sunscreen when you're in the bright sunshine.
擦上防曬乳

❷ 悶熱

Taipei is usually very sultry on summer evenings.

❸ 中暑

Irene was outside in the sun all day. We shouldn't be surprised she collapsed with heatstroke.
因為中暑而倒下

❹ 曬傷

I was out in the sun too long, so now I've got sunburn.

❺ 流汗

Get ready to sweat; it's going to be hot today.

❻ 冰品

I often eat cold desserts on hot afternoons.

❼ 細肩帶上衣

Your shoulders will be exposed to the sun in that top with spaghetti straps.
肩膀會暴露於陽光底下

學更多

❶ make sure〈確定〉・put on〈擦上〉・sunscreen〈防曬乳〉・bright〈明亮的〉
❷ usually〈通常〉・summer〈夏天〉・evening〈傍晚〉
❸ outside〈在外面〉・all day〈整天〉・collapsed〈collapse（暈倒）的過去式〉
❹ out〈出外〉・long〈長久地〉・got〈get（得到）的過去分詞〉
❺ get ready〈準備好〉・hot〈熱的〉・today〈今天〉
❻ often〈時常〉・eat〈吃〉・cold〈冰凍的〉・dessert〈甜點〉・afternoon〈下午〉
❼ exposed〈expose（暴露於）的過去分詞〉・top〈上衣〉・spaghetti strap〈細肩帶〉

中譯

❶ 當你要待在豔陽下時，要確定你有擦防曬乳。
❷ 在夏季的傍晚，台北通常都很悶熱。
❸ Irene 一整天都待在太陽底下，她因中暑而暈倒，我們並不感到意外。
❹ 我待在太陽底下太久，所以已經曬傷了。
❺ 準備好流汗吧，今天將會很熱。
❻ 我經常在炎熱的午後享用冰品。
❼ 你穿著那件細肩帶上衣，肩膀會遭受陽光曝曬。

071

火
(1)

MP3 071

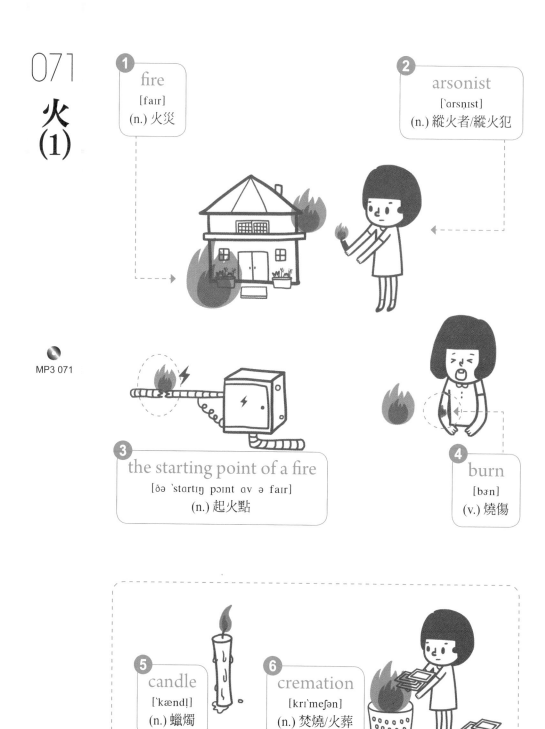

1 fire
[faɪr]
(n.) 火災

2 arsonist
[ˈɑrsṇɪst]
(n.) 縱火者/縱火犯

3 the starting point of a fire
[ðə ˈstɑrtɪŋ pɔɪnt ɑv ə faɪr]
(n.) 起火點

4 burn
[bɜn]
(v.) 燒傷

5 candle
[ˈkændḷ]
(n.) 蠟燭

6 cremation
[krɪˈmeʃən]
(n.) 焚燒/火葬

❶ 火災

There is a fire in that building. Call 119.

❷ 縱火者 / 縱火犯

Bob's an arsonist. He set his parents' home on fire.

放火燒父母的家

❸ 起火點

The investigators found that the starting point of the fire was in the kitchen.

❹ 燒傷

I fell onto the fire and burnt myself quite badly.

嚴重地燒傷了自己

❺ 蠟燭

People used to use wax candles to see with at night.

使用蠟燭來看

❻ 焚燒 / 火葬

I like the idea of cremation. There isn't enough room for everyone to be buried underground.

沒有足夠的空間

被埋在地底下

學更多

❶ building〈建築物〉・ call〈打電話〉

❷ set on fire〈set on fire（放火）的過去式〉・ parents〈雙親〉

❸ investigator〈調查員〉・ starting〈開始〉・ point〈位置〉・ kitchen〈廚房〉

❹ fell〈fall（跌倒）的過去式〉・ fire〈火〉・ burnt〈burn（燒傷）的過去式〉・ myself〈我自己〉・ quite〈相當地〉・ badly〈嚴重地〉

❺ used to〈過去經常〉・ wax〈蠟製的〉・ see〈看〉・ night〈晚上〉

❻ room〈空間〉・ buried〈bury（埋葬）的過去分詞〉・ underground〈在地下〉

中譯

❶ 那棟建築物發生火災，快打 119。

❷ Bob 是名縱火犯，他放火燒了自己父母的家。

❸ 調查員發現起火點位於廚房。

❹ 我跌進火中，讓自己嚴重燒傷了。

❺ 過去人們在夜間經常使用蠟燭照明來看東西。

❻ 我喜歡火葬這個概念。因為沒有足夠的空間讓每個人都能埋葬在地底下。

072

火
(2)

MP3 072

1 flame
[flem]
(n.) 火焰

2 campfire
[ˋkæmp.faɪr]
(n.) 營火

3 oxidizer
[ˋɑksə.daɪzɚ]
(n.) 助燃物

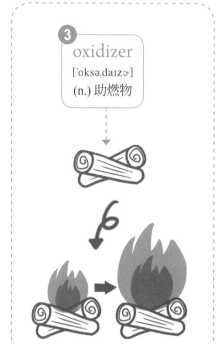

4 fuel
[ˋfjʊəl]
(n.) 燃料

5 log
[lɔg]
(n.) 木材

6 forest fire
[ˋfɔrɪst faɪr]
(n.) 森林大火

❶ 火焰

After lighting the fire, I sat back and watched the flames rise into the air.
坐下來休息

❷ 營火

The campers sat around the campfire and told stories.
圍坐在營火旁

❸ 助燃物

The oxidizer helped the fire burn more strongly.
火燃燒得更旺

❹ 燃料

We're going to use these branches as fuel for the fire.
使用這些樹枝當作燃料

❺ 木材

Throw this thick log onto the fire.

❻ 森林大火

The forest fire is covering a huge area of land now.
一片龐大的區域

學更多

❶ lighting〈light（點燃）的 ing 型態〉‧ sat back〈sit back（坐下休息）的過去式〉‧ rise〈升起〉‧ air〈空氣〉

❷ camper〈露營者〉‧ around〈圍繞〉‧ told〈tell（說）的過去式〉‧ story〈故事〉

❸ helped〈help（幫助）的過去式〉‧ fire〈火〉‧ burn〈燃燒〉‧ strongly〈強烈地〉

❹ use〈使用〉‧ branch〈樹枝〉

❺ throw〈丟〉‧ thick〈粗的〉

❻ forest〈森林〉‧ covering〈cover（覆蓋）的 ing 型態〉‧ huge〈龐大的〉‧ land〈土地〉

中譯

❶ 點火之後，我坐下來休息，看著火焰在空氣中升起。

❷ 露營者圍坐在營火旁說故事。

❸ 助燃物讓火焰燃燒得更旺盛。

❹ 我們要使用這些樹枝當作生火的燃料。

❺ 把這片厚木材丟進火裡。

❻ 目前森林大火蔓延到一片遼闊的土地上。

駕車(1)

1 speed limit
[spid `lɪmɪt]
(n.) 速限

2 speed camera
[spid `kæmərə]
(n.) 測速照相機

3 speeding
[`spidɪŋ]
(n.) 超速

MP3 073

4 run a red light
[rʌn ə rɛd laɪt]
(phr.) 闖紅燈

5 driving without a license
[`draɪvɪŋ wɪ`ðaut ə `laɪsn̩s]
(phr.) 無照駕駛

6 driver's license
[`draɪvɚz `laɪsn̩s]
(n.) 駕照

7 ticket
[`tɪkɪt]
(n.) 罰單

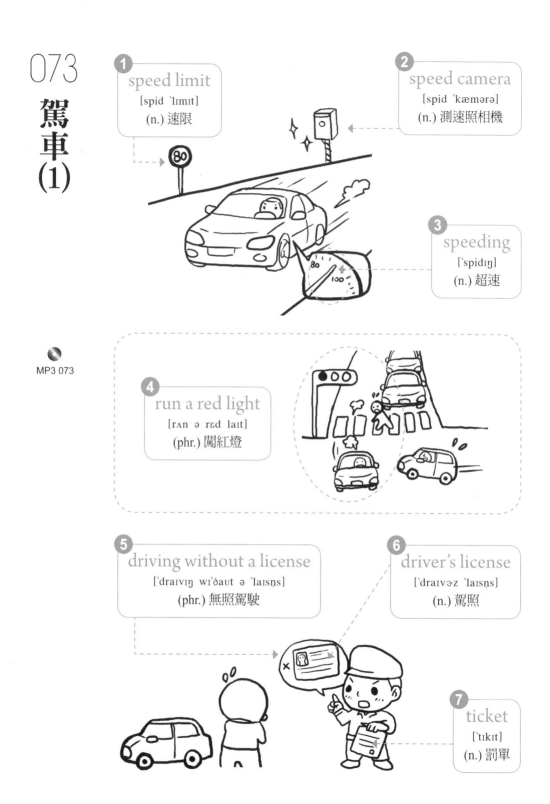

❶ 速限

The speed limit is 70 km/h on these roads. You can't drive faster than that.

速限是每小時 70 公里　　　　　　　　　　　　　　速度比 70 km/h 還快

❷ 測速照相機

Drivers usually slow down when they see speed cameras.

❸ 超速

Trevor always drives too fast, so no one was surprised when the police stopped him for speeding.

警察因超速而攔下他

❹ 闖紅燈

Darren nearly hit some cars when he ran a red light.

差一點撞上其他車子

❺ 無照駕駛

Jamie got into a lot of trouble when he was caught driving without a license.

當他因無照駕駛被抓

❻ 駕照

Les was happy when he passed his driving test and got his driver's license.

通過駕駛測驗

❼ 罰單

The police officer told me I was driving too fast and gave me a ticket.

給了我一張罰單

學更多

❶ speed〈速度〉・limit〈限制〉・drive〈開車〉・faster〈更快地，fast（快地）的比較級〉
❷ driver〈駕駛〉・slow down〈減速〉・see〈看到〉・camera〈照相機〉
❸ surprised〈感到意外的〉・police〈警察〉・stopped〈stop（阻止）的過去式〉
❹ nearly〈幾乎〉・hit〈hit（碰撞）的過去式〉・ran〈run（衝過）的過去式〉
❺ trouble〈麻煩〉・caught〈catch（抓）的過去分詞〉・without〈沒有〉・license〈執照〉
❻ passed〈pass（通過）的過去式〉・driving〈駕駛〉・test〈測驗〉
❼ driving〈drive（駕駛）的 ing 型態〉・gave〈give（給）的過去式〉

中譯

❶ 這些路段的速限是每小時 70 公里，開車時你不能超過這個速度。
❷ 駕駛們看到測速照相機時，通常會減速。
❸ Trevor 開車總是太快，所以當警察因超速而攔下他時，沒人感到意外。
❹ Darren 闖紅燈時，差點撞上其他車子。
❺ Jamie 因無照駕駛被抓，讓自己惹上大麻煩。
❻ Les 很開心自己通過了駕駛測驗，並拿到駕照。
❼ 警察說我開車開得太快，並給了我一張罰單。

駕車(2)

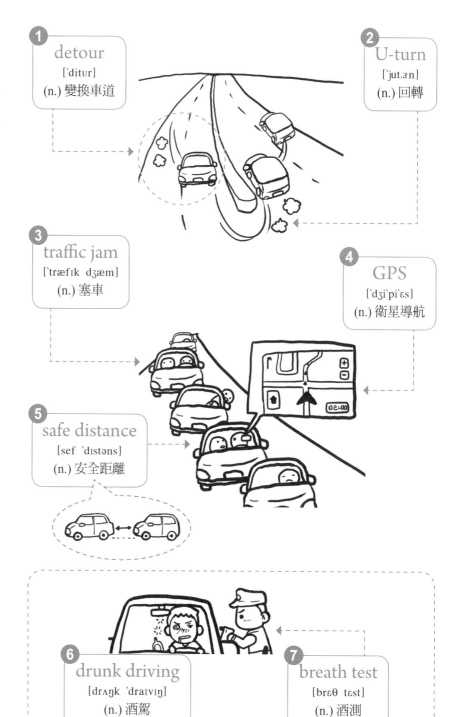

1 detour
['ditʊr]
(n.) 變換車道

2 U-turn
['jut.ɜn]
(n.) 回轉

3 traffic jam
['træfɪk dʒæm]
(n.) 塞車

4 GPS
['dʒi'pi'ɛs]
(n.) 衛星導航

5 safe distance
[sef 'dɪstəns]
(n.) 安全距離

6 drunk driving
[drʌŋk 'draɪvɪŋ]
(n.) 酒駕

7 breath test
[brɛθ tɛst]
(n.) 酒測

❶ 變換車道

Lindsey took a detour because the road was blocked.
　　　　　　　　　　　　　　　　　　　　道路被封鎖

❷ 回轉

Vivian realized she was going the wrong way, so she did a U-turn.
　　　　　　　　　　　她走錯方向

❸ 塞車

Sorry I took so long to get here. I was stuck in a traffic jam.
　　　　花了這麼久的時間

❹ 衛星導航

Your GPS will tell you exactly where you are.
　　　　　　　　　　　　　　　　你在哪裡

❺ 安全距離

Don't drive too close to the car in front. Keep a safe distance.
　　　　　　　開得太靠近前方的車子

❻ 酒駕

Drunk driving is dangerous and stupid. You can't concentrate properly
after drinking alcohol.　　　　　　　　無法好好地專注

❼ 酒測

The police officer thought Ginny had been drinking so he gave her a breath test.
　　　　　　　　　　　　　　喝了酒

學更多

❶ road〈路〉・blocked〈被封鎖的〉
❷ realized〈realize（領悟）的過去式〉・wrong〈錯誤的〉・way〈方向〉
❸ long〈久的〉・stuck〈stick（阻塞）的過去分詞〉・traffic〈交通〉・jam〈堵塞〉
❹ tell〈顯示某訊息〉・exactly〈確切地〉
❺ close〈接近的〉・in front〈在前面〉・keep〈保持〉・safe〈安全的〉・distance〈距離〉
❻ drunk〈喝醉的〉・dangerous〈危險的〉・concentrate〈集中〉・alcohol〈酒〉
❼ thought〈think（認為）的過去式〉・gave〈give（做）的過去式〉・breath〈一口氣〉

中譯

❶ Lindsey 因道路封閉而變換車道。
❷ Vivian 發現自己開錯方向了，所以她做了回轉。
❸ 很抱歉我這麼久才抵達這裡，我被塞車困住了。
❹ 你的衛星導航能顯示出你目前的確切位置。
❺ 別開得太靠近前方的車子，要保持安全距離。
❻ 酒駕既危險又愚蠢，喝酒後你根本無法好好地保持專注。
❼ 警察認為 Ginny 喝了酒，所以對她進行酒測。

163

075

搭飛機(1)

MP3 075

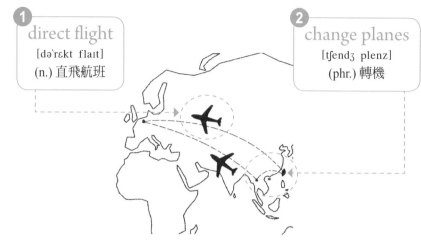

1 direct flight
[dəˋrɛkt flaɪt]
(n.) 直飛航班

2 change planes
[tʃendʒ plenz]
(phr.) 轉機

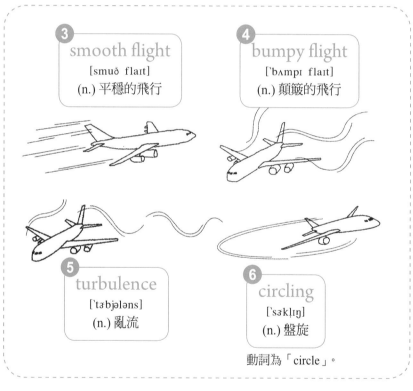

3 smooth flight
[smuð flaɪt]
(n.) 平穩的飛行

4 bumpy flight
[ˋbʌmpɪ flaɪt]
(n.) 顛簸的飛行

5 turbulence
[ˋtɝbjələns]
(n.) 亂流

6 circling
[ˋsɝklɪŋ]
(n.) 盤旋

動詞為「circle」。

7 airsickness
[ˋɛr͵sɪknɪs]
(n.) 暈機

❶ 直飛航班

It's a direct flight; there are no stops.

❷ 轉機

Sam had to change planes in Singapore, so he picked up his things and got off the plane.
_{下飛機}

❸ 平穩的飛行

We had a smooth flight; it was very comfortable.

❹ 顛簸的飛行

That was such a bumpy flight. I've never been more scared.
_{從未如此驚嚇}

❺ 亂流

The airplane shook when it passed through an area of turbulence.
_{通過亂流區域}

❻ 盤旋

The airplane was circling over the airport while the pilot was waiting to land.
_{飛機在機場上空盤旋}

❼ 暈機

Candy suffers with airsickness, so she always makes sure she has some sick bags with her when she flies.
_{她身上有帶一些嘔吐袋}

學更多

❶ direct〈直接的〉‧ flight〈航班〉‧ stop〈停靠站〉
❷ change〈更改〉‧ plane〈飛機〉‧ picked up〈pick up（拿起）的過去式〉
❸ smooth〈平穩的〉‧ flight〈飛行〉‧ comfortable〈舒適的〉
❹ such〈這樣的〉‧ bumpy〈顛簸的〉‧ scared〈嚇壞的〉
❺ shook〈shake（晃動）的過去式〉‧ passed through〈pass through（通過）的過去式〉
❻ over〈在…之上〉‧ airport〈機場〉‧ while〈當…的時候〉‧ pilot〈飛行員〉‧ land〈降落〉
❼ suffer〈受苦〉‧ make sure〈確定〉‧ sick bag〈嘔吐袋〉‧ fly〈飛行〉

中譯

❶ 這是直飛航班，沒有任何停靠站。
❷ Sam 必須在新加坡轉機，所以他帶著隨身行李下了飛機。
❸ 我們有一趟平穩的飛行，那非常舒適。
❹ 那真是一趟顛簸的飛行，我從來沒有這麼驚嚇過。
❺ 飛機通過亂流區域時，出現了晃動。
❻ 當飛行員在等待降落時，飛機就在機場上空盤旋。
❼ Candy 會暈機，所以她搭飛機時，總會確認身邊備有一些嘔吐袋。

076

搭飛機(2)

MP3 076

1 estimated time of arrival
[ˋɛstəˏmetɪd taɪm ɑv əˋraɪvḷ]
(n.) 預計抵達時間

2 actual arrival time
[ˋæktʃʊəl əˋraɪvḷ taɪm]
(n.) 實際抵達時間

「estimated time of arrival」可縮寫為「ETA」。

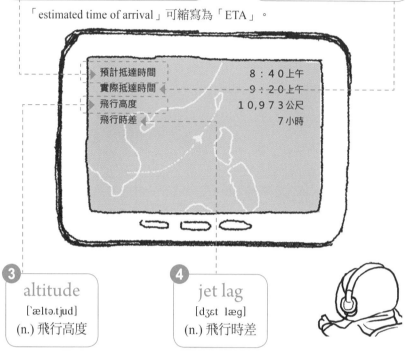

預計抵達時間	8：40上午
實際抵達時間	9：20上午
飛行高度	10,973公尺
飛行時差	7小時

3 altitude
[ˋæltəˏtjud]
(n.) 飛行高度

4 jet lag
[dʒɛt læg]
(n.) 飛行時差

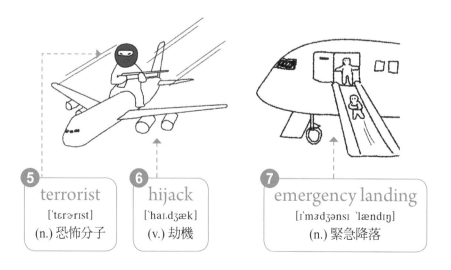

5 terrorist
[ˋtɛrərɪst]
(n.) 恐怖分子

6 hijack
[ˋhaɪˏdʒæk]
(v.) 劫機

7 emergency landing
[ɪˋmɝdʒənsɪ ˋlændɪŋ]
(n.) 緊急降落

❶ 預計抵達時間

Our estimated time of arrival is 8:30, so we should see you then.
到時候見

❷ 實際抵達時間

Dean thought he'd arrive at 1pm, but he was delayed so his actual arrival
他會在下午 1 點抵達（= he would arrive at 1pm）　　　　　他被延誤

time was 3pm.

❸ 飛行高度

Airplanes fly at a high altitude.

❹ 飛行時差

Fiona is suffering with jet lag after flying from Taiwan to Paris.
感受到飛行時差的不適

❺ 恐怖分子

The terrorists were arrested before they could blow up the embassy.
在他們可能炸毀大使館之前

❻ 劫機

The bad men hijacked the plane and told the pilot to fly to a different airport.
飛到另一座機場

❼ 緊急降落

The pilot made an emergency landing when one of the engines stopped working.
其中一具引擎停止運轉

學更多

❶ our〈我們的〉‧ estimated〈估計的〉‧ arrival〈到達〉‧ see〈見面〉
❷ thought〈think（以為）的過去式〉‧ delayed〈delay（延誤）的過去分詞〉‧ actual〈實際的〉
❸ airplane〈飛機〉‧ fly〈飛行〉‧ high〈高的〉
❹ suffering〈suffer（遭受）的 ing 型態〉‧ jet〈噴射機〉‧ lag〈落後〉
❺ arrested〈arrest（逮捕）的過去分詞〉‧ blow up〈炸毀〉‧ embassy〈大使館〉
❻ men〈man（人）的複數〉‧ pilot〈飛行員〉‧ different〈另外的〉‧ airport〈機場〉
❼ made〈make（做）的過去式〉‧ emergency〈緊急情況〉‧ landing〈降落〉‧ engine〈引擎〉

中譯

❶ 我們的預計抵達時間是 8 點 30 分，我們到時候見。
❷ Dean 原本以為會在下午 1 點抵達，但因為延誤，所以他的實際抵達時間是下午 3 點。
❸ 飛機在很高的飛行高度上飛行。
❹ 從台灣飛到巴黎後，Fiona 感受到飛行時差的不適。
❺ 在炸毀大使館之前，恐怖分子就遭到逮捕。
❻ 壞人劫持飛機，並要求飛行員將飛機開往另一個機場。
❼ 當其中一具引擎停止運轉，飛行員將飛機緊急降落。

077

聚餐(1)

MP3 077

1 reservation
[ˌrɛzəˈveʃən]
(n.) 預訂

2 order
[ˈɔrdɚ]
(v.) 點菜

3 menu
[ˈmɛnju]
(n.) 菜單

4 serve
[sɝv]
(v.) 上菜

5 drunk
[drʌŋk]
(adj.) 酩酊大醉

6 toast
[tost]
(n.) 敬酒

7 cheers
[tʃɪrz]
(n.) 乾杯

❶ 預訂

Andy called the restaurant and made a reservation for Saturday night.
做了預訂

❷ 點菜

Are you ready to order your food yet, sir?

❸ 菜單

Julie looked at the menu before ordering her food.
在她點餐之前

❹ 上菜

The food was served on a dirty plate. It was terrible.
食物被用骯髒的盤子端上來

❺ 酩酊大醉

After drinking 10 glasses of beer, Mike was drunk.
10 杯啤酒

❻ 敬酒

The man raised his glass and offered a toast to his host.
給予敬酒

❼ 乾杯

The friends picked up their beers, said cheers, and started drinking.
拿起他們的啤酒

學更多

❶ called〈call（打電話）的過去式〉・restaurant〈餐廳〉・Saturday〈星期六〉
❷ ready〈準備好的〉・food〈食物〉・yet〈已經〉・sir〈先生〉
❸ looked at〈look at（看）的過去式〉・ordering〈order（點菜）的 ing 型態〉
❹ dirty〈髒的〉・plate〈盤子〉・terrible〈糟糕的〉
❺ drinking〈drink（喝）的 ing 型態〉・glass〈杯〉・beer〈啤酒〉
❻ raised〈raise（舉起）的過去式〉・glass〈玻璃杯〉・offered〈offer（給予）的過去式〉
❼ picked up〈pick up（拿起）的過去式〉・started〈start（開始）的過去式〉

中譯

❶ Andy 撥電話到餐廳，預訂了星期六晚上。
❷ 先生，請問您已經準備好要點餐了嗎？
❸ 點餐前，Julie 先看了菜單。
❹ 用骯髒的盤子上菜，真是糟糕。
❺ 灌下 10 杯啤酒之後，Mike 就酩酊大醉了。
❻ 這個男人舉起酒杯，給主人敬酒。
❼ 這群朋友拿起他們的啤酒，說聲：「乾杯」，就喝起酒來。

078

聚餐 (2)

MP3 078

1 good mood
[gʊd mud]
(n.) 心情好

2 reunion
[riˋjunjən]
(n.) 聚會

3 delicious
[dɪˋlɪʃəs]
(adj.) 美味

yummy

4 doggy bag
[ˋdɔgɪ bæg]
(n.) 打包

5 pay cash
[pe kæʃ]
(phr.) 付現

500

250 + 250

CREDIT CARD

6 split
[splɪt]
(v.) 分攤費用

7 pay by credit card
[pe baɪ ˋkrɛdɪt kɑrd]
(phr.) 刷卡付費

❶ 心情好

Ben looks like he's in a good mood; I've never seen him so happy.

❷ 聚會

The old classmates had a reunion dinner last night. They haven't seen each other for 10 years.

❸ 美味

This food is delicious. Can I have some more?

❹ 打包

Daisy didn't finish her food, so she asked for a doggy bag.

❺ 付現

Ian decided to pay cash, so he handed over a bill.
他遞出一張鈔票

❻ 分攤費用

Let's split the bill. We'll just pay for what we ate.
支付我們自己所吃的

❼ 刷卡付費

Amy had to sign her name because she was paying by credit card.

學更多

❶ look like〈看起來像⋯〉・mood〈心情〉・seen〈see（看到）的過去分詞〉

❷ old〈舊交的〉・classmate〈同學〉・dinner〈晚餐〉・each other〈互相〉

❸ food〈食物〉・have〈吃〉・some〈一些〉・more〈更多的〉

❹ finish〈吃完〉・asked〈ask（要求）的過去式〉・doggy〈狗的〉・bag〈袋子〉

❺ pay〈支付〉・cash〈現金〉・handed over〈hand over（交出）的過去式〉・bill〈鈔票〉

❻ bill〈帳單〉・ate〈eat（吃）的過去式〉

❼ had to〈have to（必須）的過去式〉・sign〈簽寫〉・credit card〈信用卡〉

中譯

❶ Ben 看起來心情很好；我從沒看過他這麼開心。

❷ 昨晚這群老同學辦了一個晚餐聚會，他們已經 10 年沒見了。

❸ 這食物真美味，我可以再吃一些嗎？

❹ Daisy 沒把餐點吃完，所以她要求打包。

❺ Ian 決定付現，於是他遞出了一張紙鈔。

❻ 大家分攤帳單費用吧，我們就支付自己所吃的部分。

❼ Amy 必須簽名，因為她是刷卡付費的。

079

美食(1)

1 delicious
[dɪ`lɪʃəs]
(adj.) 美味的

2 delicacy
[`dɛləkəsɪ]
(n.) 精緻餐點

3 exotic cuisine
[ɛg`zɑtɪk kwɪ`zin]
(n.) 異國料理

MP3 079

4 appetizing
[`æpə.taɪzɪŋ]
(adj.) 食慾大振

5 secret ingredient
[`sikrɪt ɪn`ɡridɪənt]
(n.) 獨家祕方

6 gravy
[`ɡrevɪ]
(n.)（肉）醬汁/肉汁

❶ 美味的

Oh, this food is delicious. Where did you buy it?

❷ 精緻餐點

Insects are considered a delicacy in some countries. People love to eat them.

　　　　昆蟲被視為精緻餐點

❸ 異國料理

One of the best things about going to another country on holiday is the chance to try exotic cuisine.

❹ 食慾大振

The food looks very appetizing. I can't wait to eat it.

　　　　　　　　　　　等不及要享用它

❺ 獨家祕方

I wish I knew the secret ingredient to this dish. I'd love to know how to make it.

　　　　　　　　　　　　　　　　我很想知道（= I would love to know）

❻ （肉）醬汁/肉汁

Gravy is a meaty sauce that's popular in the West.

　　　　在西方國家很流行

學更多

❶ food〈食物〉・buy〈買〉

❷ insect〈昆蟲〉・considered〈consider（認為）的過去分詞〉・country〈國家〉

❸ another〈另外的〉・chance〈機會〉・exotic〈異國情調的〉・cuisine〈菜餚〉

❹ look〈看起來〉・wait〈等待〉

❺ wish〈希望〉・knew〈know（知道）的過去式〉・secret〈祕密的〉・ingredient〈原料〉・dish〈餐點〉

❻ meaty〈肉的〉・sauce〈醬汁〉・popular〈流行的〉・the West〈西方國家〉

中譯

❶ 噢！這食物真美味。你在哪裡買的？

❷ 昆蟲在某些國家被視為精緻餐點，人們喜歡享用它們。

❸ 出國渡假最棒的事情之一，就是有機會嘗試異國料理。

❹ 這道菜看起來令人食慾大振，我等不及要享用了。

❺ 真希望我知道這道餐點的獨家祕方，我很想知道如何做出這道料理。

❻ 「gravy」是西方國家很流行的一種肉製醬汁。

080

美食(2)

1 foodie
[ˈfudɪ]
(n.) 饕客

2 gourmet
[gurˋme]
(n.) 美食家 (adj.) 美食的

MP3 080

3 restaurant
[ˈrɛstərənt]
(n.) 餐館

4 rating
[ˈretɪŋ]
(n.) 等級/評價

5 local cuisine
[ˋlokḷ kwɪˋzin]
(n.) 當地小吃

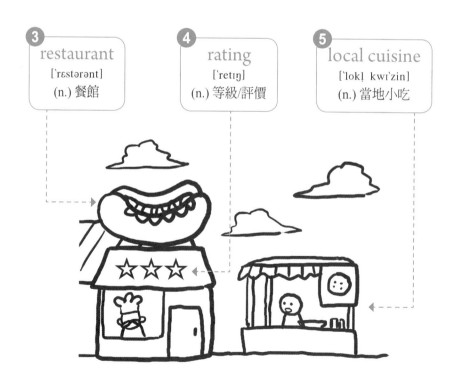

❶ 饕客

Ryan's a real foodie. All he thinks about is eating good food.

他所想的全部都有關…

❷ 美食家 / 美食的

Gordon Ramsay is a famous gourmet chef.

❸ 餐館

This is my favorite restaurant. I love the food here.

❹ 等級 / 評價

This restaurant received an excellent rating by a famous food critic. We should go there.

得到非常好的評價

❺ 當地小吃

When you go to new countries, don't eat burgers and sandwiches. Try the local cuisine.

學更多

❶ real〈真正的〉‧ think〈想〉‧ eating〈eat（吃）的 ing 型態〉‧ food〈食物〉

❷ famous〈出名的〉‧ chef〈主廚〉

❸ favorite〈特別喜愛的〉‧ love〈喜愛〉‧ here〈這裡〉

❹ received〈receive（得到）的過去式〉‧ excellent〈傑出的〉‧ critic〈評論家〉

❺ burger〈漢堡〉‧ sandwich〈三明治〉‧ try〈嘗試〉‧ local〈當地的〉‧ cuisine〈菜餚〉

中譯

❶ Ryan 是個貨真價實的饕客，他滿腦子都想著要享受美食。

❷ Gordon Ramsay 是一位知名的美食家主廚。

❸ 這是我最喜歡的餐館，我喜愛這裡的食物。

❹ 一位知名的美食評論家給了這間餐廳非常好的評價，我們該去瞧瞧。

❺ 當你到新的國家時，別只是吃漢堡和三明治，嘗試一下當地小吃。

081

烹調

1 peel
[pil]
(v.) 削皮

2 cubed
[kjubd]
(adj.) 切丁狀的

3 cut
[kʌt]
(v.) 切

4 slice
[slaɪs]
(v.) 切片

5 taste
[test]
(v.) 嘗試味道

MP3 081

6 ingredient
[ɪnˋɡridɪənt]
(n.) 食材

7 cookware
[ˋkʊk.wɛr]
(n.) 鍋具

❶ 削皮
June peeled the skin off the potato.

❷ 切丁狀的
I want my carrots cubed; I like them in squares.
<u>它們呈現方塊狀</u>

❸ 切
Can you cut these carrots into small pieces?
<u>把紅蘿蔔切成小片</u>

❹ 切片
Ian asked for the loaf of bread to be sliced.
<u>這塊麵包</u>

❺ 嘗試味道
Can you taste this sauce and tell me if it needs salt?
<u>它是否需要鹽巴</u>

❻ 食材
I don't have all the ingredients I need for this cake. I need sugar.
<u>所有我需要的食材</u>

❼ 鍋具
Dave bought some new cookware to cook his food in.
<u>用來烹煮食物的新鍋具</u>

學更多

❶ skin〈外皮〉・off〈離開〉・potato〈馬鈴薯〉
❷ want〈想要〉・carrot〈紅蘿蔔〉・square〈方塊〉
❸ small〈小的〉・piece〈一片〉
❹ asked〈ask（要求）的過去式〉・loaf〈一塊〉・bread〈麵包〉
❺ sauce〈醬料〉・tell〈告訴〉・if〈是否〉・need〈需要〉・salt〈鹽巴〉
❻ all〈所有的〉・cake〈蛋糕〉・sugar〈糖〉
❼ bought〈buy（買）的過去式〉・some〈一些〉・new〈新的〉・cook〈烹調〉

中譯

❶ June 替這些馬鈴薯削皮。
❷ 我要切丁狀的紅蘿蔔，我喜歡它們呈現方塊狀的樣子。
❸ 你能將這些紅蘿蔔切成小片的嗎？
❹ Ian 要求將這塊麵包切片。
❺ 你能幫我嘗試這個醬料的味道，然後告訴我是否需要加鹽巴嗎？
❻ 我沒有做這個蛋糕需要的所有食材，我還需要糖。
❼ Dave 買了一些新鍋具來烹煮食物。

082

飲
酒
(1)

1
liquor
[`lɪkə]
(n.) 酒精性飲料/烈酒

2
alcohol content
[`ælkəˌhɔl kən`tɛnt]
(n.) 酒精濃度

MP3 082

3
cheers
[tʃɪrz]
(n.) 敬酒時乾杯

4
toast
[tost]
(v.) 敬酒

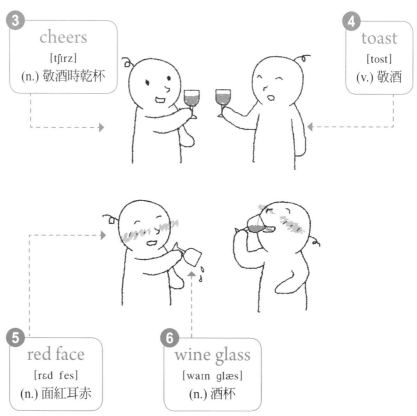

5
red face
[rɛd fes]
(n.) 面紅耳赤

6
wine glass
[waɪn glæs]
(n.) 酒杯

❶ 酒精性飲料 / 烈酒

Liquor is much stronger than wine, so don't drink too much.
比葡萄酒還濃烈

❷ 酒精濃度

This wine has a high alcohol content, so be careful how much you drink.
高酒精濃度　　　　　　　　　　　　　你喝了多少

❸ 敬酒時乾杯

The two friends said cheers and then drank their beer.

❹ 敬酒

Ian raised his glass and toasted his host.
舉起他的酒杯

❺ 面紅耳赤

Have you been drinking? You have a red face.

❻ 酒杯

Dan bought some new wine glasses to drink red wine from.
從…裡喝紅酒

學更多

❶ stronger〈更強烈的，strong（強烈的）的比較級〉・wine〈葡萄酒〉・drink〈喝〉

❷ high〈高的〉・alcohol〈酒精〉・content〈含量〉・careful〈留意的〉

❸ friend〈朋友〉・said〈say（說）的過去式〉・drank〈drink（喝）的過去式〉・beer〈啤酒〉

❹ raised〈raise（舉起）的過去式〉・host〈主人〉

❺ drinking〈drink（喝酒）的 ing 型態〉・red〈通紅的〉・face〈臉〉

❻ bought〈buy（買）的過去式〉・new〈新的〉

中譯

❶ 烈酒比葡萄酒濃烈許多，所以別喝太多。

❷ 這種酒的酒精濃度高，所以得留意自己喝了多少。

❸ 兩個朋友互說「乾杯」，然後灌下各自的啤酒。

❹ Ian 舉起他的酒杯向主人敬酒。

❺ 你剛喝了酒嗎？你面紅耳赤。

❻ Dan 買了一些新酒杯用來喝紅酒。

083 飲酒(2)

MP3 083

1 **talk nonsense**
[tɔk `nɑnsɛns]
(phr.) 胡言亂語

2 **spin**
[spɪn]
(v.) 天旋地轉

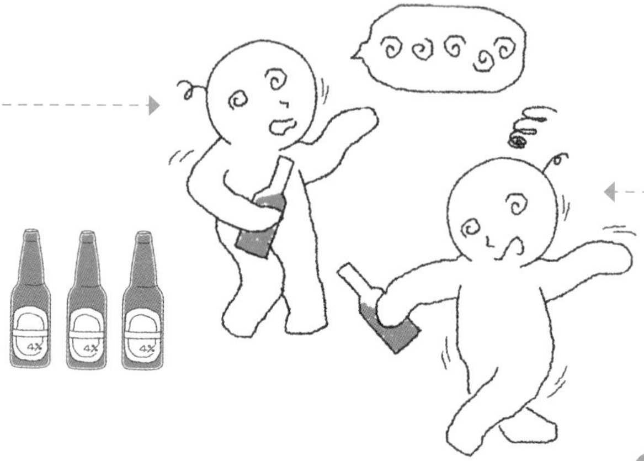

3 **throw up**
[θro ʌp]
(phr.) 嘔吐

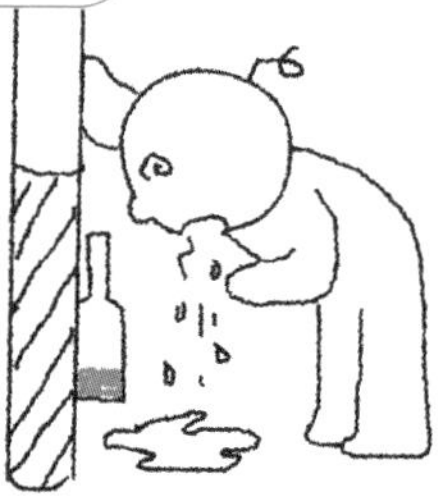

4 **wasted**
[`westɪd]
(adj.) 爛醉

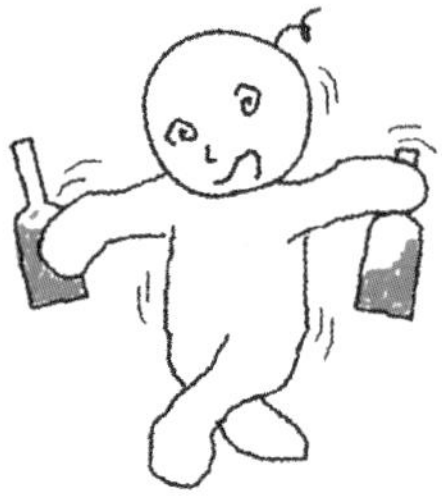

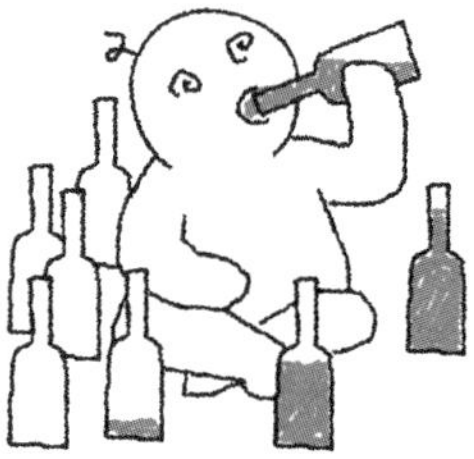

5 **alcoholism**
[`ælkəhɔl͵ɪzəm]
(n.) 酗酒

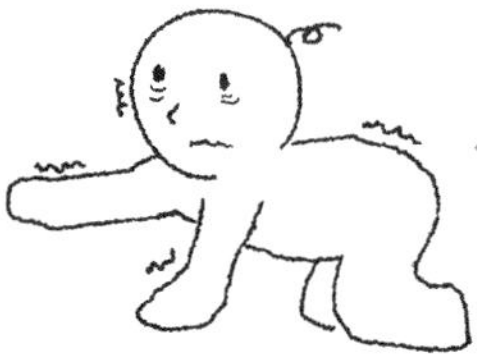

6 **alcohol poisoning**
[`ælkə͵hɔl `pɔɪzn̩ɪŋ]
(n.) 酒精中毒

❶ 胡言亂語

When people are drunk, they usually talk nonsense.

❷ 天旋地轉

After drinking too much, Mandy felt her head spinning.

覺得她的頭在旋轉

❸ 嘔吐

After eating so much food, it was inevitable that he would throw up.

這是必然的

❹ 爛醉

After drinking half the bottle of whisky, he's wasted.

半瓶威士忌

❺ 酗酒

Brian suffers with alcoholism. He feels like he needs to drink.

染上酗酒的毛病

❻ 酒精中毒

Graham drinks a lot every night. He's got alcohol poisoning now.

學更多

❶ drunk〈喝醉的〉・usually〈通常〉・talk〈講話〉・nonsense〈胡說〉
❷ drinking〈drink（喝酒）的 ing 型態〉・felt〈feel（覺得）的過去式〉・head〈頭〉
❸ eating〈eat（吃）的 ing 型態〉・inevitable〈不可避免的〉
❹ half〈一半的〉・bottle〈瓶〉・whisky〈威士忌〉
❺ suffer〈患上〉・feel like〈感覺好像〉・need〈需要〉
❻ got〈get（得到）的過去分詞〉・alcohol〈酒精〉・poisoning〈中毒〉

中譯

❶ 人們喝醉時，通常都會胡言亂語。
❷ 喝了太多酒後，Mandy 感到天旋地轉。
❸ 在吃了那麼多食物之後，他會嘔吐也是必然的。
❹ 喝了半瓶的威士忌後，他就爛醉了。
❺ Brian 染上酗酒的毛病，他總覺得自己需要喝酒。
❻ Graham 每晚都喝很多酒，他現在有酒精中毒的症狀。

084

飲食習慣(1)

MP3 084

1 picky
[`pɪkɪ]
(adj.) 挑食

2 malnutrition
[ˌmælnjuˋtrɪʃən]
(n.) 營養失調

3 food allergy
[fud ˋæləʤɪ]
(n.) 食物過敏

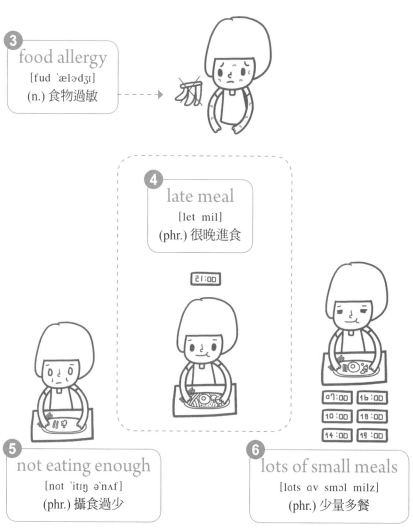

4 late meal
[let mil]
(phr.) 很晚進食

5 not eating enough
[nɑt ˋitɪŋ əˋnʌf]
(phr.) 攝食過少

6 lots of small meals
[lɑts ɑv smɔl milz]
(phr.) 少量多餐

182

❶ 挑食

Tina is very picky with her food. There's a lot she won't eat.
　　　　　　　　對食物挑剔

❷ 營養失調

Lionel hasn't eaten properly for weeks, so he's suffering with malnutrition
now.　　　　　沒有好好吃飯

❸ 食物過敏

Mike has a food allergy. If he eats wheat, he'll get sick.
　　　　　　　　　　　　　　　　　　生病

❹ 很晚進食

Dean was hungry when he got back from the party so he had a late meal.
　　　　　　　　　　　　　　當他從派對回來

❺ 攝食過少

Vinny isn't eating enough. He looks ill.

❻ 少量多餐

I don't like big meals, so I have lots of small meals.
　　　　　　豐盛的大餐

學更多

❶ very〈相當〉‧ food〈食物〉‧ a lot〈很多〉‧ eat〈吃〉

❷ eaten〈eat（吃）的過去分詞〉‧ properly〈恰當地〉‧ suffering〈suffer（受苦）的 ing 型態〉

❸ allergy〈過敏〉‧ if〈如果〉‧ wheat〈小麥〉‧ sick〈病的〉

❹ hungry〈飢餓的〉‧ got back〈get back（回來）的過去式〉‧ party〈派對〉‧ late〈晚的〉

❺ eating〈eat（吃）的 ing 型態〉‧ enough〈足夠地〉‧ look〈看起來〉‧ ill〈生病的〉

❻ like〈喜歡〉‧ big〈大量的〉‧ meal〈餐點〉‧ lots of〈許多〉‧ small〈少量的〉

中譯

❶ Tina 對於食物相當挑食，有很多東西她都不吃。

❷ Lionel 已經好幾週沒有好好吃飯了，因此他正為營養失調所苦。

❸ Mike 有食物過敏的問題。如果吃小麥類的食物，他就會生病。

❹ Dean 從派對回來時覺得很餓，所以他很晚進食。

❺ Vinny 攝食過少，他看起來病懨懨的。

❻ 我不喜歡一餐吃很多，因此我都少量多餐。

085

飲食習慣(2)

MP3 085

1 eat slowly
[it `slolɪ]
(phr.) 細嚼慢嚥

2 binge
[bɪndʒ]
(v.) 暴飲暴食

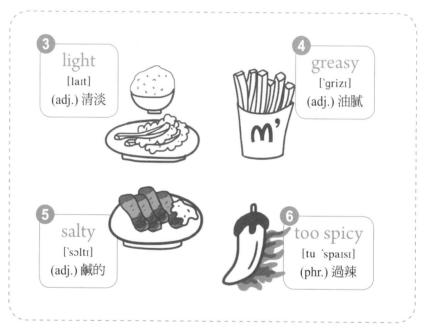

3 light
[laɪt]
(adj.) 清淡

4 greasy
[`grizɪ]
(adj.) 油膩

5 salty
[`sɔltɪ]
(adj.) 鹹的

6 too spicy
[tu `spaɪsɪ]
(phr.) 過辣

7 junk food
[dʒʌŋk fud]
(n.) 垃圾食物

❶ 細嚼慢嚥

Stacey eats slowly because she's heard it helps you to lose weight.
幫助你減肥

❷ 暴飲暴食

Chris likes to binge on food on Friday nights. He always eats too much then.

❸ 清淡

In the summer, people are more likely to want a light meal, like a salad.
更有可能想吃清淡的餐點

❹ 油膩

I don't want more fried food. It's too greasy.
油炸食物

❺ 鹹的

Soy sauce tastes very salty.
醬油

❻ 過辣

This is too spicy; my mouth's burning.

❼ 垃圾食物

Junk food, like hamburgers and pizza, is bad for you.

學更多

❶ slowly〈緩慢地〉・heard〈hear（聽說）的過去分詞〉・help〈幫助〉・lose weight〈減重〉
❷ food〈食物〉・night〈晚上〉・always〈總是〉・eat〈吃〉・then〈那時〉
❸ summer〈夏天〉・likely〈很可能的〉・meal〈餐點〉・like〈像是〉・salad〈沙拉〉
❹ want〈想要〉・more〈更多的〉・fried〈油炸的〉
❺ soy〈醬油、大豆〉・sauce〈醬汁〉・taste〈嚐起來〉
❻ too〈太〉・spicy〈辛辣的〉・mouth〈嘴〉・burning〈發熱的〉
❼ junk〈垃圾〉・hamburger〈漢堡〉・pizza〈披薩〉・bad〈不好的〉

中譯

❶ Stacey 都細嚼慢嚥，因為她聽說這樣有助於減肥。
❷ Chris 喜歡在週五晚上暴飲暴食，他總是會在那時候吃太多。
❸ 夏季時，人們更有可能想吃清淡的食物，像是沙拉。
❹ 我不想再吃油炸食品了，它們太油膩了。
❺ 醬油嚐起來非常鹹。
❻ 這東西過辣，我的嘴都在發燙了。
❼ 像漢堡和披薩這種垃圾食物，對你的身體很不好。

086

食物保存(1)

MP3 086

1 fresh
[frɛʃ]
(adj.) 新鮮的

2 rotten
['ratn̩]
(adj.) 腐壞的

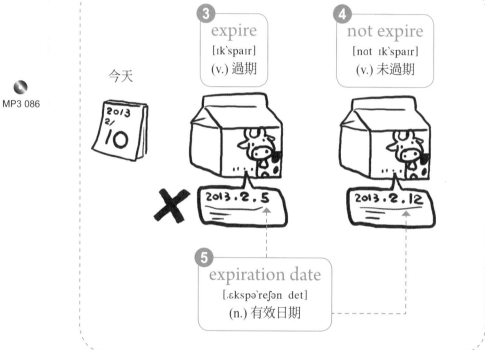

今天

3 expire
[ɪk'spaɪr]
(v.) 過期

4 not expire
[nɑt ɪk'spaɪr]
(v.) 未過期

5 expiration date
[ˌɛkspə'reʃən det]
(n.) 有效日期

5 leftovers
['lɛft.ovəz]
(n.) 未吃完的食物

7 sealing clip
['silɪŋ klɪp]
(n.) 封口夾

❶ 新鮮的

Make sure that fruit is fresh before you buy it.

❷ 腐壞的

How old are these vegetables? They're rotten.

❸ 過期

The best before date has expired; you can't eat this.

保存期限

❹ 未過期

This food has not expired. It's still OK to eat it.

❺ 有效日期

The man checked the expiration date on the food and then threw it away. It was two days ago.

❻ 未吃完的食物

Ewan is going to reheat the leftovers from yesterday for his dinner tonight.

重新加熱昨天的剩菜

❼ 封口夾

After you've opened the packet, please keep it closed with a sealing clip.

你已經打開過包裝　　　　保持密封

學更多

❶ make sure〈確認〉・fruit〈水果〉・before〈在…之前〉・buy〈買〉
❷ old〈長時間的〉・vegetable〈蔬菜〉
❸ best〈最好的〉・date〈日期〉・expired〈expire（過期）的過去分詞〉・eat〈吃〉
❹ food〈食物〉・still〈仍然〉
❺ expiration〈期滿〉・threw away〈throw away（丟掉）的過去式〉・ago〈在…以前〉
❻ reheat〈重新加熱〉・yesterday〈昨天〉・dinner〈晚餐〉
❼ opened〈open（打開）的過去分詞〉・packet〈包裝〉・sealing〈密封〉・clip〈夾子〉

中譯

❶ 買水果之前，務必確認它是新鮮的。
❷ 這些蔬菜放了多久？它們都是腐壞的。
❸ 保存期限已經過期，你不能食用。
❹ 這食物未過期，它仍可以食用。
❺ 這個男人查看食物上的有效日期，然後把它丟了。那東西已經過期兩天。
❻ Ewan 要重新加熱昨天未吃完的食物，作為今晚的晚餐。
❼ 在你開封之後，請用封口夾讓它保持密封。

087

食物保存(2)

MP3 087

1 keep out of the sun
[kip aut ɑv ðə sʌn]
(phr.) 避免日曬

2 food poisoning
[fud ˋpɔɪznɪŋ]
(n.) 食物中毒

3 turn moldy
[tɝn ˋmoldɪ]
(phr.) 發霉

4 preservative
[prɪˋzɝvətɪv]
(n.) 防腐劑

5 bacteria
[bækˋtɪrɪə]
(n.) 細菌

6 sterilize
[ˋstɛrəˌlaɪz]
(v.) 高溫殺菌

❶ 避免日曬

Keep **this** out of the sun or it will go bad.

❷ 食物中毒

If meat or fish isn't cooked properly, you can get food poisoning.
<u>沒有被適當地烹調</u>

❸ 發霉

This bread is really old. It's turning moldy.
<u>很不新鮮</u>

❹ 防腐劑

Preservatives are put in food to keep it fresh longer.
<u>能更長久地保持它的鮮度</u>

❺ 細菌

You should cook food properly to kill any bacteria.
<u>殺死任何細菌</u>

❻ 高溫殺菌

The mother sterilized the baby bottle by putting it in boiling water.
<u>滾燙的水</u>

學更多

❶ keep out of〈不讓某人或物進入⋯範圍〉・or〈否則〉・go〈變成〉・bad〈壞的〉

❷ meat〈肉〉・cooked〈cook（烹煮）的過去分詞〉・get〈變成〉・poisoning〈中毒〉

❸ bread〈麵包〉・old〈不新鮮的〉・turning〈turn（變為）的 ing 型態〉・moldy〈發霉的〉

❹ put〈put（放）的過去分詞〉・keep〈保持〉・fresh〈新鮮的〉・
longer〈較長久地，long（長久地）的比較級〉

❺ properly〈適當地〉・kill〈殺死〉・any〈任一、每一〉

❻ mother〈母親〉・bottle〈奶瓶〉・putting〈put（放）的 ing 型態〉・boiling〈沸騰的〉

中譯

❶ 要避免日曬，否則它會壞掉。

❷ 肉類或魚類如果沒有經過適當烹調，你可能會食物中毒。

❸ 這麵包很不新鮮，它已經開始發霉了。

❹ 為了能更長久保鮮，食品中被添加了防腐劑。

❺ 你應該適當地烹煮食物，以殺死所有細菌。

❻ 這名母親將嬰兒的奶瓶放入滾水中高溫殺菌。

088

咖啡(1)

MP3 088

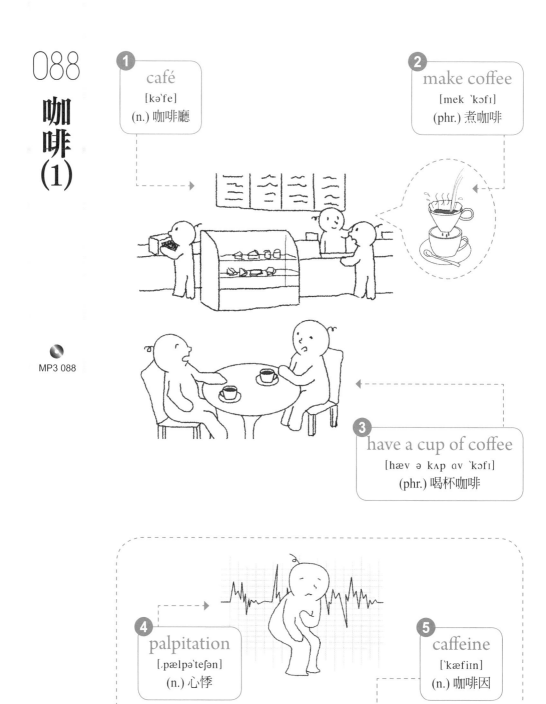

1 café
[kə`fe]
(n.) 咖啡廳

2 make coffee
[mek `kɔfɪ]
(phr.) 煮咖啡

3 have a cup of coffee
[hæv ə kʌp ɑv `kɔfɪ]
(phr.) 喝杯咖啡

4 palpitation
[.pælpə`teʃən]
(n.) 心悸

突然感覺到心跳變快、變慢、或不規則跳動的症狀。

5 caffeine
[`kæfiɪn]
(n.) 咖啡因

存在於茶葉、可可及咖啡中的植物鹼。有提神、利尿等作用。

① 咖啡廳

Imran and his wife went into a café to get a drink.

② 煮咖啡

Fearne takes making coffee very seriously. She loves the drink.

非常認真看待煮咖啡這件事

③ 喝杯咖啡

It's been a while since we've had a cup of coffee together.

已經有一段時間（＝ It has been a while）

④ 心悸

Mike had palpitations when he saw the beautiful woman.

⑤ 咖啡因

The caffeine in coffee will help to wake you up in the morning.

幫助你提神

學更多

① wife〈妻子〉・went〈go（去）的過去式〉・get〈買到〉・drink〈飲料〉

② take〈把⋯看作〉・making〈make（製作）的 ing 型態〉・seriously〈認真地〉・
love〈喜愛〉

③ while〈一段時間〉・since〈自從〉・had〈have（吃、喝）的過去分詞〉・
a cup of〈一杯〉・together〈一起〉

④ had〈have（患有）的過去式〉・saw〈see（看見）的過去式〉・beautiful〈美麗的〉・
woman〈女人〉

⑤ coffee〈咖啡〉・help〈幫助〉・wake...up〈使⋯提神〉・morning〈早上〉

中譯

① Imran 和他太太去咖啡廳點了杯飲料喝。

② Fearne 非常認真地看待煮咖啡這件事，她十分鍾情這種飲料。

③ 自從上次我們一起喝杯咖啡後，已經過了好一段時間。

④ Mike 看見這位美女時，心悸了一下。

⑤ 咖啡所含的咖啡因，有助於你在早晨時打起精神。

089
咖啡(2)

1 instant coffee
[`ɪnstənt `kɔfɪ]
(n.) 即溶咖啡

將牛奶打發成綿密狀，加在咖啡上可增添口感。

2 foam
[fom]
(n.) 奶泡

3 iced coffee
[aɪst `kɔfɪ]
(n.) 冰咖啡

4 hot coffee
[hɑt `kɔfɪ]
(n.) 熱咖啡

5 short
[ʃɔrt]
(n.) 小杯

6 tall
[tɔl]
(n.) 中杯

7 grande
[græn`de]
(n.) 大杯

❶ 即溶咖啡

Instant coffee is so much quicker and easier than fresh coffee.
　　　　　　　　　更快速、簡單多了　　　　　　　現煮咖啡

❷ 奶泡

Ginny used hot milk to make a foam on top of the coffee.
　　　　　　　　　　　　　　　在咖啡上打奶泡

❸ 冰咖啡

In the summertime, Keith likes to relax with an iced coffee.

❹ 熱咖啡

Amy loves a hot coffee on a cold day.

❺ 小杯
❻ 中杯
❼ 大杯

How big do you want your coffee to be—short, tall, or grande?
　　你想要多大杯

學更多

❶ instant〈即溶的〉・coffee〈咖啡〉・quicker〈更迅速的，quick（迅速的）的比較級〉・
easier〈更容易的，easy（容易的）的比較級〉・fresh〈新的〉

❷ used〈use（使用）的過去式〉・hot〈熱的〉・milk〈牛奶〉・top〈上方〉

❸ summertime〈夏季〉・relax〈放鬆〉・iced〈冰鎮的〉

❹ love〈喜愛〉・cold〈寒冷的〉

❺❻❼ big〈大的〉・want〈想要〉・your〈你的〉・or〈或是〉

中譯

❶ 即溶咖啡比現煮咖啡更快速、更簡單。

❷ Ginny 用熱牛奶在咖啡上打了奶泡。

❸ Keith 喜歡在夏日裡喝杯冰咖啡放鬆一下自己。

❹ Amy 喜愛在寒冷的天氣裡品嚐熱咖啡。

❺❻❼ 你的咖啡要多大杯的？小杯、中杯或大杯？

090

咖啡(3)

MP3 090

1 coffee bean
[ˈkɔfɪ bin]
(n.) 咖啡豆

2 coffee grinder
[ˈkɔfɪ ˈɡraɪndɚ]
(n.) 磨豆機

3 filter
[ˈfɪltɚ]
(n.) 濾紙

4 coffee grounds
[ˈkɔfɪ ɡraʊndz]
(n.) 咖啡渣

咖啡渣含豐富的抗氧化物及生物鹼，經曝曬乾燥後可用於吸附異味、除濕、或放置土壤作為肥料。

5 bake
[bek]
(v.) 烘焙

❶ 咖啡豆

Coffee beans have to be ground before you can use them to make coffee.
<u>在你可以使用它們之前</u>

❷ 磨豆機

Graham put his beans in a coffee grinder and turned it on.

❸ 濾紙

Use a filter when you pour the coffee into a cup, it will take out all the bits.
<u>當你把咖啡倒入杯中</u> <u>去除所有的咖啡渣</u>

❹ 咖啡渣

After finishing his coffee, Rich threw away the coffee grounds.
<u>扔掉咖啡渣</u>

❺ 烘焙

Janet plans to use fresh coffee to bake a coffee cake.
<u>現煮的咖啡</u>

學更多

❶ coffee〈咖啡〉‧ bean〈豆〉‧ have to〈必須〉‧ ground〈磨碎的〉‧ before〈在…之前〉‧ use〈使用〉

❷ put〈put（放）的過去式〉‧ grinder〈研磨機〉‧ turned on〈turn on（開啟開關）的過去式〉

❸ pour〈倒〉‧ cup〈杯子〉‧ take out〈除去〉‧ bit〈小塊〉

❹ after〈在…之後〉‧ finishing〈finish（喝完）的 ing 型態〉‧ threw away〈throw away（扔掉）的過去式〉‧ ground〈渣滓〉

❺ plan〈計劃〉‧ fresh〈新的〉‧ cake〈蛋糕〉

中譯

❶ 咖啡豆必須先經過研磨，你才能拿它們來沖泡咖啡。

❷ Graham 將咖啡豆放入磨豆機，並開啟開關。

❸ 當你要把咖啡倒入杯中時，使用濾紙將能過濾掉所有的咖啡渣。

❹ 喝完咖啡後，Rich 清掉了咖啡渣。

❺ Janet 計劃用現煮的咖啡來烘焙一個咖啡蛋糕。

091

看電影 (1)

MP3 091

1 popcorn
[ˋpɑpˌkɔrn]
(n.) 爆米花

2 release date
[rɪˋlis det]
(n.) 上映日期

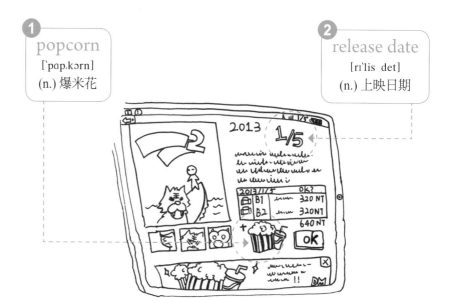

4 bad movie
[bæd ˋmuvɪ]
(n.) 爛片

3 sequel
[ˋsikwəl]
(n.) 續集

5 blockbuster
[ˋblɑkˌbʌstɚ]
(n.) 熱門鉅片

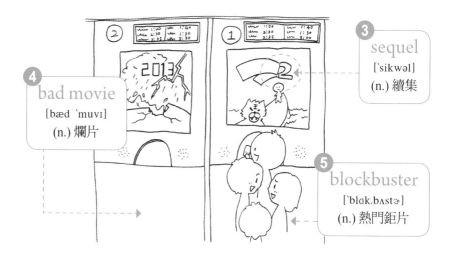

6 length
[lɛŋθ]
(n.) 片長

7 subtitle
[ˋsʌbˌtaɪtl̩]
(n.) 字幕

❶ 爆米花

Alex always eats popcorn while he watches movies.

❷ 上映日期

The release date for the movie is June 23. You'll be able to see it after that.
<u>你能夠去看</u>

❸ 續集

I loved the first movie; I hope the sequel is just as good.
<u>續集一樣好</u>

❹ 爛片

That was a bad movie. I can't believe I wasted my time watching it.
<u>我浪費我的時間去看它</u>

❺ 熱門鉅片

This movie is a drama; it's not a big blockbuster.

❻ 片長

The length of the movie puts me off. It lasts for four hours.
<u>讓我提不起興致</u>

❼ 字幕

When Emma watches foreign movies, she reads the subtitles at the bottom of the screen.
<u>螢幕下方的字幕</u>

學更多

❶ always〈總是〉‧ while〈當⋯的時候〉‧ watch〈觀看〉
❷ release〈發行〉‧ date〈日期〉‧ June〈六月〉‧ able〈能、可以〉‧ after〈在⋯之後〉
❸ loved〈love（喜愛）的過去式〉‧ first〈最先的〉‧ hope〈希望〉
❹ bad〈不好的〉‧ believe〈相信〉‧ wasted〈waste（浪費）的過去式〉‧ time〈時間〉
❺ drama〈戲劇〉‧ big〈大受歡迎的〉
❻ put off〈使⋯失去興趣〉‧ last〈持續〉‧ hour〈小時〉
❼ foreign〈外國的〉‧ read〈讀〉‧ bottom〈下方〉‧ screen〈螢幕〉

中譯

❶ Alex 總會邊看電影邊吃爆米花。
❷ 這部電影的上映日期是 6 月 23 日，那天之後你就可以去觀賞了。
❸ 我很喜歡這部電影的第一集，希望續集也一樣棒。
❹ 那是一部爛片，不敢相信我竟然會浪費時間去看。
❺ 這部電影就只是一齣戲劇，並非強檔的熱門鉅片。
❻ 這部電影的片長讓我提不起興致，它長達四個小時。
❼ Emma 觀賞外語片時，她會看螢幕下方的字幕。

092

看電影(2)

MP3 092

① currently showing
[ˈkɝəntlɪ ˈʃoɪŋ]
(n.) 院線片

② movie listings
[ˈmuvɪ ˈlɪstɪŋz]
(n.) 電影時刻表

③ movie rating
[ˈmuvɪ ˈretɪŋ]
(n.) 電影分級

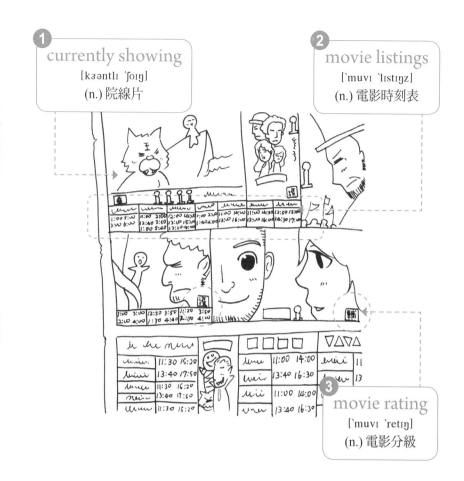

④ box office
[bɑks ˈɔfɪs]
(n.) 票房

⑤ critic
[ˈkrɪtɪk]
(n.) 影評

⑥ rating
[ˈretɪŋ]
(n.) 評價

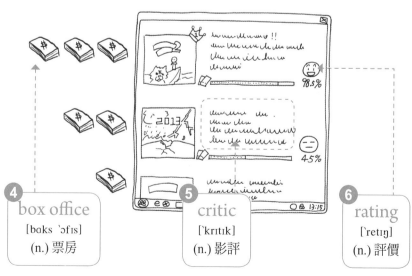

❶ 院線片

What movies are currently showing? I'd like to see a movie tonight.

<u>我想要看一場電影（= I would like to see a movie）</u>

❷ 電影時刻表

Neil didn't know what movies were on so he checked the movie listings.

<u>什麼電影正在上映</u>

❸ 電影分級

Movie rating standards in Taiwan are quite different from the United States.

<u>電影分級標準</u>

❹ 票房

The movie took in over 300 million dollars at the box office.

<u>得到超過 3 億美元的收入</u>

❺ 影評

Movie critics said it was bad, but I liked it.

❻ 評價

The newspaper gives it a rating of four stars.

<u>四顆星的評價</u>

學更多

❶ currently〈現在〉・showing〈放映〉・would like〈想要〉・tonight〈今晚〉
❷ on〈正在上映的〉・checked〈check（檢查）的過去式〉・listing〈列表〉
❸ rating〈等級〉・standard〈標準〉・quite〈相當〉・different〈不同的〉
❹ took in〈take in（賺到收入）的過去式〉・over〈超過〉・million〈百萬〉
❺ said〈say（說）的過去式〉・bad〈不好的〉・liked〈like（喜歡）的過去式〉
❻ newspaper〈報紙〉・give〈給〉・star〈星級〉

中譯

❶ 現正上映的院線片有哪些？今晚我想去看場電影。
❷ Neil 不知道上映中的電影有哪些，所以他查了電影時刻表。
❸ 台灣的電影分級標準，跟美國大不相同。
❹ 這部電影的票房收入超過 3 億美元。
❺ 影評說這部片很糟，但我挺喜歡的。
❻ 這份報紙給予這部片四顆星的評價。

093

看電視 (1)

MP3 093

1 change the channel
[tʃendʒ ðə ˋtʃænḷ]
(phr.) 轉台

2 channel
[ˋtʃænḷ]
(n.) 頻道

3 remote control
[rɪˋmot kənˋtrol]
(n.) 遙控器

4 volume
[ˋvɑljəm]
(n.) 音量

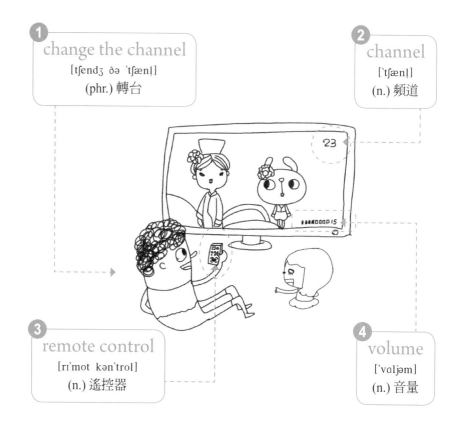

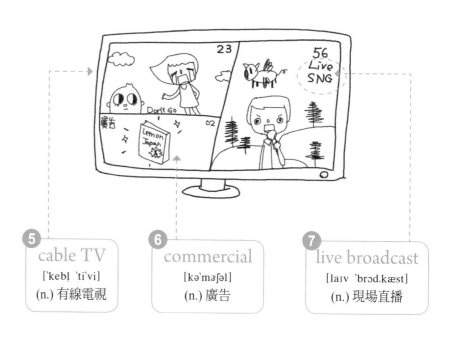

5 cable TV
[ˋkebḷ ˋtiˋvi]
(n.) 有線電視

6 commercial
[kəˋmɝʃəl]
(n.) 廣告

7 live broadcast
[laɪv ˋbrɔd͵kæst]
(n.) 現場直播

❶ 轉台
This show's boring. Please change the channel.

❷ 頻道
I think Discovery is my favorite TV channel.

❸ 遙控器
Colin picked up the remote control and changed the channel.
　　　　　　拿起遙控器

❹ 音量
It's a bit loud. Can you turn the volume down, please?
　　　　　　　　　　　　　把音量調小

❺ 有線電視
There are hundreds of channels on cable TV.
　　　　　　數百個頻道

❻ 廣告
Companies advertise their products on TV commercials.
　　　　　　　　　宣傳他們的產品

❼ 現場直播
This is a live broadcast. Everything you see is happening right now.
　　　　　　　　　　所有你看到的

學更多

❶ show〈節目〉・boring〈無聊的〉・change〈更改〉・channel〈頻道〉
❷ think〈認為〉・favorite〈特別喜愛的〉・TV〈television（電視）的縮寫〉
❸ picked up〈pick up（拿起）的過去式〉・remote〈遙控的〉・control〈控制裝置〉
❹ a bit〈有一點〉・loud〈大聲的〉・turn down〈調低、調小〉
❺ hundreds of...〈數以百計的…〉・cable〈電纜〉
❻ company〈廠商〉・advertise〈做宣傳〉・product〈產品〉
❼ live〈現場的〉・broadcast〈播送〉・everything〈一切事物〉・right now〈就是現在〉

中譯

❶ 這個節目很無聊，請轉台。
❷ 我想 Discovery 就是我最喜歡的電視頻道了。
❸ Colin 拿起遙控器轉台。
❹ 有一點大聲，可以請你將音量調小嗎？
❺ 有線電視有數百個頻道。
❻ 公司會透過電視廣告來為他們的產品做宣傳。
❼ 這是現場直播，你所看到的，都是正在發生的事。

094

看電視(2)

1 TV schedule
[ˈtiˈvi ˈskɛdʒʊl]
(n.) 節目表

2 time slot
[taɪm slɑt]
(n.) 時段

MP3 094

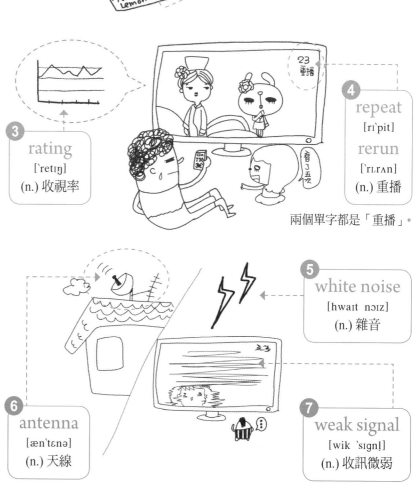

3 rating
[ˈretɪŋ]
(n.) 收視率

4 repeat
[rɪˈpit]
rerun
[ˈrɪˌrʌn]
(n.) 重播

兩個單字都是「重播」。

5 white noise
[hwaɪt nɔɪz]
(n.) 雜音

6 antenna
[ænˈtɛnə]
(n.) 天線

7 weak signal
[wik ˈsɪgnḷ]
(n.) 收訊微弱

1 節目表
Grace wasn't sure what to watch, so she looked at the TV schedule.
要看什麼

2 時段
The show has a new time slot; it's now going to be shown at 7pm.
在晚上 7 點被播出

3 收視率
This show is not popular, according to the ratings, only 500,000 people watch it.

4 重播
This show is a repeat. I've seen it before.
我之前已經看過它了（= I have seen it before）

5 雜音
When nothing is being shown on a TV channel, you might hear white noise.
沒有東西正被播放、沒有任何畫面

6 天線
Old TVs had antennas to pick up signals.

7 收訊微弱
Julie couldn't make phone calls on her cellphone because she had a weak signal.
用她的手機打電話

學更多

1 sure〈確定的〉・TV〈television（電視）的縮寫〉・schedule〈時刻表〉
2 show〈節目〉・slot〈時段〉・shown〈show（播出）的過去分詞〉
3 popular〈受歡迎的〉・according to...〈根據…〉・only〈只〉・watch〈觀看〉
4 seen〈see（看）的過去分詞〉・before〈以前〉
5 nothing〈沒什麼〉・channel〈頻道〉・hear〈聽到〉・white〈白色的〉・noise〈噪音〉
6 old〈舊型的〉・pick up〈接收訊號〉・signal〈訊號〉
7 make phone calls〈打電話〉・cellphone〈手機〉・weak〈虛弱的〉

中譯

1 Grace 不知道要看什麼節目，所以她看了節目表。
2 這個節目換了新時段，它目前將會在晚上 7 點播出。
3 這個節目不太受歡迎，根據收視率，它只有五十萬人收看。
4 這個節目是重播的，我之前已經看過了。
5 當電視頻道上沒有任何畫面時，你可能會聽到雜音。
6 舊型電視都有天線，用來接收訊號。
7 Julie 沒辦法用自己的手機撥打電話，因為收訊微弱。

095

電視新聞 (1)

MP3 095

1 newscaster / anchor
[`njuz͵kæstɚ] / [`æŋkɚ]
(n.) 新聞主播

兩個單字都是「新聞主播」。

2 tongue-tied
[`tʌŋ͵taɪd]
(adj.) 吃螺絲

3 live broadcast
[laɪv `brɔd͵kæst]
(n.) 現場直播

4 breaking news
[`brekɪŋ njuz]
(n.) 新聞快報

5 news ticker
[njuz tɪkɚ]
(n.) 新聞跑馬燈

❶ 新聞主播

The newscaster is responsible for reading the news.

❷ 吃螺絲

Oliver often gets tongue-tied and doesn't know what to say.

要說什麼

❸ 現場直播

This is a live broadcast, so what you can see is actually happening right now.

你看得到的

❹ 新聞快報

We have some breaking news. The president has just been shot.

總統剛剛遭到槍擊

❺ 新聞跑馬燈

Thomas hates looking at the news ticker at the bottom of the TV screen.

討厭看新聞跑馬燈

學更多

❶ responsible〈承擔責任的〉‧ reading〈read（播報）的 ing 型態〉

❷ often〈經常〉‧ tongue〈舌頭〉‧ tied〈打結的〉‧ know〈知道〉‧ say〈說〉

❸ live〈現場的〉‧ broadcast〈播送〉‧ actually〈實際上〉‧ right now〈就是現在〉

❹ some〈一些〉‧ breaking〈突發〉‧ president〈總統〉‧ just〈剛才〉‧
shot〈shoot（射傷）的過去分詞〉

❺ hate〈討厭〉‧ looking at〈look at（看）的 ing 型態〉‧ ticker〈跑馬燈〉‧
bottom〈下方〉‧ TV〈television（電視）的縮寫〉‧ screen〈螢幕〉

中譯

❶ 新聞主播負責播報新聞內容。

❷ Oliver 經常吃螺絲，而且不知道該說什麼。

❸ 這是現場直播，你看得到的，都是正在發生的事。

❹ 我們有幾則新聞快報，總統剛剛遭到槍擊。

❺ Thomas 討厭看電視螢幕下方的新聞跑馬燈。

096

電視新聞(2)

MP3 096

1 hourly news
[ˈaʊrlɪ njuz]
(n.) 整點新聞

2 exclusive
[ɪkˈsklusɪv]
(adj.) 獨家

3 interview
[ˈɪntɚˌvju]
(n.) 採訪

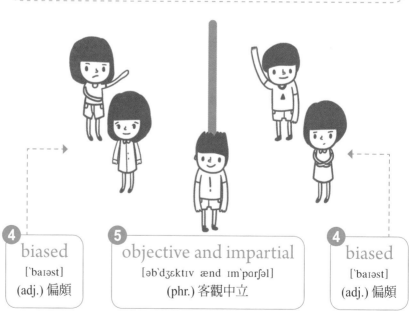

4 biased
[ˈbaɪəst]
(adj.) 偏頗

5 objective and impartial
[əbˈdʒɛktɪv ænd ɪmˈpɑrʃəl]
(phr.) 客觀中立

4 biased
[ˈbaɪəst]
(adj.) 偏頗

❶ 整點新聞

The big stories come up every hour in the hourly news.

❷ 獨家

The TV show has an exclusive interview with the star. He's not talking
to anyone else.
　　　　　　　　　　獨家專訪

❸ 採訪

Our top journalist had an interview with Beyonce. He asked her lots of
　　　　　首席記者

questions.

❹ 偏頗

These newspapers are biased. They never criticize the president.
　　　　　　　　　　　　　　　　　　　批評總統

❺ 客觀中立

Newspapers should be objective and impartial. They shouldn't
support one political party.
　　　支持某個政黨

學更多

❶ big〈重大的〉‧ story〈報導〉‧ come up〈出現〉‧ every〈每一個〉‧ hour〈小時〉‧
hourly〈每小時的〉‧ news〈新聞〉

❷ star〈明星〉‧ talking〈talk（談話）的 ing 型態〉‧ anyone〈任何人〉‧ else〈其他〉

❸ top〈首席〉‧ journalist〈記者〉‧ asked〈ask（詢問）的過去式〉‧ question〈問題〉

❹ newspaper〈報紙〉‧ never〈從未〉‧ criticize〈批評〉‧ president〈總統〉

❺ objective〈客觀的〉‧ impartial〈公正的〉‧ support〈支持〉‧ political〈政治的〉‧
party〈黨派〉

中譯

❶ 每小時的整點新聞中，都會播出這些重大新聞。

❷ 這個電視節目做了這個明星的獨家專訪；除此之外，他不接受其他人的訪問。

❸ 我們的首席記者對 Beyonce 做了採訪，問了她許多問題。

❹ 這些報紙很偏頗，他們從不批評總統。

❺ 報紙應該客觀中立，它們不該支持某個政黨。

097

旅行(1)

MP3 097

1 hotel
[hoˋtɛl]
(n.) 旅館

2 backpacker
[ˋbæk͵pækɚ]
(n.) 背包客

3 independent travel
[͵ɪndɪˋpɛndənt ˋtrævḷ]
(n.) 自由行

4 lost
[lɔst]
(adj.) 迷路

5 ask for directions
[æsk fɔr dəˋrɛkʃənz]
(phr.) 問路

❶ 旅館

Yasmine didn't have much money, so she stayed in a cheap hotel.

❷ 背包客

The backpacker picked up his huge bag and got on a train.
上了火車

❸ 自由行

The family didn't come with a tour group. It's independent travel.
跟團旅行

❹ 迷路

If you're lost, ask a police officer to help you.

❺ 問路

If you are lost, asking for directions from the locals is a good idea.
向當地人問路

學更多

❶ much〈許多〉・money〈錢〉・stayed〈stay（暫住）的過去式〉・cheap〈廉價的〉
❷ picked up〈pick up（拿起）的過去式〉・huge〈巨大的〉・bag〈旅行袋〉・
 got on〈get on（上車）的過去式〉
❸ family〈家庭〉・tour〈旅行〉・group〈團體〉・independent〈獨立的〉・travel〈旅行〉
❹ ask〈請求〉・police officer〈警察〉・help〈幫助〉
❺ asking〈ask（詢問）的 ing 型態〉・directions〈指路〉・local〈當地人〉・idea〈主意〉

中譯

❶ Yasmine 沒有帶很多錢，所以她住在一間廉價旅館。
❷ 背包客拿起他的大包行李，並上了火車。
❸ 這一家人沒有跟團旅行，他們是自助旅行。
❹ 如果你迷路了，就向警察求助。
❺ 如果你迷路了，跟當地人問路是個好方法。

098

旅行(2)

MP3 098

1 local
[`lokḷ]
(n.) 當地人

2 tour guide
[tʊr gaɪd]
(n.) 導遊

3 local guide
[`lokḷ gaɪd]
(n.) 地陪

4 tourist
[`tʊrɪst]
(n.) 遊客

5 working holiday
[`wɜkɪŋ `hɑlə.de]
(n.) 打工遊學

TAIWAN

❶ 當地人

If you want to know what a city is really like, you should do what the
locals do.　　　　　　一個城市實際上是什麼樣子　　　　　　做當地人做的事

❷ 導遊

Angela is a tour guide, so she helps tourists have a great holiday.
　　　　　　　　　　　　　　　　　　　　　　有個美好的假期

❸ 地陪

The tourists hired a local guide to show them around the city.
　　　　　　　　　　　　　　　　　帶領他們遊覽這座城市

❹ 遊客

An unlucky tourist was struck and killed by a falling rock.
　　　　　　　　　　　　　　　　　　　落石

❺ 打工遊學

Derrick's on a working holiday. He's picking fruit in Australia.
　　　　　　　　　　　　　他正在採水果

學更多

❶ know〈瞭解〉・city〈城市〉・really〈真地、實際上〉・like〈像〉

❷ tour〈旅行〉・guide〈嚮導〉・help〈幫助〉・great〈美好的〉・holiday〈假期〉

❸ tourist〈觀光客〉・hired〈hire（雇用）的過去式〉・show around〈帶…到處參觀〉

❹ unlucky〈不幸的〉・struck〈strike（攻擊）的過去分詞〉・
killed〈kill（殺死）的過去分詞〉・falling〈落下的〉・rock〈岩石〉

❺ working〈工作的〉・picking〈pick（採）的 ing 型態〉・fruit〈水果〉・Australia〈澳洲〉

中譯

❶ 如果你想瞭解一個城市真正的樣貌，你應該去體驗當地人所做的事。

❷ Angela 是名導遊，她幫助遊客們享受一個美好假期。

❸ 這些觀光客雇用一名地陪，帶他們到這座城市的各處參觀。

❹ 一名不幸的遊客遭落石擊中而身亡。

❺ Derrick 正在打工遊學。他目前在澳洲採水果。

099

藝人 (1)

MP3 099

1 actor / actress
[`æktɚ] / [`æktrɪs]
(n.) 男演員/女演員

2 variety show
[vəˈraɪətɪ ʃo]
(n.) 綜藝節目

3 agency
[ˈedʒənsɪ]
(n.) 經紀公司

4 manager
[ˈmænɪdʒɚ]
(n.) 經紀人

5 contract
[ˈkɑntrækt]
(n.) 合約

6 promotion
[prəˈmoʃən]
(n.) 宣傳/宣傳期

❶ 男演員 / 女演員

The actor and actress fell in love while making the movie.
<u>在拍電影的時候</u>

❷ 綜藝節目

You see many kinds of performers on variety shows.
<u>許多種類</u>

❸ 經紀公司

The talent agency has hundreds of stars.
<u>上百位的明星</u>

❹ 經紀人

The singer's manager books her performances for her.
<u>替她接下表演</u>

❺ 合約

The man signed a one-year contract with his new employer.
<u>為期一年的合約</u>

❻ 宣傳 / 宣傳期

As part of the promotion for the movie, the stars gave interviews on TV
<u>作為宣傳的一部分</u>
and radio.

學更多

❶ fell in love〈fall in love（愛上）的過去式〉‧while〈當…的時候〉

❷ many〈許多的〉‧kind〈種類〉‧performer〈表演者〉‧variety〈綜藝表演〉‧
show〈節目〉

❸ talent〈演藝〉‧hundreds of...〈數以百計的…〉‧star〈明星〉

❹ singer〈歌手〉‧book〈預約〉‧performance〈表演〉

❺ man〈男人〉‧signed〈sign（簽下）的過去式〉‧employer〈雇主〉

❻ part〈部分〉‧gave〈give（給予）的過去式〉‧interview〈採訪〉‧radio〈電台〉

中譯

❶ 在拍片過程中，這部電影的男演員和女演員墜入了愛河。

❷ 在綜藝節目中，你會看到各種表演者。

❸ 這間演藝經紀公司的旗下，有上百位明星。

❹ 這名歌手的經紀人，會替她接洽演出事宜。

❺ 這名男子與他的新雇主簽訂為期一年的合約。

❻ 作為電影宣傳的一部分，明星們接受了電視及電台的採訪。

100

藝人(2)

1 paparazzi
[ˌpɑpəˈrɑtsɪ]
(n.) 狗仔隊

2 gossip
[ˈɡɑsəp]
(n.) 八卦

MP3 100

3 idol
[ˈaɪdl̩]
(n.) 偶像

4 fan
[fæn]
(n.) 粉絲

5 singer
[ˈsɪŋɚ]
(n.) 歌手

6 concert tour
[ˈkɑnsət tʊr]
(n.) 巡迴演唱會

① 狗仔隊

Paparazzi follow stars and try to take pictures of them.

拍照

② 八卦

Gossip stories about stars are popular. People want to know about stars'
private lives.

私生活

③ 偶像

The people clapped and cheered when their idol came on stage.

人們鼓掌並歡呼

④ 粉絲

This singer has millions of fans. They all love her.

⑤ 歌手

This singer has a beautiful voice.

⑥ 巡迴演唱會

Lady Gaga came to Taiwan as part of her worldwide concert tour.

作為她世界巡迴演唱會的一部分

學更多

① follow〈跟蹤〉・star〈明星〉・try〈嘗試〉・take pictures〈拍照〉

② story〈報導〉・popular〈受歡迎的〉・private〈私人的〉・lives〈life（生活）的複數〉

③ clapped〈clap（鼓掌）的過去式〉・cheered〈cheer（歡呼）的過去式〉・
came〈come（來）的過去式〉・stage〈舞台〉

④ millions of...〈數百萬的…〉・all〈全部〉・love〈喜愛〉

⑤ beautiful〈美麗的〉・voice〈嗓音〉

⑥ part〈部分〉・worldwide〈全球的〉・concert〈音樂會〉・tour〈巡迴演出〉

中譯

① 狗仔隊跟蹤明星，並試圖捕捉一些照片。

② 關於明星的八卦報導很受歡迎，人們都想知道明星們的私生活。

③ 當他們的偶像現身舞台，人們鼓掌並歡呼。

④ 這名歌手擁有上百萬的粉絲，他們都很喜愛她。

⑤ 這名歌手有一副美妙的嗓音。

⑥ 女神卡卡將台灣列為她世界巡迴演唱會的其中一站。

101
逛街(1)

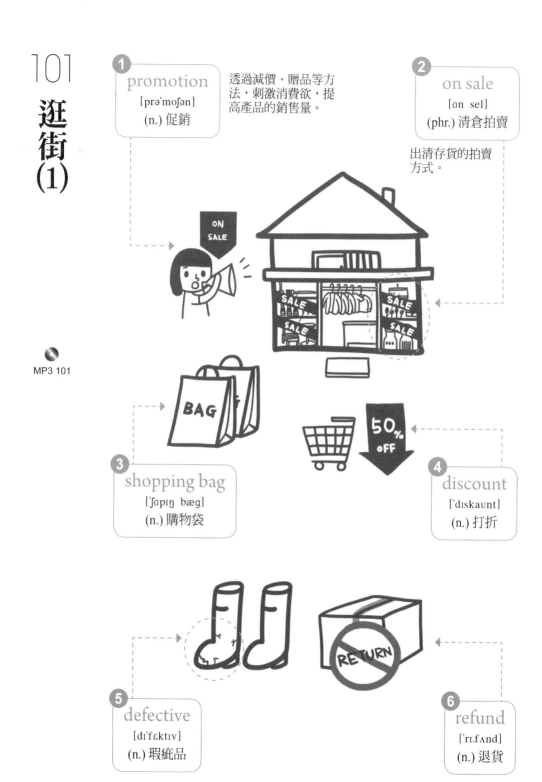

1 promotion
[prəˋmoʃən]
(n.) 促銷

透過減價、贈品等方法，刺激消費欲，提高產品的銷售量。

2 on sale
[ɑn sel]
(phr.) 清倉拍賣

出清存貨的拍賣方式。

MP3 101

3 shopping bag
[ˋʃɑpɪŋ bæg]
(n.) 購物袋

4 discount
[ˋdɪskaʊnt]
(n.) 打折

5 defective
[dɪˋfɛktɪv]
(n.) 瑕疵品

6 refund
[ˋrɪfʌnd]
(n.) 退貨

216

❶ 促銷

There's a promotion on butter. It's very cheap right now.

❷ 清倉拍賣

Shirts are on sale at the store. They're all 30% off.

<u>打 7 折</u>

❸ 購物袋

After leaving the supermarket, Beth had a lot of shopping bags.

❹ 打折

It's a good time to buy milk, because there's a discount on it now.

牛奶有折扣

❺ 瑕疵品

This machine is defective. I'd like to swap it for one that works.

我想要用它來交換（＝ I would like to swap it）

❻ 退貨

The shopper asked for a refund on her MP3 player because it doesn't work.

要求她的 MP3 播放器要退貨

學更多

❶ butter〈奶油〉．cheap〈便宜的〉．right now〈就是現在〉

❷ shirt〈襯衫〉．store〈店〉．all〈全部〉．off〈折價〉

❸ leaving〈leave（離開）的 ing 型態〉．supermarket〈超級市場〉．a lot of...〈許多…〉．shopping〈購物〉．bag〈袋子〉

❹ time〈時機〉．buy〈買〉．milk〈牛奶〉．now〈現在〉

❺ machine〈機器〉．swap〈交換〉．work〈運作〉

❻ shopper〈顧客〉．asked〈ask（要求）的過去式〉．player〈播放器〉

中譯

❶ 奶油正在做促銷，它現在非常便宜。

❷ 這間店的襯衫正在清倉拍賣，現在全部都打 7 折。

❸ 離開超級市場之後，Beth 的手上多了許多購物袋。

❹ 現在是購買牛奶的好時機，因為它們現在有折扣。

❺ 這台機器是瑕疵品，我想要換一台能正常運作的。

❻ 這名顧客要求她的 MP3 播放器要退貨，因為它不能正常播放。

102

逛街(2)

MP3 102

1 shopping mall
[`ʃɑpɪŋ mɔl]
(n.) 購物中心

2 window shopping
[`wɪndo ʃɑpɪŋ]
(phr.)（只看不買）逛街

3 shopping
[`ʃɑpɪŋ]
(n.) 購物

動詞為「shop」。

4 price
[praɪs]
(n.) 價格

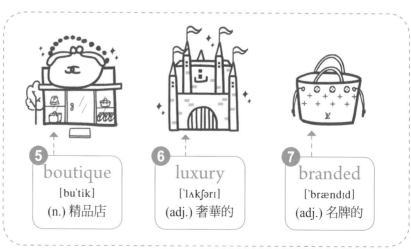

5 boutique
[bu`tik]
(n.) 精品店

6 luxury
[`lʌkʃərɪ]
(adj.) 奢華的

7 branded
[`brændɪd]
(adj.) 名牌的

❶ 購物中心

This is a huge shopping mall. There are hundreds of stores here.
大型購物中心

❷ （只看不買）逛街

I hate window shopping. I only want to look around stores if I'm going
to buy something.
如果我要買些什麼

❸ 購物

Crystal was shopping all day. She's spent a lot of money on clothes.

❹ 價格

To find out how much the jeans cost, Les asked for the price.
這條牛仔褲要花費多少錢

❺ 精品店

A little boutique store has opened down the road.
在這條路的盡頭

❻ 奢華的

Most people don't have enough money to buy luxury goods.

❼ 名牌的

Branded goods are usually more expensive.

學更多

❶ huge〈巨大的〉．mall〈購物中心〉．hundreds of...〈數以百計的…〉．store〈商店〉
❷ hate〈討厭〉．window〈櫥窗〉．look around〈四下環顧〉．buy〈買〉
❸ all day〈整天〉．spent〈spend（花費）的過去分詞〉．clothes〈衣服〉
❹ find out〈查明〉．jeans〈牛仔褲〉．asked〈ask（詢問）的過去式〉
❺ little〈小的〉．opened〈open（開幕）的過去分詞〉．down〈在…盡頭、沿著〉
❻ most〈大部分的〉．people〈人們〉．enough〈足夠的〉．goods〈商品〉
❼ usually〈通常〉．expensive〈昂貴的〉

中譯

❶ 這是一間大型購物中心，裡面有上百間商店。
❷ 我討厭只看不買的逛街。我只有在要買些東西時，才會想去商店逛逛。
❸ Crystal 整天都在購物，她已經在衣服上花費大筆金錢了。
❹ 為了知道要花多少錢買這條牛仔褲，Les 開口詢問了價格。
❺ 在這條路的盡頭，有間小精品店開幕了。
❻ 大部分的人沒有足夠的錢購買奢華的精品。
❼ 名牌的商品通常價格比較昂貴。

103

聽音樂(1)

1 live concert
[laɪv ˋkɑnsət]
(n.) 現場演唱會

2 online music
[ˋɑn͵laɪn ˋmjuzɪk]
(n.) 線上音樂

MP3 103

3 radio
[ˋredɪo]
(n.) 電台

4 radio host
[ˋredɪo host]
(n.) 電台主持人

一種黑色圓盤膠片,利用
盤面的凹凸坑紋記錄聲音。
須用唱盤機播放。

5 music video
[ˋmjuzɪk ˋvɪdɪo]
(n.) 音樂錄影帶

6 listen
[ˋlɪsn̩]
(v.) 聆聽

7 vinyl record
[ˋvaɪnɪl ˋrɛkəd]
(n.) 黑膠唱片

❶ 現場演唱會
Everyone cheered when the band started playing at the live concert.
<u>樂團開始表演</u>

❷ 線上音樂
Online music can easily be downloaded onto your computer.
<u>容易地被下載至你的電腦</u>

❸ 電台
I like listening to the radio because you can hear a lot of new music.

❹ 電台主持人
The radio host is very funny. He makes his listeners laugh every day.

❺ 音樂錄影帶
Pop stars spend a lot of time making music videos to go with their songs.
<u>花費很多時間製作</u>　　　　　　　　　　　　<u>搭配他們的歌曲</u>

❻ 聆聽
Harry turned on his stereo and listened to some music.
<u>打開他的立體音響</u>

❼ 黑膠唱片
The old man loves his old vinyl records from the 1980s.

學更多

❶ cheered〈cheer（歡呼）的過去式〉・band〈樂團〉・live〈現場的〉
❷ online〈線上的〉・easily〈容易地〉・downloaded〈download（下載）的過去分詞〉
❸ listening〈listen（聆聽）的 ing 型態〉・hear〈聽〉・a lot of〈許多〉・new〈新的〉
❹ host〈主持人〉・funny〈有趣的〉・listener〈聽眾〉・laugh〈笑〉
❺ pop〈流行的〉・star〈明星〉・spend〈花費〉・video〈錄影帶〉・go with〈搭配〉
❻ turned on〈turn on（打開）的過去式〉・stereo〈立體音響〉・music〈音樂〉
❼ old〈老的、舊的〉・man〈男人〉・love〈喜愛〉・vinyl〈乙烯基〉・record〈唱片〉

中譯

❶ 當樂團在現場演唱會上開始表演時，所有人都在歡呼。
❷ 線上音樂能夠簡單地下載到你的電腦。
❸ 我喜歡收聽電台，因為能聽到許多新歌。
❹ 這個電台主持人非常風趣，他每天都能讓聽眾歡笑。
❺ 流行音樂歌手花費很多時間製作音樂錄影帶，用來搭配他們的歌曲。
❻ Harry 打開他的立體音響聆聽音樂。
❼ 這個老人鍾愛他那些 1980 年代的舊黑膠唱片。

104

聽音樂(2)

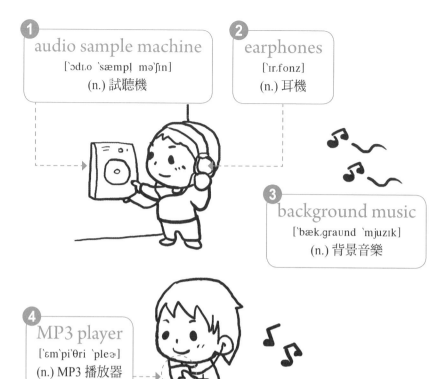

1 audio sample machine
[ˈɔdɪo ˈsæmpḷ məˈʃɪn]
(n.) 試聽機

2 earphones
[ˈɪrˌfonz]
(n.) 耳機

3 background music
[ˈbækˌgraʊnd ˈmjuzɪk]
(n.) 背景音樂

MP3 104

4 MP3 player
[ˈɛmˈpiˈθri ˈpleɚ]
(n.) MP3 播放器

5 tune
[tjun]
(n.) 音調/歌曲

【音調】:指聲音的高低聲調。

6 off-key
[ˈɔfˈki]
(adj.) (adv.) 走音

7 melodic
[məˈlɑdɪk]
(adj.) 悅耳

❶ 試聽機

I like to check out a CD's tunes before I buy it by using the store's audio sample machine.

❷ 耳機

If you don't want other people to hear your music, use earphones.
<u>戴耳機</u>

❸ 背景音樂

The waiter chose a CD to play as background music in the restaurant.
挑選一張 CD 撥放作為背景音樂

❹ MP3 播放器

The iPod is one kind of MP3 player.
是一種…

❺ 音調 / 歌曲

Sam played the tune on his guitar.
彈奏歌曲

❻ 走音

He's singing off-key. He sounds terrible.

❼ 悅耳

This tune is very melodic. It sounds nice.

學更多

❶ check out〈檢查〉・audio〈聲音的〉・sample〈樣品〉・machine〈機器〉
❷ want〈想要〉・other〈其他的〉・hear〈聽見〉・music〈音樂〉・use〈使用〉
❸ waiter〈服務生〉・chose〈choose（挑選）的過去式〉・as〈當作〉・background〈背景〉
❹ one〈一〉・kind〈種類〉・player〈播放機〉
❺ played〈play（彈奏）的過去式〉・guitar〈吉他〉
❻ singing〈sing（唱歌）的 ing 型態〉・sound〈聽起來〉・terrible〈糟糕的〉
❼ very〈非常〉・nice〈好的〉

中譯

❶ 在我購買 CD 之前，我喜歡先用試聽機聽看看裡面的歌曲。
❷ 如果你不想讓其他人聽到你的音樂，就戴上耳機。
❸ 服務生挑選了一張 CD 播放作為餐廳的背景音樂。
❹ iPod 是一種 MP3 播放器。
❺ Sam 用吉他彈奏了歌曲。
❻ 他唱歌走音，聽起來相當糟糕。
❼ 這首曲調相當悅耳，聽起來很舒服。

105

歌曲(1)

1 lyrics
[ˋlɪrɪks]
(n.) 歌詞

2 mix
[mɪks]
(v.) 編曲

3 melody
[ˋmɛlədɪ]
(n.) 旋律

4 rhythm
[ˋrɪðəm]
(n.) 節奏

5 chorus
[ˋkorəs]
(n.) 副歌

6 verse
[vɝs]
(n.) 主歌

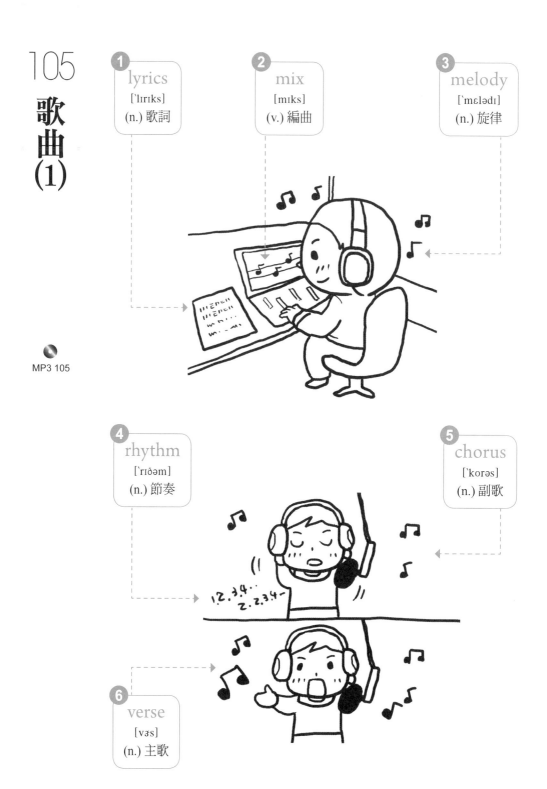

❶ 歌詞
I love the lyrics to this song; they tell a beautiful story.

❷ 編曲
The DJ mixed two different songs together.

❸ 旋律
Eric played the melody on his piano.
　　　　　彈奏一段旋律

❹ 節奏
The drummer beat a slow, steady rhythm.
　　　　　　　　緩慢、穩定的節奏

❺ 副歌
A chorus is usually repeated several times in a song.
　　　　　　　　　　　　　　　　好幾次

❻ 主歌
This is a simple song; it runs verse, chorus, verse, chorus, and then chorus again.

❶ love〈喜愛〉‧ song〈歌曲〉‧ tell〈訴說〉‧ beautiful〈美麗的〉
❷ mixed〈mix（編曲）的過去式〉‧ different〈不同的〉‧ together〈合起來〉
❸ played〈play（演奏）的過去式〉‧ piano〈鋼琴〉
❹ drummer〈鼓手〉‧ beat〈敲擊〉‧ slow〈緩慢的〉‧ steady〈穩定的〉
❺ usually〈通常〉‧ repeated〈repeat（重複）的過去分詞〉‧ several〈數個的〉‧ time〈次〉
❻ simple〈簡單的〉‧ run〈進行〉‧ again〈再一次〉

中譯

❶ 我很愛這首歌的歌詞，它們訴說一個美麗的故事。
❷ DJ 將兩首歌編曲成一首。
❸ Eric 用鋼琴彈奏了一段旋律。
❹ 鼓手敲擊著緩慢、穩定的節奏。
❺ 一首歌的副歌通常會重複好幾次。
❻ 這首歌很簡單——依照主歌、副歌、主歌、副歌，然後再一次副歌的順序進行。

106
歌曲 (2)

MP3 106

1 album
['ælbəm]
(n.) 專輯

2 title song
['taɪtl̩ sɔŋ]
(n.) 主打歌

3 release
[rɪ'lis]
(v.) 發行

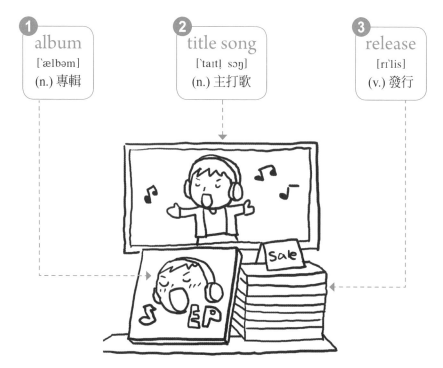

4 Billboard
['bɪl.bord]
(n.) （美國）告示牌排行榜

5 title
['taɪtl̩]
(n.) 歌名

6 single
['sɪŋɡl̩]
(n.) 單曲

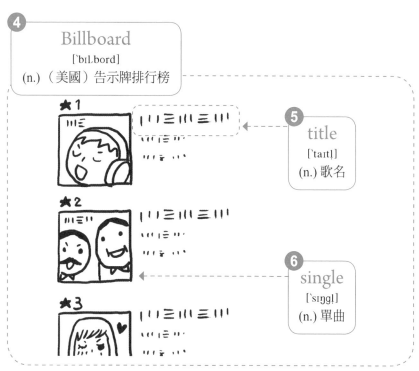

❶ 專輯

All 12 songs on this album are great.

❷ 主打歌

This is the title song; it has the same name as the album.

  　　　　　　　　　　　　　　　　　它的名字和專輯一樣

❸ 發行

The singer said she'll release her new album in June.

  　　　　　　　　她將會發行她的新專輯

❹ （美國）告示牌排行榜

My new song made it onto the Billboard Hot 100 list.

  　　　　　　　　　　　　　告示牌排行榜 100 強

❺ 歌名

The title of the song is "Beautiful Day."

❻ 單曲

The singer said that this song will be her first single.

學更多

❶ all〈全部〉・song〈歌曲〉・great〈極好的〉
❷ title〈標題〉・same〈同樣的〉・name〈名字〉
❸ singer〈歌手〉・said〈say（說）的過去式〉・new〈新的〉・June〈六月〉
❹ made it〈make it（成功）的過去式〉・hot〈熱門的〉・list〈名單〉
❺ beautiful〈美麗的〉
❻ first〈第一的〉

中譯

❶ 這張專輯裡的 12 首歌都很棒。
❷ 這是主打歌，它的歌名和這張專輯的名稱一樣。
❸ 這名歌手表示，她將在六月發行新專輯。
❹ 我的新歌成功進入了告示牌排行榜的前 100 強。
❺ 這首歌的歌名是「Beautiful Day」。
❻ 這名歌手表示，這首歌將是她的第一支單曲。

107

時尚 (1)

MP3 107

1 brand
[brænd]
(n.) 名牌

2 trend
[trɛnd]
(n.) 潮流

3 fashion magazine
[ˈfæʃən ˌmæɡəˈzin]
(n.) 時尚雜誌

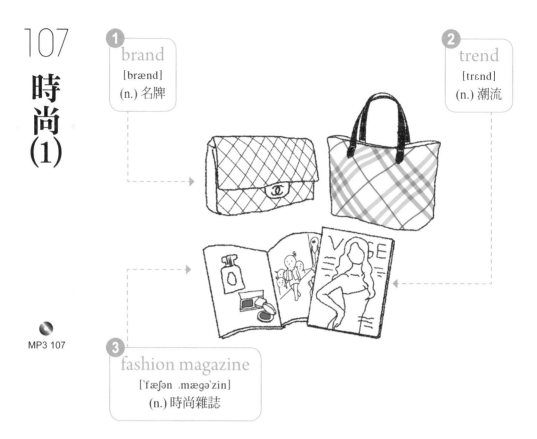

4 luxurious
[lʌɡˈʒurɪəs]
(adj.) 奢華的

5 Fifth Avenue
[fɪfθ ˈævəˌnju]
(n.) 第五大道

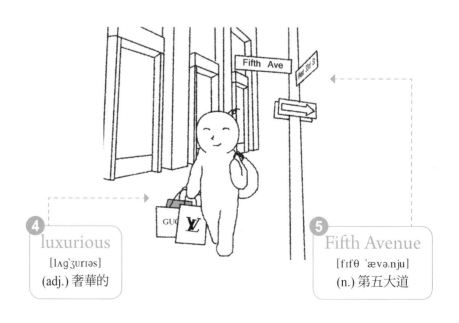

❶ 名牌

Rene is always going to the Prada store. She loves that brand.

❷ 潮流

There is a trend at the moment for men to wear skinny pants.
　　　　　　現在正有股潮流

❸ 時尚雜誌

Fashion magazines, like "Vogue", give people advice on what they should
wear.
　　　　　　　　　　　　　　　　　他們該穿什麼的建議

❹ 奢華的

The fashion store is luxurious. It's well decorated and there are lots of
nice chairs to sit on.
　　　很多好椅子可以坐

❺ 第五大道

Some of the world's best fashion stores can be found on New York's Fifth
Avenue.
　　　　　　　　　　　可以在紐約第五大道上被找到

學更多

❶ always〈經常〉・store〈店〉・love〈喜愛〉
❷ moment〈時刻〉・men〈man（男人）的複數〉・wear〈穿著〉・skinny pants〈緊身褲〉
❸ fashion〈時尚〉・magazine〈雜誌〉・like〈像〉・give〈給予〉・advice〈建議〉
❹ well〈很好地〉・decorated〈decorate（裝潢）的過去分詞〉・chair〈椅子〉
❺ some〈一些〉・world〈世界〉・best〈最好的〉・found〈find（找到）的過去分詞〉・
New York〈紐約〉・fifth〈第五的〉・avenue〈大道〉

中譯

❶ Rene 時常光顧 Prada 專賣店，她喜愛這個品牌。
❷ 現在在男性之間，有一股穿緊身褲的潮流。
❸ 時尚雜誌──如「Vogue」，給予大眾穿著上的建議。
❹ 這間時尚潮流店相當奢華，店內有精心設計的裝潢，還有許多高級座椅可以坐。
❺ 在紐約第五大道上，可以找到一些全球最棒的時尚潮流店。

108

時尚(2)

MP3 108

1 model
[ˋmɑdl̩]
(n.) 模特兒

2 walk
[wɔk]
(n.) 走秀

3 fashion show
[ˋfæʃən ʃo]
(n.) 時裝秀

4 catwalk / runway
[ˋkæt͵wɔk] / [ˋrʌn͵we]
(n.) 伸展台

兩個單字都是「伸展台」。

5 fashion designer
[ˋfæʃən dɪˋzaɪnɚ]
(n.) 時裝設計師

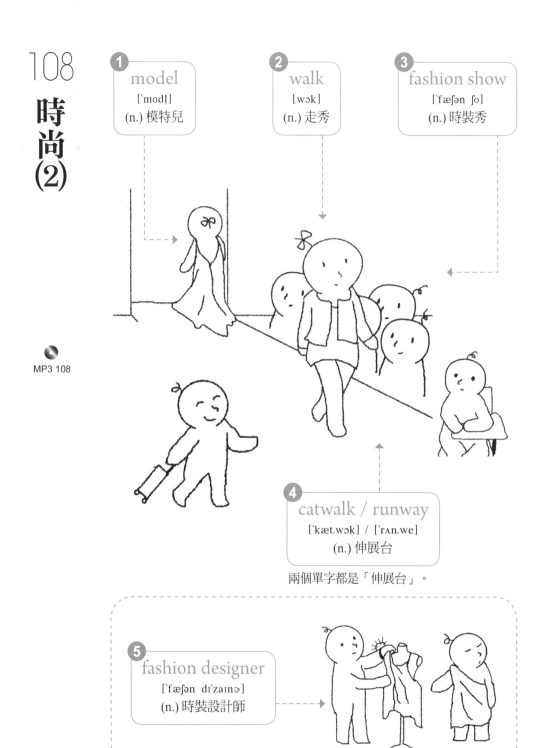

❶ 模特兒

That model has a beautiful face. Designers love to work with her.

跟她一同工作

❷ 走秀

Models need to have a strong runway walk.

具備出色的伸展台走秀能力

❸ 時裝秀

At fashion shows, models wear new clothes and walk down a catwalk.

沿著伸展台行走

❹ 伸展台

The new model was nervous while walking down the runway.

當她沿著伸展台行走

❺ 時裝設計師

Michael Kors is a famous fashion designer.

學更多

❶ beautiful〈美麗的〉‧ face〈臉〉‧ designer〈設計師〉‧ love〈喜愛〉‧ work〈工作〉

❷ need〈需要〉‧ strong〈出色的〉

❸ fashion〈時裝〉‧ show〈秀〉‧ wear〈穿著〉‧ new〈新的〉‧ clothes〈服裝〉‧ walk〈走〉‧ down〈沿著〉

❹ nervous〈緊張的〉‧ while〈當…的時候〉‧ walking〈walk（走）的 ing 型態〉

❺ famous〈知名的〉

中譯

❶ 那位模特兒有一張漂亮的臉蛋，設計師都愛跟她合作。

❷ 模特兒必須具備出色的伸展台走秀能力。

❸ 在時裝秀中，模特兒們穿著新款服飾在伸展台上走台步。

❹ 那名新人模特兒在走伸展台時，顯得很緊張。

❺ Michael Kors 是一位知名的時裝設計師。

109

唱歌(1)

MP3 109

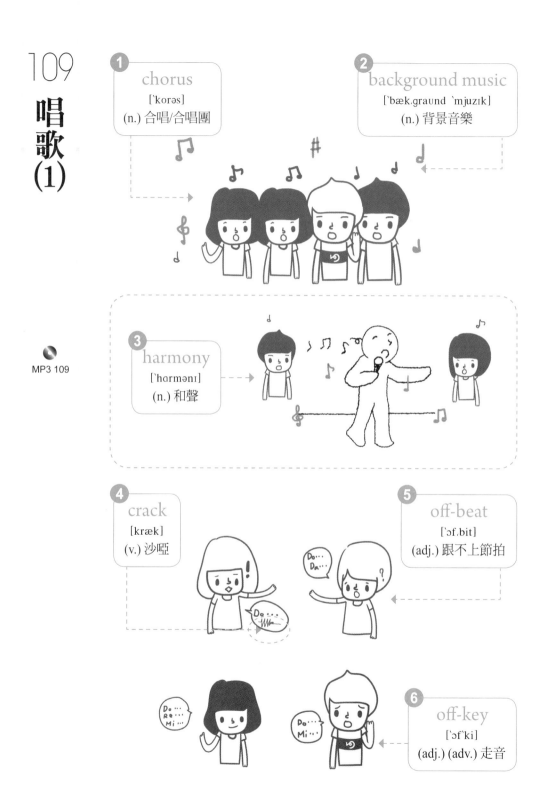

1 chorus
[ˋkorəs]
(n.) 合唱/合唱團

2 background music
[ˋbæk͵graʊnd ˋmjuzɪk]
(n.) 背景音樂

3 harmony
[ˋhɑrmənɪ]
(n.) 和聲

4 crack
[kræk]
(v.) 沙啞

5 off-beat
[ˋɔf͵bit]
(adj.) 跟不上節拍

6 off-key
[ˋɔfˋki]
(adj.) (adv.) 走音

❶ 合唱 / 合唱團

The members of the chorus sang their part very well.
把他們的聲部唱得非常好

❷ 背景音樂

The background music made the movie more exciting.

❸ 和聲

The two singers sang in perfect harmony.

❹ 沙啞

Her voice cracked and suddenly became too deep.
變得太低沉

❺ 跟不上節拍

You're a little off-beat. Try speeding up a little.
試著加快一點速度

❻ 走音

She's singing off-key. Her voice sounds terrible.

學更多

❶ member〈成員〉・sang〈sing（唱）的過去式〉・part〈聲部〉・well〈很好地〉

❷ background〈背景〉・music〈音樂〉・made〈make（使得）的過去式〉・
movie〈電影〉・exciting〈令人興奮的〉

❸ singer〈歌手〉・perfect〈完美的〉

❹ voice〈聲音〉・suddenly〈突然〉・became〈become（變得）的過去式〉・
deep〈低沉的〉

❺ a little〈一點〉・try〈嘗試〉・speeding up〈speed up（加快速度）的 ing 型態〉

❻ singing〈sing（唱）的 ing 型態〉・sound〈聽起來〉・terrible〈糟糕的〉

中譯

❶ 合唱團的團員們把他們負責的聲部唱得非常好。

❷ 背景音樂讓電影更激動人心。

❸ 這兩位歌手以完美的和聲演唱。

❹ 她的聲音沙啞了，而且突然變得過於低沉。

❺ 你有點跟不上節拍，試著把速度加快一點。

❻ 她的歌聲走音，聲音聽起來糟透了。

110
唱歌 (2)

MP3 110

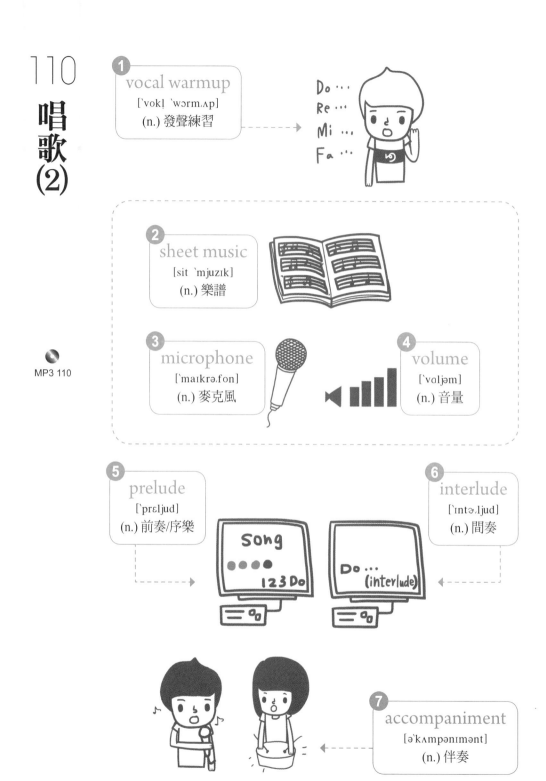

1 vocal warmup
[`vokḷ `wɔrmˌʌp]
(n.) 發聲練習

2 sheet music
[sit `mjuzɪk]
(n.) 樂譜

3 microphone
[`maɪkrəˌfon]
(n.) 麥克風

4 volume
[`vɑljəm]
(n.) 音量

5 prelude
[`prɛljud]
(n.) 前奏/序樂

6 interlude
[`ɪntɚˌljud]
(n.) 間奏

7 accompaniment
[ə`kʌmpənɪmənt]
(n.) 伴奏

1 發聲練習

The singer did a few vocal warmups before the show began.
　　　　　　　　　做了一些發聲練習

2 樂譜

The musicians looked at the sheet music and began to play.

3 麥克風

My microphone was broken so no one could hear me.

4 音量

The TV's a bit loud. Can you turn the volume down?
　　　　　　　　　　　　　　　把音量調小

5 前奏 / 序樂

There is always beautiful organ prelude music before our church service
starts.　　　　　　　　　　　　　　　　　　　　　　　　禮拜

6 間奏

There was a musical interlude in the middle of the performance.

7 伴奏

The guitar player provided an accompaniment for the singer.
　吉他手

學更多

1 vocal〈聲音的〉 · warmup〈做準備的練習〉 · began〈begin（開始）的過去式〉
2 musician〈樂師〉 · looked at〈look at（看）的過去式〉 · sheet〈一張紙〉 · play〈演奏〉
3 broken〈損壞的〉 · no one〈沒有一個人〉 · hear〈聽見〉
4 a bit〈有點〉 · loud〈大聲的〉 · turn down〈調小〉
5 organ〈管風琴〉 · church〈教堂〉 · service〈宗教儀式〉 · start〈開始〉
6 musical〈音樂的〉 · middle〈中間〉 · performance〈表演〉
7 guitar〈吉他〉 · provided〈provide（提供）的過去式〉 · singer〈歌手〉

中譯

1 表演開始前，歌手先做了一些發聲練習。
2 樂手看了樂譜後開始演奏。
3 我的麥克風壞了，所以沒有人聽得到我的聲音。
4 電視有點大聲，你可以把音量調小一點嗎？
5 在我們的禮拜儀式開始之前，都會有悅耳的管風琴序樂。
6 在表演的中間，有一段音樂間奏。
7 吉他手替這位歌手做伴奏。

111 線上購物 (1)

MP3 111

1 online catalog
[ˋɑn.laɪn ˋkætələg]
(n.) 線上型錄

2 price
[praɪs]
(n.) 價格

3 webstore
[ˋwɛb.stɔr]
(n.) 網路商店

4 watch list
[wɑtʃ lɪst]
(n.) 追蹤清單

5 shopping cart
[ˋʃɑpɪŋ kɑrt]
(n.) 購物車

6 coupon
[ˋkupɑn]
(n.) 禮券

7 member
[ˋmɛmbə]
(n.) 會員

❶ 線上型錄

I visited the website to look at the online catalog.

❷ 價格

What's the price of these CDs? I don't know if I've got enough money.

我是否有足夠的錢（ = If I have got enough money）

❸ 網路商店

We don't need to go to the shopping mall. We can just visit the webstore instead.

逛網路商店作為替代

❹ 追蹤清單

I use my watch list on ebay.com to follow items I may buy in the future.

ebay 網站　　　　　　　　　我未來可能會購買的項目

❺ 購物車

Steve added three items he wanted to buy to his shopping cart.

三件他想買的物品

❻ 禮券

I have a coupon for this product, so I can get it cheaper.

❼ 會員

You have to become a member to shop on this website.

學更多

❶ visited〈visit（拜訪）的過去式〉‧website〈網站〉‧online〈線上的〉‧catalog〈目錄〉
❷ know〈知道〉‧if〈是否〉‧enough〈足夠的〉‧money〈錢〉
❸ need〈需要〉‧shopping mall〈購物中心〉‧just〈只〉‧instead〈作為替代〉
❹ watch〈觀察〉‧list〈清單〉‧follow〈密切注意〉‧item〈項目〉‧future〈未來〉
❺ added〈add（增加）的過去式〉‧item〈物品〉‧shopping〈購物〉‧cart〈手推車〉
❻ product〈產品〉‧get〈買到〉‧cheaper〈較便宜地，cheap（便宜地）比較級〉
❼ have to〈必須〉‧become〈成為〉‧shop〈購物〉

中譯

❶ 我造訪了網站去看線上型錄。
❷ 這些 CD 的價格是多少？我不知道我是否有足夠的錢。
❸ 我們不需要去購物中心，我們可以只逛網路商店就好。
❹ 我利用 ebay 網站上的追蹤清單，來密切注意我之後可能會買的東西。
❺ Steve 追加了三件想買的商品到購物車。
❻ 我有這個商品的禮券，所以我可以用比較便宜的價格買到它。
❼ 你必須成為這個網站的會員，才能在這購物。

112

線上購物(2)

MP3 112

1 cash on delivery
[kæʃ ɑn dɪˈlɪvərɪ]
(phr.) 貨到付款

「cash on delivery」
可縮寫為「COD」。

2 shipping cost
[ˈʃɪpɪŋ kɔst]
(n.) 運費

3 remittance
[rɪˈmɪtn̩s]
(n.) 匯款

4 pay by credit card
[pe baɪ ˈkrɛdɪt kɑrd]
(phr.) 線上刷卡

5 in-store pickup
[ɪnˈstɔr ˈpɪkʌp]
(phr.) 來店取貨

6 fake
[fek]
(n.) 假貨

7 bid
[bɪd]
(n.) 競標

❶ 貨到付款

I've chosen a cash on delivery option, so I'll pay when it gets here.
<u>當它抵達這裡</u>

❷ 運費

There's a US$10 shipping cost if you want it sent to you.
<u>如果你想要它被寄送給你</u>

❸ 匯款

The writer called the company to ask where his remittance was. He needed the money.
<u>他的匯款在哪</u>

❹ 線上刷卡

I usually pay by credit card because it's so much easier than a wire transfer.

❺ 來店取貨

In-store pickup means you go to the store to collect your goods.
<u>領取你的商品</u>

❻ 假貨

This item isn't real; it's fake.

❼ 競標

I made a bid for a book in an online auction.
<u>我競標了一本書</u>

學更多

❶ chosen〈choose（選擇）的過去分詞〉· cash〈現金〉· delivery〈交貨〉· option〈選擇〉
❷ shipping〈運輸〉· cost〈費用〉· want〈想要〉· sent〈send（寄送）的過去分詞〉
❸ writer〈作者〉· called〈call（打電話）的過去式〉· company〈公司〉· money〈錢〉
❹ usually〈通常〉· pay〈支付〉· credit card〈信用卡〉· wire transfer〈電匯〉
❺ mean〈表示…的意思〉· store〈店〉· collect〈領取〉· goods〈商品〉
❻ item〈物品〉· real〈真正的〉
❼ made〈make（做）的過去式〉· book〈書〉· online〈線上的〉· auction〈拍賣〉

中譯

❶ 我選擇了貨到付款，因此當貨物送達時，我才會付錢。
❷ 如果把物品寄送給您，運費是 10 美金。
❸ 作者打電話到公司，詢問要給他的匯款在哪裡。他需要這筆錢。
❹ 我通常都線上刷卡，因為這比使用電匯簡單多了。
❺ 來店取貨的意思是：你要親自到店裡領取你的商品。
❻ 這個東西不是正品，它是假貨。
❼ 我在拍賣網站上競標了一本書籍。

113

線上遊戲 (1)

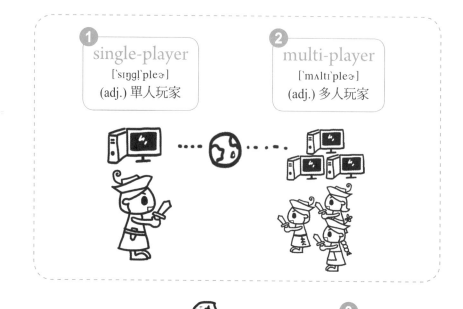

❶ single-player
[ˈsɪŋɡlˌpleɚ]
(adj.) 單人玩家

❷ multi-player
[ˈmʌltɪˌpleɚ]
(adj.) 多人玩家

MP3 113

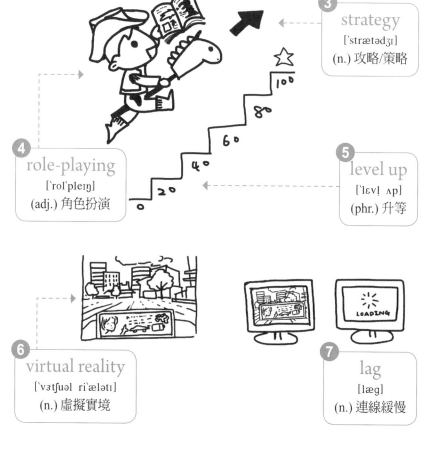

❸ strategy
[ˈstrætədʒɪ]
(n.) 攻略/策略

❹ role-playing
[ˈrolˌpleɪŋ]
(adj.) 角色扮演

❺ level up
[ˈlɛvl ʌp]
(phr.) 升等

❻ virtual reality
[ˈvɝtʃuəl rɪˈælətɪ]
(n.) 虛擬實境

❼ lag
[læg]
(n.) 連線緩慢

❶ 單人玩家

Rich likes spending time alone, so he prefers single-player games.
  獨自花費時間

❷ 多人玩家

This is a multi-player game, so we can all join in.

❸ 攻略 / 策略

The gamer is trying out a new strategy in the hope of beating his opponent.
                                              希望打敗他的對手

❹ 角色扮演

What's your character like in this role-playing game?
    你的角色是什麼樣子

❺ 升等

After playing for a few hours, Lee was able to level up.
                              幾個小時

❻ 虛擬實境

Using virtual reality allows you to feel like you're in a different place.

❼ 連線緩慢

The gamer bought a powerful computer so that he wouldn't suffer with lag.
                                                              為連線緩慢所苦

學更多

❶ alone〈獨自地〉‧ prefer〈更喜歡〉‧ single〈單個〉‧ player〈玩家〉‧ game〈遊戲〉
❷ multi〈多個〉‧ all〈全部〉‧ join in〈參與〉
❸ trying out〈try out（試驗）的 ing 型態〉‧ hope〈希望〉‧ beating〈beat（打敗）的 ing 型態〉
❹ character〈角色〉‧ like〈像〉‧ role〈角色〉‧ playing〈扮演〉
❺ playing〈play（玩）的 ing 型態〉‧ able〈可以〉‧ level〈等級〉‧ up〈提高〉
❻ virtual〈虛擬的〉‧ reality〈真實〉‧ allow〈使成為可能〉‧ different〈不同的〉
❼ gamer〈玩家〉‧ powerful〈強大的〉‧ so that〈因此〉‧ suffer〈受苦〉

中譯

❶ Rich 喜歡一個人獨處，所以他比較喜歡單人玩家的遊戲。
❷ 這是一款多人玩家的遊戲，所以我們全都可以參與。
❸ 這名玩家正在嘗試一個新策略，希望能夠打敗對手。
❹ 在這款角色扮演遊戲裡，你扮演什麼角色？
❺ 玩了幾個小時後，Lee 可以升等了。
❻ 運用虛擬實境會使你感覺彷彿身處不同環境。
❼ 這名玩家買了一台性能強大的電腦，因此他不會再為連線緩慢所苦。

114

線上遊戲(2)

MP3 114

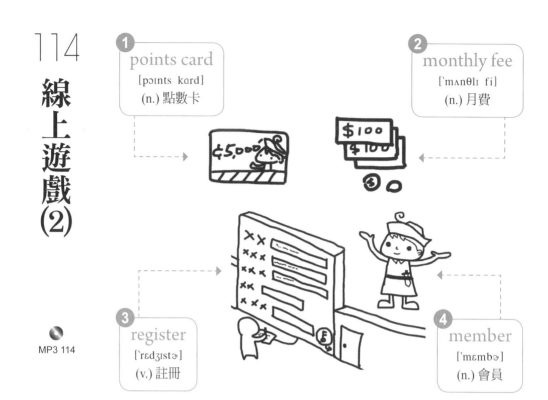

1 points card
[pɔɪnts kɑrd]
(n.) 點數卡

2 monthly fee
[ˈmʌnθlɪ fi]
(n.) 月費

3 register
[ˈrɛdʒɪstə]
(v.) 註冊

4 member
[ˈmɛmbə]
(n.) 會員

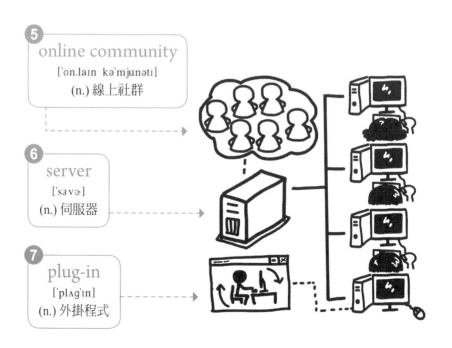

5 online community
[ˈɑnˌlaɪn kəˈmjunətɪ]
(n.) 線上社群

6 server
[ˈsɝvə]
(n.) 伺服器

7 plug-in
[ˈplʌɡˌɪn]
(n.) 外掛程式

❶ 點數卡
Points cards used for online games are not redeemable for cash.
被使用於線上遊戲　　　　　　　　　兌換成現金

❷ 月費
How much is the monthly fee for this game?

❸ 註冊
In order to play online games, you must first register for an account.

❹ 會員
I'm a member at this store, so I can get some money off.
得到一些折扣

❺ 線上社群
The online community contains people from all over the world.
來自世界各地的人

❻ 伺服器
When the server crashed, the gamers couldn't play their games anymore.
伺服器當機　　　　　　　　　　　再也不能玩他們的遊戲

❼ 外掛程式
Plug-ins allow you to do more things on your computer.

學更多

❶ point〈點〉．online〈線上的〉．redeemable〈可兌換的、可贖回的〉．cash〈現金〉
❷ monthly〈每月的〉．fee〈費用〉．game〈遊戲〉
❸ in order to〈為了〉．play〈玩〉．must〈必須〉．first〈首先〉．account〈帳戶〉
❹ store〈商店〉．some〈一些〉．money〈錢〉．off〈折價〉
❺ community〈社區〉．contain〈包含〉．people〈人們〉．all over〈在…各處〉
❻ crashed〈crash（當機）的過去式〉．gamer〈玩家〉．anymore〈再也〉
❼ allow〈使成為可能〉．more〈更多的〉．computer〈電腦〉

中譯

❶ 線上遊戲使用的點數卡不能兌換成現金。
❷ 這款遊戲的月費是多少？
❸ 為了玩線上遊戲，你必須先註冊一個帳號。
❹ 我是這家商店的會員，所以我可以得到一些折扣。
❺ 這個線上社群包含了來自世界各地的人。
❻ 當伺服器當機，所有玩家就無法再繼續他們的遊戲了。
❼ 外掛程式讓你能在電腦上做更多的事情。

115

電影幕後(1)

MP3 115

1 choose locations
[tʃuz loˋkeʃənz]
(phr.) 勘景

2 shot
[ʃɑt]
(n.) 鏡頭/拍攝

3 casting
[ˋkæstɪŋ]
(n.) 演員試鏡

4 score
[skor]
(n.) 配樂

5 edit
[ˋɛdɪt]
(n.) 剪輯

6 screenplay
[ˋskrin‚ple]
(n.) 劇本

❶ 勘景

The director and producer are visiting different places to choose locations.

❷ 鏡頭 / 拍攝

The director carefully set up the angle of the camera to get a great shot.
　　　　　　　　　　　　　調整攝影機角度

❸ 演員試鏡

During casting, the director saw hundreds of different actors.
　　　　　　　　　　　　　　　　　　好幾百位演員

❹ 配樂

A famous composer wrote the score for the movie.
　　知名作曲家

❺ 剪輯

We need to edit the movie because it's too long right now.

❻ 劇本

Dan has written a few novels, but he wants to write screenplays.

學更多

❶ director〈導演〉‧ producer〈製作人〉‧ visiting〈visit（參觀）的 ing 型態〉‧
different〈不同的〉‧ place〈地方〉‧ choose〈挑選〉‧ location〈外景拍攝地〉

❷ carefully〈仔細地〉‧ set up〈放好〉‧ angle〈角度〉‧ camera〈攝影機〉

❸ during〈在…的期間〉‧ saw〈see（看）的過去式〉‧ actor〈演員〉

❹ famous〈知名的〉‧ composer〈作曲家〉‧ wrote〈write（寫）的過去式〉

❺ too〈太〉‧ long〈長的〉‧ right now〈就是現在〉

❻ written〈write（寫）的過去分詞〉‧ novel〈小說〉

中譯

❶ 導演與製作人參訪許多不同的地點，來為電影勘景。

❷ 導演細心調整攝影機的角度，以取得絕佳鏡頭。

❸ 演員試鏡期間，導演看了好幾百位演員。

❹ 一位知名作曲家替這部電影撰寫了配樂。

❺ 我們必須剪輯這部電影，因為目前它太長了。

❻ Dan 已經寫了好幾本小說，不過他其實想要寫劇本。

116

電影幕後(2)

MP3 116

1 narration
[næˋreʃən]
(n.) 電影旁白

2 trailer
[ˋtrelɚ]
(n.) 預告片

coming soon

3 behind the scenes
[bɪˋhaɪnd ðə sinz]
(phr.) 幕後

4 special effect
[ˋspɛʃəl ɪˋfɛkt]
(n.) 特效

5 crew
[kru]
(n.) 工作人員

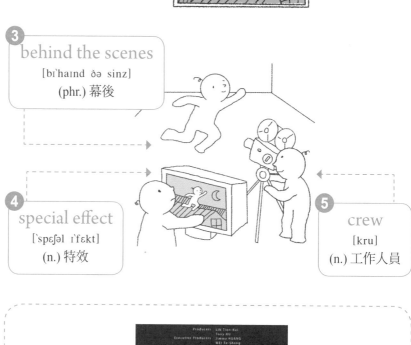

6 crew credits
[kru ˋkrɛdɪts]
(n.) 工作人員表

7 film credits
[fɪlm ˋkrɛdɪts]
(n.) 感謝名單

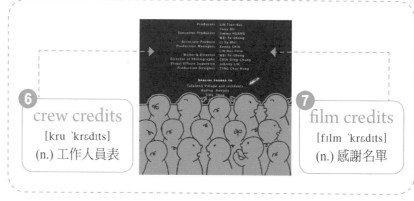

Producers   LIN Tien-Kui
             Tony KU
Executive Producers   Jimmy HUANG
             WEI Te-Sheng
Associate Producers   Li Ya-Mei
Production Managers   Kenny SHIU
             LIN Nui-Chin
Writer & Director   WEI Te-Sheng
Director of Photography   CHIN Ding-Chong
Visual Effects Supervisor   Johnny LIN
Production Designer   TSNG Chia-Hung

SPECIAL THANKS TO

Talaiong Village and residents
Kating Mongay
Siku

❶ 電影旁白

The narration in the movie was voiced by the main character.
<u>由主要角色配音</u>

❷ 預告片

After watching the trailer, everyone wants to see the movie.

❸ 幕後

Ray works in movies, but he's not an actor. He works behind the scenes.
<u>在電影界工作</u>

❹ 特效

The special effects in this movie are great. The explosions look brilliant.

❺ 工作人員

Bill works on the crew making a movie. He makes sure the lighting is OK.
<u>拍攝電影的工作人員</u>

❻ 工作人員表

Everyone who worked on the movie is listed in the crew credits.
<u>被列入工作人員表</u>

❼ 感謝名單

The film credits list everyone who worked on the movie.

學更多

❶ movie〈電影〉‧ voiced〈voice（配音）的過去分詞〉‧ main〈主要的〉‧ character〈角色〉
❷ after〈在…之後〉‧ watching〈watch（觀看）的 ing 型態〉‧ everyone〈每個人〉
❸ work〈工作〉‧ movie〈電影業〉‧ actor〈演員〉‧ behind〈在…的後面〉‧ scene〈鏡頭〉
❹ special〈特別的〉‧ effect〈效果〉‧ explosion〈爆破〉‧ brilliant〈出色的〉
❺ make sure〈確認〉‧ lighting〈燈光〉
❻ listed〈list（列入名單）的過去分詞〉‧ credits〈拍攝人員名單〉
❼ film〈電影〉‧ worked〈work（工作）過去式〉

中譯

❶ 這部電影的旁白，是由片中的主角擔綱。
❷ 看完預告片後，所有人都想去看這部電影。
❸ Ray 在電影界工作，不過他不是演員，而是從事幕後工作。
❹ 這部電影的特效很棒，爆破效果看起來十分壯觀。
❺ Bill 是電影工作人員，他負責確認所有的燈光都沒問題。
❻ 所有參與這部電影的人員，都被列入工作人員表。
❼ 在感謝名單中，會列出所有參與這部電影的人員。

117

飯店住宿(1)

1 reservation
[ˌrɛzɚˋveʃən]
(n.) 預訂

2 bed and breakfast
[bɛd ænd ˋbrɛkfəst]
(n.) 住宿並供早餐的民宿

3 check in
[tʃɛk ɪn]
(phr.) 入住

4 extended stay
[ɪkˋstɛndɪd ste]
(n.) 續住

5 check out
[tʃɛk aut]
(phr.) 退房

❶ 預訂

I've got a reservation at the hotel for tomorrow night.

我已經預約了（＝ I have got a reservation）

❷ 住宿並供早餐的民宿

The family turned its home into a bed and breakfast for people to stay in.

把他們的家改裝成住宿並供早餐的民宿

❸ 入住

After checking in, the woman went to her room.

❹ 續住

Is there a discount for an extended stay?

…有折扣嗎？

❺ 退房

You need to check out of your room before noon.

學更多

❶ got〈get（得到）的過去式〉・hotel〈飯店〉・tomorrow〈明天〉

❷ family〈家庭〉・turned into〈turn into（變成）的過去式〉・home〈家〉・
bed〈床〉・breakfast〈早餐〉・people〈人們〉・stay〈暫住〉

❸ after〈在…之後〉・checking in〈check in（入住）的 ing 型態〉・woman〈女人〉・
went〈go（去）的過去式〉・room〈房間〉

❹ discount〈折扣〉・extended〈延長的〉・ stay〈停留〉

❺ need〈需要〉・before〈在…之前〉・noon〈中午〉

中譯

❶ 我已經預訂了明天晚上要住宿這間飯店。

❷ 這家人把他們的房子改裝成一間住宿並供早餐的民宿，讓人們可以投宿。

❸ 辦理入住之後，這位女士走去了她的房間。

❹ 續住有優惠嗎？

❺ 您必須在中午之前為您的房間辦理退房。

118

飯店住宿(2)

MP3 118

1 resort
[rɪ`zɔrt]
(n.) 渡假村

2 motel
[mo`tɛl]
(n.) 汽車旅館

3 capsule hotel
[`kæpsḷ ho`tɛl]
(n.) 膠囊旅館

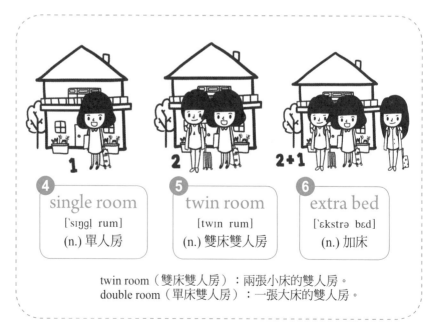

4 single room
[`sɪŋgḷ rum]
(n.) 單人房

5 twin room
[twɪn rum]
(n.) 雙床雙人房

6 extra bed
[`ɛkstrə bɛd]
(n.) 加床

twin room（雙床雙人房）：兩張小床的雙人房。
double room（單床雙人房）：一張大床的雙人房。

250

1 渡假村

We're staying at a resort hotel, so there should be swimming pools and restaurants there.　　　　　　　游泳池

2 汽車旅館

Ron was tired of driving, so he stopped to sleep for a few hours at a motel.
　　　　　　　　停車去睡覺

3 膠囊旅館

The sleeping areas at the capsule hotel are tiny.

4 單人房

It's just me, so I'll get a single room please.

5 雙床雙人房

My friend and I asked for a twin room.

6 加床

The three friends asked for an extra bed in their twin room.
　　　　　　要求加床

學更多

1 staying〈stay（暫住）的 ing 型態〉・hotel〈飯店〉・restaurant〈餐廳〉

2 tired〈疲倦的〉・driving〈drive（開車）的 ing 型態〉・stopped〈stop（停止）的過去式〉・sleep〈睡覺〉・a few〈幾個〉・hour〈小時〉

3 sleeping〈供睡覺用的〉・area〈區域〉・capsule〈膠囊〉・tiny〈極小的〉

4 just〈只〉・so〈所以〉・single〈單一的〉・room〈房間〉

5 friend〈朋友〉・asked〈ask（要求）的過去式〉・twin〈成雙的〉

6 extra〈額外的〉・bed〈床〉・their〈他們的〉

中譯

1 我們要入住一間渡假村飯店,所以那裡應該會有游泳池和餐廳。

2 Ron 開車開得很累,所以他在一間汽車旅館停下來,睡了幾個小時。

3 膠囊旅館裡,給人睡覺的空間非常小。

4 就只有我一個人,所以請給我一間單人房。

5 我和我的朋友要了一間雙床雙人房。

6 三名同行友人要求在他們的雙人房裡加床。

119

故事 (1)

MP3 119

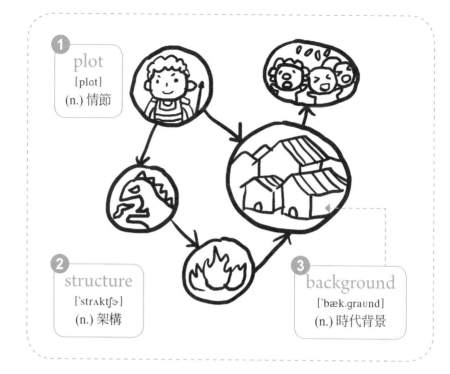

1 plot
[plɑt]
(n.) 情節

2 structure
[`strʌktʃɚ]
(n.) 架構

3 background
[`bæk.graʊnd]
(n.) 時代背景

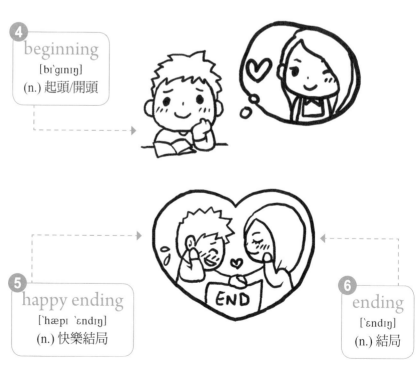

4 beginning
[bɪ`gɪnɪŋ]
(n.) 起頭/開頭

5 happy ending
[`hæpɪ `ɛndɪŋ]
(n.) 快樂結局

6 ending
[`ɛndɪŋ]
(n.) 結局

❶ 情節
The book has a great plot. So many things happen in it.

❷ 架構
The story has an interesting structure, as it jumps backwards and
forwards in time.   在時間上前後跳躍

❸ 時代背景
The background to the story is set up in the first 10 minutes of the movie.
                                         在電影的前 10 分鐘被架構出來

❹ 起頭 / 開頭
Main characters are usually introduced at the beginning of a story.

❺ 快樂結局
I love a happy ending; it's great when good things happen to the good
characters.

❻ 結局
The ending was so sad that I cried when I put the book down.
                                         我放下書

學更多

❶ book〈書〉・great〈極好的〉・happen〈發生〉
❷ story〈故事〉・interesting〈有趣的〉・as〈因為〉・jump〈跳躍〉・
   backwards〈向後〉・forwards〈向前〉・time〈時間〉
❸ set up〈set up（建造）的過去分詞〉・first〈最前面的〉・movie〈電影〉
❹ main〈主要的〉・character〈角色〉・introduced〈introduce（介紹）的過去分詞〉
❺ love〈喜愛〉・thing〈事情〉・happen〈發生〉
❻ sad〈悲傷的〉・cried〈cry（哭）的過去式〉・put down〈put down（放下）的過去式〉

中譯

❶ 這本書有絕佳的情節，內容非常豐富。
❷ 這個故事的架構很有趣，因為它在時間點上採取前後跳躍的敘事手法。
❸ 在電影開始的前 10 分鐘，就清楚呈現了整個故事的時代背景。
❹ 主要角色通常在故事開頭就會被介紹。
❺ 我喜歡快樂結局。當好事發生在善良的角色身上時，是最棒的。
❻ 這個結局如此悲傷，所以當我放下書本時，哭得很傷心。

120

故事(2)

MP3 120

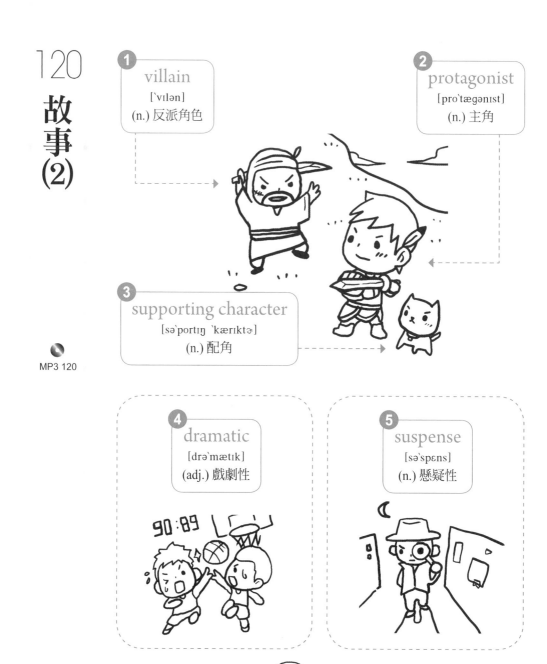

1 villain
[ˋvɪlən]
(n.) 反派角色

2 protagonist
[proˋtægənɪst]
(n.) 主角

3 supporting character
[səˋportɪŋ ˋkærɪktɚ]
(n.) 配角

4 dramatic
[drəˋmætɪk]
(adj.) 戲劇性

5 suspense
[səˋspɛns]
(n.) 懸疑性

6 bedtime story
[ˋbɛd.taɪm ˋstorɪ]
(n.) 床邊故事

❶ 反派角色

Sadly for Isabel, her husband is a bad man. He is the main villain of the story.
對 Isabel 來說很不幸

❷ 主角

The protagonist of the story is a woman called Isabel Archer.
故事的主角

❸ 配角

The supporting characters are Isabel's friends and family.

❹ 戲劇性

Much of the story is quite slow, but there are some very dramatic sections.
非常戲劇性的部分

❺ 懸疑性

There is a lot of suspense at the end of the story, because it's unclear
充滿懸疑性
what Isabel will do next.
Isabel 接下來會做什麼

❻ 床邊故事

The parent read her son a bedtime story to help him sleep.
唸一則床邊故事給兒子聽

學更多

❶ sadly〈不幸〉‧ husband〈丈夫〉‧ bad〈壞的〉‧ main〈主要的〉‧ story〈故事〉
❷ woman〈女人〉‧ called〈call（稱呼）的過去分詞〉
❸ supporting〈配角的〉‧ character〈角色〉‧ friend〈朋友〉‧ family〈家人〉
❹ quite〈很〉‧ slow〈緩慢的〉‧ some〈一些〉‧ section〈部分〉
❺ end〈最後部分〉‧ unclear〈不清楚的〉‧ next〈接下來〉
❻ parent〈父親、母親〉‧ read〈朗讀〉‧ bedtime〈就寢時間〉‧ sleep〈睡覺〉

中譯

❶ 對 Isabel 來說，很不幸的她的丈夫是個壞人，他是故事裡主要的反派角色。
❷ 這個故事的主角，是一位名叫 Isabel Archer 的女子。
❸ 配角是 Isabel 的朋友和家人。
❹ 故事的進展大部分都很緩慢，但也有一些非常戲劇性的情節。
❺ 故事的最後充滿懸疑性，因為不清楚 Isabel 下一步會採取什麼行動。
❻ 母親唸一則床邊故事給兒子聽，幫助他入睡。

121

颱風天 (1)

MP3 121

1 eye
[aɪ]
(n.) 颱風眼/風眼

2 cover
[ˋkʌvɚ]
(v.)（颱風）籠罩

3 turning
[ˋtɝnɪŋ]
(n.)（颱風）轉向

動詞為「turn」。

4 landfall
[ˋlænd͵fɔl]
(n.)（颱風）登陸

5 path
[pæθ]
(n.)（颱風）路徑

256

❶ 颱風眼 / 風眼

The conditions are calm in the eye of the storm.
　　　情況很平靜

❷ （颱風）籠罩

The typhoon is covering the whole of Taiwan right now.

❸ （颱風）轉向

The typhoon is turning, so it may now miss Taiwan.

❹ （颱風）登陸

The storm is expected to make landfall in the northeast.
　　　　　　　　　在東北方登陸

❺ （颱風）路徑

The path of the storm took it right past Taiwan.
　　　　　　　　正好通過了台灣

學更多

❶ condition〈情況〉‧ calm〈平靜的〉‧ storm〈暴風雨、風暴〉
❷ typhoon〈颱風〉‧ covering〈cover（籠罩）的 ing 型態〉‧ whole〈整個的〉‧
right now〈就是現在〉
❸ turning〈turn（轉向）的 ing 型態〉‧ may〈可能〉‧ now〈現在〉‧ miss〈避開〉
❹ expected〈expect（預計）的過去分詞〉‧ northeast〈東北〉
❺ took〈take（行進）的過去式〉‧ right〈直接地〉‧ past〈通過〉

中譯

❶ 暴風圈的風眼區域，氣候狀況很平靜。
❷ 颱風目前正籠罩全台灣。
❸ 颱風正在轉向，因此目前它可能不會侵襲台灣。
❹ 暴風圈預計會在東北邊登陸。
❺ 暴風範圍的路徑正好通過台灣。

122

颱風天(2)

MP3 122

1 typhoon warning
[taɪˈfun ˈwɔrnɪŋ]
(n.) 颱風警報

2 day off
[de ɔf]
(phr.) 颱風假

3 heavy rain
[ˈhɛvɪ ren]
(n.) 豪雨/大雨

4 heavy wind
[ˈhɛvɪ wɪnd]
(n.) 強風

5 speed
[spid]
(n.) 風速

6 rainfall
[ˈrenˌfɔl]
(n.) 降雨量

❶ 颱風警報

The authorities have issued a typhoon warning for tomorrow.

官方已經發布颱風警報

❷ 颱風假

Because of the typhoon, everyone's got a day off tomorrow.

大家都得到了一個颱風假

❸ 豪雨 / 大雨

I'm going to get wet if I go out in the heavy rain.

我會被淋濕

❹ 強風

A few trees were blown over in the heavy wind.

一些樹被吹倒

❺ 風速
❻ 降雨量

It was a terrible storm; the wind speed was high, and there was a lot of rainfall.

學更多

❶ authority〈官方〉・issued〈issue（發布）的過去分詞〉・warning〈警報〉

❷ because of〈因為〉・typhoon〈颱風〉・everyone〈每個人〉・
got〈get（得到）的過去分詞〉

❸ get〈變成〉・wet〈濕的〉・go out〈外出〉・heavy〈大量的〉・rain〈雨水〉

❹ a few〈幾個〉・tree〈樹〉・blown〈blow（吹）的過去分詞〉・over〈倒下〉・
heavy〈劇烈的〉・wind〈風〉

❺❻ terrible〈嚴重的〉・storm〈暴風雨〉・high〈強勁的〉・a lot of〈大量〉

中譯

❶ 政府相關單位已經針對明天發布了颱風警報。

❷ 因為颱風的關係，明天每個人都休颱風假。

❸ 如果在大雨中出門，我全身都會被淋濕。

❹ 有些樹在強風中被吹倒了。

❺❻ 那是場嚴重的暴風雨；風速強勁，還挾帶充沛的降雨量。

123

颱風天(3)

1
typhoon intensity
[taɪˈfun ɪnˈtɛnsətɪ]
(n.) 颱風強度

MP3 123

2
rescue team
[ˈrɛskju tim]
(n.) 搜救隊

3
mudslide
[ˈmʌd.slaɪd]
(n.) 土石流

4
blackout
[ˈblæk.aʊt]
(n.) 停電

5
flood
[flʌd]
(n.) 淹水

❶ 颱風強度
The typhoon intensity is lessening, so everyone needs to work tomorrow.

❷ 搜救隊
A rescue team was sent to the affected area to help save the survivors.
　　　　　　　　被派遣至受影響的地區

❸ 土石流
It seems like every time a major storm hits Taiwan, at least one road
　　　　似乎
gets blocked by mudslides.
　　　　　　　　被土石流阻斷

❹ 停電
I used a flashlight to read a book during the blackout.

❺ 淹水
During the flood, the street was under about a meter of water.
　　　　　　　　　　　　　　　　　　在大約一公尺高的水中

學更多

❶ intensity〈強度〉．lessening〈lessen（減輕）的 ing 型態〉．work〈工作〉
❷ rescue〈援救〉．team〈團隊〉．sent〈send（派遣）的過去分詞〉．affected〈受到影響的〉．
　area〈地區〉．help〈幫助〉．save〈救〉．survivor〈生還者〉
❸ every time〈每次〉．major storm〈強颱〉．hit〈襲擊〉．at least〈至少〉．
　road〈道路〉．blocked〈堵塞的〉
❹ used〈use（使用）的過去式〉．flashlight〈手電筒〉．read〈閱讀〉．during〈在…期間〉
❺ street〈街道〉．under〈在…下方〉．about〈大約〉．meter〈公尺〉．water〈水〉

中譯

❶ 颱風強度正在減緩，所以明天每個人都得去上班。
❷ 一支搜救隊已經出發到受影響的地區，幫忙救出生還者。
❸ 似乎每當強颱侵襲台灣，就會造成至少一條道路遭土石流沖斷。
❹ 停電時，我使用手電筒看書。
❺ 淹水期間，街道都浸泡在大約一公尺高的水中。

124

火災
(1)

MP3 124

1 wet towel
[wɛt `tauəl]
(n.) 濕毛巾

2 smoke
[smok]
(n.) 濃煙

3 carbon dioxide
[`kɑrbən daɪ`ɑksaɪd]
(n.) 二氧化碳

CO_2

4 suffocation
[ˌsʌfə`keʃən]
(n.) 窒息

Exit

5 emergency exit
[ɪ`mɝdʒənsɪ `ɛksɪt]
(n.) 逃生門

6 evacuation route
[ɪˌvækjʊ`eʃən rut]
(n.) 疏散路線

❶ 濕毛巾

Small fires can sometimes be put out with a wet towel.
被濕毛巾撲滅

❷ 濃煙

Chris coughed when he breathed in the smoke from the fire.
當他吸入濃煙

❸ 二氧化碳

When humans breathe, we produce carbon dioxide.

❹ 窒息

It can be hard to breathe in smoke-filled rooms, so people often die of
容易呼吸困難　　　　　　充滿濃煙的房間

suffocation when there's a fire.
當發生火災時

❺ 逃生門

If there's a fire, leave the building through the emergency exits.

❻ 疏散路線

Office buildings should have an evacuation route so people know where
to go if there's an emergency.
如果發生緊急狀況

學更多

❶ small〈小的〉‧ fire〈火〉‧ sometimes〈有時〉‧ put out〈put out（撲滅）的過去分詞〉‧
wet〈濕的〉‧ towel〈毛巾〉
❷ coughed〈cough（咳嗽）的過去式〉‧ breathed〈breathe（呼吸）的過去式〉‧ fire〈火災〉
❸ human〈人類〉‧ produce〈產生〉‧ carbon〈碳〉‧ dioxide〈二氧化物〉
❹ hard〈困難的〉‧ filled〈充滿…的〉‧ room〈房間〉‧ die〈死〉
❺ leave〈離開〉‧ building〈建築物〉‧ through〈憑藉〉‧ emergency〈緊急情況〉‧
exit〈出口〉
❻ office building〈辦公大樓〉‧ evacuation〈疏散〉‧ route〈路線〉

中譯

❶ 小火有時候可以用濕毛巾撲滅。
❷ 一吸入火場的濃煙，Chris 就咳嗽了。
❸ 人類呼吸時，會產生二氧化碳。
❹ 在濃煙瀰漫的房間裡容易讓人呼吸困難，所以發生火災時，人們經常是死於窒息。
❺ 如果發生火災，就從建築物的逃生門離開。
❻ 辦公大樓應該要有一條疏散路線，當發生緊急狀況，人們才知道該往哪裡走。

125

火災(2)

MP3 125

1 extinguish a fire
[ɪkˋstɪŋgwɪʃ ə faɪr]
(phr.) 滅火

2 fire alarm
[faɪr əˋlɑrm]
(n.) 火災警鈴

3 sprinkler system
[ˋsprɪŋklə ˋsɪstəm]
(n.) 自動灑水系統

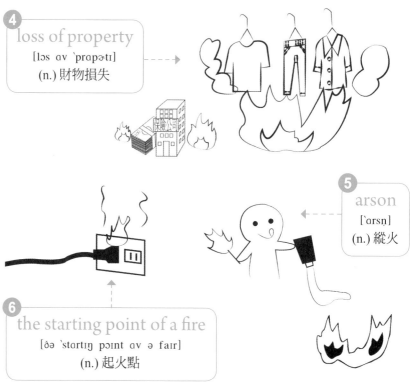

4 loss of property
[lɔs ɑv ˋprɑpətɪ]
(n.) 財物損失

5 arson
[ˋɑrsn̩]
(n.) 縱火

6 the starting point of a fire
[ðə ˋstɑrtɪŋ pɔɪnt ɑv ə faɪr]
(n.) 起火點

❶ 滅火

Chris got a bucket of water to extinguish the fire in his kitchen.
<u>一桶水</u>

❷ 火災警鈴

When the fire alarm started ringing, everyone had to leave the building.
<u>離開建築物</u>

❸ 自動灑水系統

When the man started smoking, it set off the sprinkler system.

❹ 財物損失

How bad was the fire? Did it cause much loss of property?

❺ 縱火

Investigators said the fire was a case of arson; it was started deliberately.
<u>一件縱火案件</u>　　　<u>它是被蓄意引起的</u>

❻ 起火點

The investigators found that the starting point of the fire was in the kitchen.

學更多

❶ got〈get（拿）的過去式〉‧ bucket〈一桶〉‧ extinguish〈熄滅〉‧ kitchen〈廚房〉

❷ alarm〈警報器〉‧ ringing〈ring（響）的 ing 型態〉‧ had to〈have to（必須）的過去式〉

❸ smoking〈smoke（抽煙）的 ing 型態〉‧ set off〈set off（啟動）的過去式〉‧
sprinkler〈灑水器〉‧ system〈系統〉

❹ bad〈嚴重的〉‧ fire〈火災〉‧ cause〈造成〉‧ loss〈損失〉‧ property〈財產〉

❺ investigator〈調查員〉‧ case〈案件〉‧ deliberately〈蓄意地〉

❻ found〈find（發現）的過去式〉‧ starting〈開始〉‧ point〈位置〉

中譯

❶ Chris 提了一桶水到他的廚房去滅火。

❷ 當火災警鈴作響，每個人都必須離開建築物。

❸ 當該名男子開始抽煙，就觸動了自動灑水系統。

❹ 火災的情況有多嚴重？是否造成很大的財務損失？

❺ 調查員表示，這場火災是一件縱火案，是有人蓄意造成的。

❻ 調查員發現起火點位於廚房。

126

山難 (1)

MP3 126

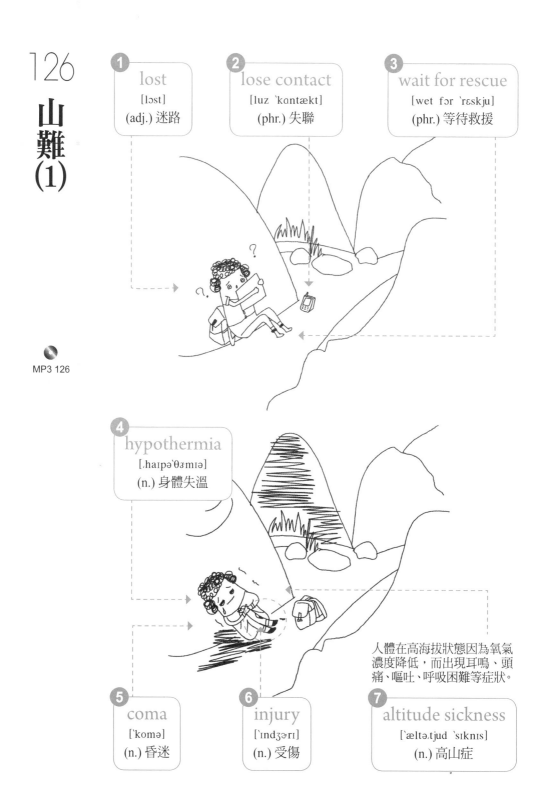

1 lost
[lɔst]
(adj.) 迷路

2 lose contact
[luz `kɑntækt]
(phr.) 失聯

3 wait for rescue
[wet fɚ `rɛskju]
(phr.) 等待救援

4 hypothermia
[ˌhaɪpə`θɝmɪə]
(n.) 身體失溫

5 coma
[`komə]
(n.) 昏迷

6 injury
[`ɪndʒɚrɪ]
(n.) 受傷

7 altitude sickness
[`æltəˌtjud `sɪknɪs]
(n.) 高山症

人體在高海拔狀態因為氧氣濃度降低，而出現耳鳴、頭痛、嘔吐、呼吸困難等症狀。

❶ 迷路

Can I have a look at the map please? I think we're lost.
看一下地圖

❷ 失聯

The hikers stayed close together. They didn't want to lose contact with
each other. 集中待在一起　　　　　　　　　　　　　　彼此失去聯繫

❸ 等待救援

A rescue team is coming for us, so we should sit here and wait for rescue.
正要來找我們

❹ 身體失溫

Make sure you wear lots of clothes. You don't want to get hypothermia.

❺ 昏迷

She's in a coma, and she's being kept alive by a machine.
她一直藉由…維持生命

❻ 受傷

Frank has an injury; I don't think he can walk.

❼ 高山症

When you climb high into the mountains, you can get altitude sickness.
爬山爬到高處

學更多

❶ have a look at〈看一看〉‧ map〈地圖〉‧ please〈請〉
❷ stayed〈stay（停留）的過去式〉‧ close〈靠近地〉‧ lose〈失去〉‧ contact〈聯繫〉
❸ rescue team〈救援隊〉‧ coming〈come（來）的 ing 型態〉‧ sit〈坐〉‧ rescue〈援救〉
❹ make sure〈確定〉‧ wear〈穿著〉‧ lots of〈很多〉‧ clothes〈衣服〉‧ get〈得到〉
❺ kept〈keep（維持某一狀態）的過去分詞〉‧ alive〈活著的〉‧ machine〈機器〉
❻ think〈認為〉‧ walk〈走路〉
❼ climb〈登上〉‧ high〈向高處〉‧ mountain〈山〉‧ altitude〈高處〉‧ sickness〈疾病〉

中譯

❶ 可以讓我看一下地圖嗎？我覺得我們迷路了。
❷ 登山客全都集中待在一起，他們不希望彼此失聯。
❸ 有支搜救隊伍正要來找我們，所以我們應該坐在這裡等待救援。
❹ 要確定你穿了很多衣服，你不會希望身體失溫的。
❺ 她處於昏迷狀態，一直藉由機器維持生命。
❻ Frank 受傷了，我不認為他能行走。
❼ 當你登上高山，你可能出現高山症。

127

山難(2)

MP3 127

1 remote mountain
[rɪˋmot ˋmauntn̩]
(n.) 深山

2 hiking group
[ˋhaɪkɪŋ grup]
(n.) 登山隊

3 radio
[ˋredɪo]
(n.) 無線電對講機/收音機

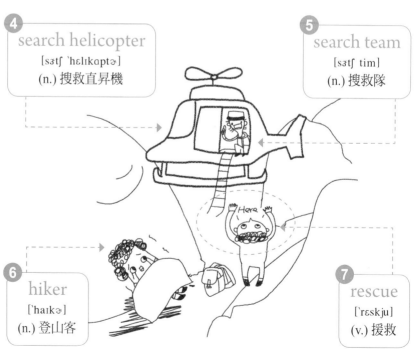

4 search helicopter
[sɜtʃ ˋhɛlɪkɑptɚ]
(n.) 搜救直昇機

5 search team
[sɜtʃ tim]
(n.) 搜救隊

6 hiker
[ˋhaɪkɚ]
(n.) 登山客

7 rescue
[ˋrɛskju]
(v.) 援救

❶ 深山

We need to drive for three hours to get to the remote mountain.

❷ 登山隊

There were seven climbers in the hiking group.

❸ 無線電對講機 / 收音機

Some hikers like to listen to music on radios when they walk.

聽收音機的音樂

❹ 搜救直昇機

The search team flew over the ocean in a search helicopter.

飛越海洋

❺ 搜救隊

A search team was sent out to find the missing hikers.

被派去尋找

❻ 登山客

The hiker climbed the mountain in a couple of hours.

兩個小時

❼ 援救

The men were so happy when they were rescued. They thought they would die.

學更多

❶ drive〈開車〉‧ hour〈小時〉‧ get〈到達〉‧ remote〈偏僻的〉‧ mountain〈山〉
❷ climber〈登山客〉‧ hiking〈健行〉‧ group〈團體〉
❸ some〈一些〉‧ listen〈聽〉‧ music〈音樂〉‧ walk〈走路〉
❹ search〈搜尋〉‧ flew〈fly（飛）的過去式〉‧ over〈越過〉‧ ocean〈海洋〉‧ helicopter〈直昇機〉
❺ team〈隊〉‧ sent out〈send out（派出）的過去分詞〉‧ find〈尋找〉‧ missing〈失蹤的〉
❻ climbed〈climb（爬）的過去式〉‧ a couple of〈兩個〉
❼ rescued〈rescue（援救）的過去分詞〉‧ thought〈think（以為）的過去式〉‧ die〈死〉

中譯

❶ 我們需要開三個小時的車，才能抵達深山。
❷ 該登山隊中，有七名登山客。
❸ 有些登山客喜歡邊走邊聽收音機的音樂。
❹ 搜救隊駕駛搜救直昇機飛越了海洋。
❺ 一支搜救隊被派去尋找失蹤的登山客。
❻ 登山客在兩個小時內就爬上了山。
❼ 這些男人獲得援救時非常高興，他們本來以為自己會沒命。

128

環保(1)

MP3 128

1 shopping bag
[ˈʃɑpɪŋ bæg]
(n.) 購物袋

2 recycled paper
[riˈsaɪkl̩d ˈpepɚ]
(n.) 再生紙

3 reduce packaging
[rɪˈdjus ˈpækɪdʒɪŋ]
(phr.) 減少包裝

4 recycle
[riˈsaɪkl̩]
(v.) 資源回收/再利用

5 waste sorting
[west ˈsɔrtɪŋ]
(n.) 垃圾分類

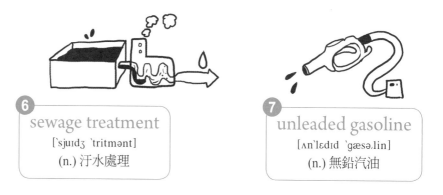

6 sewage treatment
[ˈsjuɪdʒ ˈtritmənt]
(n.) 汙水處理

7 unleaded gasoline
[ʌnˈlɛdɪd ˈgæsəˌlin]
(n.) 無鉛汽油

❶ 購物袋

After coming back from the supermarket, Tom took his food out of the shopping bags.
從購物袋裡拿出他的食物

❷ 再生紙

This is recycled paper, so no trees were cut down to make it.
沒有樹木被砍伐

❸ 減少包裝

Companies should reduce packaging to use less paper and plastic.

❹ 資源回收 / 再利用

Dean likes to recycle his shopping bags. He always uses them again and again.

❺ 垃圾分類

The waste sorting system separates paper from plastic.
區分紙張和塑膠

❻ 汙水處理

Sewage treatment processes clean dirty water.
淨化髒水

❼ 無鉛汽油

Unleaded gasoline is cleaner than older forms of gasoline.
以往的汽油

學更多

❶ coming back〈come back（回來）的 ing 型態〉・took〈take（拿）的過去式〉
❷ recycled〈再利用的〉・cut down〈cut down（砍倒）的過去分詞〉・make〈製作〉
❸ reduce〈減少〉・packaging〈包裝〉・less〈較少的〉・paper〈紙〉・plastic〈塑膠〉
❹ shopping〈購物〉・bag〈袋〉・always〈總是〉・again and again〈一再地〉
❺ waste〈廢棄物〉・sorting〈分類〉・system〈方法、制度〉・separate〈區分〉
❻ sewage〈汙水〉・treatment〈處理〉・process〈過程〉・clean〈把…弄乾淨〉・dirty〈髒的〉
❼ unleaded〈無鉛的〉・cleaner〈較乾淨的，clean（乾淨的）的比較級〉・form〈種類〉

中譯

❶ 從超市回來之後，Tom 從購物袋裡拿出他買的食物。
❷ 這是再生紙，所以不需要砍伐樹木來造紙。
❸ 企業應該用更少量的紙和塑膠來減少包裝。
❹ Dean 喜歡再利用他的購物袋，他總是一再地重複使用。
❺ 垃圾分類的方法，是將紙張和塑膠分為不同類。
❻ 汙水處理過程會淨化髒水。
❼ 無鉛汽油比以往的汽油更乾淨。

129

環保(2)

MP3 129

1 solar energy
[`solǝ `ɛnǝdʒɪ]
(n.) 太陽能

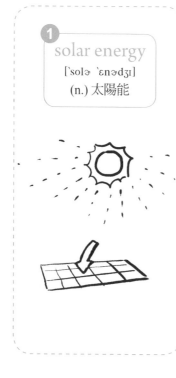

2 save energy
[sev `ɛnǝdʒɪ]
(phr.) 節能

3 carbon reduction
[`kɑrbǝn rɪ`dʌkʃǝn]
(n.) 減碳

4 earth
[ɝθ]
(n.) 地球

5 Earth Day
[ɝθ de]
(n.) 世界地球日

每年的4月22日,為
全球性的環境保護
節日。

6 ecosystem
[`ɛko,sɪstǝm]
(n.) 生態系統

7 vegetarian food
[,vɛdʒǝ`tɛrɪǝn fud]
(n.) 素食

1 太陽能

People in hot, sunny countries should make use of solar energy.
　　　　　　　　　　　　　　　　　　　　　　　應該利用太陽能

2 節能

Turn lights off when you're not using them; it will help you save energy.
把燈關掉

3 減碳

If you're interested in carbon reduction, try to use less energy.
　　　　　　　　　如果你關心減碳

4 地球

We only have one earth, so we need to look after our planet.

5 世界地球日

On Earth Day, we should all try harder to look after our world.

6 生態系統

Forests and jungles are two types of ecosystems.
　　　　　　　　　　　　　　兩種類型的生態系統

7 素食

I don't eat meat, so I always buy vegetarian food.

學更多

1 sunny〈陽光充足的〉・make use of〈利用〉・solar〈太陽的〉・energy〈能量〉
2 turn off〈關掉〉・light〈燈〉・help〈幫助〉・save〈節省〉
3 be interested in〈對…關心〉・carbon〈碳〉・reduction〈減少〉・less〈較少的〉
4 only〈只〉・look after〈照顧〉・planet〈行星〉
5 try〈嘗試〉・harder〈較努力地，hard（努力地）的比較級〉・world〈世界〉
6 forest〈森林〉・jungle〈叢林〉・type〈類型〉
7 eat〈吃〉・meat〈肉〉・buy〈買〉・vegetarian〈素菜的〉

中譯

1 居住在炎熱、陽光充足國度的人們，應該善用太陽能。
2 沒有在使用的時候，就把燈關掉，那會幫助你節能。
3 如果你關心減碳問題，就試著減少使用能源。
4 我們只有一個地球，所以必須好好照顧這個屬於你我的星球。
5 在世界地球日，我們都應該更努力地愛護我們的生存空間。
6 森林和叢林是兩種類型的生態系統。
7 我不吃肉，所以我總是買素食。

130

環境汙染 (1)

MP3 130

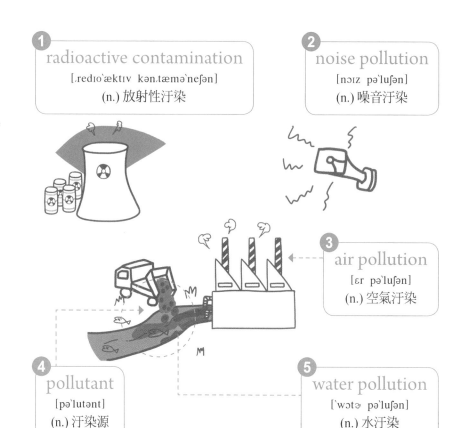

1 radioactive contamination
[͵redɪoˋæktɪv kən͵tæməˋneʃən]
(n.) 放射性汙染

2 noise pollution
[nɔɪz pəˋluʃən]
(n.) 噪音汙染

3 air pollution
[ɛr pəˋluʃən]
(n.) 空氣汙染

4 pollutant
[pəˋlutənt]
(n.) 汙染源

5 water pollution
[ˋwɔtɚ pəˋluʃən]
(n.) 水汙染

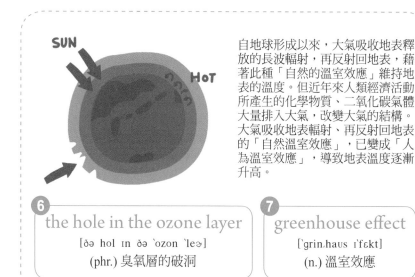

自地球形成以來，大氣吸收地表釋放的長波輻射，再反射回地表，藉著此種「自然的溫室效應」維持地表的溫度。但近年來人類經濟活動所產生的化學物質、二氧化碳氣體大量排入大氣，改變大氣的結構。大氣吸收地表輻射、再反射回地表的「自然溫室效應」，已變成「人為溫室效應」，導致地表溫度逐漸升高。

6 the hole in the ozone layer
[ðə hol ɪn ðə ˋozon ˋleɚ]
(phr.) 臭氧層的破洞

7 greenhouse effect
[ˋgrin͵haʊs ɪˋfɛkt]
(n.) 溫室效應

❶ 放射性汙染

Everyone was worried about radioactive contamination after the nuclear disaster in Japan.

❷ 噪音汙染

There are a few pubs and clubs around here, so the noise pollution can
　　　　　這裡有一些酒吧和夜店
be pretty bad.

❸ 空氣汙染

The smoke from the new factory adds to the city's air pollution problems.

❹ 汙染源

You can't put those chemicals in the river. They're pollutants.
　　　　　　　　把那些化學物品排放到河裡

❺ 水汙染

All the fish in the river have died because of water pollution.
　　　河裡所有的魚都死亡

❻ 臭氧層的破洞

Scientists say the hole in the ozone layer is getting bigger every year.
　　　　　　　　　　　　臭氧層的破洞一直在擴大

❼ 溫室效應

The earth is getting hotter due to the greenhouse effect.
　　　地球變得越來越熱

學更多

❶ radioactive〈放射性的〉・contamination〈汙染〉・nuclear〈核能的〉・disaster〈災害〉
❷ a few〈有一些〉・pub〈酒吧〉・club〈夜店〉・noise〈噪音〉・pretty〈很〉
❸ smoke〈煙〉・factory〈工廠〉・add to〈增加〉・city〈城市〉・problem〈問題〉
❹ put〈排放〉・chemical〈化學物品〉・river〈河〉
❺ fish〈魚〉・died〈die（死）的過去分詞〉・because of〈因為〉・pollution〈汙染〉
❻ scientist〈科學家〉・hole〈破洞〉・ozone〈臭氧〉・layer〈層〉
❼ getting〈get（變成）的 ing 型態〉・due to〈由於〉・greenhouse〈溫室〉・effect〈影響〉

中譯

❶ 在日本發生核能災害之後，每個人都很擔憂放射性汙染。
❷ 這附近有一些酒吧和夜店，所以噪音汙染可能很嚴重。
❸ 新工廠排放的汙煙，加劇了城市的空氣汙染問題。
❹ 你不能將化學物質排放到河裡，那是汙染源。
❺ 河裡所有的魚因為水汙染而死亡。
❻ 科學家說臭氧層的破洞每年都在擴大。
❼ 由於溫室效應，地球的溫度越來越高。

131

環境汙染(2)

MP3 131

1 carbon dioxide
[ˋkɑrbən daɪˋɑksaɪd]
(n.) 二氧化碳

2 exhaust fumes
[ɪgˋzɔst fjumz]
(n.) 汽機車廢氣

3 acid rain
[ˋæsɪd ren]
(n.) 酸雨

4 deforestation
[ˌdifɔrəsˋteʃən]
(n.) 砍伐森林

5 climate anomaly
[ˋklaɪmɪt əˋnɑməlɪ]
(n.) 氣候異常

6 extinction
[ɪkˋstɪŋkʃən]
(n.) 物種滅絕

溫室效應造成全球氣溫上昇，專家預測在可見的將來，北極冰層將完全溶解，危及北極熊的覓食與棲息，可能導致滅絕。

7 mercury poisoning
[ˋmɝkjərɪ ˋpɔɪznɪŋ]
(n.) 汞中毒

❶ 二氧化碳

Plants have the ability to use up carbon dioxide.
　　　　　　　　　　　　　消耗二氧化碳

❷ 汽機車廢氣

The exhaust fumes from the back of that car are making me choke.
　　　　　　　　那輛車後方排放的廢氣

❸ 酸雨

Acid rain is caused by pollution.

❹ 砍伐森林

Deforestation is a huge issue in Brazil, where trees are cut down for farmland.
　　砍伐森林是一個嚴重的問題

❺ 氣候異常

A climate anomaly is defined as being the difference between the future
　　　　　　　　　　被定義為

climate compared to the present climate.
　　　未來的氣候相較於目前的氣候

❻ 物種滅絕

Many people believe the extinction of the dinosaurs was caused by a meteor.
　　　　　　　　　　恐龍的滅絕

❼ 汞中毒

Thousands of fish have died due to mercury poisoning.
　　　數千條魚隻死亡

學更多

❶ ability〈能力〉‧ use up〈使某事物衰竭〉‧ carbon〈碳〉‧ dioxide〈二氧化物〉
❷ exhaust〈排氣〉‧ fumes〈煙〉‧ back〈後面〉‧ car〈車〉‧ choke〈呼吸困難〉
❸ acid〈酸性的〉‧ caused〈cause（造成）的過去分詞〉‧ pollution〈汙染〉
❹ huge〈巨大的〉‧ issue〈問題〉‧ tree〈樹〉‧ cut down〈砍倒〉‧ farmland〈農田〉
❺ anomaly〈異常現象〉‧ difference〈差異〉‧ compared〈compare（比較）的過去分詞〉
❻ believe〈相信〉‧ dinosaur〈恐龍〉‧ meteor〈隕石〉
❼ died〈die（死）的過去分詞〉‧ due to〈由於〉‧ mercury〈汞〉‧ poisoning〈中毒〉

中譯

❶ 植物有吸收二氧化碳的能力。
❷ 那輛車後方排放的廢氣，讓我呼吸困難。
❸ 汙染造成了酸雨。
❹ 在巴西，砍伐森林是一個嚴重的問題。那兒的樹木都被砍掉變成農田。
❺ 氣候異常的定義是：將未來的氣候狀況對比目前的，兩者呈現差異。
❻ 許多人相信恐龍的物種滅絕，是由於隕石撞擊造成的。
❼ 數以千計的魚隻死於汞中毒。

132

地震(1)

MP3 132

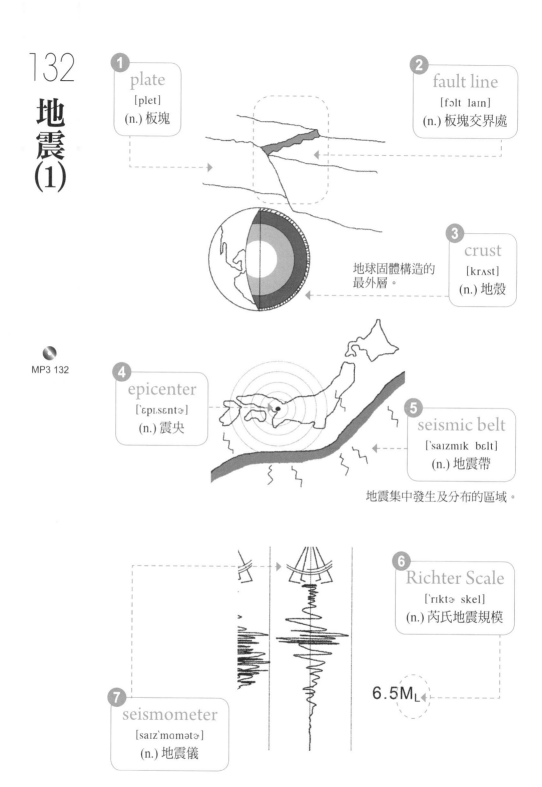

1 plate
[plet]
(n.) 板塊

2 fault line
[fɔlt laɪn]
(n.) 板塊交界處

3 crust
[krʌst]
(n.) 地殼

地球固體構造的最外層。

4 epicenter
[ˈɛpɪˌsɛntɚ]
(n.) 震央

5 seismic belt
[ˈsaɪzmɪk bɛlt]
(n.) 地震帶

地震集中發生及分布的區域。

6 Richter Scale
[ˈrɪktɚ skel]
(n.) 芮氏地震規模

6.5ML

7 seismometer
[saɪzˈmɑmətɚ]
(n.) 地震儀

❶ 板塊

The two plates rubbing past one another caused an earthquake.
<u>互相摩擦擠壓</u>

❷ 板塊交界處

The city stands on a fault line, so earthquakes are common events.
<u>位在板塊交界處</u>

❸ 地殼

The crust is the top layer of the earth.
<u>地球的最外層</u>

❹ 震央

There was an earthquake in California last night, and the epicenter was in San Francisco.

❺ 地震帶

A seismic belt is a thin area of land where earthquakes usually occur.
<u>陸地上的細長區域</u>

❻ 芮氏地震規模

The earthquake measured 7.4 on the Richter Scale.

❼ 地震儀

The seismometer measured the strength of the earthquake.
<u>地震強度</u>

學更多

❶ rubbing〈rub（磨擦）的 ing 型態〉・one another〈互相〉
❷ stand〈坐落〉・fault〈斷層〉・line〈線〉・common〈常見的〉・event〈事件〉
❸ top〈頂部的〉・layer〈層〉・earth〈地球〉
❹ California〈美國加州〉・last night〈昨晚〉・San Francisco〈舊金山〉
❺ seismic〈地震的〉・belt〈地帶〉・thin〈細的〉・land〈陸地〉・occur〈發生〉
❻ measured〈measure（測量）的過去式〉・scale〈規模〉
❼ strength〈強度〉・earthquake〈地震〉

中譯

❶ 兩塊板塊互相摩擦擠壓，引發了地震。
❷ 這座城市位於板塊交界處，所以地震是常有的事。
❸ 地殼是地球的最外層。
❹ 昨晚加州發生了地震，震央位於舊金山。
❺ 地震帶是地表陸地上經常發生地震的細長區域。
❻ 這場地震測得芮氏地震規模 7.4。
❼ 這個地震儀測得了地震的強度。

133

地震(2)

MP3 133

1 eruption
[ɪˋrʌpʃən]
(n.)（火山）爆發

2 landslide
[ˋlænd.slaɪd]
(n.) 山崩

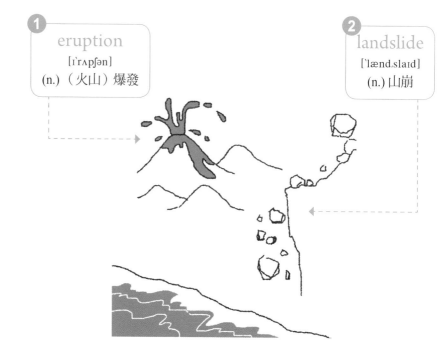

3 intensity
[ɪnˋtɛnsətɪ]
(n.) 震度

地震發生時，地表上人們
所感受到的震動程度。

4 shake
[ʃek]
(v.) 搖晃

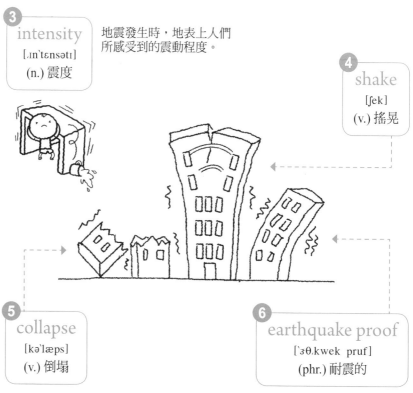

5 collapse
[kəˋlæps]
(v.) 倒塌

6 earthquake proof
[ˋɝθ.kwek pruf]
(phr.) 耐震的

❶（火山）爆發
The volcanic eruption produced a huge cloud of ash.
　　　　　　　　　　　　　　 巨大的火山灰雲

❷ 山崩
Rocks and soil rolled down the mountain in the landslide.
　　　　　　　　　滾下山

❸ 震度
There was an intensity 5 earthquake in Japan last night.

❹ 搖晃
The building shook from side to side in the earthquake.
　　　　　　　　左右搖晃

❺ 倒塌
Hundreds of buildings collapsed in the earthquake.

❻ 耐震的
The building is earthquake proof, so it won't fall down in an earthquake.

學更多

❶ volcanic〈火山引起的〉・produced〈produce（產生）的過去式〉・huge〈巨大的〉・
cloud〈雲狀物〉・ash〈灰燼〉
❷ soil〈泥土〉・rolled〈roll（滾動）的過去式〉・down〈向下〉・mountain〈山〉
❸ earthquake〈地震〉・last night〈昨晚〉
❹ building〈建築物〉・shook〈shake（搖晃）的過去式〉・side〈一邊〉
❺ hundreds of〈數以百計的〉・collapsed〈collapse（倒塌）的過去式〉
❻ so〈所以〉・fall down〈倒塌〉

中譯

❶ 火山爆發產生了巨大的火山灰雲。
❷ 山崩時，岩石和泥土從山上滾落下來。
❸ 昨晚日本發生了震度 5 級的地震。
❹ 這棟建築物在地震發生時左右搖晃。
❺ 數百棟建築物在地震中倒塌。
❻ 這棟建築是耐震的，所以它不會在地震時倒塌。

134

戰爭 (1)

MP3 134

1 death
[dɛθ]
(n.) 死亡

2 destructive
[dɪ`strʌktɪv]
(adj.) 毀滅性

3 biochemical weapon
[`baɪo`kɛmɪkl̩ `wɛpən]
(n.) 生化武器

利用化學物質的毒性，或細菌、病毒等，所製成的武器。

4 conflict
[`kɑnflɪkt]
(n.) 衝突

5 genocide
[`dʒɛnə,saɪd]
(n.) 屠殺

6 armed forces
[ɑrmd fɔrsɪz]
(n.) 武裝部隊

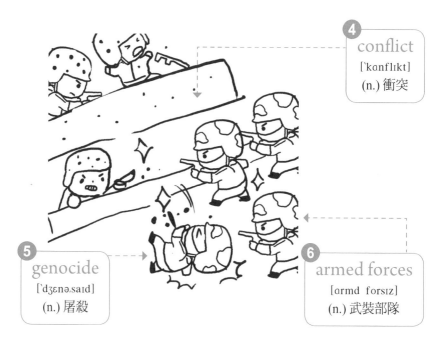

❶ 死亡

The explosion caused the death of 200 people.

❷ 毀滅性

These bombs have a huge destructive power.
<u>　　　　　　　　　　</u>
　　　　　　　強大的毀滅性威力

❸ 生化武器

Soldiers fell ill after being exposed to biochemical weapons.

❹ 衝突

The conflict between the two countries has led to 2,000 deaths since
the start of the year.　　　　　　　　<u>已經導致 2000 人的死亡</u>

❺ 屠殺

Thousands of people have been killed, and many are calling it genocide.
<u>　　　　　　　　</u>
　　數以千計的人

❻ 武裝部隊

There is a navy, army, and air force in most countries' armed forces.
<u>　　　　　　　　　　　　　　　</u>
　　　海軍、陸軍、空軍

學更多

❶ explosion〈爆炸〉‧ caused〈cause（造成）的過去式〉
❷ bomb〈炸彈〉‧ huge〈巨大的〉‧ power〈力量〉
❸ fell ill〈fall ill（生病）的過去式〉‧ exposed〈expose（接觸到）的過去分詞〉‧
　 biochemical〈生物化學的〉‧ weapon〈武器〉
❹ between〈在兩者之間〉‧ led to〈lead to（導致）的過去分詞〉‧ since〈自⋯以來〉
❺ killed〈kill（殺害）的過去分詞〉‧ many〈許多人〉‧ calling〈call（稱呼）的 ing 型態〉
❻ navy〈海軍〉‧ army〈陸軍〉‧ air force〈空軍〉‧ armed〈武裝的〉‧ force〈軍隊〉

中譯

❶ 這場爆炸造成了 200 人死亡。
❷ 這些炸彈具有強大的毀滅性威力。
❸ 接觸到生化武器之後，士兵們就病倒了。
❹ 從今年年初開始，這兩個國家之間的衝突已經造成 2000 人死亡。
❺ 已經有數千人遭到殺害，許多人稱之為屠殺。
❻ 大部分國家的武裝部隊都包含海軍、陸軍和空軍。

135
戰爭(2)

1 bombing
[`bɑmɪŋ]
(n.) 轟炸

2 battlefield
[`bætl̩.fild]
(n.) 戰場

3 blitz
[blɪts]
(v.) 突襲

4 tactic
[`tæktɪk]
(n.) 戰術

5 cruel
[`kruəl]
(adj.) 殘酷

6 violent
[`vaɪələnt]
(adj.) 暴力

MP3 135

284

❶ 轟炸

The airplanes went on a bombing raid over the foreign city.
　　　　　　　　　　　　進行轟炸襲擊

❷ 戰場

Ten soldiers died on the battlefield.

❸ 突襲

The army blitzed its opponents in a quick attack.
　　　　　　　　　　　　　　　在一次快速攻擊中

❹ 戰術

The general thinks about tactics for hours before deciding where to use his
troops.　　　　　　思考戰術好幾個小時　　　　　　　　　　　　要把他的軍隊運用在何處

❺ 殘酷

The cruel man beats his dog every day.

❻ 暴力

Rich seems like a violent guy. I always think he's ready to hit someone.

學更多

❶ airplane〈飛機〉‧went on〈go on（進行）的過去式〉‧raid〈襲擊〉‧
over〈在…之上〉‧foreign〈外國的〉

❷ soldier〈士兵〉‧died〈die（死亡）的過去式〉

❸ army〈軍隊〉‧opponent〈敵人〉‧quick〈迅速的〉‧attack〈進攻〉

❹ general〈將軍〉‧deciding〈decide（決定）的 ing 型態〉‧troop〈軍隊〉

❺ beat〈打〉‧dog〈狗〉‧every day〈每天〉

❻ seem〈似乎〉‧like〈像〉‧guy〈人、傢伙〉‧ready〈準備好的〉‧hit〈打〉

中譯

❶ 飛機在他國城市上空進行了轟炸襲擊。

❷ 十名士兵在戰場上陣亡了。

❸ 在一次快攻中，軍隊突襲了敵軍。

❹ 將軍決定如何用兵之前，先用幾個小時思考戰術。

❺ 那個殘酷的男人每天都打他的狗。

❻ Rich 似乎是個暴力分子，我總覺得他隨時都會打人。

136

懷孕 (1)

MP3 136

1 test tube baby
[tɛst tjub ˋbebɪ]
(n.) 試管嬰兒

2 infertility
[ɪnfəˋtɪlətɪ]
(n.) 不孕

3 pregnancy test
[ˋprɛgnənsɪ tɛst]
(n.) 驗孕棒

4 prenatal checkup
[priˋnetḷ ˋtʃɛkˏʌp]
(n.) 產檢

縮寫為「EDD」。

5 EDD [ˋiˋdiˋdi]
(expected date of delivery)
[ɪkˋspɛktɪd det ɑv dɪˋlɪvərɪ]
(n.) 預產期

6 maternity leave
[məˋtɜnətɪ liv]
(n.) 產假

❶ 試管嬰兒

To make test tube babies, eggs are fertilized outside the body.
卵子在體外受精

❷ 不孕

The man and woman took infertility tests to see if they could have children.
做了不孕檢查　　　　　　　　　　　他們是否能有小孩

❸ 驗孕棒

The woman used a pregnancy test to check whether she was pregnant or not.
她是否懷孕

❹ 產檢

The pregnant mother went to a prenatal checkup to make sure her baby was OK.
去做產檢

❺ 預產期

Mary will probably become a mother on September 4. That's the
Mary 可能會成為一名母親

expected date of delivery.

❻ 產假

The woman had three months of maternity leave after having her baby.
她生完孩子之後

學更多

❶ make〈製造〉‧ test tube〈試管〉‧ baby〈嬰兒〉‧ egg〈卵子〉‧
fertilized〈fertilize（受精）的過去分詞〉‧ outside〈在外面〉‧ body〈身體〉

❷ took〈take（做）的過去式〉‧ test〈試驗〉‧ see〈知道〉‧ children〈child（孩子）的複數〉

❸ pregnancy〈懷孕〉‧ check〈檢查〉‧ whether〈是否〉‧ pregnant〈懷孕的〉

❹ prenatal〈產前的〉‧ checkup〈檢查〉‧ make sure〈確認〉

❺ probably〈很可能〉‧ become〈成為〉‧ expected〈預期要發生的〉‧ delivery〈分娩〉

❻ month〈月〉‧ maternity〈產婦的〉‧ leave〈假期〉‧ after〈在…之後〉

中譯

❶ 為了做試管嬰兒，卵子會在體外進行受精。

❷ 那對男女為了知道自己能否有小孩，做了不孕檢查。

❸ 那名女子用驗孕棒檢測自己是否懷孕。

❹ 孕婦為了確認她的寶寶一切健康，去做了產檢。

❺ Mary 可能在 9 月 4 號那天成為一名母親，那天是她的預產期。

❻ 那名女子在生完小孩後，休了三個月的產假。

287

137
懷孕⑵

MP3 137

1 pregnant woman
[ˈprɛgnənt ˈwumən]
(n.) 孕婦

2 morning sickness
[ˈmɔrnɪŋ ˈsɪknɪs]
(n.) 害喜

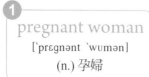

3 prenatal education
[priˈnetḷ ˌɛdʒʊˈkeʃən]
(n.) 胎教

4 labor
[ˈlebɚ]
(n.) 陣痛

5 childbirth
[ˈtʃaɪd.bɝθ]
(n.) 分娩

6 miscarry
[mɪsˈkærɪ]
(v.) 流產

7 abortion
[əˈbɔrʃən]
(n.) 墮胎

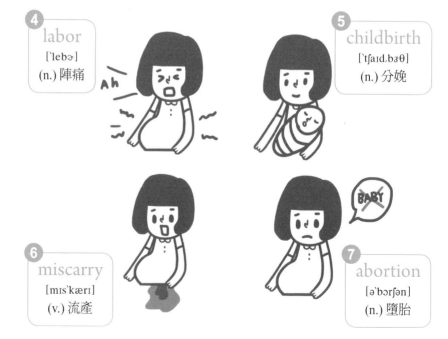

❶ 孕婦

If you're on the bus or an MRT train and you see a pregnant woman standing up, you should give her your seat.

你看見一位孕婦站著

❷ 害喜

Pregnant mothers often suffer really badly with morning sickness.

經歷很嚴重的害喜

❸ 胎教

The parents went to prenatal education classes before their baby was born.

父母親參加了胎教課程

❹ 陣痛

Sarah was in labor for 10 hours before she had her baby.

Sarah 陣痛了 10 個小時

❺ 分娩

Women go through a lot of pain during childbirth.

經歷許多痛苦

❻ 流產

The woman was very sad when she miscarried and lost her baby.

❼ 墮胎

The woman didn't want her baby, so she had an abortion.

她進行墮胎

學更多

❶ pregnant〈懷孕的〉‧ standing up〈stand up（站起）的 ing 型態〉‧ seat〈座位〉
❷ suffer〈經歷〉‧ badly〈嚴重地〉‧ morning〈早晨〉‧ sickness〈嘔吐〉
❸ parents〈父母〉‧ prenatal〈產前的〉‧ education〈教育〉‧ born〈出生的〉
❹ hour〈小時〉‧ before〈在…之前〉‧ had〈have（生育）的過去式〉
❺ women〈woman（女人）的複數〉‧ go through〈經歷〉‧ a lot of〈許多〉‧ pain〈痛苦〉
❻ sad〈悲傷的〉‧ miscarried〈miscarry（流產）的過去式〉‧ lost〈lose（失去）的過去式〉
❼ want〈想要〉‧ baby〈嬰兒〉‧ had〈have（進行）的過去式〉

中譯

❶ 如果你在公車或捷運上看見孕婦站著，你應該要讓座給她。
❷ 孕婦通常會經歷很嚴重的害喜。
❸ 父母親在小孩出生前，參加了胎教課程。
❹ Sarah 生產前，陣痛了 10 個小時。
❺ 女人在分娩時，會經歷許多痛苦。
❻ 那個女人流產失去了孩子時，她非常難過。
❼ 那名女子不想要小孩，所以她做了墮胎。

138

減肥(1)

MP3 138

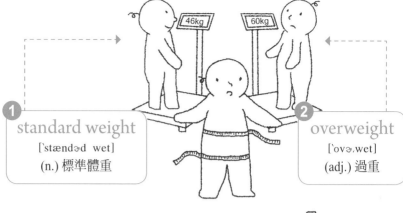

1 standard weight
[ˋstændəd wet]
(n.) 標準體重

2 overweight
[ˋovɚ,wet]
(adj.) 過重

BMI 的計算公式為：體重（公斤）/ 身高^2（公尺^2）。理想範圍為 18.5 至 24 之間。

3 BMI (body mass index)
[ˋbiˋɛmˋaɪ] [ˋbɑdɪ mæs ˋɪndɛks]
(n.) 身體質量指數

4 body fat
[ˋbɑdɪ fæt]
(n.) 體脂肪

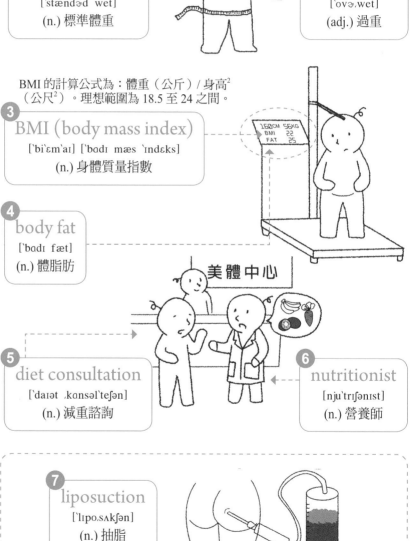

美體中心

5 diet consultation
[ˋdaɪət ,kɑnsəlˋtefən]
(n.) 減重諮詢

6 nutritionist
[njuˋtrɪʃənɪst]
(n.) 營養師

7 liposuction
[ˋlɪpo,sʌkʃən]
(n.) 抽脂

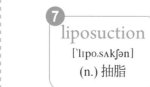

1 標準體重

Lisa doesn't need to go on a diet, she's the standard weight for her height.

符合她的身高的標準體重

2 過重

Sam's really overweight. He needs to stop eating fatty foods.

停止吃油膩的食物

3 身體質量指數

She took advice from a licensed nutritionist and got back to her standard

接受了認證合格的營養師的建議

weight and normal BMI.

4 體脂肪

Tom has a lot of body fat. How much does he weigh?

5 減重諮詢

Andy saw an expert for a diet consultation to ask about what he should eat.

他應該吃什麼

6 營養師

The nutritionist will tell you what foods you should eat.

哪些食物是你應該吃的

7 抽脂

Frank's having liposuction to suck the fat out of his body.

把脂肪抽出他的身體之外

學更多

1 go on a diet〈節食〉・standard〈標準〉・weight〈體重〉・height〈身高〉
2 really〈確實〉・stop〈停止〉・eating〈eat（吃）的 ing 型態〉・fatty〈油膩的〉
3 advice〈勸告〉・licensed〈有執照的〉・normal〈正常的〉・mass〈質量〉・index〈指數〉
4 a lot of...〈許多…〉・body〈身體〉・fat〈脂肪〉・weigh〈有…重量〉
5 saw〈see（訪問）的過去式〉・expert〈專家〉・diet〈節食〉・consultation〈諮詢〉
6 tell〈告訴〉・food〈食物〉
7 suck〈吸取〉・out of〈自…離開〉

中譯

1 Lisa 不需要節食，她已經是符合身高的標準體重。
2 Sam 確實是過重，他需要禁食油膩的食物。
3 她聽取合格營養師的建議，並慢慢回復標準體重和正常的身體質量指數。
4 Tom 的體脂肪很高，他的體重是多少？
5 Andy 向一位專家尋求減重諮詢，詢問他應該吃些什麼。
6 營養師會告訴你應該吃哪些食物。
7 Frank 要去做抽脂手術抽出身體的脂肪。

139

減肥(2)

1 low-calorie
[loˈkæləri]
(adj.) 低卡路里

2 weight loss diet
[wet lɔs ˈdaɪət]
(n.) 減肥餐

MP3 139

3 slimming diet
[ˈslɪmɪŋ ˈdaɪət]
(n.) 代餐

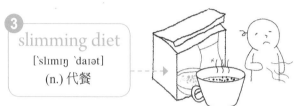

代餐為取代部分或全部正餐的食物。具高纖、低熱量、有飽足感等特質,可藉此控制食量及熱量。

4 fake
[fek]
(n.) 誇大不實

5 diet pill
[ˈdaɪət pɪl]
(n.) 減肥藥

6 anorexia
[ˌænəˈrɛksɪə]
(n.) 厭食症

7 bulimia
[bjuˈlɪmɪə]
(n.) 貪食症

❶ 低卡路里

This is a low-calorie cake, so you can eat it without worrying about getting fat.

擔心變胖

❷ 減肥餐

I need to go on a weight loss diet. I'm too fat.

持續吃減肥餐一段時間

❸ 代餐

I'm on a slimming diet, and I've already lost a few kilos.

我已經減下好幾公斤了

❹ 誇大不實

Many ads about weight loss are fake.

減肥廣告

❺ 減肥藥

She tried a diet pill, but it brought some serious side effects and an eating disorder.

它帶來一些嚴重的副作用

❻ 厭食症

People suffering with anorexia believe that they need to lose weight,

受厭食症所苦的人

even if they're very thin.

❼ 貪食症

People with bulimia eat too much food and then make themselves sick.

貪食症患者

學更多

❶ low〈低的〉・calorie〈卡路里〉・worrying〈worry（擔心）的 ing 型態〉
❷ go on〈持續進行〉・weight〈體重〉・loss〈減少〉・diet〈飲食〉・fat〈肥胖的〉
❸ slimming〈減肥〉・lost〈lose（失去）的過去分詞〉・kilo〈kilogram（公斤）的簡稱〉
❹ many〈許多的〉・ad〈廣告〉・weight loss〈減肥〉
❺ pill〈藥丸〉・brought〈bring（招致）的過去式〉・side effect〈副作用〉・disorder〈失調〉
❻ suffering〈suffer（受苦）的 ing 型態〉・believe〈認為〉・even if〈即使〉・thin〈瘦的〉
❼ food〈食物〉・make〈使得〉・themselves〈他們自己〉・sick〈病的〉

中譯

❶ 這是低卡路里蛋糕,所以你不必擔心吃了會變胖。
❷ 我需要開始吃一段時間的減肥餐,我太胖了。
❸ 我目前在吃代餐,而且已經瘦了好幾公斤。
❹ 很多減肥廣告都誇大不實。
❺ 她嘗試使用減肥藥,卻引發嚴重的副作用和飲食失調。
❻ 飽受厭食症之苦的人認為他們需要減肥,即使他們已經非常瘦了。
❼ 貪食症患者會飲食過量,並使自己的身體出現問題。

健康(1)

1 metabolism
[mɛ`tæbḷˌɪzəm]
(n.) 新陳代謝

2 sufficient sleep
[sə`fɪʃənt slip]
(n.) 睡眠充足

3 physical health
[`fɪzɪkḷ hɛlθ]
(n.) 生理健康

4 mental health
[`mɛntḷ hɛlθ]
(n.) 心理健康

5 biological clock
[ˌbaɪə`lɑdʒɪkḷ klɑk]
(n.) 生理時鐘

6 health evaluation
[hɛlθ ˌɪvæljuˋeʃən]
(n.) 健康檢查

7 blood pressure
[blʌd `prɛʃɚ]
(n.) 血壓

❶ 新陳代謝
People with a high metabolism use up calories a lot more quickly.
高代謝、代謝速度快

❷ 睡眠充足
If you don't get sufficient sleep, you won't be able to concentrate.
獲得充足的睡眠

❸ 生理健康
Eric's mother is worried about his physical health. He never exercises.

❹ 心理健康
Your mental health will suffer if you don't sleep enough.

❺ 生理時鐘
Your biological clock gets mixed up when you fly east or west.
生理時鐘會混亂

❻ 健康檢查
Ian went to the hospital for a full health evaluation.
全身健康檢查

❼ 血壓
Anyone with high blood pressure should see a doctor.
高血壓

學更多

❶ use up〈消耗〉・calorie〈卡路里〉・a lot〈很多〉・quickly〈迅速地〉
❷ if〈如果〉・sufficient〈充分的〉・sleep〈睡眠〉・able〈能〉・concentrate〈專心〉
❸ worried〈擔心的〉・physical〈身體的〉・health〈健康〉・exercise〈運動〉
❹ mental〈心理的〉・suffer〈受損害〉・enough〈充足地〉
❺ biological〈生物的〉・mixed up〈mix up（混亂）的過去分詞〉・east〈東〉・west〈西〉
❻ went〈go（去）的過去式〉・hospital〈醫院〉・full〈完整的〉・evaluation〈評估〉
❼ high〈高的〉・blood〈血液〉・pressure〈壓力〉・see a doctor〈看醫生〉

中譯

❶ 新陳代謝快的人，能夠更快速地消耗大量的卡路里。
❷ 如果沒有睡眠充足，你將無法專心。
❸ Eric 的媽媽擔心他的生理健康，因為他從來不運動。
❹ 如果睡眠不足，會影響你的心理健康。
❺ 搭飛機飛往東邊或西邊時，你的生理時鐘就會混亂。
❻ Ian 去醫院做全身健康檢查。
❼ 高血壓的人都應該去看醫生。

141

健康
(2)

MP3 141

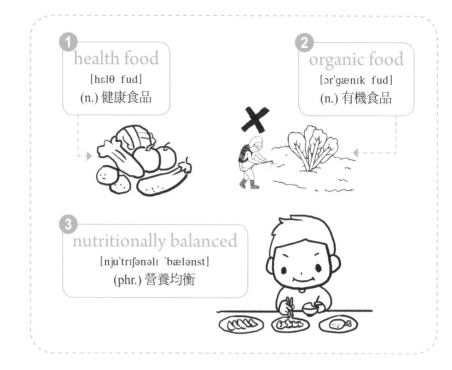

1 health food
[hɛlθ fud]
(n.) 健康食品

2 organic food
[ɔrˋgænɪk fud]
(n.) 有機食品

3 nutritionally balanced
[njuˋtrɪʃənlɪ ˋbælənst]
(phr.) 營養均衡

4 weight control
[wet kənˋtrol]
(n.) 控制體重

5 quit smoking
[kwɪt ˋsmokɪŋ]
(phr.) 戒煙

6 aerobic exercise
[eəˋrobɪk ˋɛksəˏsaɪz]
(n.) 有氧運動

7 exercise
[ˋɛksəˏsaɪz]
(n.) 運動

❶ 健康食品

If you're worried about your weight or your heart, you should eat more health foods.

❷ 有機食品

Organic foods are not sprayed with chemicals.
<u>沒有被噴灑化學藥品</u>

❸ 營養均衡

These meals are nutritionally balanced. They have everything you need.
<u>所有你需要的</u>

❹ 控制體重

People can take weight control pills if they want to lose weight.
<u>服用控制體重的藥</u>

❺ 戒煙

Cigarettes are bad for you; you should quit smoking.
<u>香煙對你有害</u>

❻ 有氧運動

When doing aerobic exercise, you should be able to breathe easily.

❼ 運動

If you want to lose some weight, do some exercise.

學更多

❶ worried〈擔心的〉・weight〈體重〉・heart〈心臟〉・health〈健康〉・food〈食物〉
❷ organic〈有機的〉・sprayed〈spray（噴灑）的過去分詞〉・chemical〈化學藥品〉
❸ meal〈飲食〉・nutritionally〈營養地〉・balanced〈均衡的〉・everything〈一切事物〉
❹ control〈控制〉・pill〈藥丸〉・want〈想要〉・lose weight〈減肥〉
❺ cigarette〈香煙〉・bad〈不好的〉・quit〈停止〉・smoking〈smoke（抽煙）的 ing 型態〉
❻ aerobic〈有氧的〉・able〈能〉・breathe〈呼吸〉・easily〈容易地〉
❼ lose〈失去〉・some〈一些〉・weight〈體重〉・do〈做〉

中譯

❶ 如果擔心體重或心臟問題，你應該多吃健康食品。
❷ 有機食品不會噴灑化學藥劑。
❸ 這些是營養均衡的飲食，它們包含所有你需要的。
❹ 如果人們想要減肥，可以服用控制體重的藥。
❺ 香煙對你有害，你應該要戒煙。
❻ 從事有氧運動時，你應該要能夠輕鬆地呼吸。
❼ 如果你想要減掉一些體重，就做些運動。

142

不健康(1)

MP3 142

1 sick
[sɪk]
(adj.) 病厭厭

2 weak
[wik]
(adj.) 虛弱

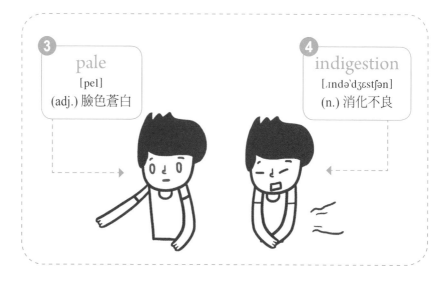

3 pale
[pel]
(adj.) 臉色蒼白

4 indigestion
[ˌɪndəˈdʒɛstʃən]
(n.) 消化不良

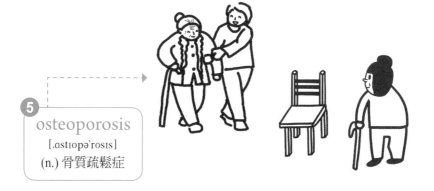

5 osteoporosis
[ˌɑstɪopəˈrosɪs]
(n.) 骨質疏鬆症

❶ 病厭厭

Jerry stayed at home today because he felt sick.

❷ 虛弱

After being ill for a month, Jim is feeling weak.
~~病了一個月之後~~

❸ 臉色蒼白

You're looking very pale. You need some sun.

❹ 消化不良

You'll get indigestion if you eat your food too quickly.
~~你會消化不良~~

❺ 骨質疏鬆症

The old woman has osteoporosis, so her bones could break easily.
~~她的骨頭可能很容易斷裂~~

學更多

❶ stayed〈stay（停留）的過去式〉‧today〈今天〉‧felt〈feel（覺得）的過去式〉

❷ after〈在…之後〉‧ill〈生病的〉‧month〈月〉‧feeling〈feel（覺得）的 ing 型態〉

❸ looking〈look（看起來）的 ing 型態〉‧need〈需要〉‧some〈一些〉‧sun〈陽光〉

❹ get〈得到〉‧eat〈吃〉‧too〈太〉‧quickly〈迅速地〉

❺ old〈上了年紀的〉‧bone〈骨頭〉‧break〈斷裂〉‧easily〈容易地〉

中譯

❶ Jerry 今天待在家裡，因為他覺得病懨懨的。

❷ 病了一個月之後，Jim 覺得很虛弱。

❸ 你看起來臉色非常蒼白，你需要曬點太陽。

❹ 如果吃東西吃得太快，你會消化不良。

❺ 那位上了年紀的女人有骨質疏鬆症，所以她可能很容易發生骨折。

143

不健康(2)

MP3 143

1 inadequate sleep
[ɪnˋædəkwɪt slip]
(n.) 睡眠不足

2 picky
[ˋpɪkɪ]
(adj.) 偏食

3 drink
[drɪŋk]
(v.) 喝酒

4 smoke
[smok]
(v.) 抽（煙）

5 high blood pressure
[haɪ blʌd ˋprɛʃɚ]
(n.) 高血壓

6 high-calorie
[haɪˋkælərɪ]
(adj.) 高熱量

7 high cholesterol
[haɪ kəˋlɛstəˌrol]
(n.) 高膽固醇

❶ 睡眠不足

I think most of your problems are because of inadequate sleep.

你大部分的問題

❷ 偏食

Chris is a picky eater. There are lots of things he won't eat.

❸ 喝酒

How much did you drink? It seems like you can't even stand up properly.

似乎

❹ 抽（煙）

Do you smoke cigarettes? It's bad for you.

抽香煙

❺ 高血壓

The doctors are worried about my high blood pressure. They say I need to reduce my stress.

❻ 高熱量

If you're going to be cycling all day, you should get some high-calorie foods.

你打算要騎腳車

❼ 高膽固醇

Potato chips and ice cream will give you high cholesterol.

學更多

❶ most〈大部分的〉・problem〈問題〉・because of〈因為〉・inadequate〈不充分的〉
❷ eater〈吃東西的人〉・lots of...〈許多〉
❸ even〈甚至〉・stand up〈站起來〉・properly〈恰當地〉
❹ cigarette〈香煙〉・bad〈不好的〉
❺ worried〈擔心的〉・blood〈血液〉・pressure〈壓力〉・reduce〈降低〉・stress〈壓力〉
❻ cycling〈cycle（騎腳踏車）的 ing 型態〉・all day〈整天〉・calorie〈卡路里〉
❼ potato chip〈薯片〉・ice cream〈冰淇淋〉・give〈帶來〉・cholesterol〈膽固醇〉

中譯

❶ 我覺得你大部分的問題都是因為睡眠不足。
❷ Chris 是一個偏食的人，有很多食物他都不吃。
❸ 你喝了多少酒？你似乎連好好站著都辦不到。
❹ 你有抽香煙嗎？那對你沒有好處。
❺ 醫生憂心我的高血壓，他們說我需要減少壓力。
❻ 如果你要騎腳踏車一整天，你應該要吃一些高熱量的食物。
❼ 薯片和冰淇淋會為你帶來高膽固醇。

144

眼睛 (1)

1 wink
[wɪŋk]
(v.) 眨眼

2 close one's eyes
[kloz wʌns aɪz]
(phr.) 閉眼

3 squint
[skwɪnt]
(v.) 瞇眼

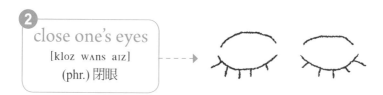

4 foldless eyelid
[ˋfoldlɪs ˋaɪ.lɪd]
(n.) 單眼皮

6 double-fold eyelid
[ˋdʌb].ˋfold ˋaɪ.lɪd]
(n.) 雙眼皮

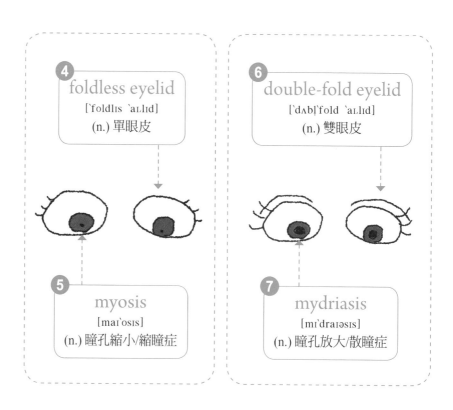

5 myosis
[maɪˋosɪs]
(n.) 瞳孔縮小/縮瞳症

7 mydriasis
[mɪˋdraɪəsɪs]
(n.) 瞳孔放大/散瞳症

❶ 眨眼

To wink at someone, you just close one of your eyes.
　　　對某個人眨眼

❷ 閉眼

Close your eyes and go to sleep.

❸ 瞇眼

You might find yourself squinting when the sun shines in your eyes.

❹ 單眼皮

Many Asians have foldless eyelids.

❺ 瞳孔縮小 / 縮瞳症

People with myosis have pupils that are too small.
　　　　　　　　　　過小的瞳孔

❻ 雙眼皮

A double-fold eyelid has a crease above the eye.
　　　　　　　　眼睛上方有一條摺縫

❼ 瞳孔放大 / 散瞳症

People with mydriasis have very large pupils.
　　　　　　　很大的瞳孔

學更多

❶ someone〈某個人〉• just〈只〉• close〈閉上〉
❷ go to sleep〈入睡〉
❸ find〈發現〉• yourself〈你自己〉• squinting〈squint（瞇眼）的 ing 型態〉• shine〈照耀〉
❹ many〈許多的〉• Asian〈亞洲人〉• foldless〈沒有皺摺的〉• eyelid〈眼皮〉
❺ pupil〈瞳孔〉• too〈太〉• small〈小的〉
❻ double〈雙層的〉• fold〈皺摺〉• crease〈摺縫〉• above〈在…上面〉
❼ very〈很〉• large〈大的〉

中譯

❶ 要對人眨眼，你只要閉上你的一隻眼睛就可以。
❷ 閉上你的眼睛睡覺。
❸ 當陽光照射到你的眼睛時，你會發現自己正瞇著眼。
❹ 很多亞洲人都是單眼皮。
❺ 縮瞳症的人有過小的瞳孔。
❻ 雙眼皮在眼睛上方有一條摺縫。
❼ 散瞳症的人有極大的瞳孔。

145

眼睛(2)

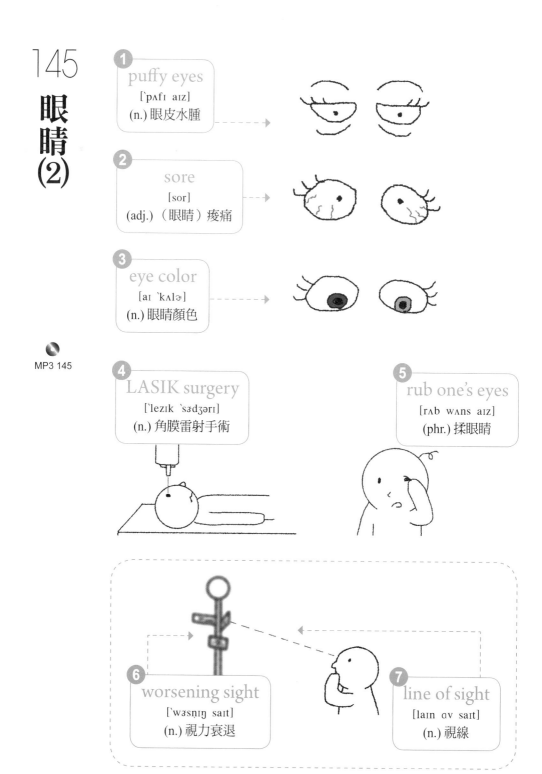

1 puffy eyes
[ˋpʌfɪ aɪz]
(n.) 眼皮水腫

2 sore
[sor]
(adj.)（眼睛）痠痛

3 eye color
[aɪ ˋkʌlɚ]
(n.) 眼睛顏色

4 LASIK surgery
[ˋlezɪk ˋsɝdʒərɪ]
(n.) 角膜雷射手術

5 rub one's eyes
[rʌb wʌns aɪz]
(phr.) 揉眼睛

6 worsening sight
[ˋwɝsnɪŋ saɪt]
(n.) 視力衰退

7 line of sight
[laɪn ɑv saɪt]
(n.) 視線

❶ 眼皮水腫

If you cry before you sleep, you might wake up with puffy eyes.
<u>醒來時眼皮水腫</u>

❷ （眼睛）痠痛

I've been looking at my computer screen too long and my eyes are too sore.
我一直在看…（＝I have been looking at）

❸ 眼睛顏色

I think a blue eye color is beautiful.

❹ 角膜雷射手術

After having LASIK surgery, you should be able to see better.
做完角膜雷射手術後

❺ 揉眼睛

The little boy rubbed his eyes when he woke up.

❻ 視力衰退

The old man's worsening sight is becoming a problem.
將會是一個問題

❼ 視線

Gina is in my line of sight every time I look up from my work, so it seems like I'm always looking at her.　我從工作中抬起頭
像是

學更多

❶ cry〈哭〉．sleep〈睡覺〉．wake up〈醒來〉．puffy〈脹大的〉
❷ looking at〈look at（看）的 ing 型態〉．screen〈螢幕〉．long〈長久地〉
❸ think〈認為〉．blue〈藍色的〉．color〈顏色〉．beautiful〈美麗的〉
❹ after〈在…之後〉．surgery〈手術〉．able〈能〉．better〈更好地〉
❺ little〈小的〉．rubbed〈rub（摩擦）的過去式〉．woke up〈wake up（醒來）的過去式〉
❻ worsening〈惡化的〉．sight〈視力〉．becoming〈become（變成）的 ing 型態〉
❼ line〈線條〉．look up〈抬頭看〉．work〈工作〉．always〈總是〉

中譯

❶ 如果你睡前哭泣，醒來時可能眼皮水腫。
❷ 我長時間一直盯著電腦螢幕看，所以我的眼睛很痠痛。
❸ 我覺得藍色的眼睛顏色很美麗。
❹ 做完角膜雷射手術之後，你應該可以看得比較清楚。
❺ 小男孩醒來時，揉了揉眼睛。
❻ 這名老人的視力衰退，將會是一個問題。
❼ 每當我從工作中抬起頭，Gina 都在我的視線範圍內，就好像我總是盯著她看一樣。

146
血液(1)

MP3 146

1 draw blood
[drɔ blʌd]
(phr.) 抽血

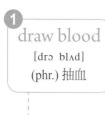

2 blood test
[blʌd tɛst]
(n.) 驗血

3 blood transfusion
[blʌd træns`fjuʒən]
(n.) 輸血

4 anemia
[ə`nimɪə]
(n.) 貧血

5 blood shortage
[blʌd `ʃɔrtɪdʒ]
(n.) 血庫缺血/血液不足

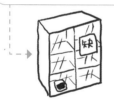

6 blood donation
[blʌd do`neʃən]
(n.) 捐血

7 rejection
[rɪ`dʒɛkʃən]
(n.) 排斥現象

醫學上的「移植物抗宿主反應」；俗稱「排斥現象」或「排斥反應」。

❶ 抽血

The nurse put a needle in my arm and drew some blood.
把一根針插進我的手臂

❷ 驗血

The doctor asked for a blood test to check whether his patient has any illnesses.
他的病患是否有任何疾病

❸ 輸血

Ben needs a blood transfusion as he has lost a lot of blood.
已經大量失血

❹ 貧血

If you don't eat enough iron, you could get anemia.
攝取足夠的鐵質

❺ 血庫缺血 / 血液不足

There is a blood shortage at the blood bank. They need people to donate blood.
捐血

❻ 捐血

Alex goes to the blood donation center every month because he knows
捐血中心
hospitals always need more blood.

❼ 排斥現象

The patient's rejection of his new liver was a problem for the doctors.
對新肝臟產生的排斥現象

學更多

❶ put〈put（放）的過去式〉‧ needle〈針〉‧ drew〈draw（抽出）的過去式〉
❷ doctor〈醫生〉‧ check〈檢查〉‧ whether〈是否〉‧ patient〈病人〉‧ illness〈疾病〉
❸ transfusion〈灌輸〉‧ as〈因為〉‧ lost〈lose（失去）的過去分詞〉‧ a lot of〈許多〉
❹ enough〈足夠的〉‧ iron〈鐵質〉‧ could〈可能〉‧ get〈得到〉
❺ blood〈血液〉‧ shortage〈不足〉‧ blood bank〈血庫〉‧ donate〈捐贈〉
❻ donation〈捐贈〉‧ center〈中心〉‧ hospital〈醫院〉‧ always〈總是〉‧ more〈更多的〉
❼ new〈新的〉‧ liver〈肝臟〉‧ problem〈問題〉

中譯

❶ 護士將一根針插進我的手臂，並抽一些血。
❷ 醫生要求驗血，來檢查病患是否患有任何疾病。
❸ Ben 需要輸血，因為他已經大量失血了。
❹ 如果你沒有攝取足夠的鐵質，你可能會貧血。
❺ 血庫裡血液不足，他們需要人們去捐血。
❻ Alex 每個月都去捐血中心捐血，因為他知道醫院總是需要更多的血。
❼ 這名病患對新肝臟產生的排斥現象，讓醫生們覺得是個問題。

147

血液(2)

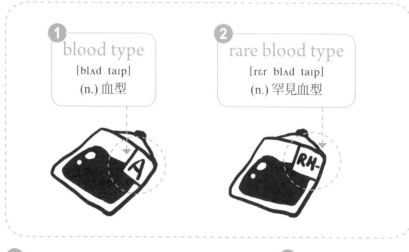

1 blood type
[blʌd taɪp]
(n.) 血型

2 rare blood type
[rɛr blʌd taɪp]
(n.) 罕見血型

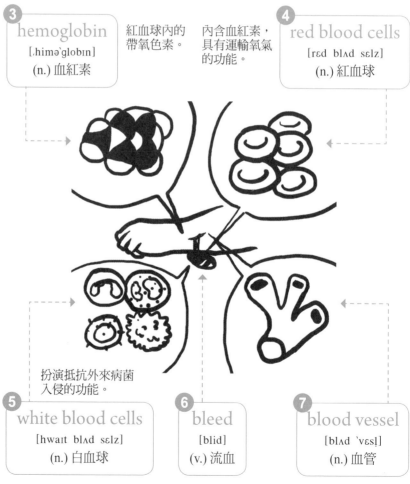

3 hemoglobin
[ˌhiməˋglobɪn]
(n.) 血紅素

紅血球內的
帶氧色素。

內含血紅素，
具有運輸氧氣
的功能。

4 red blood cells
[rɛd blʌd sɛlz]
(n.) 紅血球

扮演抵抗外來病菌
入侵的功能。

5 white blood cells
[hwaɪt blʌd sɛlz]
(n.) 白血球

6 bleed
[blid]
(v.) 流血

7 blood vessel
[blʌd ˋvɛsl]
(n.) 血管

❶ 血型

Wayne's blood type is A+.

❷ 罕見血型

He has a rare blood type, so I hope he never needs a transfusion.
<u>永遠不需要輸血</u>

❸ 血紅素

Red blood cells contain hemoglobin which gives blood its red color.
<u>讓血液呈現紅色</u>

❹ 紅血球

Red blood cells carry oxygen through the body.
<u>通過人體各處</u>

❺ 白血球

White blood cells help your body to fight disease.
<u>對抗疾病</u>

❻ 流血

Ian's finger started to bleed after he cut it.

❼ 血管

Blood travels around the body in blood vessels.
<u>血液在身體裡到處移動</u>

學更多

❶ blood〈血液〉・type〈類型〉
❷ rare〈罕見的〉・hope〈希望〉・never〈從未〉・transfusion〈輸血〉
❸ cell〈細胞〉・contain〈包含〉・give〈給〉・color〈顏色〉
❹ red〈紅色的〉・carry〈攜帶〉・oxygen〈氧氣〉・through〈在…各處〉
❺ white〈白色的〉・help〈幫助〉・body〈身體〉・fight〈打架〉・disease〈疾病〉
❻ finger〈手指〉・started〈start（開始）的過去式〉・cut〈cut（切）的過去式〉
❼ travel〈移動〉・around〈到處〉・vessel〈血管〉

中譯

❶ Wayne 的血型是 A 型 Rh 陽性。
❷ 他是罕見血型，所以我希望他永遠不需要輸血。
❸ 紅血球含有血紅素，使血液呈現紅色。
❹ 紅血球攜帶氧氣流經人體各處。
❺ 白血球幫助你的身體對抗疾病。
❻ Ian 切到手指之後，手指就開始流血。
❼ 血液透過血管在身體各處流動。

148

看診(1)

1 sick
[sɪk]
(adj.) 生病

2 emergency
[ɪˈmɝdʒənsɪ]
(n.) 急診

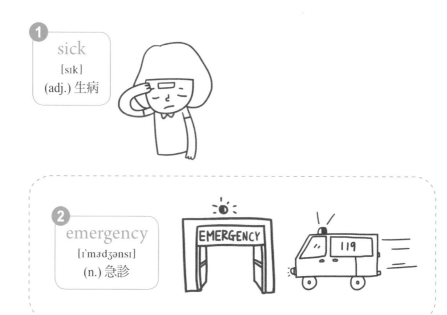

EMERGENCY

119

MP3 148

3 registration
[ˌrɛdʒɪˈstreʃən]
(n.) 掛號

422
REGISTRY
①

4 intravenous drip
[ˌɪntrəˈvinəs drɪp]
(n.) 打點滴

A ➘ B

5 referral
[rɪˈfɝəl]
(n.) 轉診

❶ 生病

Rich didn't come to school today because he's sick.

❷ 急診

It's an emergency. I think he could die.

❸ 掛號

When you arrive at a hospital, you need to go to the registration desk to make an appointment.

去掛號櫃檯做預約

❹ 打點滴

By using an intravenous drip, the doctors let the liquid flow straight into the patient's veins.

讓液體直接流進…

❺ 轉診

My doctor gave me a referral to see a cancer specialist.

幫我轉診

學更多

❶ come〈來〉‧ school〈學校〉‧ today〈今天〉‧ because〈因為〉

❷ think〈認為〉‧ die〈死亡〉

❸ arrive〈到達〉‧ hospital〈醫院〉‧ desk〈櫃檯〉‧ appointment〈預約〉

❹ using〈use（使用）的 ing 型態〉‧ intravenous〈靜脈注射的〉‧ drip〈點滴〉‧ liquid〈液體〉‧ flow〈流動〉‧ straight〈直接地〉‧ patient〈病患〉‧ vein〈靜脈〉

❺ gave〈give（給）的過去式〉‧ cancer〈癌症〉‧ specialist〈專科醫生〉

中譯

❶ Rich 今天沒到學校，因為他生病了。

❷ 這是急診，我覺得他可能會死亡。

❸ 當你到達醫院，你需要先去掛號櫃檯做預約。

❹ 醫生利用打點滴，讓液體直接流進病患的靜脈。

❺ 我的醫生幫我轉診去看癌症專科醫生。

149

看診(2)

1 consulting room
[kən`sʌltɪŋ rum]
(n.) 診療室

2 history
[`hɪstərɪ]
(n.) 病歷

3 prescription
[prɪ`skrɪpʃən]
(n.) 處方

4 measure body temperature
[`mɛʒɚ `bɑdɪ `tɛmprətʃɚ]
(phr.) 量體溫

5 injection
[ɪn`dʒɛkʃən]
(n.) 打針

6 symptom
[`sɪmptəm]
(n.) 症狀

7 drug allergy
[drʌg `ælədʒɪ]
(n.) 藥物過敏

❶ 診療室
The doctor checked on his patients in a consulting room.
　　　　　　　　檢視他的病人

❷ 病歷
The doctors asked the patient questions to get his medical history.
　　　　　　　　　　　　　　　　　　　　　醫療病歷

❸ 處方
The doctor gave the man a prescription for some medicine.

❹ 量體溫
The doctor used a thermometer to measure my body temperature.

❺ 打針
The doctor looked for a vein in my arm so he could give me an injection.
　　　　　　　　　　　　　　　　　　　　　　　　　給我打針

❻ 症狀
Doctors have to check on a patient's symptoms to know what's wrong
with them.　　　　　　　　　　　　　他們有什麼問題

❼ 藥物過敏
Eric can't have penicillin because he has a drug allergy. It would make
him very ill.

❶ checked on〈check on（檢查）的過去式〉・patient〈病人〉・consulting〈專門診視的〉
❷ asked〈ask（詢問）的過去式〉・question〈問題〉・medical〈醫療的〉
❸ gave〈give（給）的過去式〉・some〈一些〉・medicine〈藥〉
❹ thermometer〈溫度計〉・measure〈測量〉・body〈身體〉・temperature〈溫度〉
❺ looked for〈look for（尋找）的過去式〉・vein〈靜脈〉・arm〈手臂〉
❻ have to〈必須〉・know〈知道〉・wrong〈不正常的〉
❼ penicillin〈盤尼西林〉・drug〈藥品〉・allergy〈過敏〉・ill〈不舒服的〉

中譯

❶ 醫生在診療室替病患看診。
❷ 醫生問了病患問題，來了解他的醫療病歷。
❸ 醫生開給那名男子一張處方，讓他去拿一些藥。
❹ 醫生使用溫度計幫我量體溫。
❺ 醫生在我手臂上找出靜脈，這樣他才能幫我打針。
❻ 醫生必須檢查病患的症狀，才能知道他們出了什麼問題。
❼ Eric 不能接受盤尼西林，因為他會藥物過敏，那會讓他非常不舒服。

150

心情不好 (1)

MP3 150

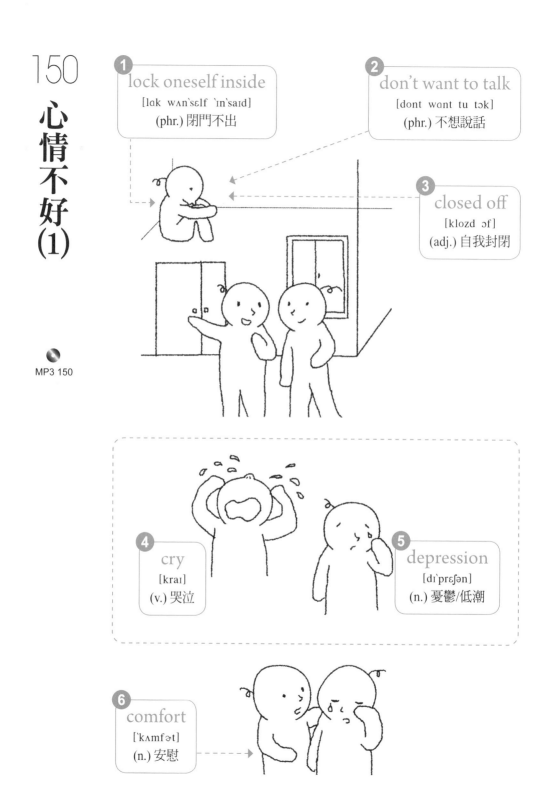

1 lock oneself inside
[lɑk wʌnˋsɛlf ˋɪnˋsaɪd]
(phr.) 閉門不出

2 don't want to talk
[dont wɑnt tu tɔk]
(phr.) 不想說話

3 closed off
[klozd ɔf]
(adj.) 自我封閉

4 cry
[kraɪ]
(v.) 哭泣

5 depression
[dɪˋprɛʃən]
(n.) 憂鬱/低潮

6 comfort
[ˋkʌmfət]
(n.) 安慰

❶ 閉門不出

After his wife's death, he locked himself inside and doesn't talk much anymore.

❷ 不想說話

Ken doesn't want to talk to anyone; he's too upset to do that right now.

太心煩以致於不想説話

❸ 自我封閉

He's very closed off to others. He doesn't talk to people very much.

對其他人非常封閉

❹ 哭泣

Jesse began to cry when she heard the bad news.

❺ 憂鬱 / 低潮

He's suffering with depression, so he finds it hard to feel good about things.

他正經歷低潮

❻ 安慰

Thanks for your kind words. They gave me a lot of comfort.

很大的安慰

學更多

❶ death〈死亡〉‧ locked〈lock（鎖住）的過去式〉‧ inside〈裡面〉‧ anymore〈再也〉
❷ talk〈說話〉‧ anyone〈任何人〉‧ too...to...〈太…以致於不…〉‧ upset〈苦惱的〉
❸ closed〈關閉的〉‧ off〈隔開〉‧ people〈人們〉
❹ began〈begin（開始）的過去式〉‧ heard〈hear（聽到）的過去式〉‧ news〈消息〉
❺ suffering〈suffer（經歷）的 ing 型態〉‧ hard〈困難的〉‧ feel〈感覺〉
❻ kind〈體貼的〉‧ word〈話〉‧ gave〈give（給）的過去式〉‧ a lot of〈很多〉

中譯

❶ 妻子過世後，他閉門不出，也不太跟人交談。
❷ Ken 不想跟任何人說話，他現在太心煩了。
❸ 他對人非常自我封閉，不太跟人們交談。
❹ 當 Jesse 聽到那則壞消息時，就開始哭泣。
❺ 他正經歷低潮，所以很難對其他事情感到開心。
❻ 謝謝你體貼的話，那帶給我很大的安慰。

151

心情不好(2)

MP3 151

1 depressed
[dɪˋprɛst]
(adj.) 沮喪的

2 sad
[sæd]
(adj.) 悲傷的/難過的

3 lonely
[ˋlonlɪ]
(adj.) 寂寞的

4 moody
[ˋmudɪ]
(adj.) 情緒化

5 tearful
[ˋtɪrfəl]
(adj.) 容易掉淚的

6 neurotic
[njuˋrɑtɪk]
(adj.) 神經質

7 suspicious
[səˋspɪʃəs]
(adj.) 多疑的/懷疑的

❶ 沮喪的

I'm depressed; good things never happen to me.

❷ 悲傷的 / 難過的

He wasn't going to cry about it, but Ted felt sad that his team lost the game.
<u>他的隊伍輸掉比賽</u>

❸ 寂寞的

Living by himself, Steve feels lonely sometimes.

❹ 情緒化

My brother is so moody. I never know if he's going to be in a good mood
or not.
<u>是否他將會是好心情</u>

❺ 容易掉淚的

Mary has been tearful for weeks. She cries whenever she sees anything sad.

❻ 神經質

Sam's been worrying so much, he's starting to go neurotic.

Sam 擔心太多了（= Sam has been worrying so much）

❼ 多疑的 / 懷疑的

Dave's suspicious of his friends. He thinks they're all talking about him.

學更多

❶ never〈從未〉・happen〈發生〉
❷ cry〈哭〉・felt〈feel（感覺）的過去式〉・team〈隊伍〉・lost〈lose（輸）的過去式〉
❸ living〈live（居住）的 ing 型態〉・himself〈他自己〉・sometimes〈有時〉
❹ brother〈兄弟〉・know〈知道〉・mood〈心情〉・in a good mood〈心情好〉
❺ week〈週〉・whenever〈每當〉・see〈看到〉・anything〈無論什麼事情〉
❻ worrying〈worry（擔心）的 ing 型態〉・starting〈start（開始）的 ing 型態〉・go〈變得〉
❼ friend〈朋友〉・all〈全部〉・talking〈talk（談論）的 ing 型態〉

中譯

❶ 我很沮喪，好事永遠不會發生在我身上。
❷ Ted 不會因為這樣就哭泣，但是他對自己隊伍輸掉比賽感到很難過。
❸ Steve 獨自生活，有時候他覺得很寂寞。
❹ 我哥哥很情緒化，我永遠不知道他下一刻的心情是好是壞。
❺ Mary 這幾週都很容易掉淚，每當她看到任何悲傷的事物時都會哭泣。
❻ Sam 擔心太多了，他開始變得神經質。
❼ Dave 對他的朋友感到懷疑，他覺得他們都在談論他。

152

感冒 (1)

MP3 152

1 cough
[kɔf]
(v.) 咳嗽

2 runny nose
[`rʌnɪ noz]
(n.) 流鼻水

3 dizzy
[`dɪzɪ]
(adj.) 暈眩

4 chills
[tʃɪlz]
(n.) 寒顫

5 fever
[`fivɚ]
(n.) 發燒

❶ 咳嗽

You should cover your mouth when you cough.
<u>遮住你的嘴巴</u>

❷ 流鼻水

The little boy has a runny nose. I wish he'd wipe it with a tissue.
<u>用衛生紙擦掉它</u>

❸ 暈眩

The little girl spun around in circles until she felt dizzy.
<u>轉圈圈</u>

❹ 寒顫

I need another blanket. I've got the chills.
我覺得很冷（= I have got the chills）

❺ 發燒

I think I have a fever; I feel really hot.

學更多

❶ should〈應該〉‧ cover〈遮住〉‧ mouth〈嘴巴〉

❷ runny〈流鼻涕的〉‧ nose〈鼻子〉‧ wish〈希望〉‧ wipe〈擦〉‧ tissue〈衛生紙〉

❸ spun〈spin（旋轉）的過去式〉‧ around〈環繞〉‧ circle〈圓圈〉‧ until〈到…為止〉‧
felt〈feel（覺得）的過去式〉

❹ another〈另外的〉‧ blanket〈毯子〉‧ got〈get（得到）的過去分詞〉

❺ think〈認為〉‧ really〈很〉‧ hot〈熱的〉

中譯

❶ 當你咳嗽時，應該遮住嘴巴。

❷ 那個小男孩流鼻水了，我希望他可以用衛生紙擦掉它。

❸ 小女孩不停地轉圈圈，直到她覺得暈眩。

❹ 我需要再一條毯子，我猛打寒顫。

❺ 我想我發燒了，我覺得好熱。

153

感冒(2)

MP3 153

1 see a doctor
[si ə `dɑktɚ]
(phr.) 看醫生

2 patient
[`peʃənt]
(n.) 病患

3 cough syrup
[kɔf `sɪrəp]
(n.) 咳嗽糖漿

4 vaccine
[`væksin]
(n.) 疫苗

5 get lots of fluids
[gɛt lɑts ɑv fluɪdz]
(phr.) 補充水分

❶ 看醫生

I think you should see a doctor about your headaches.

❷ 病患

Once a patient is admitted to the hospital, they will receive good care.

病人被送進醫院

❸ 咳嗽糖漿

This cough syrup will help soothe your throat.

舒緩你的喉嚨

❹ 疫苗

Vaccines protect you against viruses.

保護你免受病毒侵害

❺ 補充水分

You have the flu, so it's important for you to get lots of fluids.

得了流行性感冒

學更多

❶ think〈認為〉‧ should〈應該〉‧ doctor〈醫生〉‧ headache〈頭痛〉

❷ once〈一旦〉‧ admitted〈admit（准許進入）的過去分詞〉‧ receive〈接受〉‧ care〈照顧〉

❸ cough〈咳嗽〉‧ syrup〈糖漿〉‧ help〈幫助〉‧ soothe〈緩和〉‧ throat〈喉嚨〉

❹ protect A against B〈保護 A 免受 B〉‧ virus〈病毒〉

❺ flu〈流行性感冒〉‧ important〈重要的〉‧ lots of〈很多〉‧ fluid〈液體〉

中譯

❶ 我認為你頭痛的毛病應該要去看醫生。

❷ 病患一旦被送進醫院，就會受到良好的照顧。

❸ 這個咳嗽糖漿，有助於舒緩你的喉嚨。

❹ 疫苗會保護你不受病毒侵害。

❺ 你得了流行性感冒，所以補充水分對你來說是很重要的。

154

籃球賽(1)

MP3 154

1 starter
['stɑrtɚ]
(n.) 先發球員

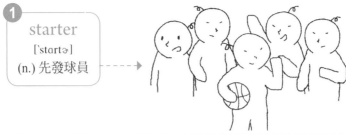

2 three-pointer
['θri`pɔɪntɚ]
(n.) 三分球

3 shoot
[ʃut]
(v.) 投籃

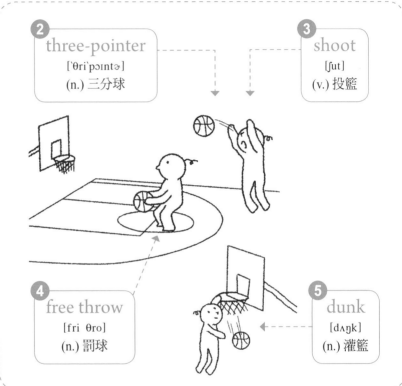

4 free throw
[fri θro]
(n.) 罰球

5 dunk
[dʌŋk]
(n.) 灌籃

6 block
[blɑk]
(v.) 蓋火鍋

7 fake
[fek]
(v.) 假動作

❶ 先發球員

I've been made a starter for the team, so I'll be playing from the beginning of the game.
從比賽一開始

❷ 三分球

You have to shoot from a long distance to score a three-pointer.
從很遠的距離射籃

❸ 投籃

Although Dan shoots a lot, he rarely scores. He's a terrible player.

❹ 罰球

Nelly was fouled so she's got two free throws.
被對手犯規

❺ 灌籃

LeBron James slammed the ball into the net. It was a great dunk.
猛力把球灌進籃網

❻ 蓋火鍋

Eric jumped up to block the other player's shot.
蓋火鍋阻擋對方球員的投籃

❼ 假動作

Kobe faked a pass and then moved to the basket.
假動作傳球

學更多

❶ made〈make（成為⋯的成員）的過去分詞〉．team〈隊伍〉．beginning〈開始〉
❷ have to〈必須〉．long〈遠的〉．distance〈距離〉．score〈得分〉
❸ although〈雖然〉．rarely〈很少〉．terrible〈極差的〉
❹ fouled〈foul（犯規）的過去分詞〉．free〈自由的〉．throw〈投擲〉
❺ slammed〈slam（猛扔）的過去式〉．ball〈球〉．net〈球網〉．great〈極好的〉
❻ jumped〈jump（跳）的過去式〉．player〈球員〉．shot〈投籃〉
❼ pass〈傳球〉．moved〈move（移動）的過去式〉．basket〈籃網〉

中譯

❶ 我已經成為隊上的先發球員，所以比賽一開始我就會上場。
❷ 你必須從很遠的距離射籃，才能以三分球得分。
❸ Dan 雖然投籃次數多，但卻很少命中得分。他是一名表現極差的球員。
❹ Nelly 被對手犯規，所以她得到兩球罰球的機會。
❺ LeBron James 猛力把球灌進籃網，那是一記絕妙的灌籃。
❻ Eric 跳起來，蓋了對方球員一記火鍋。
❼ Kobe 做了一個假動作假裝要傳球，接著就移動到籃下。

155

籃球賽(2)

MP3 155

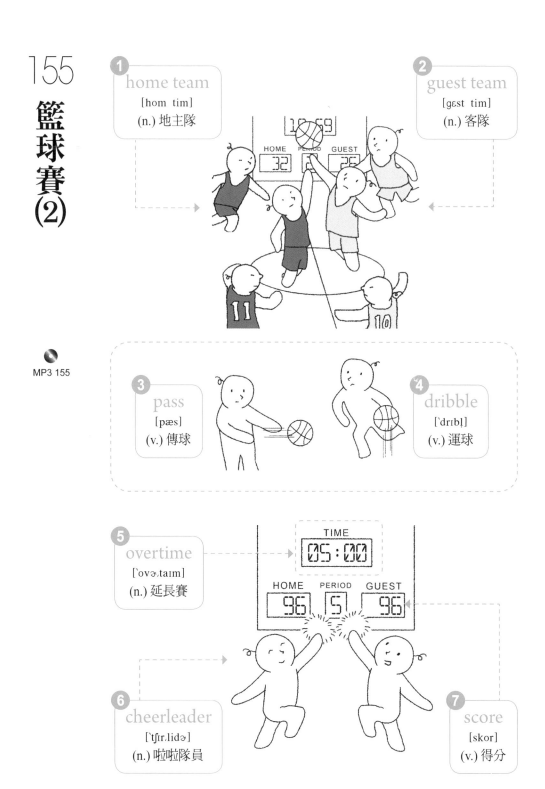

1 home team
[hom tim]
(n.) 地主隊

2 guest team
[gɛst tim]
(n.) 客隊

3 pass
[pæs]
(v.) 傳球

4 dribble
[ˋdrɪb!]
(v.) 運球

5 overtime
[ˋovɚˌtaɪm]
(n.) 延長賽

6 cheerleader
[ˋtʃɪrˌlidɚ]
(n.) 啦啦隊員

7 score
[skor]
(v.) 得分

❶ 地主隊

The players on the home team were happy to be playing at their own school.

❷ 客隊

The guest team had traveled a long way for the game.
　　　　　　　　　　　走了很遠的路

❸ 傳球

Steve's a selfish player; he doesn't pass the ball very much.

❹ 運球

After you stop dribbling, you're only allowed to take two steps with the ball.
　　　　　　　　　　　　　　　　　　　　　　　　　帶球走兩步

❺ 延長賽

The game was tied at the end of the game, so it went into overtime.
比賽被打成平手　　　　　　　　　　　　　　　　進入了延長賽

❻ 啦啦隊員

The cheerleaders danced at halftime to entertain the crowd.

❼ 得分

Michael Jordan scored thousands of points in his career.
　　　　　　得到無數千的分數

學更多

❶ player〈球員〉・home〈本地的〉・playing〈play（打球）的 ing 型態〉・own〈自己的〉
❷ guest〈客人的〉・team〈隊伍〉・traveled〈travel（走過）的過去分詞〉・way〈路程〉
❸ selfish〈自私的〉・ball〈球〉
❹ stop〈停止〉・only〈只〉・allowed〈allow（允許）的過去分詞〉・step〈一步〉
❺ game〈比賽〉・tied〈tie（打成平手）的過去分詞〉・end〈結束〉
❻ halftime〈中場休息〉・entertain〈使娛樂〉・crowd〈人群〉
❼ thousands of...〈無數千的…〉・point〈分數〉・career〈生涯〉

中譯

❶ 地主隊的球員很高興能在自己的學校進行比賽。
❷ 客隊為了比賽長途跋涉。
❸ Steve 是一名自私的球員，他不常傳球。
❹ 停止運球之後，你只能帶球走兩步。
❺ 比賽結束時雙方打成平手，於是進入延長賽。
❻ 啦啦隊員們在中場休息時跳舞，娛樂現場觀眾。
❼ 在 Michael Jordan 的籃球職業生涯裡，得分超過上萬分。

156

足球賽(1)

MP3 156

1 goalkeeper
[ˈgolˌkipɚ]
(n.) 守門員

2 goal
[gol]
(n.) 球門/（足球或曲棍球的）得分

3 shot
[ʃɑt]
(n.) 射門

4 penalty area
[ˈpɛn̩tɪ ˈɛrɪə]
(n.) 罰球區

5 throw-in
[ˈθroɪn]
(n.) 界外球

6 penalty shootout
[ˈpɛn̩tɪ ˈʃutˌaʊt]
(n.) 十二碼罰球（PK大戰）

❶ 守門員

The goalkeeper is the only player who can use his hands.
可以使用手的人

❷ 球門／（足球或曲棍球的）得分

Sam kicked the ball into the net for a brilliant goal.
踢球進網

❸ 射門

I took a shot, but I wasn't able to score a goal.
得分

❹ 罰球區

The penalty area is a rectangular space in front of the goal.
球門前的長方形區域

❺ 界外球

If a player kicks the ball out of play at the side of the field, the other team gets a throw-in.
把球踢出球場邊界

❻ 十二碼罰球（PK大戰）

The game finished in a tie, so it was settled by a penalty shootout.
以十二碼罰球決勝負

學更多

❶ only〈唯一的〉‧ player〈球員〉‧ use〈使用〉‧ hand〈手〉
❷ kicked〈kick（踢）的過去式〉‧ net〈球網〉‧ brilliant〈出色的〉
❸ took〈take（做）的過去式〉‧ able〈能〉‧ score〈得分〉
❹ penalty〈罰球〉‧ area〈區域〉‧ rectangular〈長方形的〉‧ in front of〈在⋯前面〉
❺ out of play〈出界〉‧ side〈邊〉‧ field〈球場〉‧ team〈隊伍〉‧ throw〈投擲〉
❻ game〈比賽〉‧ tie〈平手〉‧ settled〈settle（解決）的過去分詞〉‧ shootout〈槍戰〉

中譯

❶ 守門員是唯一能使用手碰球的球員。
❷ Sam 踢球進網，一記漂亮的射門得分。
❸ 我踢了一記射門，卻沒有得分。
❹ 罰球區是指球門前長方形的區域。
❺ 如果球員把球踢出界外，另一隊就能獲得一個界外球。
❻ 比賽結束時雙方平手，因此以十二碼罰球決勝負。

157

足球賽(2)

🔊 MP3 157

1 header
[ˈhɛdə]
(n.) 頭錘

2 kick
[kɪk]
(v.) 踢球

3 catch
[kætʃ]
(v.) 接球

4 offside
[ˈɔfˈsaɪd]
(adj.) 越位

裁判用來「將嚴重犯規的球員驅逐出場」的紅色牌子。

裁判用來「警告球員」的黃色牌子。

5 red card
[rɛd kɑrd]
(n.) 紅牌

6 yellow card
[ˈjɛlo kɑrd]
(n.) 黃牌

328

① 頭錘

The ball was flying in the air, so I scored with a header instead of kicking it.
代替踢球

② 踢球

I always kick the ball with my right foot. I never use my left.
從不使用我的左腳

③ 接球

The goalkeeper caught the ball and kicked it down the field.
將它踢進球場裡

④ 越位

Joe ran past the last defender before I passed the ball to him, so he was
跑過最後一個後衛　　　　　　　　　　　　我傳球給他
offside.

⑤ 紅牌

The player was shown a red card, so he had to leave the field.
被亮了一張紅牌

⑥ 黃牌

Being given a yellow card is like receiving a warning.
被給了一張黃牌

學更多

① flying〈fly（飛）的 ing 型態〉・air〈空中〉・instead of〈代替〉

② always〈總是〉・right〈右邊的〉・never〈從未〉・left〈左邊的〉

③ goalkeeper〈守門員〉・caught〈catch（接球）的過去式〉・down〈到〉・field〈球場〉

④ ran〈run（跑）的過去式〉・past〈越過〉・last〈最後的〉・defender〈後衛〉

⑤ shown〈show（出示）的過去分詞〉・had to〈have to（必須）的過去式〉・leave〈離開〉

⑥ given〈give（給）的過去分詞〉・receiving〈receive（收到）的 ing 型態〉・
warning〈警告〉

中譯

① 球在空中飛，所以我不用腳踢，改以一記頭錘得分。

② 我總是用右腳踢球，從不使用左腳。

③ 守門員接住球，並將球踢進球場。

④ 我傳球給 Joe 之前，他從對方最後一名後衛身旁跑過，所以他越位了。

⑤ 那名球員被亮了一張紅牌，所以他必須離開球場。

⑥ 得到一張黃牌，就等同收到一個警告。

158

棒球場 (1)

MP3 158

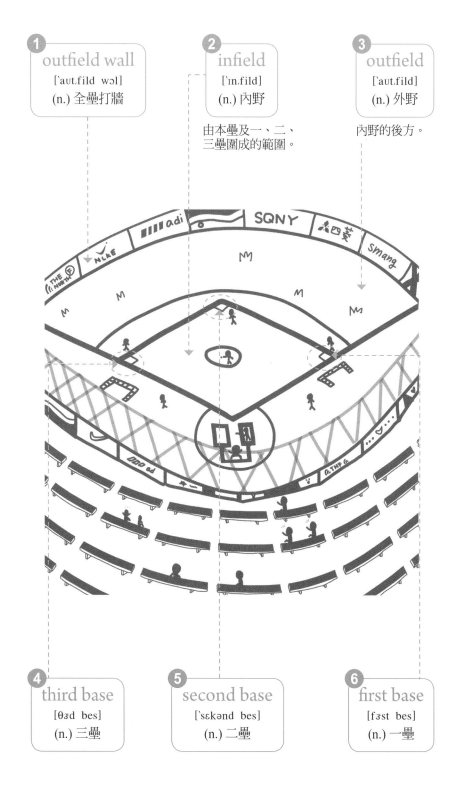

1 outfield wall
['aʊt.fild wɔl]
(n.) 全壘打牆

2 infield
['ɪn.fild]
(n.) 內野

由本壘及一、二、
三壘圍成的範圍。

3 outfield
['aʊt.fild]
(n.) 外野

內野的後方。

4 third base
[θɝd bes]
(n.) 三壘

5 second base
['sɛkənd bes]
(n.) 二壘

6 first base
[fɝst bes]
(n.) 一壘

❶ 全壘打牆

To score a home run, you have to hit the ball over the outfield wall.
要打全壘打得分

❷ 內野

The infield is the area inside and just around the diamond.
在內部且恰好圍成菱形

❸ 外野

Players in the outfield usually have to run farther than the ones in the
infield.
在內野的球員

❹ 三壘
❺ 二壘
❻ 一壘

He hit the ball hard and ran around first, second, and third bases before
用力地擊球

completing his home run.

學更多

❶ score〈得分〉‧ home run〈全壘打〉‧ have to〈必須〉‧ over〈越過〉‧ wall〈圍牆〉
❷ area〈區域〉‧ inside〈在內部〉‧ just〈恰好〉‧ around〈環繞〉‧ diamond〈菱形〉
❸ player〈球員〉‧ usually〈通常〉‧ farther〈更遠地〉‧ than〈比〉
❹❺❻ hit〈打擊〉‧ hard〈猛力地〉‧ ran〈run（跑）的過去式〉‧
first〈第一的〉‧ second〈第二的〉‧ third〈第三的〉‧ base〈壘〉‧
completing〈complete（完成）的 ing 型態〉

中譯

❶ 要打全壘打得分，你必須將球擊出超過全壘打牆。
❷ 內野是球場內恰好圍成菱形的區域。
❸ 外野的球員通常要跑得比內野的球員遠。
❹❺❻ 他用力擊出球，並在完成這支全壘打前，繞著一壘、二壘和三壘跑。

159

棒球場(2)

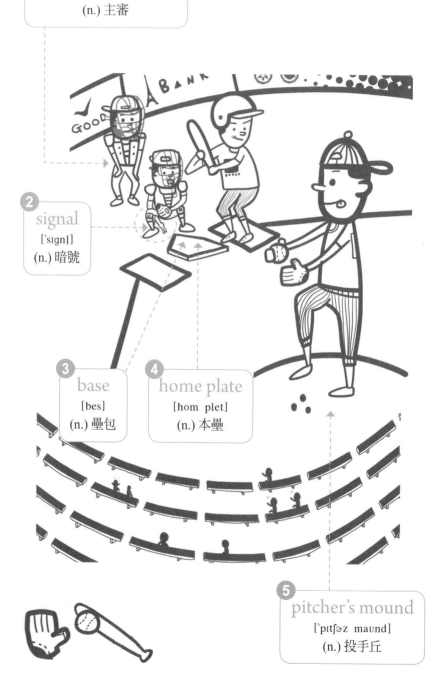

MP3 159

1 home plate umpire
[hom plet `ʌmpaɪr]
(n.) 主審

2 signal
[`sɪgnḷ]
(n.) 暗號

3 base
[bes]
(n.) 壘包

4 home plate
[hom plet]
(n.) 本壘

5 pitcher's mound
[`pɪtʃɚz maʊnd]
(n.) 投手丘

❶ 主審

The home plate umpire decides whether a pitch is a strike or a ball.
<u>一記投球是好球還是壞球</u>

❷ 暗號

Coaches use hand signals to communicate with their pitchers.
<u>手勢暗號</u>

❸ 壘包

The first, second, and third basemen stand in the infield, near their bases.

❹ 本壘

Batters stand at home plate when they face pitches.

❺ 投手丘

I stood on the pitcher's mound and threw the ball towards the batter.
<u>把球投向打擊者</u>

學更多

❶ umpire〈裁判員〉‧ decide〈決定〉‧ pitch〈投過來的球〉‧ strike〈好球〉‧ ball〈壞球〉

❷ coach〈教練〉‧ use〈使用〉‧ hand〈手〉‧ communicate〈溝通〉‧ pitcher〈投手〉

❸ first〈第一〉‧ second〈第二〉‧ third〈第三〉‧ basemen〈baseman（壘手）的複數〉‧
stand〈站立〉‧ infield〈內野〉‧ near〈接近〉

❹ batter〈打者〉‧ plate〈投手板〉‧ face〈面對〉

❺ stood〈stand（站立）的過去式〉‧ mound〈小丘、投手踏板〉‧
threw〈throw（投擲）的過去式〉‧ towards〈向、朝〉

中譯

❶ 主審會決定投手的投球是好球還是壞球。

❷ 教練們利用手勢暗號，來跟投手們溝通。

❸ 一壘、二壘和三壘手站在內野，且靠近各自的壘包。

❹ 打者面對投過來的球時，會站在本壘。

❺ 我站在投手丘，將球投向打者。

160

棒球選手

MP3 160

1 left fielder
[lɛft `fildə]
(n.) 左外野手

2 center fielder
[`sɛntə `fildə]
(n.) 中外野手

3 right fielder
[raɪt `fildə]
(n.) 右外野手

4 shortstop
[`ʃɔrt,stɑp]
(n.) 游擊手

5 second baseman
[`sɛkənd `besmən]
(n.) 二壘手

6 third baseman
[θɜd `besmən]
(n.) 三壘手

7 first baseman
[fɜst `besmən]
(n.) 一壘手

8 batter
[`bætə]
(n.) 打者

9 catcher
[`kætʃə]
(n.) 捕手

10 pitcher
[`pɪtʃə]
(n.) 投手

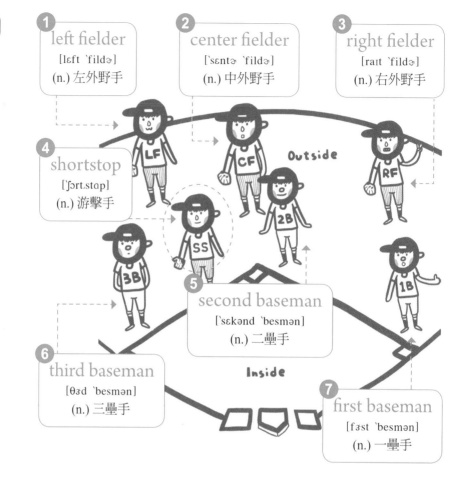

❶ 左外野手
❷ 中外野手
❸ 右外野手
The left, right, and center fielders stand in the outfield.

❹ 游擊手
The shortstop stands between the second and third bases.
<u>站在二壘和三壘之間</u>

❺ 二壘手
❻ 三壘手
❼ 一壘手
The first, second, and third basemen stand in the infield, near their bases.

❽ 打者
This batter's having a great game. He's had four hits already.
<u>比賽表現持續良好</u>

❾ 捕手
The catcher squatted behind the batter and waited for the pitch.
<u>蹲在打者後方</u>

❿ 投手
The pitcher couldn't play because his throwing arm was injured.
<u>他投球的手臂</u>

學更多

❶❷❸ left〈左方的〉．right〈右方的〉．center〈中央〉．fielder〈外野手〉．
outfield〈外野〉
❹ stand〈站著〉．second〈第二〉．third〈第三〉．between〈在…之間〉．base〈壘包〉
❺❻❼ first〈第一〉．basemen〈baseman（壘手）的複數〉．infield〈內野〉．near〈靠近〉
❽ game〈比賽〉．hit〈安打〉．already〈已經〉
❾ squatted〈squat（蹲）的過去式〉．behind〈在…後面〉．pitch〈投過來的球〉
❿ play〈比賽〉．throwing〈投擲〉．arm〈手臂〉．injured〈受傷的〉

中譯

❶❷❸ 左外野手、右外野手和中外野手站在外野。
❹ 游擊手站在二壘和三壘之間。
❺❻❼ 一壘、二壘和三壘手站在內野，且靠近各自的壘包。
❽ 這名打者的表現正好，他已經擊出了四支安打。
❾ 捕手蹲在打者後方，等候投手投過來的球。
❿ 那名投手無法進行比賽，因為他投球的手臂受傷了。

161
運動(1)

1 run
[rʌn]
(v.) 跑步

2 speed walk
[spid wɔk]
(n.) 快走

3 sports shoes
[spɔrts ʃuz]
(n.) 運動鞋

4 muscle strength
[`mʌsl̩ strɛŋθ]
(n.) 肌耐力

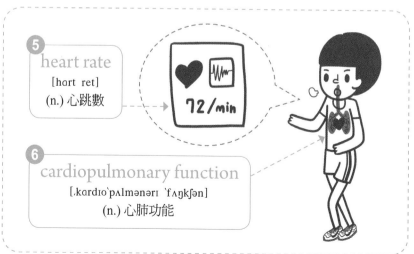

5 heart rate
[hɑrt ret]
(n.) 心跳數

72/min

6 cardiopulmonary function
[ˌkɑrdɪoˈpʌlmənərɪ ˈfʌŋkʃən]
(n.) 心肺功能

❶ 跑步
He's a great runner; he can run 1,500 meters in three and a half minutes.
三分半鐘

❷ 快走
People in the speed walk must keep at least one foot on the floor all the time.
至少一隻腳著地

❸ 運動鞋
Wear sports shoes when you exercise. If you don't, you might hurt your feet.

❹ 肌耐力
The gym teacher designed an exercise to test the students' muscle strength.
體育老師設計一種運動

❺ 心跳數
After running, your heart rate will be higher.

❻ 心肺功能
The doctor checked my cardiopulmonary function by listening to my heart and lungs.
檢查我的心肺功能

學更多

❶ runner〈跑步者〉‧meter〈公尺〉‧half〈一半〉‧minute〈分鐘〉
❷ speed〈加速〉‧at least〈至少〉‧foot〈腳〉‧floor〈地面〉‧all the time〈一直〉
❸ exercise〈運動〉‧hurt〈傷害〉‧feet〈foot（腳）的複數〉
❹ gym〈體育〉‧designed〈design（設計）的過去式〉‧muscle〈肌肉〉‧strength〈力量〉
❺ after〈在…之後〉‧running〈跑步〉‧heart〈心臟〉‧rate〈速度〉
❻ checked〈check（檢查）的過去式〉‧cardiopulmonary〈心肺的〉‧function〈功能〉‧listening〈listen（聽）的 ing 型態〉‧lung〈肺〉

中譯

❶ 他是一名優秀的跑者，他能在三分半內跑一千五百公尺。
❷ 快走的人必須隨時保持至少一隻腳著地。
❸ 運動時要穿運動鞋，如果不穿，你的腳可能會受傷。
❹ 體育老師設計了一種運動，來測試學生們的肌耐力。
❺ 跑步後，你的心跳數會高於平常。
❻ 醫生聽我的心跳和肺部，檢查我的心肺功能。

162

運動(2)

MP3 162

1 catch one's breath
[kætʃ wʌns brɛθ]
(phr.) 喘息調整呼吸

2 sweat
[swɛt]
(v.) 流汗

3 burning fat
[ˋbɝnɪŋ fæt]
(phr.) 燃脂

4 weight loss
[wet lɔs]
(n.) 減肥

5 sports injury
[spɔrts ˋɪndʒɪrɪ]
(n.) 運動傷害

6 sore muscle
[sor ˋmʌsḷ]
(n.) 肌肉痠痛

1 喘息調整呼吸

Can we stop running for a minute? I need to catch my breath.
　　　　　　　　　　稍微一下

2 流汗

I'm sweating so much, my clothes are completely wet.
　　　　　　　　　　　　　我的衣服全都濕了

3 燃脂

When you work out hard for a long time, you will start burning fat.
　　　　　　　　努力運動鍛鍊一段時間

4 減肥

These people are overweight. They come to the gym because weight loss is important to them.

5 運動傷害

The pain in my leg is a sports injury; I hurt myself by running too much.
　　　　　　　　　　　　　　　　　我因為跑步太多而受傷

6 肌肉痠痛

I was running yesterday, so I've got sore muscles today.
　　　　　　　　　　　　　我肌肉痠痛（＝I have got sore muscles）

學更多

1 stop〈停止〉・running〈run（跑步）的 ing 型態〉・minute〈分鐘〉・catch〈抓住〉・breath〈氣息〉

2 sweating〈sweat（流汗）的 ing 型態〉・completely〈完全地〉・wet〈濕的〉

3 work out〈大量運動鍛鍊〉・hard〈努力地〉・burning〈燃燒〉

4 overweight〈過重的〉・gym〈健身房〉・loss〈減少〉・important〈重要的〉

5 pain〈疼痛〉・leg〈腿〉・injury〈傷害〉・hurt〈傷害〉・myself〈我自己〉

6 yesterday〈昨天〉・so〈所以〉・sore〈痛的〉・muscle〈肌肉〉・today〈今天〉

中譯

1 我們可不可以稍微停下跑步？我需要喘息調整呼吸。

2 我流很多汗，我的衣服全都濕了。

3 當你努力運動鍛鍊一段時間之後，就會開始燃脂。

4 這些人都過重，他們來到健身房，是因為減肥對他們而言很重要。

5 我腿上的疼痛是運動傷害，我因為跑步過多而受傷。

6 我昨天有跑步，因此今天肌肉痠痛。

163
游泳(1)

MP3 163

1 cramp
[kræmp]
(n.) 抽筋

2 drown
[draʊn]
(v.) 溺水/溺斃

3 choke
[tʃok]
(v.) 嗆到/噎住

4 CPR
[ˋsiˋpiˋɑr]
(n.) 心肺復甦術

5 artificial respiration
[ˌɑrtəˋfɪʃəl ˌrɛspəˋreʃən]
mouth-to-mouth resuscitation
[mauθ tu mauθ rɪˌsʌsəˋteʃən]
(n.) 人工呼吸/口對口急救

兩個單字都是「人工呼吸」。

6 swimming coach
[ˋswɪmɪŋ kotʃ]
(n.) 游泳教練

7 lifeguard
[ˋlaɪfˌgɑrd]
(n.) 救生員

❶ 抽筋

Don't swim too soon after eating; otherwise, you might get a cramp.

不要太快就去游泳

❷ 溺水 / 溺斃

Four people drowned when their boat suddenly sank.

他們的船突然沉了

❸ 嗆到 / 噎住

Jenny took a drink of water too quickly, and began choking.

喝了一口水

❹ 心肺復甦術

All lifeguards must take a CPR training course.

接受心肺復甦術的訓練課程

❺ 人工呼吸 / 口對口急救

Artificial respiration or mouth-to-mouth resuscitation can save someone's life.

拯救一個人的生命

❻ 游泳教練

My swimming coach is famous because he swam in the 2008 Olympics.

他參加了 2008 年奧運的游泳項目

❼ 救生員

Johnny became a lifeguard the summer after he graduated from high school.

他高中畢業的那個夏天

學更多

❶ swim〈游泳〉‧ soon〈快〉‧ eating〈eat（吃）的 ing 型態〉‧ otherwise〈不然〉
❷ drowned〈drown（溺水）的過去式〉‧ boat〈船〉‧ sank〈sink（下沉）的過去式〉
❸ took〈take（喝）的過去式〉‧ drink〈一口〉‧ choking〈choke（嗆到）的 ing 型態〉
❹ take〈接受〉‧ training〈訓練〉‧ course〈課程〉
❺ artificial〈人工的〉‧ respiration〈呼吸〉‧ resuscitation〈搶救〉‧ save〈拯救〉
❻ coach〈教練〉‧ swam〈swim（游泳）的過去式〉‧ Olympics〈奧林匹克運動會〉
❼ became〈become（成為）的過去式〉‧ graduated〈graduate（畢業）的過去式〉

中譯

❶ 吃東西後不要太快下水游泳，不然你可能會抽筋。
❷ 船隻突然沉船，造成四個人溺斃。
❸ Jenny 一口水喝得太快，接著就嗆到了。
❹ 所有的救生員都必須接受心肺復甦術的訓練課程。
❺ 人工呼吸或口對口急救可以拯救一個人的生命。
❻ 我的游泳教練很有名，因為他參加了 2008 年奧林匹克運動會的游泳項目。
❼ Johnny 在高中畢業的那個夏天，成為了救生員。

164

游泳(2)

MP3 164

1 warm up
[wɔrm ʌp]
(phr.) 暖身

2 diving
[ˋdaɪvɪŋ]
(n.) 跳水

3 flutter kick
[ˋflʌtɚ kɪk]
(n.) 打水

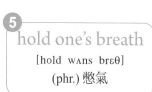

4 arm stroke
[ɑrm strok]
(n.) 划水

5 hold one's breath
[hold wʌns brɛθ]
(phr.) 憋氣

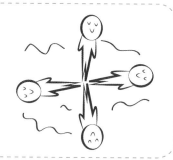

6 synchronized swimming
[ˋsɪŋkrənaɪzd ˋswɪmɪŋ]
(n.) 水上芭蕾

7 disinfectant
[͵dɪsɪnˋfɛktənt]
(n.) 池水消毒劑

❶ 暖身

Before Jared goes jogging, he warms up his leg muscles.
他會暖身腿部肌肉

❷ 跳水

Scott was thrilled to learn he made the diving team.
成為跳水隊的成員

❸ 打水

If you want to learn to swim freestyle, you need to practice the flutter kick.
游自由式

❹ 划水

In swimming, correct arm strokes are just as important as kicking your legs correctly.
就跟…一樣重要

❺ 憋氣

After practicing for weeks, Missy could hold her breath under water for two minutes.
在水裡憋氣

❻ 水上芭蕾

Synchronized swimming is beautiful, but requires a lot of dedication and breath control.
需要很多專注

❼ 池水消毒劑

Keeping a public pool clean requires a lot of disinfectant.
保持公共泳池乾淨

學更多

❶ jogging〈慢跑〉・warm〈使暖和〉・leg〈腿〉・muscle〈肌肉〉
❷ thrilled〈非常興奮的〉・learn〈得知〉・made〈make（成為…的成員）的過去式〉
❸ learn〈學習〉・freestyle〈自由式〉・practice〈練習〉・flutter〈拍打〉・kick〈踢〉
❹ correct〈正確的〉・arm〈手臂〉・stroke〈划法〉・kicking〈kick（踢）的 ing 型態〉
❺ practicing〈practice（練習）的 ing 型態〉・under〈在…下面〉・minute〈分鐘〉
❻ synchronized〈同步的、步驟一致的〉・require〈需要〉・dedication〈專心致力〉
❼ keeping〈keep（保持某狀態）的 ing 型態〉・public〈公共的〉・clean〈乾淨的〉

中譯

❶ Jared 慢跑前，都會暖身腿部肌肉。
❷ Scott 得知他錄取跳水隊時，非常興奮。
❸ 如果你要學游自由式，你需要練習打水。
❹ 游泳時，正確的划水動作和正確的踢水動作一樣重要。
❺ 練習了幾週之後，Missy 可以在水裡憋氣兩分鐘。
❻ 水上芭蕾很美，但是需要非常專注並控制呼吸。
❼ 要讓公共游泳池保持乾淨，需要大量的池水消毒劑。

165

競
選
(1)

MP3 165

1 candidate
['kændədet]
(n.) 候選人

2 party
['partɪ]
(n.) 政黨

3 staff
[stæf]
(n.) 幕僚

4 slogan
['slogən]
(n.) 競選口號

5 advertisement
[͵ædvɚ'taɪzmənt]
(n.) 競選文宣

6 campaign van
[kæm'pen væn]
(n.) 競選宣傳車

7 campaign commercial
[kæm'pen kə'mɝʃəl]
(n.) 競選廣告

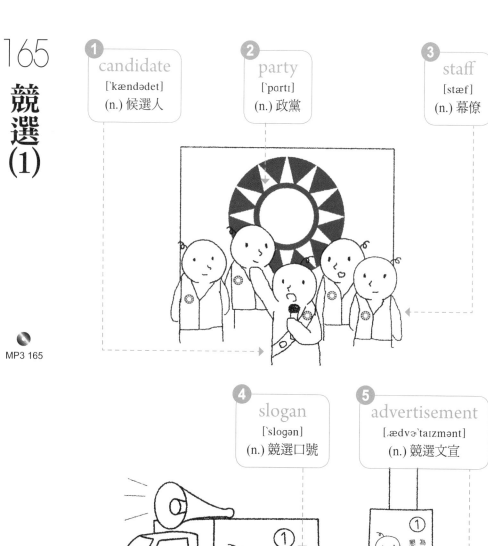

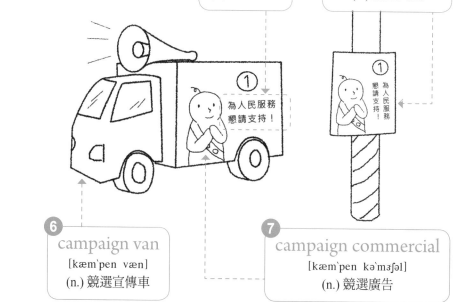

❶ 候選人
There are three candidates in this year's presidential election.
總統選舉

❷ 政黨
Barack Obama is a member of the US Democratic Party.
民主黨

❸ 幕僚
I was given the chance to be on the president's staff, but I didn't want to
我曾經被給予機會
work for him.

❹ 競選口號
A slogan is a short phrase that should be easy to remember.

❺ 競選文宣
The advertisement showed the president giving the thumbs-up sign.
總統比大拇指的手勢

❻ 競選宣傳車
The candidate's voice was played from the campaign van as it drove around
聲音被播放   在市區穿梭行駛
the city.

❼ 競選廣告
The campaign commercial on TV last night showed the president talking
about his achievements.   總統談論他的政績

學更多

❶ presidential〈總統的〉・election〈選舉〉
❷ member〈成員〉・democratic〈民主的〉
❸ given〈give（給予）的過去分詞〉・chance〈機會〉・president〈總統〉・work〈工作〉
❹ short〈短的〉・phrase〈話語〉・easy〈容易的〉・remember〈記得〉
❺ showed〈show（展示）的過去式〉・thumbs-up〈翹拇指〉・sign〈手勢〉
❻ campaign〈競選活動〉・van〈箱型車〉・drove〈drive（駕駛）的過去式〉
❼ commercial〈廣告〉・talking〈talk（談論）的 ing 型態〉・achievement〈成績〉

中譯

❶ 今年的總統大選，有三位候選人。
❷ Barack Obama 是美國民主黨的成員之一。
❸ 我曾經有機會成為總統的幕僚，但是我並不想替他工作。
❹ 競選口號應該是一句讓人容易記得的簡短話語。
❺ 競選文宣上印著總統比出大拇指的手勢。
❻ 競選宣傳車在市區穿梭時，播放著候選人的聲音。
❼ 昨晚的電視競選廣告中，出現了總統談論政績的內容。

166

競選(2)

MP3 166

1 political donation
[pə'lɪtɪkl̩ do'neʃən]
(n.) 政治獻金

2 scandal
['skændl̩]
(n.) 醜聞

3 bribery
['braɪbərɪ]
(n.) 賄選

4 smear campaign
[smɪr kæm'pen]
(n.) 黑函

5 announce one's policy
[ə'naʊns wʌns 'pɑləsɪ]
(phr.) 發表政見/宣布政策

6 poll
[pol]
(n.) 民調

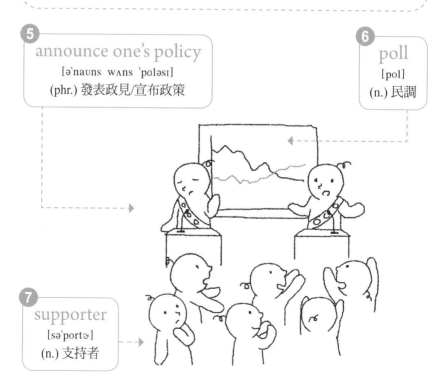

7 supporter
[sə'portɚ]
(n.) 支持者

❶ 政治獻金

The businesswoman made a political donation to help fund her favorite party's election campaign.
幫助她支持的政黨作為選舉競選資金

❷ 醜聞

Stories have come out suggesting that the candidate was speeding last
有一些傳言暗指…

week, and the scandal could finish him.
可能毀滅他

❸ 賄選

The politician was accused of bribery, but he denies giving anyone any money.
被指控賄選

❹ 黑函

The smear campaign was designed to let the opposition look bad.
讓對手難堪

❺ 發表政見 / 宣布政策

The president held a meeting to announce his policies.

❻ 民調

All the polls suggest that the opposition party will win the election.
所有的民調顯示

❼ 支持者

I'm a supporter of that party. I'll vote for its candidate.

學更多

❶ political〈政治的〉‧ donation〈捐獻〉‧ fund〈提供資金〉‧ election〈選舉〉
❷ come out〈come out（傳出）的過去分詞〉‧ suggesting〈suggest（暗示）的 ing 型態〉
❸ politician〈政治人物〉‧ accused〈accuse（控告）的過去分詞〉‧ deny〈否認〉
❹ smear〈誹謗〉‧ designed〈design（設計）的過去分詞〉‧ opposition〈對手〉
❺ held〈hold（舉行）的過去式〉‧ announce〈宣布〉‧ policy〈政策〉
❻ all〈所有的〉‧ suggest〈顯示〉‧ opposition party〈反對黨〉‧ win〈贏〉
❼ party〈政黨〉‧ vote〈投票〉‧ candidate〈候選人〉

中譯

❶ 女商人提供一筆政治獻金，幫助她支持的政黨作為選舉競選資金。
❷ 有些傳言暗指那名候選人上週開車超速，這個醜聞可能會毀滅他。
❸ 那名政治人物被指控賄選，但他否認有給任何人錢。
❹ 製造黑函是為了讓對手難堪。
❺ 總統召開會議宣布他的政策。
❻ 所有的民調都顯示，反對黨將贏得選戰。
❼ 我是那個政黨的支持者，我會投票給他們的候選人。

167

投票(1)

MP3 167

1 suffrage
[ˋsʌfrɪdʒ]
(n.) 投票權

2 swing voters
[swɪŋ ˋvotɚz]
(n.) 中間選民

3 ballot
[ˋbælət]
(n.) 選票/投票

4 voting booth
[ˋvotɪŋ buθ]
(n.) 投票亭

5 ballot box
[ˋbælət bɑks]
(n.) 投票箱

6 secret ballot
[ˋsikrɪt ˋbælət]
(n.) 不記名投票

投票時，選舉人不在選票上簽寫自己的姓名。

7 display one's ballot
[dɪˋsple wʌns ˋbælət]
(phr.) 亮票

公開出示投票結果的違法行為。

（選票放大圖）

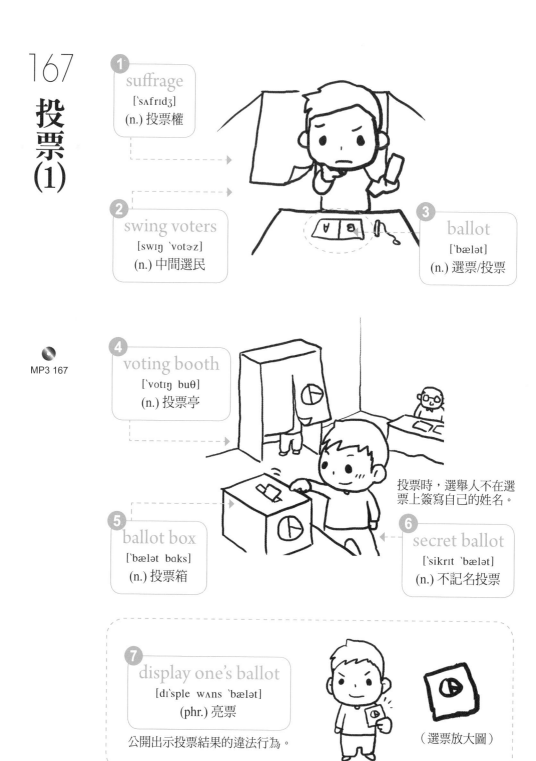

❶ 投票權

Saudi Arabian women were granted suffrage in 2011, and they're
沙烏地阿拉伯的女人

excited about being able to vote.

❷ 中間選民

The swing voters haven't decided who to support yet.

❸ 選票 / 投票

The 10 names on the ballot represent the 10 different candidates.
代表 10 位不同的候選人

❹ 投票亭

Step inside the voting booth so that people can't see who you vote for.
走進投票亭

❺ 投票箱

After you've marked the ballot paper, drop it into the ballot box.
你在選票上做記號

❻ 不記名投票

This is a secret ballot; no one will know who you voted for.

❼ 亮票

After voting, Neil displayed his ballot for people to see.

學更多

❶ Saudi Arabian〈沙烏地阿拉伯的〉・granted〈grant（授予）的過去分詞〉・excited〈興奮的〉
❷ swing〈搖動〉・voter〈選舉人〉・decided〈decide（決定）的過去分詞〉・support〈支持〉
❸ name〈名字〉・represent〈代表〉・different〈不同的〉・candidate〈候選人〉
❹ step〈走〉・inside〈往裡面〉・booth〈投票站〉・see〈看〉・vote〈投票〉
❺ marked〈mark（做記號）的過去分詞〉・ballot paper〈選票紙張〉・drop〈投〉
❻ secret〈祕密的〉・no one〈沒有人〉・know〈知道〉
❼ after〈在…之後〉・voting〈vote（投票）的 ing 型態〉・displayed〈display（顯露）的過去式〉

中譯

❶ 沙烏地阿拉伯的女性在 2011 年被賦予投票權，能夠投票令她們感到很興奮。
❷ 中間選民還沒有決定要支持誰。
❸ 選票上的十個名字，代表十位不同的候選人。
❹ 走進投票亭，這樣別人就看不到你投給誰。
❺ 你在選票上蓋上記號後，就將它投入投票箱。
❻ 這是一個不記名投票，沒有人會知道你投給誰。
❼ 投票後，Neil 亮票給其他人看。

168

投票(2)

MP3 168

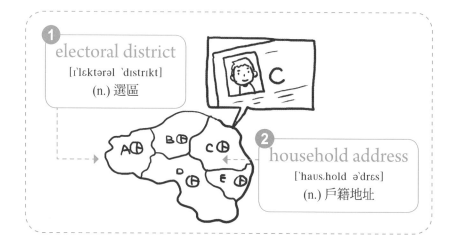

1 electoral district
[ɪˋlɛktərəl ˋdɪstrɪkt]
(n.) 選區

2 household address
[ˋhaʊsˏhold əˋdrɛs]
(n.) 戶籍地址

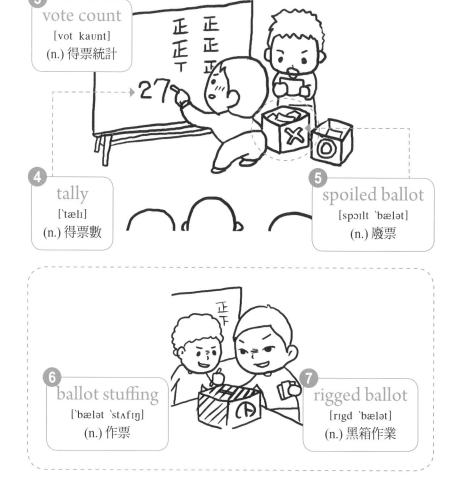

3 vote count
[vot kaʊnt]
(n.) 得票統計

4 tally
[ˋtælɪ]
(n.) 得票數

5 spoiled ballot
[spɔɪlt ˋbælət]
(n.) 廢票

6 ballot stuffing
[ˋbælət ˋstʌfɪŋ]
(n.) 作票

7 rigged ballot
[rɪgd ˋbælət]
(n.) 黑箱作業

❶ 選區

This city is split into two electoral districts.
<u>被劃分為兩個選區</u>

❷ 戶籍地址

I need to send something to you. What's your household address?

❸ 得票統計

My candidate had a vote count of 10,895.

❹ 得票數

About half the votes have been counted, and the current tally shows
<u>大約半數的選票已經被計算</u>

that the president is leading.

❺ 廢票

The angry voter turned in a spoiled ballot after he expressed his disgust with

the candidates by drawing a big line across it.　表達他對候選人的厭惡
<u>畫一條粗線穿過它</u>

❻ 作票

Ballot stuffing involves putting fake ballots into the ballot box.

❼ 黑箱作業

People believe this was a rigged ballot; they think the results were decided

before the vote began.　結果被決定了

學更多

❶ city〈城市〉• split〈spilt（劃分）的過去分詞〉• electoral〈選舉的〉• district〈區域〉
❷ send〈寄〉• something〈某些東西〉• household〈家庭的〉• address〈地址〉
❸ candidate〈候選人〉• vote〈選票〉• count〈總數〉
❹ counted〈count（統計）的過去分詞〉• current〈目前的〉• leading〈領先的〉
❺ turned in〈turn in（交出）的過去式〉• spoiled〈作廢的〉• disgust〈厭惡〉• across〈穿過〉
❻ ballot〈選票〉• stuffing〈填充物〉• involve〈包括〉• fake〈假的〉
❼ believe〈相信〉• rigged〈作弊的〉• result〈結果〉• began〈begin（開始）的過去式〉

中譯

❶ 這個城市被劃分為兩個選區。
❷ 我要寄東西給你，你的戶籍地址是哪裡？
❸ 我所支持的候選人得票統計是 10,859 票。
❹ 大約一半的選票都已經計算完成，目前的得票數顯示總統領先。
❺ 那位憤怒的選民在選票上候選人的地方，畫過一條粗線表達厭惡之後，便投了一張
　 廢票出去。
❻ 作票包括了將偽造的選票放入投票箱。
❼ 人們相信這是一個黑箱作業，他們認為投票開始前就已經內定好結果。

169

離婚 (1)

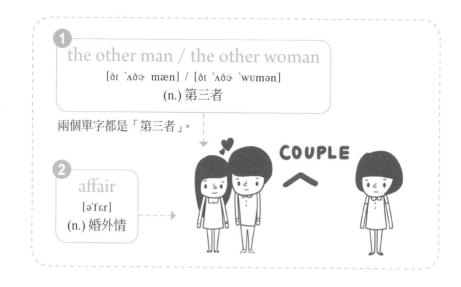

① the other man / the other woman
[ðɪ `ʌðɚ mæn] / [ðɪ `ʌðɚ `wumən]
(n.) 第三者

兩個單字都是「第三者」。

② affair
[ə`fɛr]
(n.) 婚外情

MP3 169

③ separation
[ˌsɛpə`reʃən]
(n.) 分居

④ lawyer
[`lɔjɚ]
(n.) 律師

⑤ law firm
[lɔ fɝm]
(n.) 律師事務所

⑥ uncontested divorce
[ʌnkən`tɛstɪd də`vors]
(n.) 協議離婚

❶ 第三者

That's not Neil's wife, that's the other woman.

❷ 婚外情

Tom's having an affair with a woman from his office.

❸ 分居

After a period of separation, the husband and wife decided to file for a divorce.
　　　　　　　　　　　　　　　　　　　　　　　　　　　決定提出離婚

❹ 律師

The lawyer argued my case in court.

❺ 律師事務所

This law firm specializes in criminal law.
　　　　　　　　　　　　專攻刑法

❻ 協議離婚

Uncontested divorces are settled more quickly because there are no big
　　　　　　協議離婚較快被解決

disagreements.

學更多

❶ wife〈太太〉・man〈男人〉・woman〈女人〉

❷ having〈have（有）的 ing 型態〉・office〈辦公室〉

❸ period〈期間〉・husband〈丈夫〉・file〈提出〉・divorce〈離婚〉

❹ argued〈argue（辯論）的過去式〉・case〈案件〉・court〈法庭〉

❺ law〈法律〉・firm〈公司〉・specialize〈專攻〉・criminal law〈刑法〉

❻ uncontested〈無爭議的〉・settled〈settle（解決）的過去分詞〉・quickly〈迅速地〉・
disagreement〈歧見〉

中譯

❶ 那不是 Neil 的太太，那是第三者。

❷ Tom 和他辦公室的一個女人，有了婚外情，

❸ 在分居一段時間後，丈夫和妻子決定訴請離婚。

❹ 律師在法庭上替我的案子辯論。

❺ 這間律師事務所專攻刑事案件。

❻ 協議離婚都能較快解決，因為沒有太大的歧見。

170

離婚(2)

MP3 170

1 distribution of property
[ˌdɪstrəˈbjuʃən ɑv ˈprɑpətɪ]
(n.) 財產分配

2 alimony
[ˈæləˌmonɪ]
(n.) 贍養費

3 child custody
[tʃaɪld ˈkʌstədɪ]
(n.) 監護權

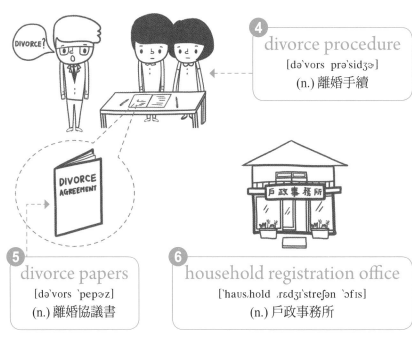

DIVORCE?

DIVORCE AGREEMENT

4 divorce procedure
[dəˈvors prəˈsidʒɚ]
(n.) 離婚手續

5 divorce papers
[dəˈvors ˈpepɚz]
(n.) 離婚協議書

6 household registration office
[ˈhausˌhold ˌrɛdʒɪˈstreʃən ˈɔfɪs]
(n.) 戶政事務所

❶ 財產分配

As part of their divorce, the couple argued over the distribution of their property. They both wanted to keep their car. 爭論他們的財產分配

❷ 贍養費

The man was ordered to pay his ex-wife NT$20,000 a month in alimony.
被命令要支付…

❸ 監護權

The child custody battle will be difficult, as both parents want to keep
監護權之爭

their child.

❹ 離婚手續

The divorce procedure is very complicated in some countries and it can take people a long time to separate.
為了分開可能會花上人們很長時間

❺ 離婚協議書

My wife's lawyers sent me divorce papers last week. She really does want to leave me.

❻ 戶政事務所

In Taiwan, divorces have to be registered at the household registration office.
離婚必須被登記

學更多

❶ divorce〈離婚〉・couple〈夫妻〉・argued over〈argue over（為某事爭執）的過去式〉・distribution〈分配〉・property〈財產〉・both〈兩個都…〉

❷ ordered〈order（命令）的過去分詞〉・pay〈支付〉・ex-wife〈前妻〉

❸ custody〈監護權〉・battle〈鬥爭〉・difficult〈困難的〉・as〈因為〉・keep〈留住〉

❹ procedure〈手續〉・complicated〈複雜的〉・country〈國家〉・separate〈分離〉

❺ wife〈太太〉・sent〈send（寄）的過去式〉・papers〈文件〉・leave〈離開〉

❻ registered〈register（登記）的過去分詞〉・household〈家庭的〉・registration〈登記〉

中譯

❶ 在離婚過程中，這對夫妻對財產分配爭論不休，他們都想要保有車子。

❷ 這男人被判決，必須支付前妻每個月兩萬元台幣的贍養費。

❸ 監護權之爭將會很辛苦，因為父母雙方都想保有孩子。

❹ 在某些國家，離婚手續非常複雜，可能需要很長的時間人們才能分開。

❺ 我太太的律師上週寄給我離婚協議書，她真的很想離開我。

❻ 在台灣，離婚必須在戶政事務所辦理登記。

171

親子關係(1)

🔊 MP3 171

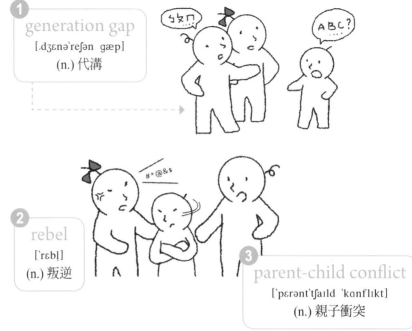

1 generation gap
[ˌdʒɛnəˈreʃən gæp]
(n.) 代溝

2 rebel
[ˈrɛbl̩]
(n.) 叛逆

3 parent-child conflict
[ˈpɛrəntˈtʃaɪld ˈkɑnflɪkt]
(n.) 親子衝突

4 intimate
[ˈɪntəmɪt]
(adj.) 親密

5 distant
[ˈdɪstənt]
(adj.) 疏離

6 family atmosphere
[ˈfæməlɪ ˈætməs.fɪr]
(n.) 家庭氣氛

356

❶ 代溝

The generation gap was difficult for the boy and his grandfather to overcome, and they sat together in silence.
他們沉默地坐在一起

❷ 叛逆

Since she turned 13, Iris has become a bit of a rebel, and she enjoys
Iris 變得有點兒叛逆
doing things that upset her parents.

❸ 親子衝突

Low grades are a common source of parent-child conflicts.
親子衝突常見的起因

❹ 親密

The two sisters are sitting in the corner having an intimate conversation.
親密的交談

❺ 疏離

Don has a very distant relationship with his parents. They rarely communicate.

❻ 家庭氣氛

The family atmosphere in Susan's house is good. They're a close family.

學更多

❶ generation〈世代〉・gap〈隔閡〉・difficult〈困難的〉・grandfather〈祖父〉・overcome〈克服〉・sat〈sit（坐）的過去式〉・silence〈沉默〉

❷ since〈自從〉・turned〈turn（變成）的過去式〉・a bit of a〈有點兒〉・upset〈使生氣〉

❸ low〈低的〉・grade〈成績〉・common〈常見的〉・source〈起因〉・conflict〈衝突〉

❹ sitting〈sit（坐）的 ing 型態〉・corner〈角落〉・conversation〈交談〉

❺ relationship〈關係〉・rarely〈很少〉・communicate〈溝通〉

❻ family〈家庭〉・atmosphere〈氣氛〉・close〈親近的〉

中譯

❶ 那個男孩和祖父之間很難克服彼此的代溝，他們沉默地坐在一起。

❷ 自從 Iris 十三歲之後，她變得有點兒叛逆，她喜歡做惹父母親生氣的事。

❸ 成績不佳是親子衝突常見的起因。

❹ 兩姊妹正坐在角落親密的交談著。

❺ Don 和父母親的關係很疏離，他們很少溝通。

❻ Susan 的家庭氣氛很好，他們一家人非常親近。

172

親子關係(2)

MP3 172

1 communication
[kə͵mjunə`keʃən]
(n.) 溝通

2 interaction
[͵ɪntə`rækʃən]
(n.) 互動

3 trusted
[`trʌstɪd]
(adj.) 信賴的/可靠的

4 filial piety
[`fɪljəl `paɪətɪ]
(n.) 孝道

5 education
[͵ɛdʒʊ`keʃən]
(n.) 教育

6 spoiled
[spɔɪlt]
(adj.) 受寵

7 only child
[`onlɪ tʃaɪld]
(n.) 獨生子女

❶ 溝通

Communication between the boy and his father is bad; they rarely speak.

❷ 互動

Tom has great interaction with his students. He chats with them all the time.

良好的互動

❸ 信賴的 / 可靠的

Chris is a trusted friend. He's helped me out several times in the past.

他已經幫過我好幾次

❹ 孝道

Confucius taught that filial piety, or respecting your parents, is very important.

孔子教導大家⋯　　　　　也就是説

❺ 教育

Mr. Davies wants his son to have a good education, so he sent him to a good school.

❻ 受寵

Josh is very spoiled; he gets everything he wants.

得到一切他想要的

❼ 獨生子女

Gina is an only child; she doesn't have any brothers or sisters.

她沒有任何兄弟姊妹

學更多

❶ between〈在⋯之間〉‧ rarely〈很少地〉‧ speak〈說話〉

❷ great〈極好的〉‧ student〈學生〉‧ chat〈聊天〉‧ all the time〈一直〉

❸ helped out〈help out（幫助⋯擺脫困難）的過去式〉‧ several times〈好幾次〉

❹ filial〈子女的〉‧ piety〈孝順〉‧ respecting〈respect（尊重）的 ing 型態〉

❺ sent〈send（使進入）的過去式〉‧ school〈學校〉

❻ get〈得到〉‧ everything〈一切事物〉

❼ only〈唯一的〉‧ child〈小孩〉‧ brother〈兄弟〉‧ sister〈姊妹〉

中譯

❶ 男孩和父親之間溝通不良，他們很少和對方說話。

❷ Tom 和學生有良好的互動，他經常和他們聊天。

❸ Chris 是一個可靠的朋友，過去他幫過我好幾次。

❹ 孔子教導大家：孝道——也就是尊重父母，是非常重要的。

❺ Davies 先生希望兒子接受良好的教育，所以把他送進一所好學校。

❻ Josh 非常受寵，他得到一切他想要的。

❼ Gina 是獨生女，她沒有任何兄弟姊妹。

173

國家&政治(1)

MP3 173

1 territorial water
[ˌtɛrəˈtorɪəl ˈwɔtə]
(n.) 領海

2 territory
[ˈtɛrəˌtorɪ]
(n.) 領土

3 people
[ˈpipl̩]
(n.) 人民

4 constitution
[ˌkɑnstəˈtjuʃən]
(n.) 憲法

5 law
[lɔ]
(n.) 法律

❶ 領海

The US was unhappy when a foreign warship sailed into its territorial waters.
一艘外國的艦艇駛入

❷ 領土

Puerto Rico is an official territory of the United States.
法定的領土

❸ 人民

The people in this country are usually very friendly.

❹ 憲法

The constitution contains a list of rules that a country's leaders should follow.
一個國家的領袖應該遵守的條例清單

❺ 法律

In Taiwan, it is against the law for 16-year-olds to drive.
這是違法的

學更多

❶ unhappy〈不滿的〉‧ foreign〈外國的〉‧ warship〈艦艇〉‧
   sailed〈sail（航行）的過去式〉‧ territorial〈領土的〉‧ water〈海域〉
❷ Puerto Rico〈波多黎各〉‧ official〈法定的〉‧ the United States〈美國〉
❸ country〈國家〉‧ usually〈通常〉‧ friendly〈友善的〉
❹ contain〈包含〉‧ a list of...〈一份…的清單〉‧ rule〈條例〉‧ leader〈領袖〉‧
   follow〈遵循〉
❺ against〈違反〉‧ drive〈駕駛〉

中譯

❶ 當一艘外國艦艇駛入美國領海時，美國相當不滿。
❷ 波多黎各是美國法定的領土。
❸ 這個國家的人民大多都很友善。
❹ 憲法包含一個國家的領袖應該遵守的條例清單。
❺ 在台灣，十六歲開車是違法的。

174

國家&政治(2)

MP3 174

1 change in the ruling party
[tʃendʒ ɪn ðə ˈrulɪŋ ˈpɑrtɪ]
(phr.) 政黨輪替

2 ruling party
[ˈrulɪŋ ˈpɑrtɪ]
(n.) 執政黨

3 opposition party
[ˌɑpəˈzɪʃən ˈpɑrtɪ]
(n.) 在野黨

4 dominant-party system
[ˈdɑmənəntˈpɑrtɪ ˈsɪstəm]
(n.) 一黨獨大

5 president
[ˈprɛzədənt]
(n.) 總統

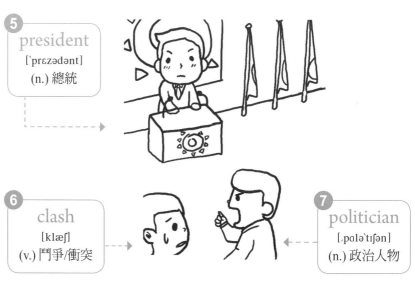

6 clash
[klæʃ]
(v.) 鬥爭/衝突

7 politician
[ˌpɑləˈtɪʃən]
(n.) 政治人物

❶ 政黨輪替

The opposition won the election, so there will be a change in the ruling party.
  在野黨贏得選舉

❷ 執政黨

The ruling party has been in government for over four years.
                          已經執政超過四年

❸ 在野黨

The opposition party criticized the government's ideas.

❹ 一黨獨大

In a dominant-party system, one party is expected to win nearly all elections.
                            某一個政黨被預期

❺ 總統

Barack Obama was elected president of the US in 2008.
                          被選為總統

❻ 鬥爭 / 衝突

The two parties clashed over their plans for the country.

❼ 政治人物

The boy wants to be a politician when he grows up. He wants to help run the country.
     管理國家

學更多

❶ opposition〈反對〉・won〈win（贏）的過去式〉・election〈選舉〉・ruling〈統治的〉
❷ party〈政黨〉・government〈政府〉・over〈超過〉
❸ criticized〈criticize（批評）的過去式〉・idea〈計劃〉
❹ dominant〈佔優勢的〉・expected〈expect（預期）的過去分詞〉・nearly〈幾乎〉
❺ elected〈elect（選舉）的過去分詞〉・the US〈美國〉
❻ clashed〈clash（鬥爭、衝突）的過去式〉・plan〈計劃、方案〉・country〈國家〉
❼ grow up〈長大〉・run〈管理〉

中譯

❶ 在野黨贏得了選舉，所以將會政黨輪替。
❷ 執政黨已經執政超過四年。
❸ 在野黨批評政府的計劃。
❹ 在一黨獨大的情況下，某一個政黨被預期幾乎會贏得所有選舉。
❺ 2008 年，Barack Obama 當選美國總統。
❻ 兩個政黨在各自的國家方案上產生衝突。
❼ 那個男孩長大後想成為政治人物，他想要幫忙管理國家。

175

犯罪行為 (1)

MP3 175

1 kidnapping
[ˈkɪdnæpɪŋ]
(n.) 綁架

2 ransom
[ˈrænsəm]
(n.) 贖金

3 kidnapper
[ˈkɪdnæpɚ]
(n.) 綁匪

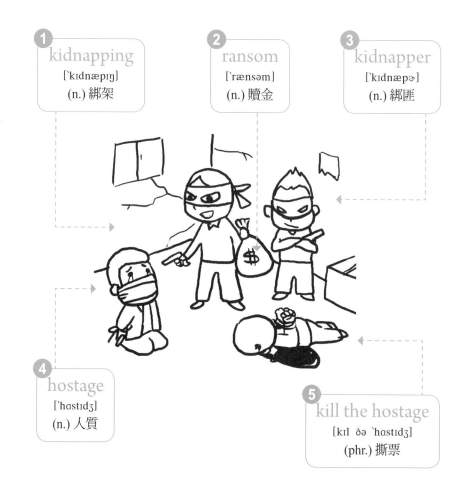

4 hostage
[ˈhɑstɪdʒ]
(n.) 人質

5 kill the hostage
[kɪl ðə ˈhɑstɪdʒ]
(phr.) 撕票

6 robbery
[ˈrɑbərɪ]
(n.) 搶劫

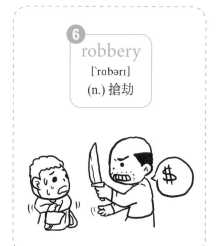

7 rape
[rep]
(n.) 強暴

❶ 綁架

Kidnapping is considered a serious offense.
　　　　　　被視為

❷ 贖金

Kidnappers demanded a ransom of NT$30 million.
　　　　　　　　　　　　　三千萬台幣

❸ 綁匪

Two kidnappers were caught by the police last night.
　　　　　　　　被警方逮捕

❹ 人質

Three hostages were taken captive when a bank was robbed yesterday.
　　　　　　　被俘虜、被挾持　　　　　一間銀行被搶

❺ 撕票

The bank robbers killed the hostages before the police could rescue them.
　　　　　　　　　　　　　　　　　在警察能拯救他們之前

❻ 搶劫

Mike served over 10 years in prison for armed robbery.
　　入監服刑超過 10 年

❼ 強暴

Rape is one of the most violent crimes possible against another human being.
　　　　　　　　　　　　　　　　　　　　　對另外一個人

❶ considered〈consider（視為）的過去分詞〉‧ serious〈嚴重的〉‧ offense〈罪行〉

❷ demanded〈demand（要求）的過去式〉‧ million〈百萬〉

❸ caught〈catch（逮捕）的過去分詞〉‧ police〈警察〉‧ last night〈昨天晚上〉

❹ taken〈take（抓）的過去分詞〉‧ captive〈被俘的〉‧ robbed〈rob（搶劫）的過去分詞〉

❺ robber〈搶匪〉‧ killed〈kill（殺死）的過去式〉‧ rescue〈拯救〉

❻ served〈serve（服刑）的過去式〉‧ over〈超過〉‧ prison〈監獄〉‧ armed〈武裝的〉

❼ violent〈暴力的〉‧ crime〈罪行〉‧ against〈對於、不利於〉‧ human being〈人〉

中譯

❶ 綁架被視為一種嚴重的犯罪行為。

❷ 綁匪要求三千萬台幣的贖金。

❸ 兩名綁匪昨晚被警方逮捕。

❹ 在昨天的銀行搶案中，三名人質遭到挾持。

❺ 在警方拯救之前，銀行搶匪已經將人質撕票。

❻ Mike 因為武裝搶劫而入監服刑 10 多年。

❼ 強暴可能是對他人最暴力的一種犯罪行為。

176

犯罪行為(2)

MP3 176

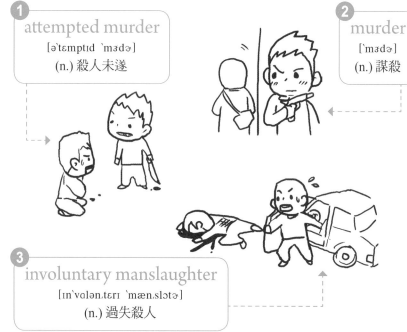

1 attempted murder
[ə`tɛmptɪd `mɝdə]
(n.) 殺人未遂

2 murder
[`mɝdə]
(n.) 謀殺

3 involuntary manslaughter
[ɪn`vɑləntɛrɪ `mænˌslɔtə]
(n.) 過失殺人

4 suspect
[`səspɛkt]
(n.) 嫌犯

5 accomplice
[ə`kɑmplɪs]
(n.) 共犯

兩個單字都是
「逃亡」。

6 on the run / flee
[ɑn ðə rʌn] / [fli]
(phr.) / (v.) 逃亡

7 wanted poster
[`wɑntɪd `postə]
(n.) 通緝海報

❶ 殺人未遂

He was charged with attempted murder after he almost beat a man to death.

他依殺人未遂被起訴

❷ 謀殺

There was a murder last night at the local convenience store during a robbery.

在當地的便利商店

❸ 過失殺人

Luke was charged with involuntary manslaughter after he ran down a man crossing the street while driving drunk.

他撞倒一位正在過馬路的男子

酒駕

❹ 嫌犯

The suspect was arrested by police after fleeing the crime scene.

嫌犯被警方逮捕

❺ 共犯

The murder suspect told the police his accomplice's name.

謀殺案的嫌犯

❻ 逃亡

After a prisoner broke out of prison, he was on the run from police for a

一名囚犯逃獄後

month before being caught.

❼ 通緝海報

Wanted posters of dangerous criminals are often put up in public areas, like post offices.

經常被張貼在公共場所

學更多

❶ charged〈charge（控告）的過去分詞〉 • attempted〈未遂的〉 • beat〈beat（打）的過去式〉
❷ local〈當地的〉 • convenience store〈便利商店〉 • during〈在⋯期間〉 • robbery〈搶劫〉
❸ involuntary〈非故意的〉 • manslaughter〈殺人〉 • ran down〈run down（撞倒）的過去式〉
❹ arrested〈arrest（逮捕）的過去分詞〉 • fleeing〈flee（逃亡）的 ing 型態〉 • scene〈現場〉
❺ told〈tell（告訴）的過去式〉 • name〈名字〉
❻ prisoner〈囚犯〉 • broke out〈break out（逃出）的過去式〉 • prison〈監獄〉
❼ wanted〈被通緝的〉 • criminal〈罪犯〉 • put up〈put up（張貼）的過去分詞〉

中譯

❶ 在他幾乎將一名男子毆打致死之後，被依殺人未遂起訴。
❷ 昨晚在當地的便利商店發生了搶劫謀殺案。
❸ 當 Luke 酒駕撞倒一名正在過馬路的男子後，被依過失殺人起訴。
❹ 嫌犯逃離犯罪現場後，就遭到警方逮捕。
❺ 謀殺案的嫌犯告訴警方共犯的名字。
❻ 一名囚犯逃獄後，逃亡了一個月才被警方抓到。
❼ 危險罪犯的通緝海報經常被張貼在公共場所，像是郵局。

177

社會福利 (1)

MP3 177

1 volunteer
[ˌvɑlənˈtɪr]
(n.) 志工

在公共、志願團體內，不受報酬貢獻心力的人。

具備專業知識及訓練，協助特定對象改善生活的社會工作人員。

2 social worker
[ˈsoʃəl ˈwɝkɚ]
(n.) 社工

3 subsidy
[ˈsʌbsədɪ]
(n.) 補助

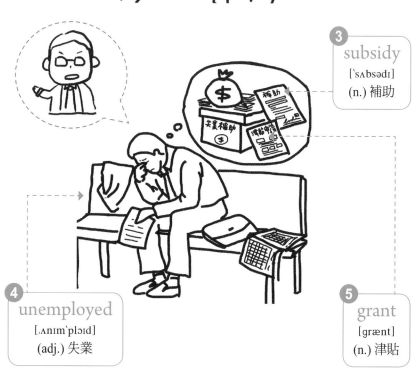

4 unemployed
[ˌʌnɪmˈplɔɪd]
(adj.) 失業

5 grant
[grænt]
(n.) 津貼

❶ 志工
Volunteers donate their time and talents to help the less fortunate.
<u>不幸的人們</u>

❷ 社工
Jenny wanted to help children, so she decided to become a social worker.

❸ 補助
New York City provides a housing subsidy to the poor.
提供住宅補貼

❹ 失業
Charlotte has been unemployed since last year.

❺ 津貼
Many governments offer school grants to students needing financial aid.
就學津貼　　　　　　　　　　需要經濟援助的學生

❶ donate〈捐贈〉‧ talent〈才能〉‧ less〈較少的〉‧ fortunate〈幸運的〉
❷ decided〈decide（決定）的過去式〉‧ become〈成為〉‧ social〈社會的〉‧
worker〈工作者〉
❸ provide〈提供〉‧ housing〈住宅〉‧ the poor〈窮人〉
❹ since〈從…至今〉‧ last year〈去年〉
❺ government〈政府〉‧ offer〈提供〉‧ financial〈財務的〉‧ aid〈援助〉

❶ 志工奉獻他們的時間和技能,幫助不幸的人們。
❷ Jenny 想要幫助孩童,所以她決定要成為一名社工。
❸ 紐約市會提供住宅補助給貧困的人。
❹ Charlotte 從去年失業至今。
❺ 許多政府會提供就學津貼給需要經濟援助的學生。

178

社會福利(2)

MP3 178

1 donation
[doˋneʃən]
(n.) 捐款

2 fundraising
[ˋfʌnd͵rezɪŋ]
(n.) 募款

3 homeless person
[ˋhomlɪs ˋpɝsn̩]
the homeless
[ðə ˋhomlɪs]
(n.) 遊民

4 disadvantaged groups
[͵dɪsədˋvæntɪdʒd grups]
(n.) 弱勢族群

兩個單字都是「遊民」。
「homeless person」的複數
是「homeless people」。

5 charitable act
[ˋtʃærətəbl̩ ækt]
(n.) 公益行為

6 public service activity
[ˋpʌblɪk ˋsɝvɪs ækˋtɪvətɪ]
(n.) 公眾服務活動

❶ 捐款

Would you like to make a donation to the Red Cross?
　　　　　　　　　　　　捐款

❷ 募款

Without fundraising, it's impossible to keep a charitable organization
functioning.
　　　　　　　　　　　　　讓慈善機構繼續運作

❸ 遊民

Many homeless people are actually war veterans.

❹ 弱勢族群

It's important that nations take care of their disadvantaged groups like
the blind.
　　　　　　　　　　　國家照顧他們的弱勢族群

❺ 公益行為

One charitable act that is relatively easy to do is to donate blood.
　　　　　　　　　　　相對容易去做

❻ 公眾服務活動

Providing free flu shots each year to the elderly is a great public service
提供免費注射流感疫苗　　　　　　　　老年人
activity.

學更多

❶ make〈做〉・Red Cross〈紅十字會〉
❷ without〈沒有〉・impossible〈不可能的〉・charitable〈慈善的〉・
organization〈組織、機構〉・functioning〈function（運作）的的 ing 型態〉
❸ homeless〈無家可歸的〉・actually〈實際上〉・war〈戰爭〉・veteran〈退役軍人〉
❹ nation〈國家〉・take care of〈照顧〉・disadvantaged〈弱勢的〉・the blind〈盲人〉
❺ relatively〈相對地〉・easy〈簡單的〉・donate〈捐獻〉・blood〈血液〉
❻ providing〈provide（提供）的 ing 型態〉・flu〈流行性感冒〉・shot〈注射〉

中譯

❶ 你想要捐款給紅十字會嗎？
❷ 沒有募款，慈善機構不可能持續運作。
❸ 許多遊民其實都是退伍的老兵。
❹ 國家對於弱勢族群——例如盲胞的照顧，是很重要的。
❺ 捐血是一項相對容易做的公益行為。
❻ 每年提供免費的流感疫苗給老年人，是一項很好的公眾服務活動。

179

借貸(1)

1 lend money
[lɛnd `mʌnɪ]
(phr.) 借（出）錢

2 borrow money
[`bɑro `mʌnɪ]
(phr.) 借（入）錢

MP3 179

「IOU」源自「I owe you」（我欠你錢）。

3 IOU
[`aɪoˋju]
(n.) 借據

4 guarantor
[`gærəntɚ]
(n.) 保證人

5 deadline
[`dɛd.laɪn]
(n.) 期限

6 return
[rɪˋtɚn]
(v.) 歸還

❶ 借（出）錢

My friend asked me to lend him some money. He wants NT$10,000.

❷ 借（入）錢

I borrowed some money from my dad last month when I couldn't pay my bills.
<small>無法支付我的帳單</small>

❸ 借據

After borrowing NT$1,000 from Sally, I gave her an IOU.

❹ 保證人

My dad is the guarantor on my loan. He'll have to pay back the money if I can't.
<small>我的貸款保證人　　　　　　　　　　　　　　　　還這筆錢</small>

❺ 期限

The deadline for this assignment is tomorrow. I have to finish it tonight.
<small>這份工作的期限</small>

❻ 歸還

I need to return some books to the library. I've already had them for a week.
<small>我已經取得它們一個禮拜了</small>

學更多

❶ asked〈ask（請求）的過去式〉・lend〈借出〉

❷ borrowed〈borrow（借入）的過去式〉・pay〈支付〉・bill〈帳單〉

❸ borrowing〈borrow（借入）的 ing 型態〉・gave〈give（給予）的過去式〉

❹ loan〈貸款〉・have to〈必須〉・pay back〈償還〉

❺ assignment〈任務、工作〉・finish〈完成〉

❻ library〈圖書館〉・already〈已經〉・had〈have（擁有、取得）的過去分詞〉

中譯

❶ 朋友要求我借他一些錢，他需要一萬元台幣。

❷ 上個月我無法支付帳單時，向父親借了一些錢。

❸ 向 Sally 借了一千元台幣之後，我給了她一張借據。

❹ 父親是我的貸款保證人，如果我無法償還，他就必須還這筆錢。

❺ 這份工作的完成期限是明天，今天晚上我必須做完。

❻ 我需要歸還圖書館一些書，我已經借了一個禮拜了。

180

借貸(2)

MP3 180

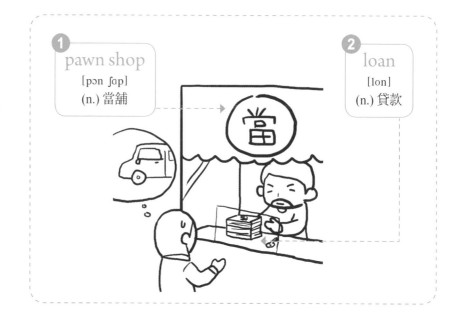

1 pawn shop
[pɔn ʃɑp]
(n.) 當舖

2 loan
[lon]
(n.) 貸款

3 debt
[dɛt]
(n.) 債務/負債

4 money dispute
[ˋmʌnɪ dɪˋspjut]
(n.) 金錢糾紛

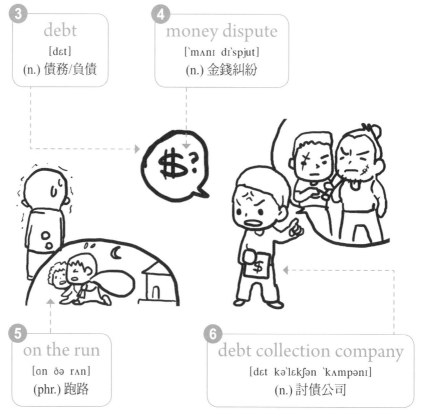

5 on the run
[ɑn ðə rʌn]
(phr.) 跑路

6 debt collection company
[dɛt kəˋlɛkʃən ˋkʌmpənɪ]
(n.) 討債公司

❶ 當舖

Hillary sold her old jewelry at the pawn shop.
　　　　　她以前的珠寶

❷ 貸款

I got a loan from the bank to pay for my car.
　　　　　從銀行申請到貸款

❸ 債務 / 負債

I'm in debt. I owe the bank about NT$50,000.

❹ 金錢糾紛

The two friends are having a money dispute. They can't agree on
who paid for dinner last week.
　　　　誰支付了上星期的晚餐

❺ 跑路

Tom owes so much money that he's decided to go on the run.
　　　　　　　　　　　　　　　　　　　　　他被迫決定要跑路

❻ 討債公司

I was contacted by a debt collection company about the money I owe.
　　　　　　　被討債公司聯絡

學更多

❶ sold〈sell（出售）的過去式〉‧ jewelry〈珠寶〉‧ pawn〈典當〉‧ shop〈商店〉

❷ got〈get（得到）的過去式〉‧ bank〈銀行〉‧ pay〈付款〉

❸ owe〈欠債〉‧ about〈大約〉

❹ dispute〈爭執〉‧ agree on...〈對…取得一致意見〉‧ paid〈pay（付款）的過去式〉‧
last week〈上星期〉

❺ decided〈decide（決定）的過去分詞〉

❻ contacted〈contact（聯絡）的過去分詞〉‧ collection〈收集〉‧ company〈公司〉

中譯

❶ Hillary 在當舖賣掉了她以前的珠寶。

❷ 我從銀行申請到貸款，用來支付車貸。

❸ 我處於負債狀況，我欠了銀行大約五萬元台幣。

❹ 那兩個朋友之間有金錢糾紛，他們對上星期的晚餐是誰付錢的有不同意見。

❺ Tom 欠了很多錢，他被迫決定要跑路。

❻ 討債公司跟我聯絡，提醒我欠的那筆錢。

181

金
錢
(1)

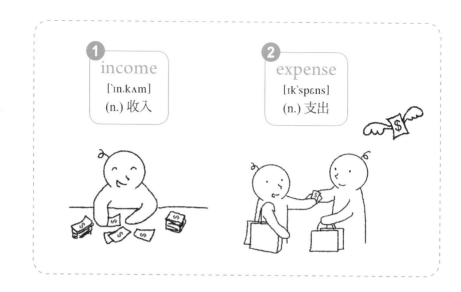

① income
[`ɪn.kʌm]
(n.) 收入

② expense
[ɪk`spɛns]
(n.) 支出

MP3 181

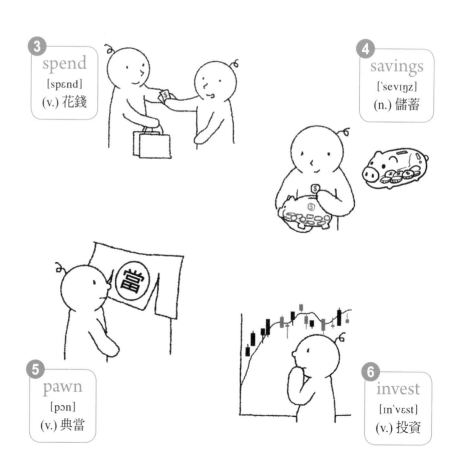

③ spend
[spɛnd]
(v.) 花錢

④ savings
[`sevɪŋz]
(n.) 儲蓄

⑤ pawn
[pɔn]
(v.) 典當

⑥ invest
[ɪn`vɛst]
(v.) 投資

❶ 收入

People with low incomes often have problems paying their bills.

低收入

❷ 支出

You have to make sure your expenses are lower than your income.

你的支出低於你的收入

❸ 花錢

Lisa spent a lot of money on her car.

❹ 儲蓄

I don't spend much money, so I've got quite a large savings account.

我已經有相當多的儲蓄

❺ 典當

Molly wants to pawn her ring to get some more money.

❻ 投資

I've invested my money in oil companies.

學更多

❶ low〈低的〉‧problem〈問題〉‧paying〈pay（支付）的 ing 型態〉‧bill〈帳單〉

❷ make sure〈確定〉‧lower〈較低的，low（低的）的比較級〉

❸ spent〈spend（花費）的過去式〉‧a lot of〈很多〉

❹ got〈get（得到）的過去分詞〉‧quite〈相當〉‧large〈大量的〉‧account〈帳戶〉‧
savings account〈儲蓄帳戶〉

❺ ring〈戒指〉‧more〈更多的〉

❻ invested〈invest（投資）的過去分詞〉‧oil〈石油〉‧company〈公司〉

中譯

❶ 收入少的人常常有支付帳單的困難。

❷ 你必須確認你的支出少於收入。

❸ Lisa 在她的車子上花了很多錢。

❹ 我不太花錢，所以我有很多儲蓄。

❺ Molly 想要典當她的戒指，來多換得一些錢。

❻ 我將錢投資於石油公司。

182

金錢(2)

MP3 182

1 appreciation
[ə͵priʃɪˋeʃən]
(n.) 升值

2 depreciation
[dɪ͵priʃɪˋeʃən]
(n.) 貶值

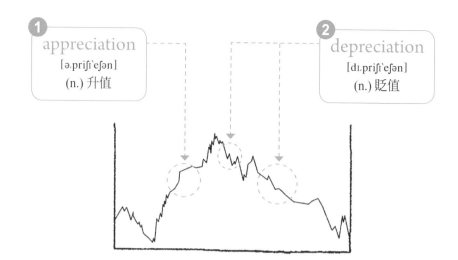

3 foreign currency
[ˋfɔrɪn ˋkɝənsɪ]
(n.) 外幣

4 coin
[kɔɪn]
(n.) 硬幣

5 bill
[bɪl]
(n.) 紙鈔

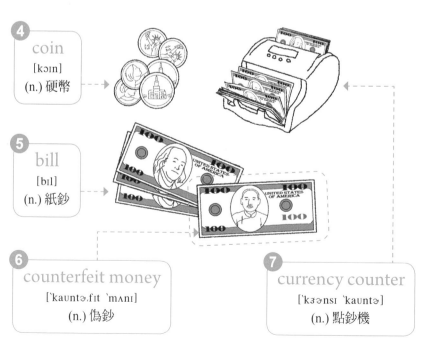

6 counterfeit money
[ˋkaʊntɚ͵fɪt ˋmʌnɪ]
(n.) 偽鈔

7 currency counter
[ˋkɝənsɪ ˋkaʊntɚ]
(n.) 點鈔機

❶ 升值

There has been a lot of appreciation in the value of houses in this area.
　　　　　　　　　　　　　　　　房價升值很多

❷ 貶值

The depreciation of my stocks caused me a lot of problems.
　　　　　我的股票貶值

❸ 外幣

Before you go on holiday, make sure you get some foreign currency.
　　　　　　　　去渡假

❹ 硬幣

Do you have any coins to put in the drinks machine?
　　　　　　　　　　　　　　　投進飲料販賣機

❺ 紙鈔

In Taiwan, the smallest bill is for NT$100.
　　　　　　　　最小的紙鈔面額

❻ 偽鈔

This is counterfeit money. It's not real.

❼ 點鈔機

Currency counters are able to count bills very quickly.
　　　　　　　　　　　快速地點算紙鈔

學更多

❶ a lot of〈很多〉‧ value〈價值〉‧ house〈房宅〉‧ area〈地區〉
❷ stock〈股票〉‧ caused〈cause（導致）的過去式〉‧ problem〈問題、麻煩〉
❸ holiday〈假期〉‧ foreign〈外國的〉‧ currency〈貨幣〉
❹ put〈放〉‧ drink〈飲料〉‧ machine〈機器〉
❺ smallest〈最小的，small（小的）的最高級〉
❻ counterfeit〈偽造的〉‧ real〈真的〉
❼ counter〈計算器〉‧ count〈計算〉‧ bill〈鈔票〉‧ quickly〈迅速地〉

中譯

❶ 這個地區的房價最近升值不少。
❷ 我的股票貶值，帶給我很大的困擾。
❸ 去渡假之前，要確認你已經準備好外幣。
❹ 你有任何硬幣可以投進飲料販賣機嗎？
❺ 在台灣，最小的紙鈔面額是一百元。
❻ 這是偽鈔，不是真的。
❼ 點鈔機可以快速地點算紙鈔。

183

儲蓄(1)

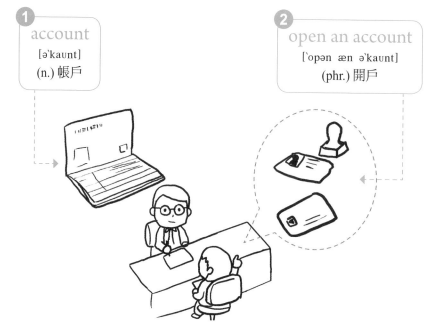

1 account
[ə`kaʊnt]
(n.) 帳戶

2 open an account
[`opən æn ə`kaʊnt]
(phr.) 開戶

MP3 183

3 deposit
[dɪ`pɑzɪt]
(v.) (n.) 存款

4 balance
[`bæləns]
(n.) 餘額

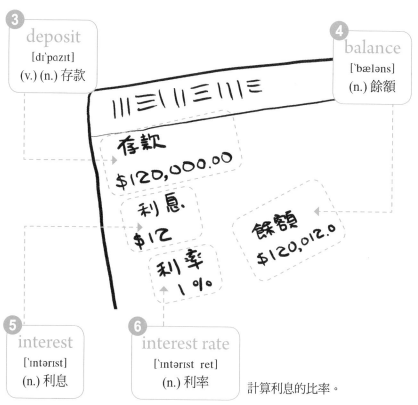

存款
$120,000.00

利息
$12

餘額
$120,012.0

利率
1%

5 interest
[`ɪntərɪst]
(n.) 利息

6 interest rate
[`ɪntərɪst ret]
(n.) 利率

計算利息的比率。

380

❶ 帳戶

Do you have an account at this bank?

❷ 開戶

The parent helped his daughter open an account at the bank.

❸ 存款

My salary is deposited straight into my account.
　　　　　　 我的薪水被直接存入

❹ 餘額

I don't know how much money I've got right now. I need to check my
balance.　　　　　　　　　　　　　　 我現在已經擁有

❺ 利息

The bank paid me NT$1,200 interest on my savings.
　　　　　　　　　　　　 我的存款利息

❻ 利率

The interest rate at my bank is terrible. I don't get anything for saving there.
　　　　　　　　　　　　　　　　　 存錢在那裡我得不到任何好處

學更多

❶ have〈擁有〉・bank〈銀行〉
❷ parent〈父親、母親〉・helped〈help（幫助）的過去式〉・daughter〈女兒〉・
　 open〈開〉
❸ salary〈薪水〉・deposited〈deposit（存款）的過去分詞〉・straight〈直接地〉
❹ got〈get（得到）的過去分詞〉・check〈檢查〉
❺ paid〈pay（支付）的過去式〉・savings〈存款〉
❻ rate〈比率〉・terrible〈極差的〉・saving〈save（儲蓄）的 ing 型態〉

中譯

❶ 你在這間銀行有帳戶嗎？
❷ 那位父親幫女兒在銀行開戶。
❸ 我的薪水都直接被存到我的帳戶裡。
❹ 我不知道我現在有多少錢，我需要查一下我的餘額。
❺ 銀行付給我一千兩百元的存款利息。
❻ 我那家銀行的利率很差，存錢在那裡一點好處也沒有。

184

儲蓄(2)

1 terminate contract
[ˋtɝməˌnet ˋkɑntrækt]
(phr.) 解約

2 time deposit
[taɪm dɪˋpɑzɪt]
(n.) 定期存款

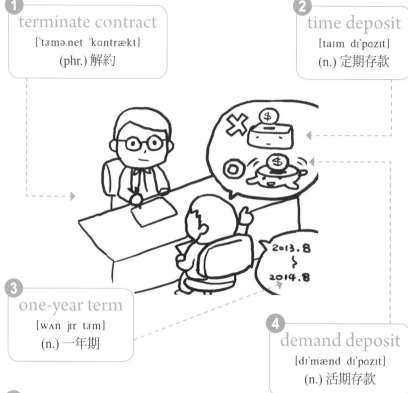

3 one-year term
[wʌn jɪr tɝm]
(n.) 一年期

4 demand deposit
[dɪˋmænd dɪˋpɑzɪt]
(n.) 活期存款

5 piggy bank
[ˋpɪgɪ bæŋk]
(n.) 撲滿

6 increase income
[ɪnˋkris ˋɪnˌkʌm]
(phr.) 增加收入

7 decrease expense
[dɪˋkris ɪkˋspɛns]
(phr.) 減少消費

❶ 解約

You haven't been paying your rent, so we're going to terminate your contract.
你一直沒有付租金　　　　　　　　　　　　　　　　　解除你的合約

❷ 定期存款

I'm saving in a time deposit account, so I can't take my money out for some time.
領出我的錢

❸ 一年期

My money has to stay in the account for a one-year term.

❹ 活期存款

With a demand deposit account, you can get your money whenever you want it.
每當你需要的時候

❺ 撲滿

Little children often save coins in a piggy bank.
把銅板存入撲滿

❻ 增加收入

Andy took on a second job to increase his income.
接下了第二份工作

❼ 減少消費

To save more money, you should decrease your expenses.

學更多

❶ paying〈pay（支付）的 ing 型態〉・rent〈租金〉・terminate〈終止〉・contract〈合約〉
❷ saving〈save（儲蓄）的 ing 型態〉・time〈定期的〉・deposit〈存款〉・account〈帳戶〉
❸ stay〈保持、停留〉・term〈期限〉
❹ demand〈需求〉・get〈取出〉・whenever〈每當〉
❺ coin〈硬幣〉・piggy〈小豬〉・bank〈銀行〉
❻ took on〈take on（接受）的過去式〉・second〈第二的〉・increase〈增加〉
❼ decrease〈減少〉・expense〈開支〉

中譯

❶ 你一直沒有付租金，所以我們打算跟你解約。
❷ 我將錢存在定期存款的帳戶，所以一段時間我都不能領錢。
❸ 我的錢必須存在帳戶一年期的時間。
❹ 把錢存在活期存款帳戶裡，每當你需要用錢時，隨時都可以領出來。
❺ 小孩子常常將銅板存入撲滿。
❻ Andy 接了第二份工作來增加收入。
❼ 為了存更多錢，你應該要減少消費。

185

投資(1)

MP3 185

③ stock
[stɑk]
(n.) 股票

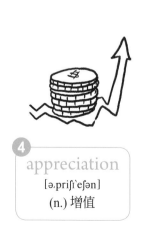

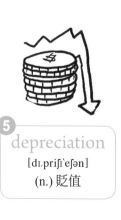

④ appreciation
[ə,priʃɪ'eʃən]
(n.) 增值

⑤ depreciation
[dɪ,priʃɪ'eʃən]
(n.) 貶值

⑥ rate of return
[ret ɑv rɪ'tɝn]
(n.) 獲利率

❶ 股本
Capital stock is the common and preferred stock a company can sell to
<u>普通股和優先股</u>
investors, and represents equity.

❷ 投資人
Taiwan is full of enthusiastic investors in the stock market.
<u>充滿許多熱情的投資者</u>

❸ 股票
Do you own any stock in Asus?

❹ 增值
A stock's appreciation is good news for any investor.

❺ 貶值
The last thing investors like to hear about is their stock's depreciation.
<u>投資人最後想聽到的事情（投資人最不想聽到的事情）</u>

❻ 獲利率
I had a 7% rate of return on my mutual funds last year.
<u>共同基金</u>

學更多

❶ capital〈資本的〉・common〈普通的〉・preferred〈優先的〉・
represent〈代表、相當於〉・equity〈股票〉
❷ full〈充滿的〉・enthusiastic〈熱情的〉・stock market〈股市〉
❸ own〈擁有〉・any〈任何〉
❹ good news〈好消息〉
❺ last〈最後的〉・hear〈聽到〉
❻ rate〈率〉・return〈利潤〉・mutual〈共同的〉・fund〈基金〉

中譯

❶ 股本是公司可以出售給投資人的普通股和優先股，相當於股票。
❷ 台灣的股市裡，充滿許多熱情的投資人。
❸ 你有任何 Asus 的股票嗎？
❹ 股票增值對任何投資人來說都是好消息。
❺ 投資人最不想聽到的事，就是他們的股票貶值。
❻ 去年我的共同基金有百分之七的獲利率。

186

投資(2)

MP3 186

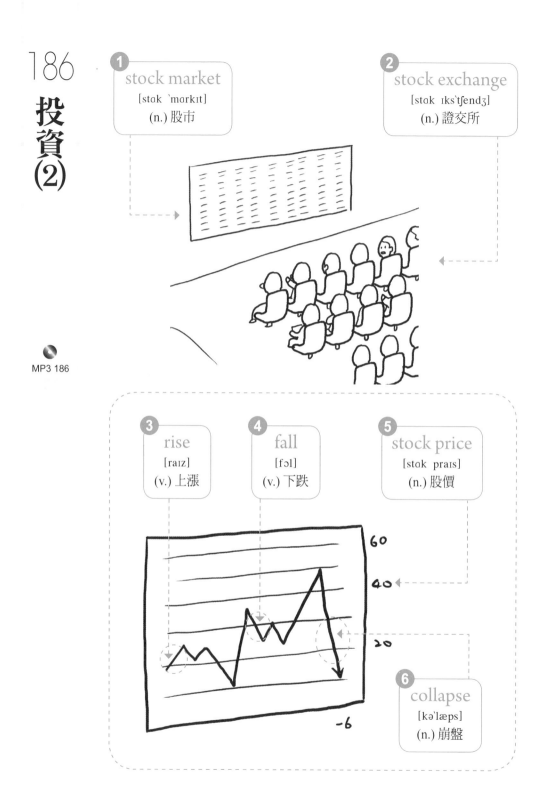

1 stock market
[stɑk ˋmɑrkɪt]
(n.) 股市

2 stock exchange
[stɑk ɪksˋtʃendʒ]
(n.) 證交所

3 rise
[raɪz]
(v.) 上漲

4 fall
[fɔl]
(v.) 下跌

5 stock price
[stɑk praɪs]
(n.) 股價

6 collapse
[kəˋlæps]
(n.) 崩盤

60

40

20

-6

❶ 股市

Investing in the stock market is a way to increase your net worth.

提升你的財富淨值

❷ 證交所

Taiwan has its own stock exchange which lists shares of stock to be traded.

被交易的股票、成交的股票

❸ 上漲
❹ 下跌

The Taiwan Stock Exchange rose almost 1% in yesterday's trading, but fell 2% today.

將近百分之一

❺ 股價

Stock prices in the oil industry have fallen sharply due to the sluggish global economy.

由於全球景氣蕭條

❻ 崩盤

A market collapse is predicted by some economists for next year.

被一些經濟學家預測

學更多

❶ investing〈invest（投資）的 ing 型態〉· stock〈股票〉· market〈市場〉· increase〈增加〉· net〈淨值的〉· worth〈價值、財富〉

❷ exchange〈交易所〉· list〈列出〉· share〈股份〉· traded〈trade（交易）的過去分詞〉

❸❹ rose〈rise（上漲）的過去式〉· trading〈交易〉· fell〈fall（下跌）的過去式〉

❺ oil〈石油〉· industry〈工業〉· fallen〈fall（下跌）的過去分詞〉· sharply〈猛烈地〉· due to〈由於〉· sluggish〈蕭條的〉· global〈全球的〉· economy〈經濟〉

❻ market〈股市〉· predicted〈predict（預測）的過去分詞〉· economist〈經濟學家〉

中譯

❶ 投資股市是提升你的財富淨值的一種方式。

❷ 台灣有自己的證交所，會列出所有成交的股票。

❸❹ 台灣證交所昨天的交易量上漲將近 1%，但是今天下跌 2%。

❺ 由於全球景氣蕭條，導致石油產業的股價急遽下跌。

❻ 一些經濟學家預測明年股市會崩盤。

187

理財

1 financial planning
[faɪˋnænʃəl ˋplænɪŋ]
(n.) 理財

2 savings
[ˋsevɪŋz]
(n.) 儲蓄/存款

MP3 187

3 insurance
[ɪnˋʃʊrəns]
(n.) 保險

4 life insurance
[laɪf ɪnˋʃʊrəns]
(n.) 壽險

5 pension fund
[ˋpɛnʃən fʌnd]
(n.) 養老金

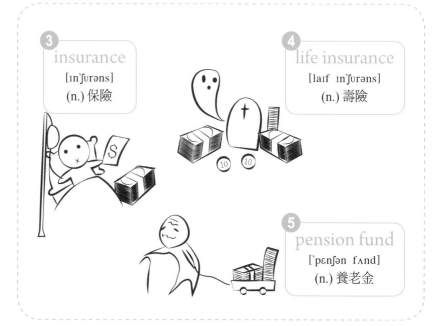

6 financial consultant
[faɪˋnænʃəl kənˋsʌltənt]
(n.) 理財顧問

7 financial planning tool
[faɪˋnænʃəl ˋplænɪŋ tul]
(n.) 理財工具

❶ 理財

Alex is interested in a career in financial planning, and helping people
Alex 對理財相關的行業有興趣
plan for their retirement.

❷ 儲蓄 / 存款

Stacy's savings are quite impressive, considering she's just 18 years old.
存款相當可觀

❸ 保險

I have renter's insurance on my apartment to protect me against floods or fires.
保障我免受淹水或火災的損失

❹ 壽險

Mr. Liu bought life insurance to take care of his family after his death.
為了照顧他的家人

❺ 養老金

The company's pension fund is very generous.
養老金很優渥

❻ 理財顧問

A financial consultant advised Derek to start saving for his future.
為他的未來做儲蓄

❼ 理財工具

Quicken software is an example of a financial planning tool.
是…的其中一例

學更多

❶ be interested in〈對…感興趣〉‧ career〈職業〉‧ plan〈計劃〉‧ retirement〈退休〉
❷ quite〈很〉‧ impressive〈令人欽佩的〉‧ considering〈就…而論、考慮到〉
❸ renter〈承租人、出租人〉‧ apartment〈公寓〉‧ protect A against B〈保障 A 免於 B〉
❹ bought〈buy（買）的過去式〉‧ life〈生命〉‧ take care of〈照顧〉‧ death〈死亡〉
❺ pension〈養老金〉‧ fund〈資金、專款〉‧ generous〈優渥的〉
❻ financial〈金融的〉‧ consultant〈顧問〉‧ advised〈advise（建議）的過去式〉
❼ software〈軟體〉‧ example〈例子、樣品〉‧ planning〈計劃〉‧ tool〈工具〉

中譯

❶ Alex 對理財相關行業有興趣，並想幫助人們規劃退休生活。
❷ 就 Stacy 才 18 歲來說，她的存款是相當可觀的。
❸ 我的公寓有投保承租保險，保障我免受淹水或火災的損失。
❹ 劉先生為了自己死後家人能得到妥善照顧，而買了壽險。
❺ 公司的養老金很優渥。
❻ 一位理財顧問建議 Derek 要開始為他的未來做儲蓄。
❼ Quicken 軟體是一種理財工具。

面試
(1)

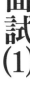

1 self-introduction
[ˌsɛlfˌɪntrəˈdʌkʃən]
(n.) 自我介紹

2 autobiography
[ˌɔtəbaɪˈagrəfɪ]
(n.) 自傳

3 education
[ˌɛdʒʊˈkeʃən]
(n.) 學歷

4 resume
[ˌrɛzjuˈme]
(n.) 履歷

5 a copy of your ID
[ə ˈkapɪ av juə ˈaɪˈdi]
(n.) 證照影本

6 letter of recommendation
[ˈlɛtə av ˌrɛkəmɛnˈdeʃɪ]
(n.) 推薦函

❶ 自我介紹

When Amy applied for the job, she wrote a short self-introduction in
her email.　　　應徵這份工作

❷ 自傳

In your autobiography, you should talk about your life.

❸ 學歷

When you apply for a job, you have to tell people about your education.
　　　應徵一份工作

❹ 履歷

Emma updated her resume to include some more information about
her work experience.　　　包含更多資訊

❺ 證照影本

Could you send me some information about yourself and a copy of
your ID?　　　關於你的資料

❻ 推薦函

When I applied for a new job, my supervisor wrote me a letter of
recommendation.　　　替我寫了一封推薦函

學更多

❶ applied〈apply（申請）的過去式〉．wrote〈write（寫）的過去式〉． short〈簡短的〉
❷ should〈應該〉．talk〈說〉．life〈生活〉
❸ have to〈必須〉．tell〈告訴〉．people〈人們〉
❹ updated〈update（更新）的過去式〉．include〈包含〉．experience〈經歷〉
❺ send〈寄〉．information〈資料、資訊〉．copy〈副本〉．ID〈身分證〉
❻ supervisor〈主管〉．letter〈函件〉．recommendation〈推薦〉

中譯

❶ 當 Amy 應徵這份工作時，她在電子郵件裡寫了一段簡短的自我介紹。
❷ 在你的自傳裡，你應該介紹你的生活經歷。
❸ 當你應徵一份工作時，你必須告訴別人你的學歷。
❹ Emma 更新了她的履歷，加入更多關於工作經驗的資訊。
❺ 你可以寄給我一些你的相關資料和證照影本嗎？
❻ 應徵新工作時，我的主管替我寫了一封推薦函。

189

面試(2)

MP3 189

1 position
[pəˈzɪʃən]
(n.) 職位

2 salary
[ˈsælərɪ]
(n.) 薪資

3 job description
[dʒɑb dɪˈskrɪpʃən]
(n.) 工作內容

4 interviewer
[ˈɪntəˌvjuə]
(n.) 面試官

5 interview
[ˈɪntəˌvju]
(n.) 口試/面試

6 written test
[ˈrɪtn̩ tɛst]
(n.) 筆試

7 recruit
[rɪˈkrut]
(v.) 錄取/雇用

❶ 職位

What's your position at the company? Are you a manager?

❷ 薪資

I get a monthly salary of NT$60,000.
　　　　　　　月薪

❸ 工作內容

After reading the job description, Graham decided to apply for the job.
　　　　　　　　　　　　　　　　　　　　　應徵這份工作

❹ 面試官

The interviewer asked a lot of questions about why I wanted the job.
　　　　　　　　　　　　　　　　　　　　為什麼我要這份工作

❺ 口試 / 面試
❻ 筆試

Before the interview started, I had to complete a written test.
　　　　　　　　　　　　　　　　　我必須完成筆試

❼ 錄取 / 雇用

My management consulting company recruits some of Harvard's best
students by interviewing them while they are still seniors.
　　　　　　　　　　　　當他們還是四年級時

學更多

❶ company〈公司〉‧ manager〈經理〉
❷ get〈得到〉‧ monthly〈每月的〉
❸ description〈描述〉‧ decided〈decide（決定）的過去式〉‧ apply〈申請〉
❹ asked〈ask（詢問）的過去式〉‧ question〈問題〉‧ wanted〈want（要）的過去式〉
❺ ❻ started〈start（開始）的過去式〉‧ complete〈完成〉‧ written〈書寫的〉
❼ management〈管理〉‧ consulting〈諮詢的、任顧問的〉‧ Harvard〈哈佛大學〉‧
　 while〈當…的時候〉‧ still〈仍然〉‧ senior〈大學四年級生〉

中譯

❶ 你在這間公司的職位是什麼？你是經理嗎？
❷ 我每個月的薪資是台幣六萬元。
❸ 看過工作內容之後，Graham 決定應徵這份工作。
❹ 面試官對於為什麼我要應徵這份工作，提出了很多問題。
❺ ❻ 面試開始前，我必須先完成筆試。
❼ 我的管理顧問公司要雇用一些哈佛大學最優秀的學生，並會在他們還是四年級時，
　 就對他們進行面試。

上班 (1)

1 meeting
[`mitɪŋ]
(n.) 開會

2 business trip
[`bɪznɪs ˏtrɪp]
(n.) 出差

3 training
[`trenɪŋ]
(n.) 培訓

4 promotion
[prə`moʃən]
(n.) 升遷

5 overtime
[`ovɚˏtaɪm]
(n.) 加班

6 salary
[`sælərɪ]
(n.) 薪水

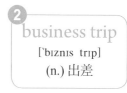

❶ 開會

I'm having a meeting with the boss later today.

❷ 出差

Peter's dad is going away on a business trip for his company.
<u>將要出差</u>

❸ 培訓

The new worker was given training to let her know how to do her job.
<u>被給予培訓</u>

❹ 升遷

Simon got a promotion, so he's doing a better job now.
<u>獲得升遷</u>

❺ 加班

Mandy couldn't get her work finished before 6pm, so she had to do some overtime.
<u>她必須加班</u>

❻ 薪水

Joe gets a good salary, so he's able to save lots of money.
<u>薪水優渥</u>

學更多

❶ boss〈老闆〉‧ later〈晚些時候〉

❷ going away〈go away（離開、外出）的 ing 型態〉‧ business〈商務〉‧ trip〈旅行〉

❸ worker〈員工〉‧ given〈give（給予）的過去分詞〉‧ job〈工作〉

❹ got〈get（獲得）的過去式〉‧ better〈更好的〉

❺ finished〈完成的〉‧ had to〈have to（必須）的過去式〉

❻ able〈能夠〉‧ save〈儲蓄〉‧ lots of〈很多〉

中譯

❶ 我今天晚點要和老闆開會。

❷ Peter 的父親要為公事出差。

❸ 對新員工進行培訓，讓她了解如何做這份工作。

❹ Simon 獲得升遷，所以他現在有了更好的工作。

❺ Mandy 無法在晚上六點前完成工作，所以她必須加班。

❻ Joe 的薪水很優渥，所以他可以存很多錢。

191

上班 (2)

1 take leave
[tek liv]
(phr.) 請假

2 punch
[pʌntʃ]
(v.) 打卡

3 unpaid leave
[ʌnˋped liv]
(n.) 留職停薪

MP3 191

4 absence
[ˋæbsn̩s]
(n.) 曠職

5 gossip
[ˋgɑsəp]
(n.) 八卦

6 sexual harassment
[ˋsɛkʃuəl ˋhærəsmənt]
(n.) 性騷擾

❶ 請假

I need to take some leave tomorrow. I need to see the dentist.
                                                    看牙醫

❷ 打卡

When you get to work, punch your timecard.
        上班

❸ 留職停薪

Oliver is taking some unpaid leave, so he won't receive any money from
his company during this time.   收到來自他公司的任何金錢

❹ 曠職

Sandy's absence can be explained by the fact that she's sick.
                        可以被解釋

❺ 八卦

There's a lot of gossip in the office. People are always talking about
everyone else.

❻ 性騷擾

Sexual harassment is a terrible thing. Even making sexual comments
about a colleague is wrong.   做出關於同事性方面的評論

學更多

❶ need〈需要〉・leave〈休假〉・tomorrow〈明天〉・dentist〈牙醫〉
❷ work〈工作〉・timecard〈工時卡〉
❸ taking〈take（執行、採取）的 ing 型態〉・unpaid〈無報酬的〉・receive〈收到〉
❹ explained〈explain（解釋）的過去分詞〉・fact〈事實〉・sick〈生病〉
❺ a lot of〈許多〉・talking about〈talk about（談論）的 ing 型態〉・else〈其他〉
❻ sexual〈性的〉・harassment〈騷擾〉・terrible〈糟糕的〉・even〈即使〉・
making〈make（做出）的 ing 型態〉・comment〈閒話、評論〉・colleague〈同事〉・
wrong〈錯誤的〉

中譯

❶ 我明天需要請假，我要去看牙醫。
❷ 當你上班時，要打卡。
❸ Oliver 將要留職停薪，所以這段期間內他不會收到公司支付的任何金錢。
❹ Sandy 曠職是有原因的，因為她生病了。
❺ 辦公室裡有很多八卦，人們總是談論著其他人。
❻ 性騷擾是一件很糟糕的事，即使評論同事關於性方面的事情，都是不對的。

192

會議(1)

1 on time
[ɑn taɪm]
(phr.) 準時

2 late
[let]
(adj.) 遲到

3 meeting notice
[ˈmitɪŋ ˈnotɪs]
(n.) 開會通知

MP3 192

4 conference room
[ˈkɑnfərəns rum]
(n.) 會議室

5 video conference
[ˈvɪdɪo ˈkɑnfərəns]
(n.) 視訊會議

6 documents
[ˈdɑkjəmənts]
(n.) 書面資料

7 minutes
[ˈmɪnɪts]
(n.) 會議記錄

❶ 準時
You should make sure you're on time for the meeting. Don't keep people waiting.
讓別人等

❷ 遲到
Ron's 10 minutes late already. I hate waiting for people.

❸ 開會通知
The boss sent out a meeting notice for the weekly staff meeting held on Fridays.
每週的員工會議

❹ 會議室
The meeting today was held in the conference room.

❺ 視訊會議
We can set up a video conference, so we'll be able to see one another.
我們將可以看見彼此

❻ 書面資料
I have some documents here. Can you make sure everyone gets a copy?
每個人都拿到一份

❼ 會議記錄
The secretary took down the minutes of the meeting.
寫下了會議記錄

學更多

❶ make sure〈確定〉・meeting〈會議〉・keep〈使…保持某狀態〉
❷ already〈已經〉・hate〈不喜歡〉・waiting for〈wait for（等待）的 ing 型態〉
❸ sent out〈send out（發送）的過去式〉・notice〈通知〉・weekly〈每週的〉・staff〈職員〉
❹ held〈hold（舉行）的過去分詞〉・conference〈會議〉
❺ set up〈設置〉・video〈視訊的〉・one another〈彼此〉
❻ everyone〈每個人〉・copy〈拷貝、相同的一份〉
❼ secretary〈秘書〉・took down〈take down（寫下、記下）的過去式〉

中譯

❶ 你務必要準時參加會議，不要讓別人等。
❷ Ron 已經遲到十分鐘了，我討厭等人。
❸ 老闆針對每週五舉行的員工會議發送了開會通知。
❹ 今天的會議是在會議室舉行的。
❺ 我們可以安排一次視訊會議，這樣我們就可以看見彼此。
❻ 我這裡有一些書面資料，可以麻煩你幫每個人都影印一份嗎？
❼ 秘書記下了會議記錄。

193

會議(2)

MP3 193

1 briefing
[ˋbrifɪŋ]
(n.) 簡報

2 proposal
[prəˋpozl̩]
(n.) 提案

3 raise your hand
[rez jʊɚ hænd]
(phr.) 舉手

4 opening remarks
[ˋopənɪŋ rɪˋmɑrks]
(n.) 致詞

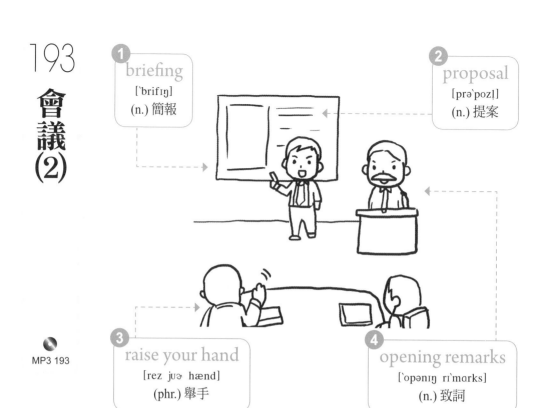

5 vote
[vot]
(n.) 投票表決

6 opinion
[əˋpɪnjən]
(n.) 意見

7 discuss
[dɪˋskʌs]
(v.) 討論

❶ 簡報

The boss gave everyone a briefing about the new project.

<u>給每個人做了簡報</u>

❷ 提案

The writer contacted an editor with a proposal for a new textbook.

<u>作者聯絡編輯</u>

❸ 舉手

There are a lot of us here, so if you have something to say, please raise

<u>今天我們有很多人在這裡</u>

your hand.

❹ 致詞

After giving his opening remarks, the boss began the meeting.

❺ 投票表決

The workers took a vote on the important issue.

投票表決

❻ 意見

The boss wanted his employee's opinion on the new product idea.

❼ 討論

The supervisor met the worker to discuss his poor attitude.

<u>不好的態度</u>

學更多

❶ gave〈give（給予）的過去式〉‧ everyone〈每個人〉‧ project〈計劃〉
❷ contacted〈contact（聯絡）的過去式〉‧ editor〈編輯〉‧ textbook〈教科書〉
❸ a lot of〈很多〉‧ raise〈舉起〉‧ hand〈手〉
❹ giving〈give（給予）的 ing 型態〉‧ opening〈開頭〉‧ remark〈話語〉
❺ worker〈員工〉‧ took〈take（採取）的過去式〉‧ important〈重要的〉‧ issue〈議題〉
❻ employee〈員工〉‧ product〈產品〉‧ idea〈概念〉
❼ supervisor〈主管〉‧ met〈meet（會見）的過去式〉‧ poor〈低劣的〉‧ attitude〈態度〉

中譯

❶ 老闆做簡報向眾人說明新計劃。
❷ 作者和編輯聯絡，討論一本新教材的提案。
❸ 今天我們有很多人在這裡，所以如果你要發言，請舉手。
❹ 致詞之後，老闆開始了會議。
❺ 員工們針對這項重要議題進行投票表決。
❻ 關於新產品的概念，老闆想知道員工們的意見。
❼ 主管和員工面對面討論他不良的工作態度。

194

一般電腦操作(1)

MP3 194

1 turn on
[tɜn ɑn]
(phr.) 開機

2 crash
[kræʃ]
(v.) 當機

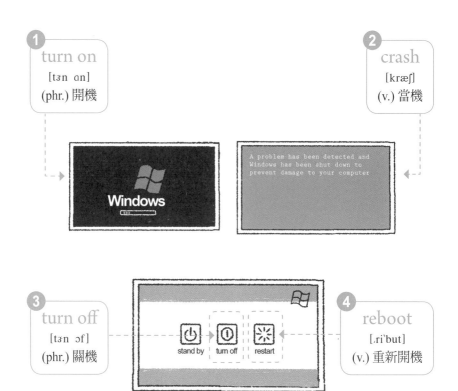

Windows

A problem has been detected and Windows has been shut down to prevent damage to your computer

3 turn off
[tɜn ɔf]
(phr.) 關機

4 reboot
[ˌriˈbut]
(v.) 重新開機

stand by   turn off   restart

5 install
[ɪnˈstɔl]
(v.) 安裝

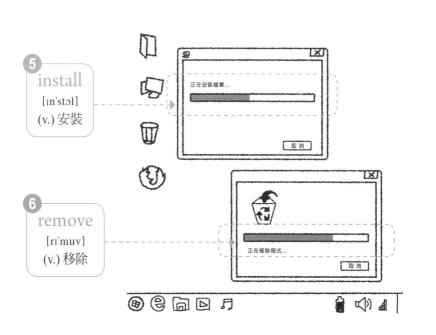

正在安裝檔案...

取消

6 remove
[rɪˈmuv]
(v.) 移除

正在移除程式...

取消

❶ 開機

Bill turned on his computer because he wanted to check something on the Internet.

❷ 當機

Tim had a lot of windows open on his computer, so it crashed.
他的電腦上開了很多視窗

❸ 關機

After finishing her work, Lillian turned off her computer.

❹ 重新開機

Jim's computer was running strangely, so he decided to reboot it.
電腦運作怪怪的

❺ 安裝

Belinda installed a new program on her computer.
安裝了一個新程式

❻ 移除

Tony has a lot of programs on his computer, so he removed some of them.

學更多

❶ turned on〈turn on（開機）的過去式〉・check〈檢查〉・Internet〈網路〉
❷ a lot of〈很多〉・window〈視窗〉・open〈打開〉・crashed〈crash（當機）的過去式〉
❸ finishing〈finish（完成）的 ing 型態〉・work〈工作、功課〉・computer〈電腦〉
❹ running〈run（運轉）的 ing 型態〉・strangely〈奇怪地〉・
　decided〈decide（決定）的過去式〉
❺ installed〈install（安裝）的過去式〉・new〈新的〉・program〈程式〉
❻ removed〈removed（移除）的過去式〉

中譯

❶ Bill 把電腦開機，因為他要上網查一些東西。
❷ Tim 的電腦上開了很多視窗，所以當機了。
❸ 完成工作之後，Lillian 把電腦關機。
❹ Jim 的電腦運作起來怪怪的，所以他決定重新開機。
❺ Belinda 在她的電腦裡安裝了一個新程式。
❻ Tony 的電腦裡有很多程式，所以他移除了一些。

195

一般電腦操作(2)

MP3 195

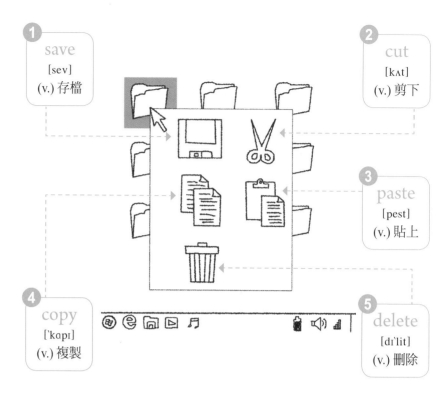

1 save
[sev]
(v.) 存檔

2 cut
[kʌt]
(v.) 剪下

3 paste
[pest]
(v.) 貼上

4 copy
[ˋkɑpɪ]
(v.) 複製

5 delete
[dɪˋlit]
(v.) 刪除

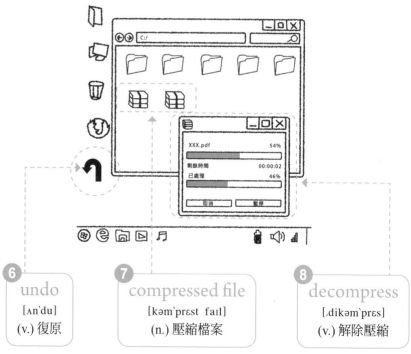

6 undo
[ʌnˋdu]
(v.) 復原

7 compressed file
[kəmˋprɛst faɪl]
(n.) 壓縮檔案

8 decompress
[ˌdikəmˋprɛs]
(v.) 解除壓縮

❶ 存檔

Save your work regularly because you don't want to lose anything.
　　　習慣性地存檔你的工作

❷ 剪下
❸ 貼上

The editor asked Dan to cut a sentence and paste it at the end of the paragraph.
　　　　　　　　　　　　　　　　　　　　貼到段落的最後面

❹ 複製

Copy the documents before you send them.

❺ 刪除

After arguing with her boyfriend, Olivia deleted all the photos of him
from her computer.　　　　　　　　　　刪除了所有他的照片

❻ 復原

It doesn't matter if you make a mistake; you can easily undo it.
　　沒有關係

❼ 壓縮檔案

Compressed files are smaller and easier to send by email.
　　　　　　　　　　　　　　　　更容易以電子郵件傳送

❽ 解除壓縮

Dean had to decompress the file before opening it.
　　　必須將檔案解除壓縮

學更多

❶ regularly〈習慣性地〉‧ lose〈失去〉‧ anything〈任何東西〉
❷ ❸ editor〈編輯〉‧ asked〈ask（請求）的過去式〉‧ sentence〈句子〉‧ paragraph〈段落〉
❹ document〈文件〉‧ before〈在…之前〉‧ send〈寄出〉
❺ arguing〈argue（爭吵）的 ing 型態〉‧ deleted〈delete（刪除）的過去式〉
❻ matter〈有關係、要緊〉‧ make a mistake〈出錯〉‧ easily〈容易地〉
❼ compressed〈壓縮的〉‧ smaller〈較小的，small（小的）的比較級〉
❽ had to〈have to（必須）的過去式〉‧ file〈檔案〉‧ opening〈open（打開）的 ing 型態〉

中譯

❶ 要習慣性地存檔你的工作，因為你不會希望失去任何進度。
❷ ❸ 編輯請 Dan 剪下一個句子，再貼上到段落的最後面。
❹ 寄出文件之前，你要先複製一份。
❺ 和男朋友吵架後，Olivia 從她的電腦裡刪除了所有他的照片。
❻ 如果你出錯也沒關係，你可以輕易地復原。
❼ 壓縮檔案比較小，更容易透過電子郵件傳送。
❽ 開啟檔案前，Dean 必須先將檔案解除壓縮。

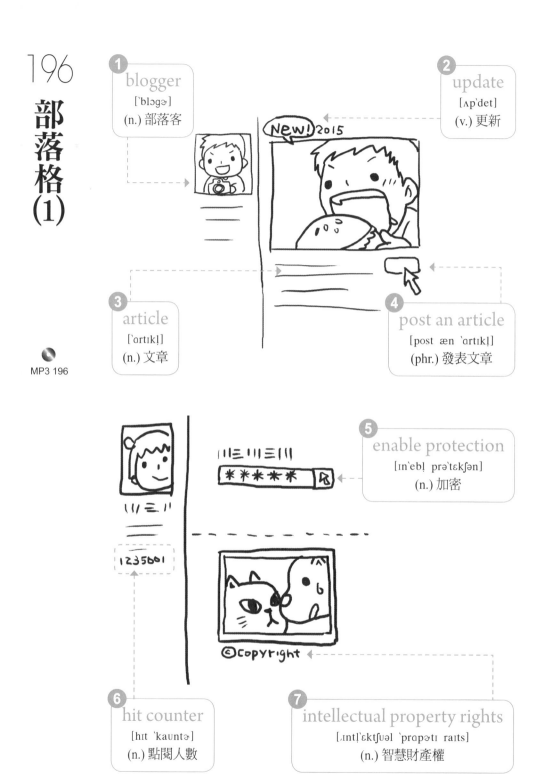

196 部落格 (1)

MP3 196

1 blogger
[ˋblɔgɚ]
(n.) 部落客

2 update
[ʌpˋdet]
(v.) 更新

3 article
[ˋɑrtɪkl]
(n.) 文章

4 post an article
[post æn ˋɑrtɪkl]
(phr.) 發表文章

5 enable protection
[ɪnˋebl prəˋtɛkʃən]
(n.) 加密

6 hit counter
[hɪt ˋkaʊntɚ]
(n.) 點閱人數

7 intellectual property rights
[ˌɪntlˋɛktʃʊəl ˋprɑpətɪ raɪts]
(n.) 智慧財產權

❶ 部落客

She's one of the world's most popular bloggers, and thousands of people read her posts every day.
成千上萬的人閱讀她張貼的文章

❷ 更新

After getting married, the woman updated the marital status on her Facebook profile.
她的臉書個人簡介的婚姻狀況

❸ 文章

John writes articles about politics for his blog.

❹ 發表文章

Whenever Sam posts an article on his blog, he tells his friends to visit his site and read his work.

❺ 加密

By enabling protection, you can keep your blog more secure.
讓你的部落格更安全

❻ 點閱人數

The hit counter goes up by one every time someone else visits the website.
數字增加 1

❼ 智慧財產權

The creator of this website owns the intellectual property rights for the programming used to run it.
用於營運網站的程式設計

學更多

❶ popular〈受歡迎的〉‧ thousands of〈成千上萬的〉‧ post〈張貼的文章〉
❷ updated〈update（更新）的過去式〉‧ marital〈婚姻的〉‧ status〈狀況〉‧ profile〈簡介〉
❸ write〈書寫〉‧ about〈關於〉‧ politics〈政治〉‧ blog〈部落格〉
❹ whenever〈每當〉‧ post〈張貼〉‧ visit〈參觀〉‧ site〈網站〉‧ work〈作品〉
❺ enabling〈enable（使能夠）的 ing 型態〉‧ protection〈保護〉‧ secure〈安全的〉
❻ hit〈點擊〉‧ counter〈計算器〉‧ go up〈上升〉‧ website〈網站〉
❼ creator〈創辦人〉‧ own〈擁有〉‧ intellectual〈智力的〉‧ property〈財產〉‧ right〈權利〉

中譯

❶ 她是全世界最受歡迎的部落客之一，每天有成千上萬的人閱讀她所張貼的文章。
❷ 結婚後，這名女子更新了她的臉書個人簡介上的婚姻狀況。
❸ John 在他的部落格寫政治相關的文章。
❹ 每當 Sam 在他的部落格發表文章，他會告訴朋友來瀏覽他的網站並閱讀文章。
❺ 藉由加密，你可以讓部落格更安全。
❻ 每次有不同的人瀏覽網站，點閱人數就會加 1。
❼ 這個網站的創辦人擁有運作自己網站的程式設計的智慧財產權。

197
部落格(2)

MP3 197

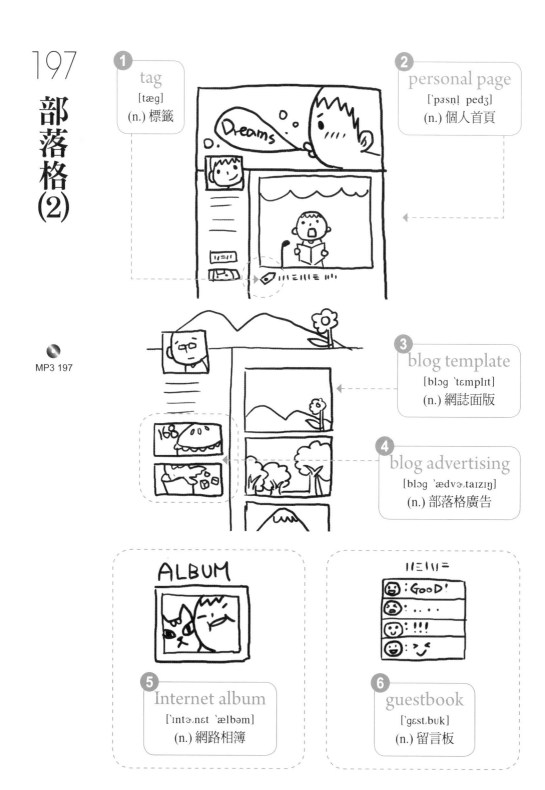

1 tag
[tæg]
(n.) 標籤

2 personal page
[ˋpɝsn̩l ˋpedʒ]
(n.) 個人首頁

3 blog template
[blɔg ˋtɛmplɪt]
(n.) 網誌面版

4 blog advertising
[blɔg ˋædvɚˌtaɪzɪŋ]
(n.) 部落格廣告

5 Internet album
[ˋɪntɚˌnɛt ˋælbəm]
(n.) 網路相簿

6 guestbook
[ˋgɛstˌbʊk]
(n.) 留言板

❶ 標籤

Dan always uses tags on his blog articles to let people know what they're
about.　　　　在他的部落格文章上使用標籤　　　　　　　　　　　　　它們是關於什麼

❷ 個人首頁

You can write a little bit about yourself on your blog's personal page.

❸ 網誌面版

The blog template you choose will determine what your blog looks like.
　　　　　　　　　　　　　　　　　　決定你的部落格看起來像什麼樣子

❹ 部落格廣告

Some writers are able to make quite a lot of money through blog
advertising.　　　　　　　　　賺很多錢

❺ 網路相簿

The pretty girl loves to post pictures of herself in her Internet album.
　　　　　　　　　　張貼她自己的照片

❻ 留言板

I found the blog really interesting, so I left a nice message in the guestbook.
　　　　　　　　　　　　　　留下一則讚美的訊息

學更多

❶ always〈總是〉・blog〈部落格〉・article〈文章〉・let〈讓〉

❷ a little bit〈一些〉・yourself〈你自己〉・personal〈個人的〉・page〈網頁〉

❸ template〈範本〉・choose〈選擇〉・determine〈決定〉・look like〈看起來像…〉

❹ writer〈作家〉・quite〈相當〉・money〈金錢〉・through〈藉由〉・advertising〈廣告〉

❺ pretty〈漂亮的〉・post〈張貼〉・picture〈照片〉・Internet〈網路〉・album〈相簿〉

❻ found〈find（發現）的過去式〉・interesting〈有趣的〉・left〈leave（留下）的過去式〉・
nice〈好的〉・message〈訊息〉

中譯

❶ Dan 總會在他的部落格文章上使用標籤，讓大家知道是關於哪一類的文章。

❷ 你可以在部落格的個人首頁上，寫一些關於你自己的事。

❸ 你選用的網誌面版，會決定你的部落格呈現的樣貌。

❹ 有些作家能藉由部落格廣告賺很多錢。

❺ 那位漂亮的女孩喜歡在網路相簿張貼自己的照片。

❻ 我發現這個部落格很有趣，所以在留言板留下了一則讚美。

198

電子郵件(1)

MP3 198

1 send
[sɛnd]
(v.) 寄送

2 forward
[ˈfɔrwəd]
(v.) 轉寄

3 reply
[rɪˈplaɪ]
(v.) 回覆

4 receive
[rɪˈsiv]
(v.) 接收

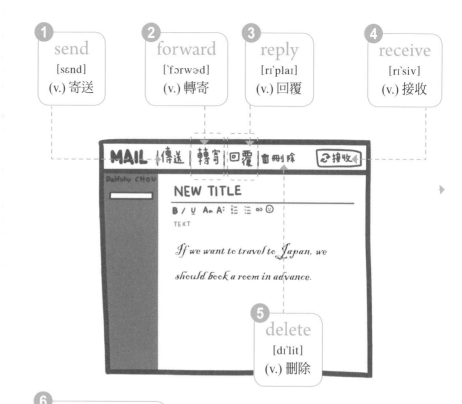

5 delete
[dɪˈlit]
(v.) 刪除

6 e-mail address
[iˈmel əˈdrɛs]
(n.) 郵件地址

Lemontree @ good.com

「carbon copy」可縮寫為「cc」。

7 cc (carbon copy)
[ˈsiˈsi] / [ˈkɑrbən ˈkɑpɪ]
(n.) 副本

「blind carbon copy」可縮寫為「bcc」。

8 bcc (blind carbon copy)
[ˈbiˈsiˈsi] / [blaɪnd ˈkɑrbən ˈkɑpɪ]
(n.) 密件副本

❶ 寄送
❷ 轉寄

I know what you wrote about me, because after you sent the email to Ken,
<u>你所寫的關於我的事</u>

he forwarded it to me.

❸ 回覆

I sent him an email yesterday, but he hasn't replied yet.

❹ 接收

Can you let me know as soon as you receive my email?
<u>當你一接收我的電子郵件，就…</u>

❺ 刪除

I never delete my emails, so I've got thousands of them now.
<u>我現在已經有上千封信</u>

❻ 郵件地址

What's your email address? It'd be good to stay in touch.
<u>能保持聯絡會是很好的（＝ It would be good to stay in touch）</u>

❼ 副本

The salesman wrote to his customer and sent a cc to his boss.
<u>寄副本給他的老闆</u>

❽ 密件副本

I don't want people knowing who I'm writing to, so I'll add the recipients
in the bcc field. <u>我會把收件人加到密件副本的地方</u>

學更多

❶❷ wrote〈write（寫）的過去式〉‧ sent〈send（寄送）的過去式〉‧ email〈電子郵件〉
❸ replied〈reply（回覆）的過去分詞〉‧ yet〈還沒〉
❹ let〈讓〉‧ know〈知道〉‧ as soon as〈一…就…〉
❺ never〈從不〉‧ got〈get（得到）的過去分詞〉‧ thousands of〈數千的〉
❻ address〈地址〉‧ stay〈保持〉‧ touch〈聯絡〉
❼ salesman〈業務員〉‧ customer〈客戶〉‧ carbon〈複寫本〉‧ copy〈副本〉‧ boss〈老闆〉
❽ add〈加〉‧ recipient〈收件人〉‧ blind〈隱蔽的〉‧ field〈領域〉

中譯

❶❷ 我知道你寫了一些關於我的事，因為你寄送那封電子郵件給 Ken 之後，他轉寄給我。
❸ 我昨天寄給他一封電子郵件時，但是他還沒有回覆。
❹ 當你接收到我的電子郵件時，可以盡快讓我知道嗎？
❺ 我從來不刪除我的電子郵件，所以我現在已經有上千封信件。
❻ 你的郵件地址是什麼？如果我們能保持聯絡是最好的。
❼ 這名業務員寫信給他的客戶，也寄了副本給他的老闆。
❽ 我不想讓別人知道我寄信給誰，所以我會把收件人加到密件副本。

199

電子郵件(2)

MP3 199

1 contact list
['kɑntækt lɪst]
(n.) 通訊錄

2 inbox
['ɪnbɑks]
(n.) 收件匣

3 sent mail
[sɛnt mel]
(n.) 寄件備份

4 draft
[dræft]
(n.) 草稿

5 spam / junk email
[spæm] / [dʒʌŋk `imel]
(n.) 垃圾郵件

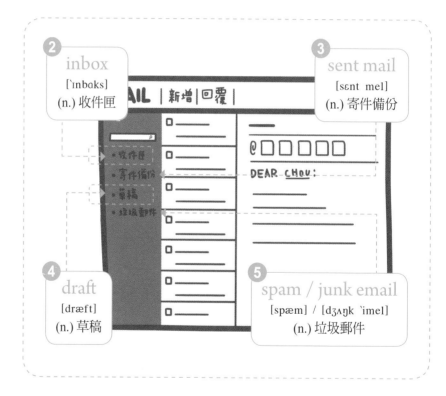

6 failed delivery
[feld dɪ`lɪvərɪ]
(n.) 寄送失敗

❶ 通訊錄

I looked for an address in my contact list, but I couldn't find it.

在我的通訊錄尋找一個地址

❷ 收件匣

Check your inbox. I just sent you an email with a link to a funny video.

有一個有趣影片的連結

❸ 寄件備份

All the emails I've written are saved in my sent mail folder.

被存放在我的寄件備份匣

❹ 草稿

I didn't have time to finish the email, so I saved it in my draft folder.

把它存在我的草稿匣

❺ 垃圾郵件

I hate getting spam, especially the emails claiming to be from my bank.

宣稱來自我的銀行的郵件

❻ 寄送失敗

I think I wrote down his email address incorrectly, because when I send him an email, it comes back to me as a failed delivery.

當作寄送失敗退回給我

學更多

❶ looked for〈look for（尋找）的過去式〉・contact〈聯絡〉・list〈目錄〉・find〈找到〉

❷ check〈檢查〉・just〈剛才〉・link〈連結〉・funny〈有趣的〉・video〈影片〉

❸ saved〈save（儲存）的過去分詞〉・sent〈已寄出〉・folder〈文件夾〉

❹ finish〈完成〉・saved〈save（儲存）的過去式〉

❺ hate〈討厭〉・getting〈get（得到）的 ing 型態〉・claiming〈claim（宣稱）的 ing 型態〉

❻ wrote down〈write down（寫下）的過去式〉・address〈地址〉・incorrectly〈錯誤地〉・come back〈回來〉・failed〈失敗的〉・delivery〈投遞〉

中譯

❶ 我在通訊錄上尋找一個地址，但是找不到。

❷ 檢查一下你的收件匣，我剛才寄給你一封郵件，裡面有一個有趣的影片連結。

❸ 所有我寫的電子郵件，都存放在我的寄件備份匣。

❹ 我沒時間完成這封郵件，所以我把它存放在我的草稿匣。

❺ 我討厭收到垃圾郵件，特別是宣稱來自我的銀行的郵件。

❻ 我想我寫錯了他的郵件地址，因為當我寄出郵件給他時，卻以寄送失敗退回。

200

繪圖

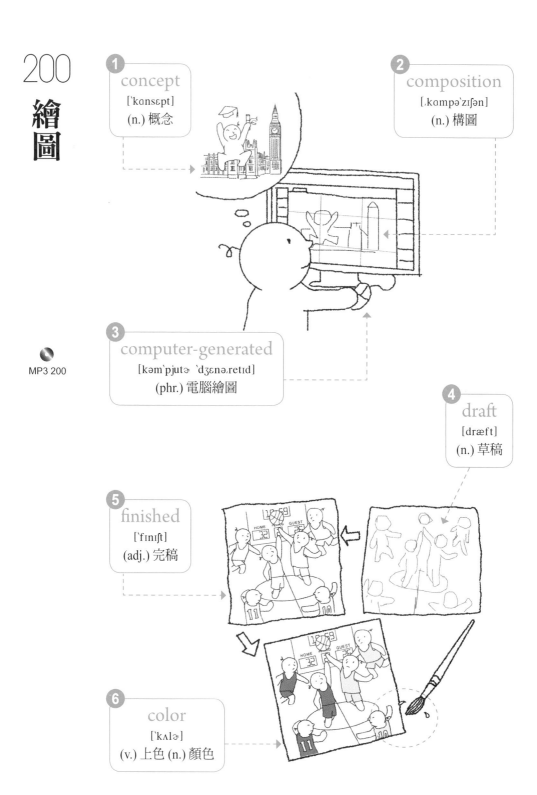

1 concept
['kɑnsɛpt]
(n.) 概念

2 composition
[ˌkɑmpə'zɪʃən]
(n.) 構圖

3 computer-generated
[kəm'pjutɚ 'dʒɛnəˌretɪd]
(phr.) 電腦繪圖

4 draft
[dræft]
(n.) 草稿

5 finished
['fɪnɪʃt]
(adj.) 完稿

6 color
['kʌlɚ]
(v.) 上色 (n.) 顏色

① 概念

I asked the painter what the concept of her picture was, but she wouldn't say what it was about.　　她的畫作的概念是什麼

② 構圖

I find the composition of this piece fascinating. I wonder why the artist placed the different objects in these positions.
把不同的物品放在這些位置

③ 電腦繪圖

These pictures weren't drawn by hand; they're computer-generated images.
這些畫不是手繪的

④ 草稿

The artist drew a quick draft, and he'll paint the scene later.
稍後他將替畫作上的景物上色

⑤ 完稿

The painter doesn't want anyone to see the picture until it's finished.
直到畫作完稿

⑥ 上色 / 顏色

The artist used crayons to color his sketch.

學更多

① asked〈ask（詢問）的過去式〉・painter〈畫家〉・picture〈畫作〉

② piece〈作品〉・fascinating〈極好的〉・wonder〈想知道〉・
placed〈place（安置）的過去式〉・object〈物品〉・position〈位置〉

③ drawn〈draw（畫）的過去分詞〉・generated〈產生的〉・image〈圖像〉

④ drew〈draw（畫）的過去式〉・quick〈快速的〉・paint〈上色〉・scene〈場面、景象〉

⑤ anyone〈任何人〉・until〈直到〉

⑥ artist〈藝術家〉・used〈use（使用）的過去式〉・crayon〈蠟筆〉・sketch〈素描〉

中譯

① 我問這名畫家她的畫作的概念是什麼，但是她不願意說。

② 我發現這個作品的構圖很棒，我想知道為什麼這名藝術家會把不同的物品放在這些位置。

③ 這些畫不是手繪的，它們是電腦繪圖的圖像。

④ 藝術家很快地畫了一張草稿，而且他稍後會替它上色。

⑤ 這名畫家不希望畫作完稿前，有任何人看過它。

⑥ 藝術家用蠟筆替他的素描上色。

201·
攝影(1)

1
wide-angle lens
[ˈwaɪdˈæŋgl̩ lɛnz]
(n.) 廣角鏡頭

2
automatic focus
[ˌɔtəˈmætɪk ˈfokəs]
(n.) 自動對焦

兩個單字都是「焦距」。

3
focal distance
[ˈfokl̩ ˈdɪstəns]
focal length
[ˈfokl̩ lɛŋθ]
(n.) 焦距

MP3 201

4
look at the camera
[lʊk æt ðə ˈkæmərə]
(phr.) 看鏡頭

5
press the shutter
[prɛs ðə ˈʃʌtə]
(phr.) 按快門

6
digital camera
[ˈdɪdʒɪtl̩ ˈkæmərə]
(n.) 數位相機

7
photoshopped image
[ˈfotoˌʃapt ˈɪmɪdʒ]
(n.) 合成相片

❶ 廣角鏡頭

Wide-angle lenses are great for landscape shots as they allow more of the scene to be included in the photo. 它們能包含更多的風景

❷ 自動對焦

Using an automatic focus makes it much easier to take great pictures. 拍出好照片

❸ 焦距

With good cameras, you can extend the focal length to take pictures of faraway objects. 拍遠處的物體

❹ 看鏡頭

OK, everyone. Look at the camera and give me a nice, big smile.

❺ 按快門

It's a simple camera, so just aim it in the right direction and press the shutter. 對準方向

❻ 數位相機

Digital cameras are great, because you don't need to use film with them.

❼ 合成相片

I think this is a photoshopped image. It doesn't look at all real. 看起來一點也不真實

學更多

❶ landscape〈風景〉・shot〈照片〉・allow〈容許〉・scene〈景象〉・included〈被包含的〉
❷ automatic〈自動的〉・focus〈調焦、聚焦〉・easier〈更容易的，easy（容易的）的比較級〉
❸ extend〈延伸〉・focal〈焦點的〉・length〈長度〉・faraway〈遠處的〉・object〈物體〉
❹ everyone〈大家〉・look at〈看〉・smile〈笑容〉
❺ simple〈簡易的〉・aim〈對準〉・direction〈方向〉・press〈按〉・shutter〈快門〉
❻ digital〈數碼的〉・film〈底片〉
❼ not at all〈完全不…〉・real〈真實的〉・image〈影像〉

中譯

❶ 廣角鏡頭很適用於拍攝風景照，因為它們能讓照片容納更大範圍的景象。
❷ 使用自動對焦更容易拍出好照片。
❸ 使用好相機，你可以延伸焦距來拍攝遠處的物體。
❹ 好，各位，看鏡頭，然後給我一個很棒的燦爛笑容。
❺ 這是台容易操作的相機，只要對準方向，然後按快門。
❻ 數位相機很方便，因為你不需要裝底片。
❼ 我覺得這是合成相片，它看起來一點也不真實。

202

攝影(2)

MP3 202

1 night mode
[naɪt mod]
(n.) 夜拍模式

2 flash
[flæʃ]
(n.) 閃光燈

3 exposure
[ɪk`spoʒɚ]
(n.) 曝光

4 backlight
[`bæk.laɪt]
(n.) 背光

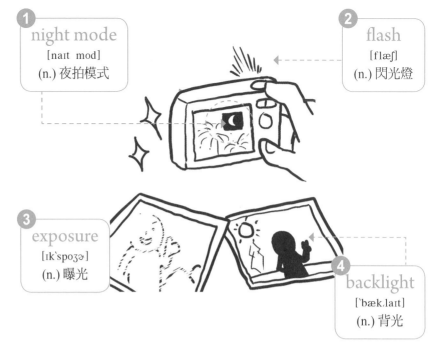

5 darkroom
[`dɑrk`rum]
(n.) 暗房

沖洗照片時，為讓底片或相紙不曝光，
經特別設計具遮光效果的房間。

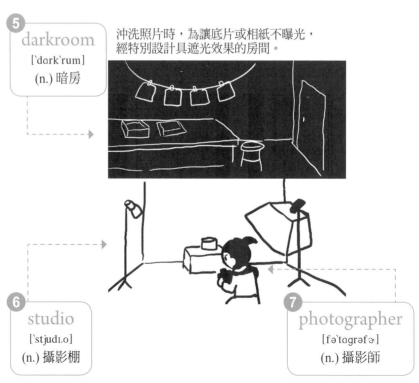

6 studio
[`stjudɪo]
(n.) 攝影棚

7 photographer
[fə`tɑgrəfɚ]
(n.) 攝影師

❶ 夜拍模式

The night mode setting on my camera is great for low-light conditions.
　　　夜拍模式設定　　　　　　　　　　　　　　　　　　　低光源環境

❷ 閃光燈

Harry felt blinded when the flash went off in his eyes.

❸ 曝光

The photographer extended the exposure to allow in more light.
　　　　　　　　　　　　　延長曝光時間

❹ 背光

If there's a strong backlight, then your subject might appear very dark.
　　　　　　　　有很明顯的背光

❺ 暗房

Neil is in the darkroom developing his photographs.
　　　　　　　　　　　　　沖洗他的照片

❻ 攝影棚

The model posed for the photographer in her studio.

❼ 攝影師

I enjoy taking photos, so I'd love to become a professional photographer.
　喜歡拍照　　　　　　我希望（= I would love to）

學更多

❶ mode〈模式〉・setting〈裝置、設定〉・condition〈情況、環境〉
❷ blinded〈blind（使看不見）的過去分詞〉・went off〈go off（閃滅）的過去式〉
❸ extended〈extend（延長）的過去式〉・allow〈容許〉・light〈光源〉
❹ strong〈強烈的〉・subject〈主體〉・appear〈顯現〉・dark〈黑暗的〉
❺ developing〈develop（沖洗）的 ing 型態〉・photograph〈照片〉
❻ model〈模特兒〉・posed〈pose（擺姿勢）的過去式〉
❼ enjoy〈喜愛〉・become〈成為〉・professional〈專業的〉

中譯

❶ 我相機裡的夜拍模式設定，在低光源的環境下很好用。
❷ 當閃光燈的閃光射入 Harry 的眼睛，他覺得自己好像看不見了。
❸ 攝影師延長曝光時間，來接收更多光源。
❹ 如果是很明顯的背光，你的拍攝主體可能會變得很暗。
❺ Neil 正在暗房沖洗照片。
❻ 模特兒在自己的攝影棚擺姿勢給攝影師拍照。
❼ 我喜歡拍照，所以我希望成為一名專業攝影師。

203

寫作(1)

MP3 203

1 writer's block
[`raɪtɚz blɑk]
(n.) 瓶頸

2 inspiration
[ˌɪnspəˈreʃən]
(n.) 靈感

3 imagination
[ɪˌmædʒəˈneʃən]
(n.) 想像力

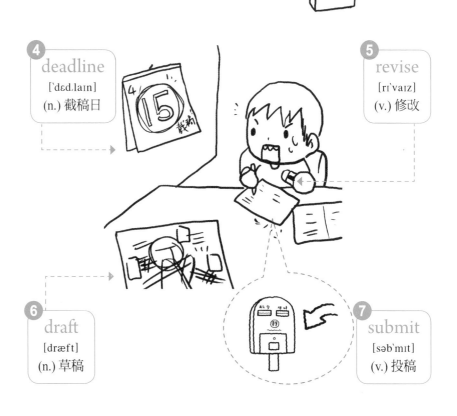

4 deadline
[ˈdɛdˌlaɪn]
(n.) 截稿日

5 revise
[rɪˈvaɪz]
(v.) 修改

6 draft
[dræft]
(n.) 草稿

7 submit
[səbˈmɪt]
(v.) 投稿

❶ 瓶頸

The author's suffering with writer's block, and she hasn't been able to write anything all day. 遇到瓶頸

❷ 靈感

The children's writer said he got the inspiration for his latest book from 童書作家 watching his daughter play with her toys.

❸ 想像力

She said she writes about real events because she doesn't have a good enough imagination to create new ones.

❹ 截稿日

Mark's working hard because the deadline for him to finish his book is coming up soon. 即將到來

❺ 修改

Paul tries to write quite quickly and then spend a lot of time revising his work. 要花很多時間修改

❻ 草稿

This is just a draft copy of my novel. I still need to make some changes. 我的小說的草稿

❼ 投稿

After completing her short story, Amy submitted it to the literary magazine.

學更多

❶ author〈作家〉・suffering〈suffer（經歷）的 ing 型態〉・block〈阻塞物〉
❷ got〈get（得到）的過去式〉・latest〈最新的〉・watching〈watch（看）的 ing 型態〉
❸ real〈真實的〉・event〈事件〉・enough〈足夠的〉・create〈創造〉
❹ working〈work（工作）的 ing 型態〉・coming up〈come up（到來）的 ing 型態〉
❺ quite〈相當〉・quickly〈迅速地〉・a lot of〈很多〉・work〈作品〉
❻ copy〈稿件〉・novel〈小說〉・change〈改變〉
❼ completing〈complete（完成）的 ing 型態〉・short〈短的〉・literary〈文學的〉

中譯

❶ 這名作家遭遇瓶頸，一整天她都無法寫出任何文字。
❷ 這名童書作家說，他最近一本書的靈感，來自於看女兒玩玩具。
❸ 她說她寫的是真實事件，因為她沒有完美而充分的想像力來創造新故事。
❹ Mark 正忙著努力工作，因為他的書的截稿日就快到了。
❺ Paul 試著很迅速地寫完，然後再花很多時間修改自己的作品。
❻ 這只是我的小說草稿，我仍需要做一些修改。
❼ 完成短篇故事後，Amy 投稿到文學雜誌。

204

寫作(2)

MP3 204

1 vocabulary
[vəˈkæbjəˌlɛrɪ]
(n.) 詞彙

2 article
[ˈɑrtɪkl]
(n.) 文章

3 writing style
[ˈraɪtɪŋ staɪl]
(n.) 寫作風格

4 creation
[krɪˈeʃən]
(n.) 創作/創造

5 outline
[ˈaʊtˌlaɪn]
(n.) 架構

6 author
[ˈɔθə]
(n.) 作者/作家

7 theme
[θim]
(n.) 主題

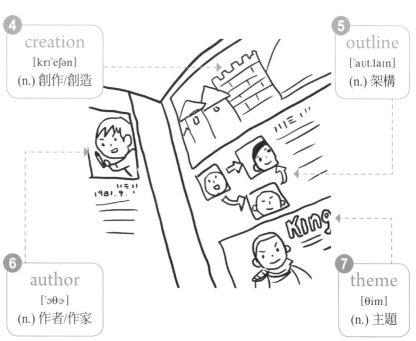

❶ 詞彙

Although most people have a fairly large vocabulary, we don't use that many words on a daily basis.

日常的基本生活

❷ 文章

The writer is working on a travel article for the local newspaper.

當地的報紙

❸ 寫作風格

Jack Kerouac has an incredible writing style. His stories are full of life and energy.

❹ 創作／創造

The writer says that the creation of new characters is the most interesting part of writing a book.

寫書中最有趣的部分

❺ 架構

Before starting to write, Alex always writes an outline for his articles.

❻ 作者／作家

My sister works as an author, and she's already written three novels.

我姊姊是位專職作家

❼ 主題

These poems are quite depressing. The theme of them is death.

學更多

❶ although〈雖然〉・fairly〈相當地〉・large〈大量的〉・daily〈日常的〉・basis〈基本〉
❷ working〈work（工作）的 ing 型態〉・travel〈旅遊〉・local〈當地的〉
❸ incredible〈意想不到的〉・be full of..〈充滿…〉・life〈生命力〉・energy〈活力、能量〉
❹ character〈角色〉・part〈部分〉・writing〈write（書寫）的 ing 型態〉
❺ before〈在…之前〉・starting〈start（開始）的 ing 型態〉
❻ as〈作為〉・already〈已經〉・written〈write（書寫）的過去分詞〉・novel〈小說〉
❼ poem〈詩〉・quite〈相當〉・depressing〈令人沮喪的〉・death〈死亡〉

中譯

❶ 雖然大部分的人都懂相當多的詞彙，但在我們每天的日常生活中，並不會用到那麼多字。
❷ 這名作家正在為當地報紙寫旅遊文章。
❸ Jack Kerouac 有讓人意想不到的寫作風格，他的故事充滿了生命力與活力。
❹ 那位作家表示，新角色的創造是寫書中最有趣的部分。
❺ 開始寫作前，Alex 總是先寫出文章的架構。
❻ 我姊姊是位專職作家，而且她已經完成三本小說。
❼ 這些詩讓人心情相當沮喪，它們的主題都是死亡。

205

聲音

MP3 205

1 noisy
[ˋnɔɪzɪ]
(adj.) 嘈雜

2 decibel
[ˋdɛsɪbɛl]
(n.) 分貝

3 volume
[ˋvɑljəm]
(n.) 音量

4 loud
[laʊd]
(adj.) 大聲

5 faint
[fent]
(adj.) 微弱

6 voice actor
[vɔɪs ˋæktɚ]
(n.) 配音員

7 aphasia
[əˋfeʒɪə]
(n.) 失語/失語症

❶ 嘈雜

My neighbors are so noisy. They're always shouting or having parties.
<u>舉辦派對</u>

❷ 分貝

Scientists measure sound in units of decibels.
<u>以分貝為單位測量聲音</u>

❸ 音量

Bob has trouble hearing, so the volume of his TV is always quite high.
<u>聽力有問題</u>

❹ 大聲

The mother asked her son to turn down his loud music.
<u>把他開得很大聲的音樂關小聲</u>

❺ 微弱

Although there was no answer at the door, Lisa could hear a faint noise
from inside. <u>沒有人應門</u>

❻ 配音員

Stephanie is a great voice actor, so she often records things for the radio.
<u>幫電台錄音</u>

❼ 失語 / 失語症

The man suffers with aphasia, so he has trouble speaking or understanding others.
<u>罹患失語症</u>

學更多

❶ shouting〈shout（喊叫）的 ing 型態〉· having〈have（從事某事）的 ing 型態〉
❷ scientist〈科學家〉· measure〈測量〉· sound〈音量〉· unit〈單位〉
❸ trouble〈困難、困境〉· hearing〈hear（聽）的 ing 型態〉· quite〈相當〉· high〈高的〉
❹ asked〈ask（要求）的過去式〉· turn down〈關小〉· music〈音樂〉
❺ although〈雖然〉· answer〈回應〉· noise〈聲響〉· inside〈裡面〉
❻ voice〈聲音〉· actor〈演員〉· record〈錄音〉· radio〈電台〉
❼ speaking〈speak（說話）的 ing 型態〉· understanding〈understand（理解）的 ing 型態〉

中譯

❶ 我的鄰居很嘈雜，他們總是一直大吼大叫或是開派對。
❷ 科學家以分貝為單位測量音量。
❸ Bob 的聽力有問題，所以他總是把電視音量開得很大聲。
❹ 媽媽要求兒子，把他開得很大聲的音樂關小聲點。
❺ 雖然沒有人應門，但是 Lisa 能聽到屋裡傳出微弱的聲音。
❻ Stephanie 是位很棒的配音員，所以她常幫電台錄音。
❼ 那位男士患有失語症，所以他在說話或理解方面都有困難。

萬聖節(1)

1 trick or treat
[trɪk ɔr trit]
(phr.) 不給糖就搗蛋

10月31日（萬聖夜）當晚，小孩們做特殊的裝扮或戴上面具，逐戶按門鈴並大叫「Trick or Treat」，主人家便會拿出糖果或小禮物。

2 jack-o'-lantern
[ˋdʒækəˌlæntən]
(n.) 南瓜燈籠

3 pumpkin
[ˋpʌmpkɪn]
(n.) 南瓜

4 ghost
[gost]
(n.) 鬼魂

5 zombie
[ˋzɑmbɪ]
(n.) 殭屍

6 skeleton
[ˋskɛlətn̩]
(n.) 骷髏

7 devil
[ˋdɛvl̩]
(n.) 惡魔

❶ 不給糖就搗蛋

The man opened the door and saw a young vampire and fairy saying "trick or treat!"
一個小吸血鬼和小精靈

❷ 南瓜燈籠

In the US, many people carve scary jack-o'-lanterns out of pumpkins.
用南瓜雕刻可怕的南瓜燈籠

❸ 南瓜

Pumpkins are associated with Halloween, and there are loads of the
南瓜被聯想到萬聖節

large, orange fruit at this time of year.

❹ 鬼魂

The boy thought he saw the ghost of his dead grandfather.
他已死去的祖父的鬼魂

❺ 殭屍

Zombies' faces are usually covered with blood because they keep eating humans.
通常滿臉都是血

❻ 骷髏

While digging in his garden, Harry found some bones, and he later realized there was a whole skeleton in the ground.
之後他發現地底下有一整副骷髏

❼ 惡魔

A lot of people think of the devil as a red man with horns and a tail.
長角並有尾巴

學更多

❶ vampire〈吸血鬼〉‧ fairy〈小精靈〉‧ trick〈惡作劇〉‧ treat〈請客〉
❷ carve〈雕刻〉‧ scary〈可怕的〉‧ lantern〈燈籠〉‧ out of〈用…做材料〉
❸ associated〈associate（聯想）的過去分詞〉‧ loads of〈許多〉‧ orange〈橘色〉
❹ thought〈think（以為）的過去式〉‧ saw〈see（看見）的過去式〉‧ dead〈死去的〉
❺ covered〈cover（覆蓋）的過去分詞〉‧ blood〈血〉‧ human〈人類〉
❻ digging〈dig（挖掘）的 ing 型態〉‧ bone〈骨頭〉‧ realized〈realize（了解）的過去式〉
❼ a lot of〈許多〉‧ as〈如同〉‧ horn〈角〉‧ tail〈尾巴〉

中譯

❶ 男子開了門，眼前一個小吸血鬼和小精靈對他說「不給糖就搗蛋」。
❷ 在美國，很多人會用南瓜雕刻出可怕的南瓜燈籠。
❸ 南瓜總會和萬聖節聯想在一起，每年此時都會看到許多這種大型的橘色蔬果。
❹ 男孩以為自己看到了死去祖父的鬼魂。
❺ 殭屍通常滿臉都是血，因為他們都吃人。
❻ 在花園挖土時，Harry 發現了一些骨頭；隨後他才知道在地底下有一整副骷髏。
❼ 很多人認為惡魔是個長角、有尾巴的血紅色男子。

萬聖節(2)

1 witch
[wɪtʃ]
(n.) 女巫

2 goblin
[ˋgɑblɪn]
(n.) 妖精

MP3 207

3 haunted house
[ˋhɔntɪd haʊs]
(n.) 鬼屋

4 black cat
[blæk kæt]
(n.) 黑貓

5 bat
[bæt]
(n.) 蝙蝠

6 owl
[aʊl]
(n.) 貓頭鷹

7 Halloween costume
[ˌhæloˋwin ˋkɑstjum]
(n.) 萬聖節服飾

❶ 女巫

The old witch got angry with the man and turned him into a frog.
<u>把他變成一隻青蛙</u>

❷ 妖精

Goblins are usually shown as being small, ugly creatures.
<u>通常被顯現為…</u>

❸ 鬼屋

That's supposed to be a haunted house; people say there are ghosts in there.
<u>那應該是…</u>

❹ 黑貓

According to a lot of old stories, witches all keep black cats.

❺ 蝙蝠

Bats hang upside down when they sleep.
<u>向下倒吊</u>

❻ 貓頭鷹

Owls are supposed to be very wise birds.
<u>被認為</u>

❼ 萬聖節服飾

The woman spent hours making Halloween costumes for her children to wear.
<u>花了好幾個小時</u>　<u>給她的孩子穿</u>

學更多

❶ angry〈生氣的〉‧ turned into〈turn into（使變成）的過去式〉‧ frog〈青蛙〉
❷ shown〈show（顯現）的過去分詞〉‧ as〈如同〉‧ ugly〈醜陋的〉‧ creature〈生物〉
❸ be supposed to〈認為應該〉‧ haunted〈鬧鬼的〉‧ ghost〈鬼魂〉
❹ according to〈根據〉‧ story〈故事〉‧ keep〈飼養〉‧ black〈黑色的〉
❺ hang〈吊著〉‧ upside〈顛倒〉‧ down〈向下〉‧ sleep〈睡覺〉
❻ supposed〈suppose（認為）的過去分詞〉‧ wise〈聰明的〉‧ bird〈鳥〉
❼ spent〈spend（花費）的過去式〉‧ making〈make（製作）的 ing 型態〉‧ costume〈服裝〉

中譯

❶ 老女巫因為這名男子而感到憤怒，把他變成了一隻青蛙。
❷ 妖精呈現的樣子，通常是又小又醜的生物。
❸ 那應該是間鬼屋，大家都說裡面有鬼。
❹ 根據很多古老的故事，女巫都會養黑貓。
❺ 蝙蝠睡覺時，都是倒吊垂掛。
❻ 貓頭鷹被認為是非常聰明的鳥類。
❼ 那名女子花了好幾個小時做萬聖節服裝給她的孩子穿。

208 農曆春節(1)

1 New Year
[nju jɪr]
(n.) 新的一年

2 holidays on consecutive days
[ˋhɑlə.dez ɑn kənˋsɛkjʊtɪv dez]
(phr.) 連續假期

MP3 208

3 cold weather
[kold ˋwɛðɚ]
(n.) 天氣冷

4 Chinese New Year
[ˋtʃaɪˋniz nju jɪr]
(n.) 農曆春節

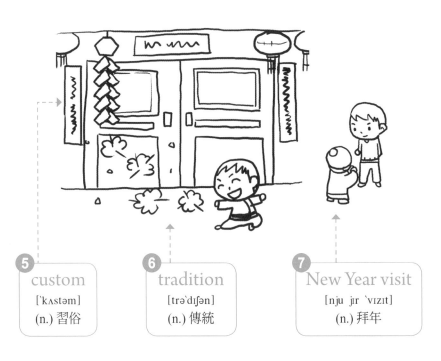

5 custom
[ˋkʌstəm]
(n.) 習俗

6 tradition
[trəˋdɪʃən]
(n.) 傳統

7 New Year visit
[nju jɪr ˋvɪzɪt]
(n.) 拜年

❶ 新的一年

Ethan wants to watch the New Year fireworks at 101 this year.

101 大樓的新年煙火

❷ 連續假期

We have holidays on consecutive days this week: Children's Day on
Tuesday and Tomb Sweeping Day on Wednesday. 兒童節

清明節

❸ 天氣冷

The cold weather over New Year means that many people stay home for
the holiday period.

❹ 農曆春節

Brad plans to travel home to see his family for Chinese New Year.

回家探望他的家人

❺ 習俗

There are many customs associated with Chinese New Year, such as
cleaning your home at that time of year. 例如

❻ 傳統

It's tradition in my family for boys to have Mark as a middle name.

作為中間名

❼ 拜年

The two sisters went to see their grandmother for a New Year visit.

去祖母家拜年

學更多

❶ watch〈看〉‧firework〈煙火〉
❷ holiday〈假期〉‧consecutive〈連續的〉‧tomb〈墓地〉‧sweeping〈清掃的〉
❸ over〈在…期間〉‧New Year〈新年〉‧mean〈表示〉‧period〈期間〉
❹ plan〈計劃〉‧travel〈行經〉‧family〈家人〉
❺ associated〈associate（聯想）的過去分詞〉‧cleaning〈clean（打掃）的 ing 型態〉
❻ boy〈男孩〉‧middle〈中間的〉‧name〈名字〉
❼ sister〈姊妹〉‧went〈go（去）的過去式〉‧grandmother〈祖母〉

中譯

❶ 今年 Ethan 想去看 101 大樓的新年煙火。
❷ 這星期我們有連續假期：星期二是兒童節，星期三是清明節。
❸ 新年期間天氣冷，那表示假期期間很多人都會待在家裡。
❹ Brad 計劃農曆春節要回家探望家人。
❺ 有很多習俗會讓人聯想到農曆新年，像是在一年的這個時候打掃家裡。
❻ 用「Mark」作為男孩的中間名，是我們家族的傳統。
❼ 那兩姊妹去了祖母家拜年。

209

農曆春節(2)

MP3 209

1 Chinese New Year's Eve
[ˈtʃaɪˈniz nju jɪrs iv]
(n.) 除夕夜

農曆 12 月 30 日的夜晚

2 gathering
[ˈgæðərɪŋ]
(n.) 團圓

3 family meal
[ˈfæməlɪ mil]
(n.) 年夜飯/團圓飯

除夕夜家人團聚,徹夜不眠地玩牌、談天說笑等,據傳有祈求雙親長壽之意。

4 see in the new year
[si ɪn ðə nju jɪr]
(phr.) 守歲

5 red envelope
[rɛd ˈɛnvəˌlop]
(n.) 紅包

❶ 除夕夜

The whole family <u>stayed up until midnight</u> on Chinese New Year's Eve.
熬夜到半夜

❷ 團圓

I'm going to <u>have a gathering at my house</u> for New Year's Eve. It'll just
在我自己家裡團圓

be a few friends, but it should be fun.

❸ 年夜飯 / 團圓飯

The old woman was upset when her son didn't <u>go to the family meal</u>.
回家吃年夜飯

❹ 守歲

The whole family is going to <u>stay up late to</u> see in the new year.
打算熬夜晚睡

❺ 紅包

<u>Children are given lots of red envelopes</u> over the New Year holiday.
小孩會獲得很多紅包

學更多

❶ whole〈全體的〉・stayed up〈stay up（不去睡覺）的過去式〉・until〈直到〉・
   midnight〈半夜〉・eve〈前夕〉

❷ house〈家〉・a few〈幾個〉・fun〈有趣的〉

❸ old〈老的〉・upset〈傷心的〉・family〈家庭、家人〉・meal〈一餐〉

❹ be going to〈即將、打算〉・late〈晚〉・new year〈新的一年〉

❺ given〈give（給予）的過去分詞〉・envelope〈信封〉・over〈在…期間〉・
   holiday〈假日〉

中譯

❶ 除夕夜當晚，全家人一直到半夜都沒睡覺。

❷ 除夕夜我會在家團圓，只有幾個朋友，但是應該會很有趣。

❸ 當兒子沒有回家吃年夜飯，老太太感到很傷心。

❹ 全家人打算熬夜晚睡來守歲。

❺ 新年期間，小孩子會收到很多紅包。

433

210

占卜 (1)

1 astrology
[əˋstrɑlədʒɪ]
(n.) 占星

2 tarot cards
[ˋtæro kɑrdz]
(n.) 塔羅牌

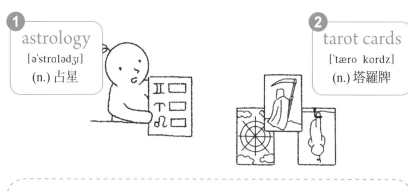

3 dream interpretation
[drim ɪn͵tɝprɪˋteʃən]
(n.) 解夢

MP3 210

4 fortune telling about relationships
[ˋfɔrtʃən ˋtɛlɪŋ əˋbaut rɪˋleʃənˋʃɪps]
(phr.) 戀愛占卜

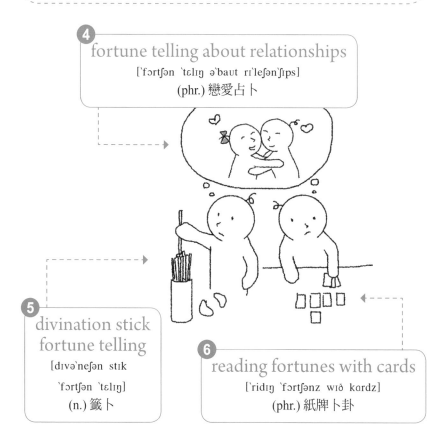

5 divination stick fortune telling
[dɪvəˋneʃən stɪk ͵fɔrtʃən ˋtɛlɪŋ]
(n.) 籤卜

6 reading fortunes with cards
[ˋridɪŋ ˋfɔrtʃənz wɪð kɑrdz]
(phr.) 紙牌卜卦

❶ 占星

Those who believe in astrology study the stars to learn about their future.
相信占星學的人

❷ 塔羅牌

The symbols of the face of tarot cards are supposed to say things about
塔羅牌面上的符號

what will happen to you.

❸ 解夢

Dream interpretation helps you learn more about your thoughts and desires.
了解更多關於…

❹ 戀愛占卜

This guy specializes in fortune telling about relationships. He'll tell you
專門研究戀愛占卜

if your boyfriend is good for you or not.

❺ 籤卜

The long sticks you sometimes see in temples are for divination stick
你偶爾在廟裡看到的長棒狀物

fortune telling.

❻ 紙牌卜卦

We played a few card games and then Bill started reading our fortunes
with the cards.

學更多

❶ believe〈相信〉‧ study〈研究〉‧ stars〈星象〉‧ learn〈得知〉‧ future〈未來〉
❷ symbol〈符號〉‧ tarot〈塔羅紙牌〉‧ supposed〈suppose（認為）的過去分詞〉‧ say〈說明〉
❸ dream〈夢〉‧ interpretation〈解釋〉‧ thought〈想法〉‧ desire〈欲望〉
❹ specialize〈專攻〉‧ fortune〈命運〉‧ telling〈敘述〉‧ relationship〈戀愛關係〉
❺ long〈長的〉‧ stick〈棒狀物〉‧ sometimes〈有時候〉‧ temple〈廟〉‧ divination〈占卜〉
❻ a few〈一些〉‧ started〈start（開始）的過去式〉‧ reading〈read（覺察）的 ing 型態〉

中譯

❶ 那些相信占星的人，會研究星象來預知他們的未來。
❷ 塔羅牌牌面上的符號，被認為可以解讀出你未來會發生什麼事。
❸ 解夢可以幫助你，更深入了解你的想法和欲望。
❹ 這個人專門研究戀愛占卜。他會告訴你對你來說，目前的男朋友是好還是壞。
❺ 你偶爾在廟裡看到的長棒狀物，是用來算命的籤卜。
❻ 我們玩了一些紙牌遊戲，然後 Bill 開始幫我們做紙牌卜卦。

211

占卜
(2)

MP3 211

1 fortune telling
[`fɔrtʃən `tɛlɪŋ]
(n.) 算命

2 omen
[`omən]
(n.) 預兆

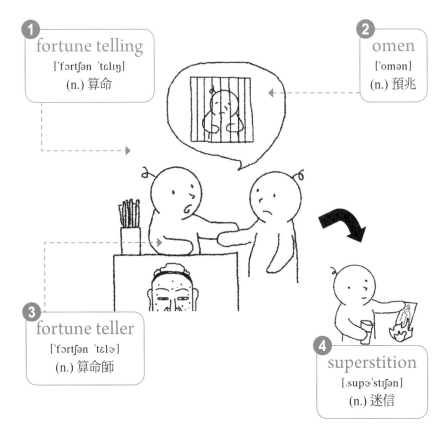

3 fortune teller
[`fɔrtʃən `tɛlə]
(n.) 算命師

4 superstition
[ˌsupə`stɪʃən]
(n.) 迷信

5 prophet
[`prɑfɪt]
(n.) 預言家

6 prediction
[prɪ`dɪkʃən]
(n.) 預言

7 Armageddon
[ˌɑrmə`gɛdn̩]
(n.) 世界末日

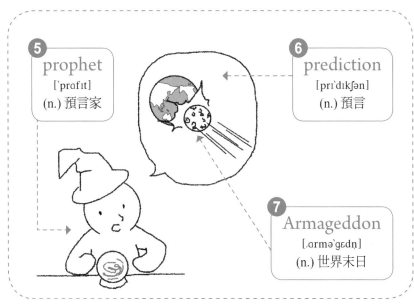

❶ 算命

Fortune telling is very popular in Taiwan, and people believe there are many different ways to see into the future.
<u>了解未來</u>

❷ 預兆

In the West, people think it's a bad omen to see a black cat.
<u>這是不好的預兆</u>

❸ 算命師

I'd love to be a fortune teller. It would be great to see into the future.

❹ 迷信

Danny believes in lots of superstitions. For example, he thinks bad things will happen if he walks under ladders.
<u>如果他從梯子下面走過</u>

❺ 預言家

The crazy old man claims to be a prophet who can see the future.
<u>是可以看見未來的預言家</u>

❻ 預言

My father made a prediction that I would be married by this time next year.
<u>做了預言</u>

❼ 世界末日

Someone told me today that the Armageddon was coming, but I don't think the world is going to end.
<u>世界末日就要來臨</u>
<u>世界即將終結</u>

學更多

❶ fortune〈命運〉‧ telling〈敘述〉‧ popular〈受歡迎的〉‧ different〈不同的〉
❷ West〈西方〉‧ think〈認為〉‧ bad〈不好的、有害的〉‧ black〈黑色的〉‧ cat〈貓〉
❸ teller〈敘述者〉‧ future〈未來〉
❹ believe〈相信〉‧ lots of〈很多〉‧ for example〈例如〉‧ happen〈發生〉‧ ladder〈梯子〉
❺ crazy〈瘋狂的〉‧ claim〈宣稱〉
❻ made〈make（做）的過去式〉‧ married〈已婚的〉‧ next year〈明年〉
❼ told〈tell（告訴）的過去式〉‧ coming〈come（來）的 ing 型態〉‧ end〈結束〉

中譯

❶ 在台灣非常流行算命，人們相信有很多不同的方法可以預見未來。
❷ 在西方，人們認為看見黑貓是不好的預兆。
❸ 我想當個算命師，能夠預見未來會是很棒的。
❹ Danny 相信很多迷信。例如，他認為自己如果從梯子下面走過，就會有壞事發生。
❺ 那位瘋狂的老人宣稱，自己是可以看見未來的預言家。
❻ 我父親預言明年的這個時候我已經結婚了。
❼ 今天有人告訴我世界末日就要來臨，但我不認為世界即將毀滅。

212
婚禮(1)

MP3 212

1 best man
[bɛst mæn]
(n.) 伴郎

2 maid of honor
[med ɑv `ɑnə]
(n.) 伴娘

3 bridegroom / groom
[`braɪd.grum] / [grum]
(n.) 新郎

4 bride
[braɪd]
(n.) 新娘

兩個單字都是「新郎」。

5 newlywed
[`njuɪ.wɛd]
(n.) 新人/新婚夫妻

6 honeymoon
[`hʌnɪ.mun]
(n.) 蜜月

❶ 伴郎

The best man is the groom's oldest friend.

❷ 伴娘

The bride asked her best friend to be the maid of honor at her wedding.

❸ 新郎

The bridegroom was really excited about his wedding.
對…感到很興奮

❹ 新娘

The bride looks beautiful in her white dress.
她身穿白色禮服

❺ 新人 / 新婚夫妻

Everybody wanted to take pictures with the newlyweds after their
wedding ceremony. 和新人拍照

❻ 蜜月

For their honeymoon, Brenda and Nate spent two weeks in Greece.

學更多

❶ oldest〈最多年的，old（多年的）的最高級〉・friend〈朋友〉
❷ asked〈ask（請求）的過去式〉・maid〈未婚女子〉・honor〈榮譽〉・wedding〈婚禮〉
❸ really〈非常〉・excited〈興奮的〉
❹ beautiful〈漂亮的〉・white〈白色的〉・dress〈禮服〉
❺ everybody〈每個人〉・take pictures〈拍照〉・ceremony〈典禮〉
❻ spent〈spend（花費）的過去式〉・Greece〈希臘〉

中譯

❶ 伴郎是新郎認識最久的老朋友。
❷ 新娘請她最好的朋友在婚禮上當伴娘。
❸ 新郎對於婚禮感到很興奮。
❹ 新娘身穿白紗，看起來非常漂亮。
❺ 每個人都想在婚禮後和新人合照。
❻ Brenda 和 Nate 到希臘兩週渡蜜月。

213 婚禮 (2)

MP3 213

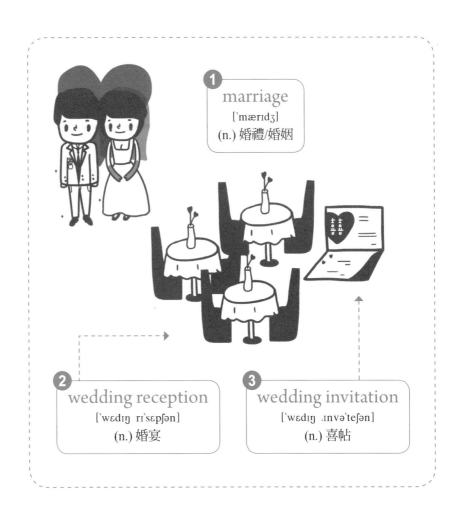

1 marriage
[ˋmærɪdʒ]
(n.) 婚禮/婚姻

2 wedding reception
[ˋwɛdɪŋ rɪˋsɛpʃən]
(n.) 婚宴

3 wedding invitation
[ˋwɛdɪŋ ͵ɪnvəˋteʃən]
(n.) 喜帖

4 wedding dress
[ˋwɛdɪŋ drɛs]
(n.) 婚紗

5 wedding ring
[ˋwɛdɪŋ rɪŋ]
(n.) 結婚戒指

6 bouquet
[buˋke]
(n.) 捧花

❶ 婚禮 / 婚姻

Charles and Diana have a wonderful marriage. They really love each other.

❷ 婚宴

After the wedding ceremony, all the guests went to a hall for the wedding reception.
　　　　　　　　　　　　　　　　　　　　　　　前往大廳參加婚宴

❸ 喜帖

The happy couple sent out wedding invitations to ask people to come to their wedding.
　　　　　　　　　　　　發送喜帖

❹ 婚紗

Traditional wedding dresses are white.

❺ 結婚戒指

As part of the wedding ceremony, the bride and groom put wedding rings on each other's fingers.
　　　　　　　　　　　　　　　　　　把結婚戒指戴在對方的手指上

❻ 捧花

The bride walked into the church holding a beautiful bouquet of flowers.
　　　　　　　　　　　　　　　　　　一束漂亮的捧花

學更多

❶ wonderful〈美滿的〉・really〈真的〉・each other〈彼此、對方〉

❷ ceremony〈儀式〉・guest〈來賓〉・hall〈大廳〉・reception〈宴會〉

❸ happy〈幸福的〉・couple〈一對、夫妻〉・sent out〈send out（發送）的過去式〉・invitation〈請帖〉・ask〈邀請〉

❹ traditional〈傳統的〉・dress〈禮服〉・white〈白色的〉

❺ as〈作為〉・bride〈新娘〉・groom〈新郎〉・put on〈戴上〉・finger〈手指〉

❻ walked into〈walk into（走入）的過去式〉・church〈教堂〉・holding〈hold（拿）的 ing 型態〉

中譯

❶ Charles 和 Diana 的婚姻生活美滿，他們真的彼此很相愛。

❷ 結婚儀式結束後，所有的來賓前往大廳參加婚宴。

❸ 那對幸福的佳偶發送喜帖，邀請大家參加他們的婚禮。

❹ 傳統的婚紗是白色的。

❺ 婚禮的其中一段，是新娘和新郎把結婚戒指戴在對方的手指上。

❻ 新娘拿著一束漂亮的捧花走進教堂。

214

幸
運
(1)

1 unplanned
[ʌnˋplænd]
(adj.) 不在計劃內

2 accidental
[ˌæksəˋdɛntl̩]
(adj.) 意外的

3 serendipitous
[ˌsɛrənˋdɪpɪtəs]
(adj.) 出乎意料

MP3 214

4 surprise
[səˋpraɪz]
(v.) 驚喜/驚嚇

5 lucky dog
[ˋlʌkɪ dɔg]
(n.) 幸運兒

❶ 不在計劃內

I took an unplanned vacation last week when I discovered my friend was
　　　請了一個非計劃內的休假　　　　　　　　　　　　　　　　我的朋友將前來附近造訪

visiting the area.

❷ 意外的

I didn't mean to eat your sandwich. It was accidental! It looked like mine.
　我不是故意做…

❸ 出乎意料

How serendipitous it is to see you here today! I thought you moved to
　　　　真是出乎意料

the US.

❹ 驚喜 / 驚嚇

You shouldn't surprise the elderly—they may have a heart attack.
　　　　　　　　　　　　　　　　　　　　　　　　心臟病發

❺ 幸運兒

You have a date with a supermodel? You lucky dog!
　　　和超級名模約會

學更多

❶ took〈take（採取、執行）的過去式〉・vacation〈休假〉・
discovered〈discover（發現）的過去式〉・visiting〈visit（拜訪）的 ing 型態〉・
area〈區域〉

❷ mean〈意圖、打算〉・sandwich〈三明治〉・
looked like〈look like（看起來像是）的過去式〉・mine〈我的〉

❸ see〈遇見〉・thought〈think（以為）的過去式〉・moved〈move（搬家）的過去式〉

❹ the elderly〈年長者〉・heart attack〈心臟病發作〉

❺ date〈約會〉・supermodel〈超級名模〉・lucky〈幸運的〉・dog〈傢伙〉

中譯

❶ 上週當我知道朋友將前來附近造訪時，我請了一個不在計劃內的休假。

❷ 我不是故意吃掉你的三明治的，這是意外！它看起來像是我的。

❸ 今天在這裡遇見你真是出乎意料！我以為你搬去美國了。

❹ 你不應該讓上了年紀的人受到驚嚇，他們可能會心臟病發。

❺ 你和超級名模約會？你這個幸運兒！

215

幸運(2)

MP3 215

1 sign
[saɪn]
(n.) 徵象/前兆

2 prediction
[prɪ`dɪkʃən]
(n.) 預言/預報

3 unpredictable
[ˌʌnprɪ`dɪktəbḷ]
(adj.) 無法預測

4 coincidence
[ko`ɪnsədəns]
(n.) 巧合

5 fate
[fet]
(n.) 命中註定/命運

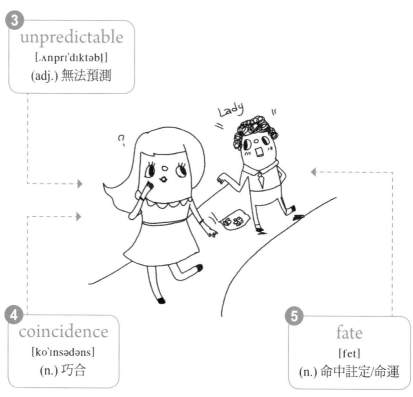

1 徵象 / 前兆

Those dark clouds are a sign that a thunderstorm is on its way.
<u>大雷雨即將來臨</u>

2 預言 / 預報

Weather predictions are often inaccurate.

3 無法預測

Earthquakes are unpredictable, so you just have to always be prepared.
<u>你就是必須隨時做好準備</u>

4 巧合

What a coincidence—running into you today and it's your birthday!
<u>巧遇你</u>

5 命中註定 / 命運

The fate of the passengers was in the hands of the pilot.
<u>在駕駛員手中</u>

學更多

1 dark cloud〈烏雲〉・thunderstorm〈大雷雨〉・way〈路途、路線〉
2 weather〈天氣〉・often〈經常〉・inaccurate〈不準確的〉
3 earthquake〈地震〉・have to〈必須〉・always〈總是〉・prepared〈有準備的〉
4 running into〈run into（偶遇）的 ing 型態〉・birthday〈生日〉
5 passenger〈乘客〉・hand〈手〉・pilot〈駕駛員〉

中譯

1 那些烏雲是大雷雨即將來臨的前兆。
2 天氣預報經常不準。
3 地震是無法預測的，所以你就是必須隨時做好準備。
4 真是巧合！今天巧遇你，又剛好是你的生日！
5 乘客的命運掌握在駕駛員手中。

216

夢想(1)

MP3 216

1 ambition
[æmˋbɪʃən]
(n.) 志願

「ambition」同時適用於表示「志願」和「野心」。

2 ambition
[æmˋbɪʃən]
(n.) 野心

3 future
[ˋfjutʃɚ]
(n.) 未來

4 goal
[gol]
(n.) 目標

5 plan
[plæn]
(n.) 計劃

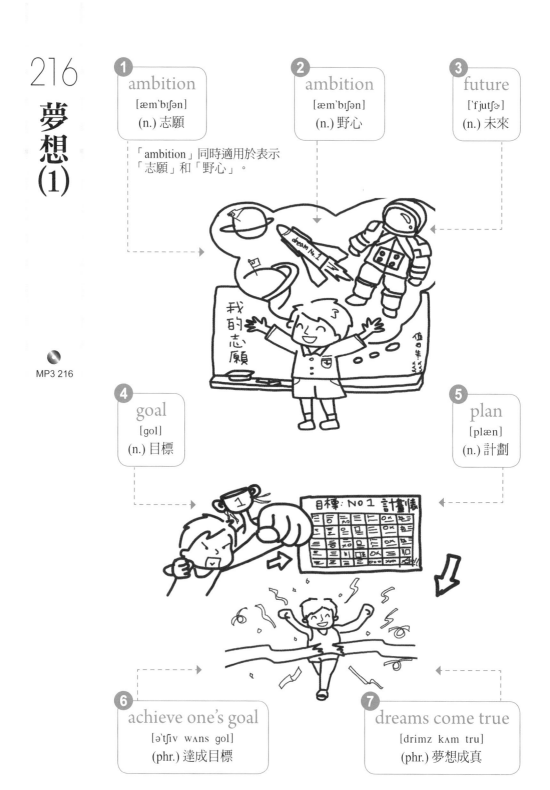

6 achieve one's goal
[əˋtʃiv wʌns gol]
(phr.) 達成目標

7 dreams come true
[drimz kʌm tru]
(phr.) 夢想成真

❶ 志願

David's life-long ambition has been to play for the New York Yankees.

為紐約洋基隊打球

❷ 野心

If you have a lot of ambition and work hard, you will go far in life.

你的人生將有所成就

❸ 未來

The future is unknown, so live every day like it's your last.

宛如那是你的最後一天

❹ 目標

My goal for today is to finish all my homework.

❺ 計劃

Do you have any plans for summer vacation yet?

❻ 達成目標

Jeremy hopes to achieve his goal of becoming a famous rock singer one day.

成為一位知名的搖滾歌手

❼ 夢想成真

The optimist believes that dreams come true through hard work and a little luck, of course.

藉由努力工作和些許運氣

學更多

❶ life-long〈一輩子的〉‧ play〈打球〉‧ New York Yankees〈紐約洋基隊〉
❷ a lot of...〈大量…〉‧ work hard〈努力工作〉‧ go far〈有成就〉‧ life〈一生〉
❸ unknown〈未知的〉‧ live〈活〉‧ last〈最後的一個〉
❹ finish〈完成〉‧ all〈全部〉‧ homework〈作業〉
❺ any〈任何一個〉‧ summer vacation〈暑假〉‧ yet〈已經〉
❻ achieve〈達到〉‧ becoming〈become（變成）的 ing 型態〉‧ one day〈有一天〉
❼ optimist〈樂觀者〉‧ believe〈相信〉‧ come true〈實現〉‧ of course〈當然〉

中譯

❶ David 一輩子的志願，就是效力於紐約洋基隊。
❷ 如果你很有野心並努力工作，你的人生將有所成就。
❸ 未來是未知的，所以要把每一天都當作是最後一天來過。
❹ 我今天的目標是完成所有的作業。
❺ 對於暑假，你已經有任何計劃了嗎？
❻ Jeremy 希望有一天能達成目標，成為一位知名的搖滾歌手。
❼ 樂觀的人相信藉由努力工作和些許運氣，自然就會夢想成真。

217

夢想(2)

MP3 217

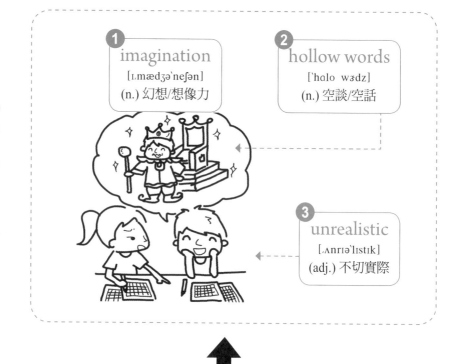

1 imagination
[ɪˌmædʒəˈneʃən]
(n.) 幻想/想像力

2 hollow words
[ˈhɑlo wɝdz]
(n.) 空談/空話

3 unrealistic
[ˌʌnrɪəˈlɪstɪk]
(adj.) 不切實際

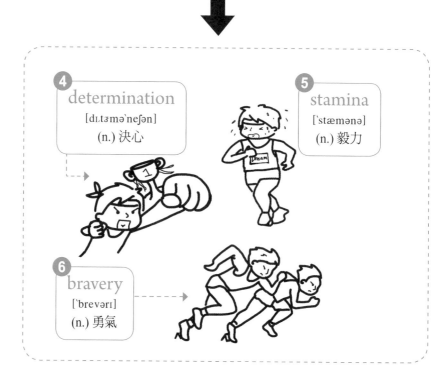

4 determination
[dɪˌtɝməˈneʃən]
(n.) 決心

5 stamina
[ˈstæmənə]
(n.) 毅力

6 bravery
[ˈbrevərɪ]
(n.) 勇氣

❶ 幻想 / 想像力

Children have a very vivid imagination.
非常生動的想像力

❷ 空談 / 空話

The boss praised Angela's excellent work, but after 10 years without a raise, she knew they were just hollow words.
10 年都沒有加薪

❸ 不切實際

It's good to be positive about your career goals, but don't be unrealistic.
正向看待你的職涯目標

❹ 決心

A strong determination to succeed is essential for anyone wanting to be an actor or actress.
任何想要成為男演員或女演員的人

❺ 毅力

Basketball players have to have amazing stamina in order to run up and down the court.
在球場上來回奔跑

❻ 勇氣

Soldiers demonstrate bravery each day in battle.
軍人展現勇氣

學更多

❶ children〈child（小孩）的複數〉‧vivid〈生動的〉
❷ praised〈praise（稱讚）的過去式〉‧excellent〈傑出的〉‧raise〈加薪〉‧knew〈know（知道）的過去式〉‧hollow〈虛偽的、空洞的〉‧word〈話語〉
❸ positive〈正向的、積極的〉‧career〈職業的〉‧goal〈目標〉
❹ strong〈強烈的〉‧succeed〈成功〉‧essential〈必要的〉‧anyone〈無論任何人〉
❺ have to〈必須〉‧amazing〈驚人的〉‧in order to〈為了〉‧up and down〈來回地〉
❻ soldier〈軍人〉‧demonstrate〈展現〉‧battle〈戰鬥〉

中譯

❶ 小孩子擁有非常生動的想像力。
❷ 老闆稱讚 Angela 傑出的工作表現，但在經過 10 年都毫無加薪之後，她便知道那些不過是空話。
❸ 正向看待你的職涯目標是很好的，但不要不切實際。
❹ 一份強烈地想要成功的決心，對於任何想成為演員的人來說，是必要的。
❺ 籃球選手必須擁有過人的毅力，才能在球場上不斷來回奔跑。
❻ 軍人們每天都在戰鬥中展現勇氣。

附錄

詞性分類 × 字母排序

詞性分類 × 字母排序

詞性分類 × 字母排序

詞性分類 × 字母排序

詞性分類 × 字母排序

詞性分類 × 字母排序

詞性分類 × 字母排序

詞性分類 × 字母排序

詞性分類 × 字母排序

檸檬樹出版社
Lemon Tree Publishing House

Fly 飛系列 10

圖解生活實用英語：腦中延伸的人事物（附 1MP3）

初版一刷　2015 年 9 月 11 日

作者	檸檬樹英語教學團隊
英語例句	Stephanie Buckley、張馨勻
插畫	許仲綺、陳博深、陳琬瑜、吳怡萱、鄭苑書、周奕伶、葉依婷、 朱珮瑩、沈諭、巫秉旂、王筑儀
封面設計	陳文德
版型設計	洪素貞
英語錄音	Stephanie Buckley
責任編輯	沈祐禎、黃冠禎
發行人	江媛珍
社長・總編輯	何聖心
出版者	檸檬樹國際書版有限公司 檸檬樹出版社 E-mail：lemontree@booknews.com.tw 地址：新北市235中和區中安街80號3樓 電話・傳真：02-29271121・02-29272336
會計・客服	方靖淳
法律顧問	第一國際法律事務所 余淑杏律師 北辰著作權事務所 蕭雄淋律師
全球總經銷・印務代理 網路書城	知遠文化事業有限公司 http://www.booknews.com.tw 博訊書網 電話：02-26648800　傳真：02-26648801 地址：新北市222深坑區北深路三段155巷25號5樓
港澳地區經銷	和平圖書有限公司 電話：852-28046687　傳真：850-28046409 地址：香港柴灣嘉業街12號百樂門大廈17樓
定價	台幣450元／港幣150元
劃撥帳號	戶名：19726702・檸檬樹國際書版有限公司 ・單次購書金額未達300元，請另付40元郵資 ・信用卡・劃撥購書需7-10個工作天

圖解生活實用英語：腦中延伸的人事物 /
檸檬樹英語教學團隊著. -- 初版. -- 新北市：
檸檬樹, 2015.09
面；　公分. --（Fly 飛系列；10）
ISBN 978-986-6703-93-5（平裝附光碟片）

1.英語　2.詞彙

805.12　　　　　　　　　　　　　104011973